CHAOS ASCENDING

A FEAST OF BETRAYAL

R.C. VIELEE

Cover designed by Miblart

Map by Inkarnate

eBook ISBN: 979-8-988-1090-4-4

Hard Cover ISBN: 979-8-988-1090-6-8

Trade ISBN: 979-8-988-1090-5-1

Library of Congress Control Number: 2024901781

For rights and permissions, please contact:

Bobalou Publishing c/o Robert Vielee

PO Box 127

Clarks Summit, PA 18411

r.c.vielee@outlook.com

For Louise, love always.

Content Advisory

Chaos Ascending: A Feast of Betrayal, journeys through the fantasy worlds of Tartica and Evidar, and explores dark themes that can be disturbing: such as fantasy violence, torture, blood, references to past childhood emotional and physical abuse, and sexual content that includes sexual violence. It is intended for mature readers.

UTOPIA FALLING: A DARKNESS RISES, RECAP

For those interested in a recap of *Utopia Falling: A Darkness Rises*, before diving into *Chaos Ascending: A Feast of Betrayal*, please navigate to a hidden page on my website that I've set up just for you. The password is chaos.

rcvielee.com/recap-utopia-falling

Tartic Ocean
Port of Aknar
Peoples Republic of Kantos
Topak
The Woodlands
Port Royal
Owls Neck
Hensdale
Teth
Lemieur Shoals
Bay of Synn
Port L
Tartic Ocean
Ferric
Jarouhar

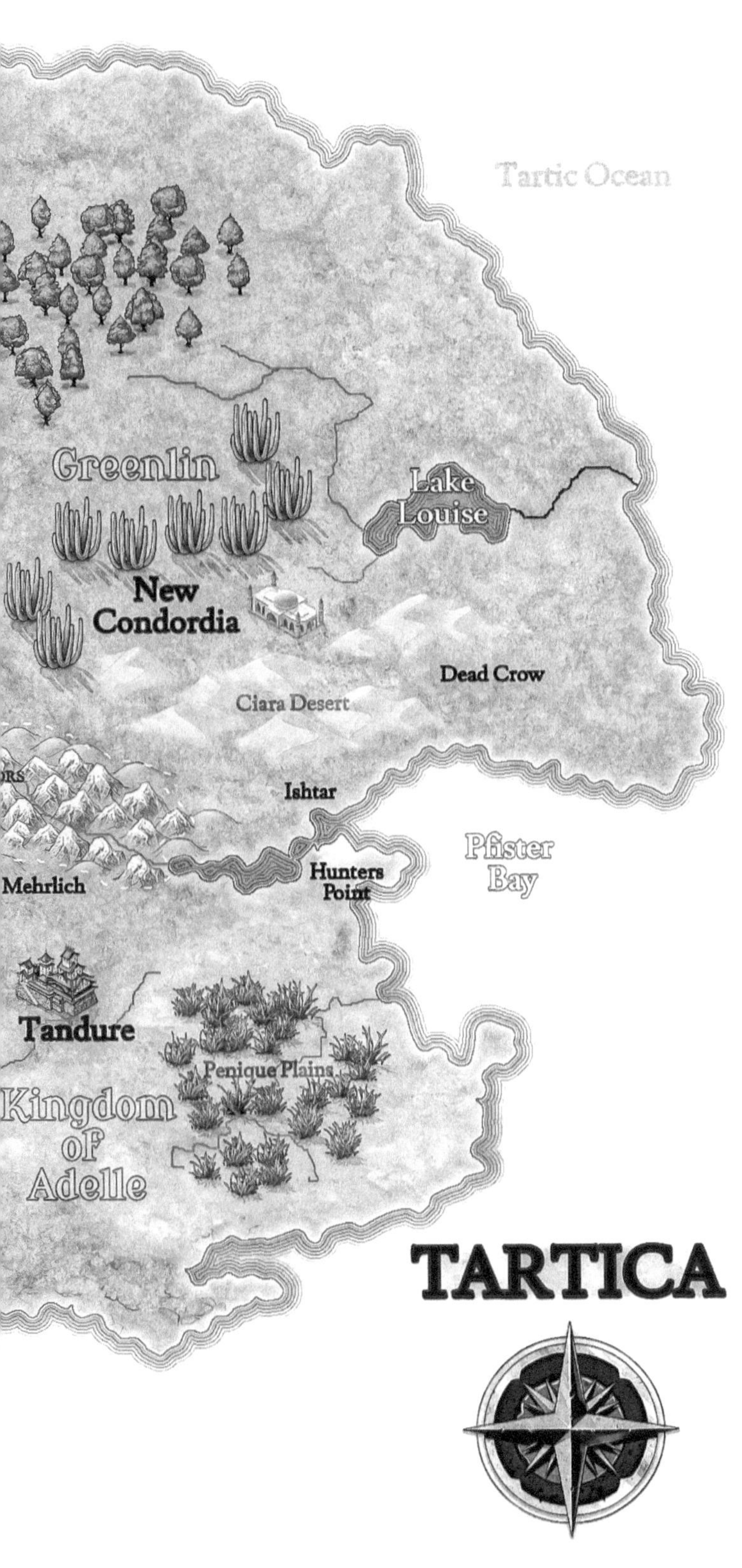

Tartic Ocean
Greenlin
Lake Louise
New Condordia
Dead Crow
Ciara Desert
Ishtar
Pfister Bay
Hunters Point
Mehrlich
Tandure
Penique Plains
Kingdom of Adelle
TARTICA

Evidar: Twenty-two Years Ago

Edruk

Edruk's sight had grown accustomed to the ever-present dark skies looming over Evidar, a brutal, foreboding world where fractional luminosity differences hardly separated night from day. He struggled to deny the gloom that pervaded every facet of life from securing a foothold on his own psyche. A desolate world in the remains of the Great Destruction, Evidar's sparsely populated inhabitants bristled against it each day to survive.

Edruk, a tall, muscular, natural-born leader in his prime, had transfigured to Evidar many times from the idyllic alternative version of Earth where he lived—Tartica. Transitioning between the dimensional realms of the two independent Earthly realities was wrought with uncertainty and was never an easy journey. First, beginning in sleep, and once achieved, accessing the astral plane, followed by the difficult task of pushing one's consciousness, absent its physical body, through an almost impenetrable barrier to enter the Void. Both risk and reward awaited one in the Void. A hub to an alternate reality or a pathway to oblivion. The danger of getting lost forever in its immersive, compelling environs was a risk all too real.

Edruk endured the difficult journey for the love of family: his three-year-old daughter and his pregnant wife. Edruk hoped for a son, and if so lucky, the couple planned to name the boy Reyne. With his wife eight and a half months pregnant, he'd learn soon whether she'd give birth to a boy or girl. Edruk would be equally happy with either a son or a daughter.

Edruk's many endeavors into the realm of Evidar forced its powers-that-be to focus on the disruptions he and his team inflicted on the enemy's goal to fold the entirety of Tartica's existence into Evidar's, subsuming the materiality of the two Earths, separated, unconnected in freestanding dimensions, into one world, one reality, with one future—Evidar's—at the cost of Tartica's very existence. A future Edruk dedicated his life to prevent from ever happening.

"Come here, Aderlee," Edruk called out to his assistant from deep inside the underground fortress his team had captured. While not strictly subterrestrial peoples, much of the populace found escape from surface conditions both safer and more conducive to blocking out the effects of the acrid environment above.

"Be right there, boss," the tall yet slight, middle-aged Aderlee replied. "I found another one lurking behind a false wall. I think this one's important. She might be the Damus we're looking for."

"Bring her here," Edruk ordered his subordinate. "She can't be allowed to complete her calculations. The future is not for anyone to see... Evidar's or Tartica's. I want a word with her before she dies."

Arms secured behind the Damus's back, Aderlee, dressed in short pants and a short-sleeved shirt, shoved the stunned captive forward, coming to a stop a few feet from Edruk.

Below ground, the fortress let in none of the diminished light from the surface, resulting in a dreary, bedimmed, lightless environment the people of Evidar accepted as a way of life. Aderlee and the Damus, Evidarian natives both, born to the dark world, were exceptionally well-sighted in crepuscular conditions. Edruk's eyesight, on an average day, bathed in the bucolic sunny skies of Tartica. However, in Evidar's environs and with the absence of sunshine, his vision proved less effective even after all his time in the alternate reality. Forms, shapes, and limited details reached into his struggling corneas, withholding any discernable minutiae or individualized characteristics from his visual perception. Everything appeared to him cloaked in a shadowy, black veil.

Edruk looked the woman up and down as best his eyesight allowed. "You surprise me," he told her. "Someone so young with the ability to do incomprehensible calculations of plotting the likelihood of a future expressed in an all-but-impossible, planet-sized Probability Wavefunction. It is amazing what you can do. Unfortunately, for an evil cause."

The woman's eyeshine, like two small round mirrors reflecting what little light existed in the dark enclosure, glared back at Edruk, but the Damus said nothing. Aderlee's eyes had it as well, as did all Evidar's natural-born inhabitants.

Hidden behind her angry, contorted expression, Edruk could almost make out the gentle features of her youthful face. "How old are you, young lady?" He turned to his assistant, Aderlee. "Are you sure this one's a Damus? Doesn't seem possible."

"She's the one, boss. Caught her hunched over, pencil in hand, computing the impact of today's events on a long timeline chart. That's good enough for me. She's the one we're looking for."

An approving grin took shape. "Nice work, Aderlee. Gather up all the documents you find. I'll want to review all of them."

"Thanks, boss. Will do."

Edruk asked his second-in-command, "You carry yellow-flame matches?"

"Yes, boss." Aderlee pulled a pack from his pocket. "I'm surprised you don't have any. You don't see so good here." He handed the matches over.

"Thanks. Mind if I keep these? I'm all out." With a flick of his thumbnail over the match-head, a faint glow appeared. The meager light struggled against the volume of blackness and reached only a few feet beyond its position between Edruk's thumb and forefinger. He moved the delicate flame toward the face of the Damus. The illuminating effects lasted only seconds before fading into ebony. Evidarian black flame's ability to consume all other colors of light didn't matter; a quick breath from the woman ended his close inspection.

"That's too bad. From what I could see, you're a pretty one. It's a shame I can't let you live." Edruk didn't have to see to sense her fear.

"Edruk!" A shout rumbled from outside the room, down the long hallway.

"What's so damned important?" Edruk demanded of the Evidarian accomplice popping her head through the doorway. Darkness concealed the fear on her face, but her oculi glowed as tiny, pallid, silvery orbs.

Terrified, the woman's words shot out in rapid succession, "Your family. I just left the Void. Got an update from my mental-connection contact back on Tartica. The Devil's Blacksmith..." she paused to catch her breath. "His people are after your family. They know where you live. My Tartican contact will try to get to your wife and daughter to save them, but she's a day away."

The Void existed as a place beyond the physical world, where reality and all the possible futures of every living thing in every dimension it touched, and it touched them all, flowed freely.

The woman, Evidar's current and only Damus, spoke up. "I calculated you being here today as only seventeen percent probable. Gaining access to this facility, even less: four percent. I'll know I'll pay the price of underestimating you. He gambled on that four percent to create an opportunity to inflict some payback on you. You don't know the damage you're doing to the future of everyone on my world. You're a demon. Now your family will pay for your crusade."

Anger roiled in his gut. The Evidarians, intent on consigning his world to devastation in their plans to enfold Evidar into his, were the evil ones from where he stood—even more so now that they threatened his family.

Edruk snapped, backhanding the Damus across the face, dropping her to the ground. Turning to Aderlee, he commanded, "Kill her. Kill them all. Aderlee, it's in your hands until I return. I've got to get to my family!"

In a panic, Edruk raced to find an empty room. Desperate to span the dimensional gap between the two alternate versions of Earth, before assassins sent by the man forging Evidar's future to his own desires, the Devil's Blacksmith, murdered his pregnant wife and his three-year-old daughter—for nothing more than spite.

In his despondent, helpless state of mind, sleep did not come easy—nor swiftly.

It's Nice to Have You Back

Evidar: Twenty-two Years After Edruk's Death

Dylla

The sky painted Dylla Weisner's home world a dim charcoal gray—normal for Evidar. She made her way through the familiar barren landscape to a particular rock pile with an embedded yellow door. She entered and traversed the long, narrow stairs to the underground compound of the Devil's Blacksmith, where even less of the coal-colored light filtered through, a welcome comfort to start an otherwise inauspicious confab. Uneasy entering his lair, her heart raced, and, for a moment, fear stole her breath away. She had bad news to deliver.

He's killed for less.

Dylla fanned her fingers through her long red hair, hoping to push aside her heightened anxiety. The Evidarian covert operations manager and onetime assassin-extraordinaire settled her middle-aged nerves and gathered her courage.

As she entered, a refined, well-built, tall man with jet black hair as dark as char and pale skin nodded in acknowledgment of her presence.

A quick gulp, and Dylla began, "Hello, sir. It's nice to be home. You adjust to the sunlight on Tartica, although it's never pleasant. I need to go back sooner than I'd like, as I'm following up on one possible loose end. That's why I'm here. To fill you in personally. No middleman." Her only comfort, a return to the near lightless environment her natural born eyesight ruled over and welcomed.

"It is wonderful to have you back, Dylla. Although I hoped for your permanent return."

The Devil's Blacksmith couldn't be granted the mantle of "Evidar's Leader," as the term implied a degree of structure or organization to the remains of humanity eking out an existence in the dismal, light-starved environs of Evidar—which possessed neither structure nor organization. Although, amongst the scattered populace, small pockets of people aligned for the common goal of survival. In the ashes of the Great Destruction, even the most fundamental form of governance never re-emerged in the fifteen hundred years that followed the near-planet-terminating event.

Dylla played a key role in that small organization with a single goal: to bring change to her home world—a version of Earth, unknown to all but a few Tarticans in the Third Age. And even those rare few could not stop the destruction Tartica faced at the hands of the Devil's Blacksmith—if successful. His singular focus, to merge two Earths from alternate dimensions, Tartica and Evidar, into one shared reality. A rescue plan of sorts for Evidar—from its ever-present gloom at the expense of the idyllic, utopian world of Tartica.

"Dylla, I am interested in hearing your report. I also have news to share. But that is for later. What is so important you needed to deliver the report yourself?" He spoke in slow, clear, educated, fully annunciated words—as he always did. Confidence and power radiated in his tone, his appearance, and in his every movement, gesture, and facial expression. It took a strong-willed person to stand up to the man's presence—without shitting one's pants.

While Dylla thought herself such a woman, she faltered when the man who coldly referred to himself as the Architect—in both title and function—gave her a look, sending chills down her spine. He created the moniker as much for his planning and manipulative successes, impacting world-driven timelines, as for his ability to lay the foundations of dread within a single word.

Not to his face, most called him the Devil's Blacksmith. Blacksmith for the symbolic hammering, forging, and compelling the future into something malleable enough to bend to his will. The inclusion of the Devil reference, bathed in blood, spoke for itself. Dylla feared his reach too much to ever use the ubiquitous title out loud. Even though the man referred to himself as the Architect, he existed as the Devil's Blacksmith in Dylla's thoughts—but never on her tongue.

Through decades of service, familiarity equipped her to detect nuances in his facial expressions. The slight rise of his left eyebrow sent her into fight-or-flight mode, pumping copious amounts of adrenaline through her system. Experience told her flight didn't exist as an option, not from the Devil's Blacksmith. When others attempted to flee his wrath, he tasked her with their deaths—never failing to deliver.

She'd yet to share her intel, and trouble had already reared its ugly head. Despite the warning signs, she clung to hopes of leaving the room alive. Her life depended on how well he'd take the news.

The Devil's Blacksmith rose from the couch and walked to his well-stocked bar near the fireplace. Deep purple, dark blue, and black flames licked at the logs spreading a faint caliginous glow across the room. The black flames grabbed at any morsel of yellow or red light that took shape. Ebony flares gobbled up and transformed the burgeoning red and yellow flames into a shade beyond the spectrum of deep space, void of any discernable color. The heat from the ominous dark fire filled the room with a subtle warmth Dylla welcomed.

"Dylla, would you like a drink?"

"Yes. Thank you. Juniper spirits would be fine," Dylla replied, familiar with what liquor he stocked. She'd been to his office many times, but never with her life hanging so precariously uncertain. Her mouth shaped the accommodating words of her reply while her brain screamed into her thoughts, *Run!*

With his back turned, Evidar's kingpin poured two juniper spirits into short stone tumblers. He handed the black stoneware to his guest. "You will enjoy this one. It has been aged several decades. Quite smooth."

Dylla reached up to accept the offering. After sipping the drink, its familiar, satisfying peppery sweetness settled her a bit. "This is really nice. Exceptional." She took another pull, a gift to her battered nerves.

The Devil's Blacksmith walked behind his desk and sat. "I am glad you like it. Now... let us get to it." He questioned in a soothing delivery, more chilling than his ice-cold, soul-piercing eyes, "What do you have to tell me?"

"Let me get straight to the reason for my visit. Reyne Brenton, the Tartican, the man your Damus fears could upset our timeline and all our plans. Ironically, his own father killed our last Damus over twenty years ago. Anyway, I've yet to confirm Reyne's death. Although, my team assures me he is, and I quote, almost certainly dead."

The Devil's Blacksmith moved a coaster to a favorite location on his desk and, with aristocratic grace, positioned his drink on it. He looked up at Dylla. Eyes as dark as any black hole prowled at her from behind his lowered brow. "Almost certainly dead is not the same as actually dead. I tasked you with the latter."

Although his visage almost caused her heart to stop beating, Dylla didn't show fear. A strong, confident leader, her practiced face didn't give anything away, but trepidation lurked beneath the surface.

Her team failed; Reyne Brenton almost certainly still lived. Duty, tinged with loyalty, compelled her to bring him the information, yet it came with great personal risk. As the team's leader, she accepted it as something she had to do, but that didn't mean she wasn't scared shitless doing it.

"Tell me why you are uncertain. The First Lord, our go-between, has reported he is confident of this Brenton man's demise. That may not be accurate?"

"Yes, sir... I mean, no, sir... What I mean is... it may not be accurate. I've got the woman you sent, Agent Arrow, Neladith Karlis, working to confirm Reyne Brenton's death, as is my entire team. Within the next day, two tops, we'll know." She took another long sip of her juniper to camouflage the gulp-of-fear riding her throat.

Deep purple and black light reached out from the hearth to dance along the rim of his cup. He ran one finger in a circle around the edge, staring intensely into the liquid.

Dylla remained silent.

Her eyes consumed his every movement.

Her ears piqued in wait of his reply.

She fought back at the terror squeezing her insides.

He asked, as a comforting father might question his frightened child, "Tell me, did our young assassin do her job?" Reassurance in his tone suggested to Dylla she had nothing to dread, yet she knew it for the false security it offered.

"Sir, Neladith performed perfectly. An amazing archer. She's young, yet every bit the prodigy you suggested. Nailed the shot from one hundred fifty yards. Dropped him without a sound." Once an assassin herself, she spoke in glowing terms of Neladith's achievement, and buried the effects of adrenaline threatening to expose the fear in her voice.

The man rested his hands on the arms of the large, high-back chair. Pushing off in one slow, graceful movement, he rose to stand behind his desk. Both palms came to rest on the workspace surface. Leaning forward, the tall man, with deep-set, lifeless, empty eyes loomed large over the seated Dylla. Black light from the dark flames flickered across his angular face and statuesque body. Dylla suspected he played it for all its sinister effects. And, she thought as her heart hammered in her chest, if he did, it worked.

"Do you trust your team?" he asked. Waiting for her reply, he walked to the bar and poured himself another drink. A proffer to refill Dylla's did not follow.

Dylla didn't like the omen, but she had a more immediate problem.

A thought exploded across her mind: *It's a trick question. Shit!*

She put the team together, minus his last-minute addition, who she just reported did an outstanding job. The only conclusion she left him, in her own words, was that the team she put together screwed it up. She was angry with herself for having stepped into the trap.

The loyal operations manager understood that her life hung on her reply. *Choose your next utterance carefully,* she told herself, paused, then answered. "Planning. Advanced intel. Execution. All perfect. We raced from Jarouhar after killing the Shifter woman named Lorique. On the very day my unit arrived in Hensdale, that son-of-a-bitch, Mera... Meratoruc, appeared out of nowhere. That night we killed someone who fit Reyne Brenton's description, but Meratoruc's presence prevented my team from completing the on-site identification of the body."

Dylla's gut clenched when he said in a calm tone, more threatening than if he screamed at her, "Go on."

"My team confirmed Reyne Brenton's brother has now gone missing. And Meratoruc appears to have surreptitiously buried the body within hours of the death before we could circle back. Reyne hasn't been seen since that night. He is likely dead, but I don't like those last two facts when put together. We most likely achieved our goals. I'm being cautious coming to you. I won't ever hide anything from you. Given how important this is, if there's the slightest chance Reyne Brenton is alive, you needed to know right away."

Reyne remained amongst the living, she knew it, and now the Devil's Blacksmith knew it too. In her attempt to soften the blow, she lied to the man who wouldn't hesitate to kill her for the offense. Dylla swallowed, no longer able to hide her growing fears. Yet, those exact words, *Reyne lived*, couldn't be uttered, as they would usher in certain death—hers. A single hope, the truth she hid behind a thin veil of uncertainty, would be enough.

She waited.

He guzzled the remaining contents in his cup and slammed it hard on his desk. Sound exploded into the silence as though a summons for Death to appear.

Dylla gripped the arms of her chair with all her strength, girding herself for his impending strike. The room's evil gloom hid her white knuckles as her nails dug into the wood secured in her palms. Her heart pounded, fearing these to be her final moments of life—knowing there would be no escape. Only the ribs in her chest kept her heart from leaping out.

Dark light reaching out from the hearth matched the vacant, threatening, death-affirming rage radiating in his eyes. And as quickly, the fury vanished from his face. His furrowed brow relaxed, and he said, "I appreciate your attention to detail. Others would have stayed away, confirming the situation one way or the other before coming to me. But you are smarter than that. You know, if he lives, I cannot wait days. I must take action immediately. Every day he lives, the chance of him making it into our world grows. I dislike what you have reported. You bear responsibility for this failure. Yet, I understand the complications Mera added to your task."

Relief pulsed through her. She considered herself fortunate to be sitting down. If knees could buckle while seated, hers did.

The leader added, "I accept your misgivings in dealing with Mera. He has been a problem ever since he stole the Soul Stone from me, at least part of it. He kept the other half. I almost killed him that day. A lost opportunity. Possession of the Soul Stone saved him. You are right to be careful around him. Mera is beyond your ability to handle. I will deal with him in time."

"Thank you, sir. I won't fail you again." Dylla withdrew the tips of her nails from the gouges she'd dug in the chair. She rode her fingers over the newly formed tiny indentations as confirmation of her own bravery, fortunate she'd survived the encounter with the Devil's Blacksmith unscathed. She'd entered his lair, faced death, and would leave a stronger leader for it. At least, that's what she told herself.

He replied, "No, you will not fail me again. Know that it would be your last."

A deep breath slowly escaped her lips in an effort to hide it from him. "What can I do beyond the immediate determination of Reyne Brenton's status?"

"I will summon my Damus. She will need to reevaluate the timeline. I broke off my connection with their former First Lord. I may have to re-establish a mental link with him through the Void. I will give it consideration. His thoughts are so tedious. But all is not lost. This Chancellor fellow's proposal to end their beloved holy Covenant will create chaos on Tartica that I can utilize to our advantage. I remain hopeful of merging our Probability Wavefunction into theirs, enjoining our two worlds as one. But... one loose end remains based on your report. Damus Emosh calculates, no matter our precautions, if Reyne Brenton steps one foot on our world, there is a seventy-nine percent probability a dimensional merger will be prevented."

"I wish I could say I understand it all. Quantum mechanics applied to planet-sized objects violates all known laws of physics."

"Yet here we are. The secrets of the universe are truly unknowable. What actual events will take place to disrupt our cause should Reyne Brenton make an appearance, I do not know. But what I do know is that Damus Emosh has calculated the probability of a disastrous outcome is all but certain if Reyne Brenton successfully transfigures here. I have guards, have taken precautions, and still her projections remain unchanged. Our recourse is to stop him while he remains on Tartica."

"We will, sir," Dylla offered, asserting an unspoken, "Thank you for letting me live."

He ignored her. "I need you on Tartica. Get back there immediately. If he remains alive, which it now appears he likely is, find him and kill him... quickly."

"Yes, sir."

"What a shame it is that in all our known population, currently only eight people can shift from our dimension into Tartica's. This tit-for-tat with Mera has been going on far too long and has drained our resources. On a positive note, you and your team have left Mera just the one threat at his disposal... Reyne Brenton. You have done well to eliminate all the other Tartican Shifters. You must finish what you have started."

"Yes, sir. With Neladith joining the team, four of our operatives are there now. I will return to Tartica immediately, and then we will be five."

"Leave one Shifter with me. The other two, I want over there post haste. Tartica is massive, and seven of you covering the entire continent leaves room for error. When you return, engage your contacts and get every available Tartican you can pay or bribe tracking down this Reyne Brenton. If he is with Mera, as you say, I am all but certain Mera is preparing him for the journey. Our time to kill him while he remains in his dimension is slipping away."

"I have a contact that is perfect for this assignment. She controls quite an extensive network. There'll be nowhere for him to hide from us."

"Good. Make it happen. One more item. Figure out where your team failed. Terminate whoever caused the problem once you have eliminated Reyne Brenton. I will not suffer incompetence. If this individual failed once, he or she will fail me again. Remove this person, or I will reevaluate the consequences of your involvement in this matter. I will not tolerate further mistakes. You showed bravery and intelligence in bringing this to me when you did. My patience with you will not hold if this is not wrapped up... immediately."

Dylla swallowed buckets of saliva. "Thank you, sir." Her gamble paid off. She'd been granted a stay of execution. Although, she suspected her reprieve grew more out of the diminished resources he had at his disposal to deal with the threat Reyne posed than from any suggestion of compassion—a quality he utterly lacked.

In her mind, she identified the linchpin, the point of failure. If prevented from confirming Reyne's kill post-op, the team needed to be one hundred percent certain of who they were going to assassinate before taking down the target. That series of decisions, failing to identify Reyne Brenton as the mark before ordering Neladith to take the kill shot, rested on one man's shoulders. His slip-up put Mera on notice, and Reyne was whisked away in the aftermath. Finding him now, hidden somewhere in the vastness of Tartica, would prove a difficult task at best.

That fuckup—which nearly cost her the rest of her days—belonged to one man... Selundra Quith.

Enter the City

Teth: 2nd Day of the Harvest Moon

Reyne

Two routes into Teth from the north included a passage through the transcontinental mountain range known as the Razors or hugging the coast, navigating the treacherous currents of the Tartic Ocean. Mera, Reyne's self-proclaimed protector, chose the Razors. Cutting through the well-worn Rickerton Passage put the duo at the northwestern entrance of Teth.

At the gates, Mera stuck out an arm. "Remember, you and I have serious business in Teth. Stay close and don't wander off."

With Mera's arm in his way, Reyne stopped. "Remind me again, what're we doin' here?"

"I'm here to uncover who ratted you out to Evidar hunters. You're here to meet Gina. She'll train you for when you get to Evidar. We spoke of this several times."

Reyne's sarcasm dripped out with every syllable. "Not sure you noticed, I've had other things on my mind. I don't always listen when you talk."

Bloodshot red lines found a temporary home in Reyne's normally effervescent, emerald-green eyes. His dark hair matted to his head, and his travel attire wore the dirt of their trek. His appearance mirrored his tattered soul. A backpack he carried seemed to weigh a thousand pounds, as if it held everything of a promised life he'd left behind. All he ever desired: marry Mithany; settle down; raise a family; enjoy a quiet life running the alphen orchard business with his brother Daedyn, had been ripped from him.

Physically tired from their journey and emotionally drained at having been forced to leave his fiancée Mithany behind, thoughts of Evidar assassins sent to kill him, who mistakenly killed his brother Daedyn instead, plagued him. Evidar operatives, if they learned of the deception, would renew their effort to end his life—or worse, Mithany's—in an effort to get to him. So he fled at Mera's insistence. Infuriated with Mera at Daedyn's death and for pulling him from his wedding only days away, Reyne held onto the anger, a welcomed companion. His focus strayed from the physical world. Every synapse carried on it thoughts of Daedyn and Mithany.

His eyes examined his surroundings, but his heart cared little for what he saw. The businessman, the young nut farmer from Hensdale, had stepped away from marrying the woman he loved to save her from his brother's fate. Yet, he couldn't let her go; love wouldn't let him.

Mera had become the focal point of his anger in spite of proclaiming to be his ally wrapped in his own self-declared good intentions. Off in the recesses of his mind, he heard Mera say, "I'm confused. There isn't anyone manning the entrance. Something's off. We need to be careful."

Jolting him back to his physical surroundings, appearing out of nowhere, a naked man running out through the administrative exit from Teth shouted at the top of his lungs, "Fuck Teth! Fuck the Covenant! Fuck Cree!" His privates bouncing and swirling as he ran, the streaker proclaimed over and over, "Fuck Teth. Fuck Cree. Fuck the Covenant."

Reyne jumped aside. The nudity didn't startle him, its existence was ever-present across Tartica: the consequence of a society founded on repopulating humanity—from the ashes of the Great Destruction—an expression of free love at almost every opportunity. Tartica's founding document, the Covenant of Absolute Universal Obligations, demanded repopulation of civilization.

A raucous cacophony followed. Additional clothing-less protesters boosted the lone sprinter's call to action and grew louder by the second. Galloping past the confused Reyne, the source of the boisterous jabbering burst through the once-manned-now-empty administrative entry portal. A hundred strong all sans clothing, repeated the same chant in unison, "Fuck Teth. Fuck the Covenant. Fuck Cree."

Reyne backed away, barely avoiding being run over. The sight stirred up the first positive emotions since his brother had been murdered. Reyne smirked at the sight of body parts flopping up and down, the larger ones the most amusing, with much of the same effect from both the men and women galloping before him. It struck Reyne that the display had some higher social purpose, but the unintended indignity of the combined wildly slapping about of dicks and tits stole all the attention from the importance of their protest.

The au naturel activists had followers, but not any they desired. Immediately after the collective display flopped and jounced past Reyne, fifteen uniformed peace officers emerged from the city gate, giving chase. Brass whistles screamed in their mouths while clubs waved wildly overhead in their hands.

After the impromptu parade of unsightly flesh thundered from view, Reyne turned back to Mera. "This is my first time in Teth. Is it always like this?"

Mera looked somewhere between dumbfounded, confused, and entertained. "Never mind all that."

"I get the first two, Teth and the Covenant, but who's Cree?"

"Jerithan Cree, First Lord of the Temple of Life. You probably know him as First Lord Jerithan."

"Yeah, he's the jerk who keeps demanding a larger tithe from us year after year since he took over a few years back. I gotta agree with the whirling dicks, fuck Cree."

Mera said, "Let's hope that's the only societal anomaly we encounter. We don't need any complications interfering with our purpose."

Mera turned from Reyne and proceeded through the empty governmental control facility normally occupied to collect entry taxes and to keep out the rabble. After emerging out the other side, gaining unfettered access to Teth, garbage littering the street of the once immaculate city welcomed them. Shoppes, normally bustling with activity, were boarded up—at least those whose windows weren't broken.

Passing one unfortunate shoppe, it became clear why those of the smashed window variety didn't bother with after-the-fact security efforts; nothing of value remained inside to protect. The contents of one unfortunate store were emptied. Rioters expressed their frustrations upon the trading post's innards. Other broken-window shoppes fared no better.

Mera said, "On a normal day the city is packed with shoppers, visitors, street vendors, and lots of people. But now, it's destitute. Empty. If I had to guess, the provost and First Lord have lost control of the city. Or, at least, this section."

Reyne continued to scan his surroundings, having little experience with big city life. In better times, it may have generated a level of excitement. Not the same man of only weeks ago, even though he was a fellow business owner, Teth's state of affairs held no interest for Reyne. The kind, joyful man who Reyne had been his entire life stayed behind in Hensdale. Replaced by a constant ache for Mithany and the torment over his brother's death. The empty shell of the man he had become weighed him down with each painful step forward.

Reyne forced himself to speak. "I agree with two points of the protesters, fuck Cree and fuck Teth. Maybe by the end of the day we can cross off that last one, the Covenant, as well. Who knows, maybe I'll join 'em."

Mera warned, "Be careful, Reyne. There is more happening here than meets the eye."

Reyne ignored the man who claimed to be his protector.

Mera continued, "I don't want to alarm you, but the city isn't safe. If Evidar hunters know what you look like, even though they think you're dead, anyone we come across who I don't know could be the last person you ever see. Stay close to me at all times."

In his state of depression, Reyne ignored Mera.

"Listen to me. This isn't a game. You lived your whole life cloistered in a rural village where every stranger who showed face, you could judge. Every person coming at us from every direction is a potential threat you can't control."

Irritation crept in at every vocalization Mera offered—well-meant or otherwise. Reyne stopped, hung his head, and reflected for a moment with eyes closed. He grasped Mera's intentions to keep him safe, yet Reyne couldn't get past Mera as the one who forced him to abandon Mithany. Mera ripped him from the life he'd been promised, and Reyne couldn't navigate his emotions around that seemingly insurmountable stumbling block.

"Like you said. If I die, Mithany's safe. Doesn't matter if it happens here or in that fantasy world of yours, Evidar." Reyne picked his head up and slowly opened his eyes. He glared hard into Mera's. "So, piss off."

Apparent to Reyne, Mera took the hint. They walked through the beaten, battered city as two mutes. Conditions remained much the same everywhere they witnessed: refuse scattered in the streets, storefronts boarded, broken, or destroyed by fire—all empty of people. With each live body they encountered, and there were only a few, Mera put himself between Reyne and whoever they passed.

Hours dragged on, and Reyne's empty husk of a body shuffled close behind Mera. The pair passed through the specter of a once beautiful city. Emptiness alone did not hold Reyne down. He'd have to feel magnitudes better to pin the blame on emptiness as the only demon causing the depth of his malaise.

Across Teth, the lingering offensive odors of flamed-out buildings, burnt homes, and the once-familiar settings of communal gatherings were all in a state of destructive decrepitude. The devastation of the city, a violation that attacked the bonds holding humanity together, now dismembered, touched Reyne's core—Teth and Reyne were the same. Both once vibrant and alive; now each a shell of what they had been. Physically and emotionally tired and raw from the treacherous journey through the Razors, mournful beyond his ability to express the depths of his loss, devoid of benevolence, of compassion, of the slightest touch of affection for anything ahead, Teth appeared to him as a representation of what had become of his soul.

Daedyn's life, all his days to come, gutted like the shattered city. His forlorn love for Mithany existed far away yet mirrored the desolate, ruined homes he passed, once filled with shared joy and playful laughter. The sight of each empty home, the fragrance of every breeze that carried smells, ashes, and memories important to people he never knew, drove hot spikes into his psyche, searing pain into his heart.

Although Reyne observed Teth for what it had become, he cared little for what he saw, its condition, or the people in it—its all-pervasive representation of his own inner being hurt too much.

Reyne's mood grew darker with each step.

Like a beast howling inside him, it fed off the anger of his diminished soul.

Intense fury from whatever it was screamed from within for release.

Reyne's inner voice wailed against what little he had left of the promised idyllic married life that, only days away, ripped from him, existed now as a dream beyond reach. With each step, Mera grew larger as the target of his rage.

Uncertain of the day, he'd given no thought as each passed, yet in his bones, today had the feeling of his forsaken wedding. He pondered the thoughts of his would-be bride, her sense of loss given the joy that should have been this day, and his nuptial-blues gave birth to even deeper remorse.

A city on a path to ruin filled his sights, yet only as an apparition, an out-of-focus theatrical set playing somewhere in the background of his mind.

Gentle winds played the charcoaled studs left standing in the aftermath like ghostly, haunting, compelling yet emotionally draining music.

Hints of the once-joyful reds, playful yellows, or religious greens that painted the city gave way to the dismally offensive grays and blacks of conflagration's story.

Aromas that might have danced along a friendly campfire into long-held memories instead spoke of devastation and the destruction of lives. The mechanics of his brain had little interest in any of it.

Voices, soft at first, became louder as the two men journeyed closer to the Temple Palace. By the time they reach the final turn, Reyne pulled himself from his ever-present morass demanded of him by the clamorous decibels escaping from the raucous crowd that had yet to reveal itself.

There, as he turned a corner, the source—a deafening mob—appeared. A thousand people or more. Angry folks with their backs to Reyne and Mera. Reyne strained to single out, to listen to individual voices as so many were screaming vile, murderous intent, all at once. He heard unidentified figures in the crowd yell out.

"Kill him!" someone shouted.

"Cut his balls off!" another yelled.

"Feed him to the hounds!" from a third voice.

Mera grabbed Reyne's arm, keeping him from moving in closer. Reyne tried to yank his arm free. Mera locked down an iron grip and with abnormal strength prevented Reyne from taking another step forward.

"What the hell, let go of me," Reyne demanded while trying to wrest free.

"No. We wait here. I don't want you seen. Remember, any single one of them—" Mera started when Reyne tried again to jerk his arm free.

Mera's grip held firm. Failing to wrest clear, Reyne said, "Let go. Alright, I get it."

From his vantage point, Reyne could make out a platform, far back, facing the crowd. An empty podium stationed off to the left only a few feet from a woman, seated in a chair, dead center of it all. A haggard-looking man, in a Temple of Life green vestment, stood with a man on either side. A third man, on a stump, loomed behind the manacled captive.

Threats from the gathered, some quite creative, poured out their antagonism at the distraught man.

Reyne asked Mera, "What's goin' on? You know any of 'em up there?"

"I do, and no, I don't know what's going on. Whatever it is, it's not good."

"Who do you know?"

"The man in the green vestment is a high-ranking lord in the Temple of Life."

"Out with it already. Who's the guy?"

"I can't believe these people have discarded the ingrained commitment to preserving life. The pillar of the Covenant. This can't be happening in Teth." Mera stopped. The look on his face spoke of uncertainty, confusion, and disbelief.

Annoyed, Reyne said, "Just tell me, who are the people up there?"

"The woman seated, she's at the top of the food chain of a loose confederation of miscreants who commit most of the crime in Teth, the Thuggery. The guy in the robe, that's Second Lord Razoal. He's the highest ranking prudent behind First Lord Jerithan Cree. I'm worried about where this is headed."

Tied Up in Lies

Hensdale: 2nd Day of the Harvest Moon

Neladith

Dark clouds rolled in across the skyline, raising the spirits of the Evidar assassins gathered in the Hensdale home of two dead apple farmers. The safe house proved infinitely useful, although no longer for the elderly couple disenfranchised from ownership because of their murders by its current occupants.

The team's on-site leader, Selundra Quith, had departed the isolated homestead earlier in search of evidence proving Reyne, in fact, had been killed. With Quith's early departure, Neladith, Grafph, and Tylus remained behind to pursue alternative means of acquiring the elusive intel. Quith tasked the trio with extracting information from the Hensdale folk's weakest link, Arek.

The cinnamon-blond Tylus, an average man who blended into any gathering and a full decade older than the youthful Neladith, popped his head up from the cellar stairway. A scar on his forehead afforded him a rugged, average, work-a-day face. His dark, teal-colored Evidarian eyes had adjusted to Tartica's light of day long ago, and, unlike Neladith, not a vestige of redness remained within them. "Let's get this done," Tylus directed.

"Did he put up any resistance?" Neladith asked, emerging from one of the bedrooms.

"Not at first. We made it most of the way here before he got suspicious. But then Grafph tripped him. Neat trick, more like half a trip, half a push and aimed his head at a rock. Grafph landed it perfectly, and Arek's head stuck the landing—out cold. We had to carry him the last half mile. He's still unconscious."

Neladith asked, "Too bad. Do you think it'll be long before he wakes up so he can be questioned?"

With a shrug Tylus replied, "Not sure, but when he does, he'll have one hell of a headache."

"That'll be the least of his worries." They both laughed.

The team didn't have to wait long. Grafph, the senior member in terms of years served yet of lower rank, being less accomplished in the realm of death and killing, shouted up from the bowels of the basement. His voice, a reflection of the man he had become, rolled out in downcast tones, "Ty. He's awake."

Shorter than his teammates, Grafph sported a once-firm physique now in a state of decline from an obvious lack of upkeep. The paunch hugging his mid-section signaled his declining dedication to the physical demands of his profession.

"Thanks, Grafph," Tylus replied. "We'll be right there." Turning to Neladith, he asked, "Would you like to take the first crack at questioning Arek?"

Neladith replied, "Ty, you're the ranking agent. You're gonna give him over to me? I'm game."

"Good. That's what I like to hear. What approach are you figuring on?"

Neladith's eyes lit up, and an evil grin crossed her face. An ulterior motive in the interrogation approach took shape in her lascivious thoughts that Tylus would never fathom. Besides, if what she was thinking didn't work, Tylus could always beat the answers out of Arek later.

"I'd like to go about it a little differently. Follow me on this. Remember, Arek's the guy I've been hooking up with to get close to Reyne. This world is obsessed with making babies to the point everyone's running around half-undressed. Their silly religion even has this adoration for what they call the Gift of Flesh, and they encourage everyone to be fucking. More babies, more people. Blah, blah. Arek downstairs, he's the worst. He ain't religious, but he's a true aficionado of all things related to flesh."

Tylus asked, "So what are you suggesting?"

"If it's okay with you, I'd like to try teasing it out of him. I'm pretty sure I can. I want to try it my way. This guy is horned up all the time. It should be easy."

Tylus said, "You could be right. The men... the women... they're all the same. The women are forever in season and the men... always on the lookout."

"Couldn't agree more. They claim to hook up with each other for the desired outcome—the whole 'We have to repopulate the world' and the baby thing. But if you ask me, it's all bullshit. Just an excuse to fornicate at will. Not that there's anything wrong with that."

"Are you sure it'll work?"

"In my short time as Arek's love interest, it's clear, I can make him do anything for the promise of sex."

Being asked to question Arek had its downside. She lamented the all-but-certain end of him filling the role as her current fuckbuddy. And Arek was as good at sex as any man or woman she had ever been with. But she couldn't pass on the opportunity Tylus offered. Not that she had feelings for Arek; she didn't. Neladith lacked feelings for anyone, except for one woman: a lover back home, lost to Neladith in a brutal death, who bore a striking resemblance to Mithany. The few days she'd spent on Tartica teased her in ways she hadn't expected. Yet, she had her job to do, and would get it done—whatever the cost.

Tylus reminded her, "The goal of Arek's interrogation is confirmation we killed Reyne, or if someone else lay dead in his grave. That's the goal."

Excited, she replied, "Yeah. I can do that... my way."

The mismatch of wills embedded at the core of her approach pitted Arek's appetite for the Gift of Flesh against her calculated use of feminine wiles, which, she concluded, skewed heavily in her favor. Competitive to a fault, she had to come away victorious, and she believed with certainty she would. Neladith expected to easily pry the information from his lips.

Tylus pushed, "What do we gain by your approach? What's the advantage?"

"We keep him as an unwilling asset if needed. Can't do that if we beat it out of him."

"Neladith, he's tied to a chair. How's that going to work?"

"Trust me, he'll think it's just kink. I'll tell him I sent you to get him here for us to play 'tie-me-up' or some plausible bullshit like that. It's all part of the game. I've tied him up before. He'll buy it. The guy's fixated on sex," Neladith told Tylus, but withheld informing him she and Arek had a lot of *fixations* in common.

Tylus stated, "Alright. Give it a shot your way. Would you like me to join you in case anything goes wrong?"

"No. He'll respond to me better if it's just the two of us."

"But don't take too long. We gotta get this done before Quith comes back."

"Thanks, Ty. I won't let you down."

She scurried away quickly into her room and dressed with purpose for the interrogation. She looked into the mirror and saw a young woman with demanding hormones like every other adult-in-the-making, be they male or female, from Tartica or Evidar. Neladith let her inner reflections wander, running her hands along her hips. She wondered about her own youthful appetites, the ones older folks seem to forget about during the days of their own post-pubescent awakening. She considered her own eagerness to answer the call of raging hormones at almost every nudging, whether alone or with a partner, and whether this would be one of those times. Death, actual or merely promised, always got her juices flowing, and she was wet just thinking about the interrogation.

Excited, she made her way to the waiting Tylus and Grafph, who positioned themselves near the door to the cellar as though part of some ceremonial reception line. "Make us proud," Grafph offered as Neladith opened, then closed the door behind her.

Neladith made her way into the basement to stand before Arek, who was tied to a large, wooden, armless chair, set in the middle of the cluttered cellar.

Pale skinned—like all from Evidar—Neladith pulled back her long, red hair into a playful ponytail. Both deadly and attractive, she approached the seated captive. She had dressed with intent, a few open buttons of her blouse highlighting her ample chest. A short skirt accentuated the meeting point of her long legs. Coupled with her other youthful assets, Neladith expected Arek to surrender quickly to her seductive offerings. Her outfit, a calculated attack aimed at what she perceived as his greatest weakness—oversexed to the point of suffocating any want for self-control. Eager to begin, she rubbed her palms together, self-aware enough to recognize the similarities she shared with Arek in the hunger to satiate carnal desires.

Excited, she began, "Arek, how are you, my dear?" A sweet voice belied her intentions. "Smells a bit musty down here, wouldn't you say?"

"Why am I tied up? The fat guy wouldn't tell me anything. Only that I tripped and here I am."

Neladith slowly paced in front of Arek. "I understand. You're a little confused, tied up and all. I can see that. Well, let me help you. We're going to play a little game. I tied you up to start the contest. You can tie me up later, but only if you win. This game is like show-and-tell, but this one is called ask-and-tell. I thought you'd like this," she said followed by a coy curtsy.

Arek scrunched his face, and Neladith could see his puzzlement. She jumped in, "Let's get started. So here's my first ask, do you like my outfit?" A slow spin gave him an overview.

"You look great."

One lone finger danced along her exposed skin above the open blouse. "So do you. I could have my way with you right now. Would you like that?"

"Would you?"

"Now, Arek, I'll be the one asking the questions."

"I'm game. Ask away."

"Well, things seemed kinda funny the other day. You know, at the Brenton family plot." She leaned in and opened another button. "Tell me what really happened, and you can get to the next level of our game. You're gonna like that part the best. So will I."

She stopped, kneeled in front of him, and rested her hands on each of his knees. Leaning in close, she said, "You know you get a reward by answering the question correctly. The prize for this one is head. So tell me, who's really under all that dirt?" Neladith moved her hand from his knee and stroked it across his crotch several times.

"You did all this for me? This game sounds like fun, but you only had to ask."

"Arek, you're getting me all wet. Let's get this behind us so we can take care of this little itch of mine."

"Now I'm taking care of your itch? What happened to the fellatio you promised?"

Laughing, she said, "Fellatio. That's a mouthful. Didn't figure you knew such big words." With a tease, she pushed her tongue against the inside of her cheek, stretching the outer skin, then released it, only to repeat it—back and forth, back and forth—several times in quick succession.

Arek smiled back at her.

She returned to rubbing her palm between his legs. "Oh, we'll get to it. Like I said, your reward for answering the question correctly. So just tell me, and we can move this along."

Arek tilted his head to the side like a bewildered puppy. "I don't know why you're asking. It's not confusing. But to answer your question, Reyne, of course. Do I win?"

She stopped her hand in mid-stroke and offered Arek a questioning look of her own. In a mocking gesture, she tilted her head, mimicking him. Cupping his groin, she said, "From experience, you should be hard by now. All I feel here is soft and mushy flesh. What's going on, Arek?"

"Maybe you're losing your touch?"

"No, that's not it. These long, thin fingers are good at this. Besides, in the short time we've been together, you get a chubby if I just look at you. And I *am* ready to go. Puddles." Neladith spoke truthfully to her captive, as the excitement of an interrogation mixed with the possibility of sex had driven her youthful desires to new heights.

"What's going on here, Arek? You thinking about something else? You trying to hide something from me? Is thinking of your lie interfering with the signals from your brain to your dick? That's what I think it is. Now, come on. Tell me. It's not really Reyne in that hole, is it?"

"Why would you think that?" His tone offered Neladith nothing in the way of suspicion. Arek projected calm strength as Neladith read it.

She admired his innocence, real or feigned. Certain, though, he offered only half-truths. But she needed proof. Hensdale's Judjurex, the guy responsible for looking into Reyne's reported death, maintained a constant presence at the orchard that hadn't left her team any opportunity to excavate his grave. They might dig later that night, yet Quith wanted answers immediately, before dark, when he expected to set out for Owls Neck to provide Dylla the update she demanded. The timing made it imperative that Neladith extracted answers from Arek before night settled in and Quith returned.

She didn't care for Arek's response to her efforts, both physical and verbal. By her calculations, he misjudged her, and his lack of an anatomical response nailed it shut in her mind. *He's lying.*

Neladith said in a friendly tone, like a couple of friends sitting and chatting, "Why would I think so, you asked? Well, it all started when you told your sister that she'd see Reyne again. You remember, just the other day, when I came out to pay my respects at the vigil and offered my condolences to you and Mithany? You told her she'd see Reyne again. You looked handsome all dressed up." She stood and twirled twice around, causing the short plackets of her skirt to fly up. "Anyway, that's why I think that. Let's cut through all this silliness. Tell me what's going on, and we can get to the part where we fuck. I always liked that part the best. Naked, you and me are soooo good together." She ran her tongue along his neck.

Arek appeared to gather his thoughts, and the delay in his response put Neladith on guard for more lies. A dozen seconds passed. Arek said, "All I meant was they'd meet up in the Community of Life. You know, when her time comes."

"You know," Neladith imitated his words, then added, "I simply don't believe you. I should leave you here and go find your sister. The two guys that brought you here could play ask-and-tell with her." Neladith raised her eyebrows, accompanied by a matching malevolent smirk, intent on putting something Arek cared about at risk: Mithany.

A Tortured Man

Hensdale: 2nd Day of the Harvest Moon

Arek | Neladith

The stakes changed for Arek the instant Neladith threatened harm to Mithany. He would never allow it, even secured in an unfamiliar basement and tied to a chair. He'd face his own death to protect her. But what he didn't understand was what interest Neladith had in Mera's ruse of Reyne's death? *Did she know it was Daedyn who died? And why would it matter to her?* Comprehension of the dynamics at play eluded Arek. Yet, it mattered little, as his only concern was for his sister.

Not usually a deep thinker—other than how to get some woman out of her clothes—Arek's synapses fired faster than usual, searching for a way out that protected both Mithany and Reyne.

Then it hit him. Mera spoke of people who wanted to kill Reyne. That was the reason for faking Reyne's death: to get them to believe they'd succeeded and to afford Reyne time to get away. *Could Neladith be one of them? No, that's not possible. But—*

"Nel, I'm pretty sure we're not playing games here."

"You found me out. Nope. No games. Just need to know who you buried, and then you can go."

He stalled. "Why do you care? Reyne got mauled by some wild animal and died."

Arek watched as Neladith looked to be in deep contemplation, staring out into the shadows of the dank room, then nodded to herself in the universal signal for *yes*, as though arriving at some important decision.

Neladith turned back to Arek, and with pursed lips, her face had changed. Playful Neladith was gone. It came through her tone as well when she said, "We both know that's not true. Nobody got mauled."

Alarms screeched in every recess of his brain. Heat exploded, turning his face the color of Neladith's fiery eyes. Unable to hide the gulp he forced down, he couldn't process any other thought. *She's one of them! She knows!* Somehow Neladith knew enough to question who'd been murdered and that no wild animal did the evil deed.

"That look on your face. You're beginning to put it together. Yes, we here in this house, we killed him. Well, more precisely, I did," she said, shaking her head up and down. Raising one eyebrow she told him, "The question you need to answer for me is who *him* is." She pushed out pouting lips. "And then you can go. After you answer me, we can still do it, if you want to." One hand, with her long, thin fingers leading the way, reached down over her skirt to rub at her groin. "I know I want to."

Arek watched with complete disinterest. She stood before him, calm, proud, and lacked any emotion other than joy. Drumbeats of blood pounded in his head so loud he was certain she could hear them. He wouldn't let Neladith see his fears or the truth of Daedyn's death. Arek pushed all concerns for his own predicament aside to allow only one purpose to prevail, to protect Mithany.

Tied to a chair, my options are limited. But I just might be able to buy her more time. After Mithany fulfilled her obligation to stand vigil, she intended to leave Hensdale behind in search of Reyne, Mera's demands to the contrary notwithstanding. Arek had planned to meet up with Mithany hours ago to start their journey, but then he'd been deceived and hijacked to his current location. He hoped Mithany had set her plan in motion to join with the Forest Maiden Inn regulars on the search—which she told them was to find Daedyn.

He prayed she had already left without him and with Spetzer et al., in tow. He needed to buy Mithany time to put distance between her and Neladith. If Mithany had time to get out of town before Neladith came looking, she would be safe.

An idea popped into his head. In spite of his thumping chest, burning ears, and red-hot face, Arek showed no fear. "I'm all tied up. Why ask? Do what you want with me." He hoped to squeeze out as much time as he could for his sister. As much as it appalled him, he knew Neladith's voracious appetite for sex might be all he needed to distract her. "Take off your clothes. Let's do it. Right here. Like you said." *This oughta take a few hours... if she bites.*

She stopped rubbing herself. "I will. After you tell me who's really in the dirt."

Arek smiled up at Neladith. "Reyne."

"Play it your way. You want me to take off my clothes? I should be taking off yours, but alright. Let's see where this leads us." Neladith unbuttoned her top. The blouse came off in quick fashion.

She cupped her bare breasts. "You do like playing with these. I gotta admit, I do too." Tightly squeezing, she jiggled them up and down for emphasis, with flesh spilling out from under each finger.

He took no pleasure in Neladith's bare-chested gesticulations.

Neladith leaned in to let her nipples brush against his cheeks as she swayed her bosom back and forth across his face. She reached down to feel Arek's crotch. "What... is this thing working?" Disappointment filled her eyes as she stared into his, with one breast pressed against his mouth.

Arek mumbled.

"Oh, I'm sorry, you can't speak." She leaned back but kept her bust front and center. "Now, what did you say?"

"I said, maybe I'm a little too constrained in these ropes."

"I thought you'd like a little bondage. We've done this before." Letting go of his privates, she reached up to roll her nipples between thumb and forefinger as she continued talking, "Tell me what happened that night. Who ended up slumped over the porch railing?"

Playing for time, while revolted at what he knew he had to do, Arek teased, "Take off your skirt. Maybe that'll get me started." And he thought, *Every minute spent with this psycho-bitch gets Mithany that much further away.*

The red-haired temptress unseated herself and fanned the front panels of her short skirt up and down several times; revealing, then hiding, what she claimed to be the prize underneath. "I'm not wearing any panties. You like that?" Standing back a few feet, Neladith allowed the raiment to drop to the ground, fulfilling Arek's request. Gingerly, each foot stepped out over the fallen garment. With a wink, she quipped, "Remember, red on top and red down below."

Arek ran his eyes over her body.

"I'm gonna cut you out of those clothes," Neladith told him, then added playfully, "Fair is fair." After cutting away his garb, Neladith stepped back, leaving Arek wearing only the ropes securing him.

"Now you and I are the same." Her eyes settled on his lap. Disappointment again painted her face when she looked up at him. "Your little soldier isn't standing at attention. Well, I have to admit, he's not so little." She stared at it, shifting and tilting her head, first to the left then to the right. In polite tones, she asked, "What's going on here, Arek?" With her hands on her hips Neladith returned to pacing back and forth in front of him, as though considering her next move. A broad grin bloomed. She stopped directly in front of him, lifted one leg, and rested her foot on his chest. "One last time, my dear," she said, her voice both sweet and seductive. "Who's in the grave?"

Arek said nothing at first. Seconds passed with her foot on his chest. He smirked.

With a little effort, given the mass of the chair and the weight Arek added, she forced it back, balancing it precariously for several heartbeats before she exerted the final push. The chair fell back, with Arek tied to it. It crashed to the ground with a bang, as did the back of his head and shoulders.

Shit, that hurt. Not wanting to give her any satisfaction, Arek looked up at her from the ground and calmly said, "Now what?"

Neladith walked over to him and stood with each foot planted on opposite sides of the fallen chair, hovering over his face.

Playing it off unimpressed, he said, "You remember, I've seen the goods before. And up a lot closer."

He watched her eyes ride over his body, coming to rest on his exposed, limp privates. She asked again, "Who'd you bury?"

Silence.

Swiveling her hips in slow circles, she asked, "What say you, Arek?"

Arek closed his eyes and said nothing, intending to drag out Neladith's every effort. She'd have to work harder for it, and he'd endure it all to prolong Neladith's time with him.

After setting the chair upright, with Arek tied to it, Neladith straddled herself across his lap. She reached down and took hold of his flaccid intromittent organ. "I'm starting to think you don't like me anymore."

With eyes aimed at his wilted penis resting on her open palm—petting it with the other hand like one would a docile cat—she said, "We're gonna be here all afternoon and into the evening if we have to. However long it takes, you *will* tell me what I want to know."

Her words, "into the evening," made him happy, even tied up.

"You know, we can do this differently. I'm playing nice, but pain can be an effective inducement." She offered him a wicked, teasing smile, moving her hand from his limp shaft to cup his balls. With the pair resting in her palm, her fingers rolled around the flesh of his scrotum and the two testes within before suddenly squeezing them—hard. While nearly crushing his testicles she leaned in and whispered in his ear, "You get the point."

His eyes bugged out the instant her viselike grip compressed his knards into a smaller space than nature ever intended, and the overwhelming compulsion to retch clenched his stomach. He coughed, gagged, and dry heaved, but nothing escaped his gut except pain.

"The guys upstairs just wanted to beat it out of you. But I told them to let me do it my way." As though to emphasize her point, she eased the pressure on his testicles, caged inside a finger-like prison cell, and instead began to gently caress them. "What's it gonna be, Arek? You gonna tell me, or should I call them down here?"

With his stomach in knots and his heart thundering in his chest, Arek knew he had only one option. For Mithany he would accept the beating Neladith promised from the two men if it dragged out the session longer. His childhood prepared him well. Pain delivered by a loveless mother in the form of frequent whippings, thrashings, and full-out battering inured him to whatever Neladith or the men upstairs could deliver—or so he thought.

He played the only card he had left. "I'm up for it. Let's just do it, here, now, you and me. We can talk when we're done. I'll tell you anything you want to know... after." Although he lied, his attempt at a conditional acceptance of her offer proved inadequate to the question she asked.

Evil bloomed across her face.

Her eyes, menacing in their redness, burned with fury. In a flash, seated across his lap, Neladith lost all control. She exploded in an attack. Her arms flailed violently. She clawed at him like a wild beast. With each strike, her nails bit into his flesh.

He howled in pain.

Blood spewed out where she dug deep, and Arek felt the warm liquid running down against his skin.

Her fists pounded his chest and face.

He tasted the coppery tang of his own blood. He wailed and spat the pool collecting in his mouth back at her. Ferociously, he squirmed, twisted, and tugged for his freedom the ropes denied him. He threw his head rabidly from side to side, becoming a wild animal himself. But blow after blow pounded his skull as her fists tracked his every movement.

With a wayward swipe, her nail, sharp and deadly, ripped across the delicate skin of his eyelid. Arek screamed.

She cuffed his ears.

Bells clanged into his skull. Burning pain turned his ears red hot. Searing agony throbbed in his temples. He hated her and couldn't fathom how he had once cared for her—only hours before. Rage consumed him and demanded of him to strike back. But he couldn't do anything to stop it.

She bit at his nose. Arek cried out in pain.

Gurgling, he spat it back at her. But she didn't stop.

The Evidar huntress bit into the soft flesh of his cheek.

Lightning-hot bolts of agony ripped across his face.

Blood sprayed into his eye. He attempted a head butt—but failed.

Wild, Neladith's teeth rendered flesh away in chunks before spitting out the pieces. She'd punched and thrashed at his body with a fury matched only by his mother's. The memories of the beatings he took from his mother aroused an uncontrollable physical response that began in the years after her death. Lightheaded and in agony, he felt what he feared even more than the pain inflicted on his body.

NO!

But it was already too late.

It had a mind of its own.

It moved.

It stirred.

It was awake—and aroused.

Suddenly, Neladith stopped. Breathing heavily, she looked down. "And what do we have here?" Surprise bled out in her tone.

Neladith scooched back in his lap, exposing an erect Arek. "My, my," she said, firmly gripping it. "It's like iron. I'd dare say we might even cut diamonds with this thing, it's so hard."

Arek had no ability to stop it. He hated himself for it. Yet he hated Neladith for revealing it, even more than for the physical torture she delivered.

Still gripping his erection in her hand, she looked into his eyes and said, "My goodness, someone in your early years must have done a number on you. Easy to guess... your father, or no... it's gotta be your mother. You like women... not men."

With an open palm, she swiped blood from his torso and used it to stroke his cock. "Imagine that, this thing just got even harder. I'm loving this," she squealed.

His hard phallus, in Neladith's hand, exposed the scars of his childhood. The consequence of his mother's frequent, furious, crazed beatings being the only real attention she ever gave him. The connection between pain and a longing for love was cemented in his psyche—somewhere deep where he couldn't root it out. Only one other person knew of Arek's anatomical secret until today, and she also experienced the ferocity of their mother's anger.

"My dear, this little quirk of yours is your undoing. I believe you're now gonna tell me what I want to know."

He feared Neladith even more now that she knew. But for Mithany, like when they were children and he stood in her place whenever he could to face their mother's torment, he'd endure Neladith's discovery of his secret and live with whatever followed. His heart thundered in response to the intense pain, in response to the sexual excitement he couldn't control, and in response to the terror of being exposed. With each squeeze of the muscle in his chest, it pulsed through his body and pushed blood oozing from the rips, cuts, and gouges to his flesh, yet did nothing to diminish the flow of blood fueling his hardened state.

All he could muster was a pathetically whimpered, "Fuck you."

"Fuck me, you say... As you wish." Before Arek could react, Neladith guided his blood-covered shaft into her. She lowered herself and slowly slipped him fully inside. Her head drifted back, her eyes fluttered, and she groaned in response to the obvious, exquisite, sensual pleasure he reluctantly delivered.

She started slowly and built up faster and faster as she rode him. After only a short time her body started quivering and shaking. Grabbing both of his shoulders as an anchor, she exploded in ecstasy as she came. She paused only several heartbeats with closed eyes and a face lit up in rapture as deep breaths filled her lungs. Slowly, Neladith began again. As she built up speed with her legs thrusting her up to the limits of his extension, then relaxing her muscles to let the weight of her body slide him deep inside with every plunge. Up and down, over and over, all the while groaning and moaning in delight.

Then, suddenly, she stopped.

"What is it with you?" she demanded, sliding back to expose his semi-flaccid penis. "You didn't come. I would've felt it." Angry, she spat, "I'm not done with you!" And in an instant, she erupted, beating, pounding, ripping at his chest and face. More blood dripped from new cuts, but she didn't stop. He became hard again, and he hated himself for it.

Neladith noticed it almost immediately and wasted no time guiding him back into her. She returned to thrusting, pumping, grinding, riding him, all the while punching, clawing, and thrashing at his body. She groaned with pleasure gratifying her carnal needs, coming again and again, her body quivering with each release. When finally exhausted, she exclaimed, "Whew, that was wild."

Neladith took in several deep breaths and slumped forward into his bloodied chest. Closing her eyes, she whispered in his ear, "If you only told me sooner of your little fetish, we could've been doing this from the day we met in Owls Neck." Her chest rose and fell as she lifted her head to face him. Then demanded, "Now, you're gonna tell me who's in the grave."

He was spent. His head slumped down to his chest. He didn't reply to her query—he couldn't. Motionless in the chair that rested on a floor spattered in blood, Arek drifted from consciousness.

Neladith swung one leg over Arek's unresponsive body and stood. Her legs were shaky, and her thigh muscles trembled as she walked. Patches of her skin were painted red in a mosaic of Arek's bodily fluids. She called up the stairway to the security detail.

The men made their way to the basement in a flash.

She shrugged. "Not sure if I killed him."

Tylus spoke up, "You're naked and covered in blood. We heard a lot of screaming and a few bangs. That must have been one hell of an interrogation. Guess you gave it both approaches. It appears you tried titillation, pun intended. And, from the looks of him, seems you tried beating it out of him as well. Couldn't ask for a better effort. But... did he talk?"

"Ty, he just gave out before I completed interrogating him. He was protecting something."

"Can't fault you for the effort. But it doesn't sound like he gave us anything useful."

"He didn't say the words, but indirectly, he confirmed Reyne's alive; I know it. Arek's useless to us now. Quith will be back soon. Can you both get this cleaned up? Not sure my legs can handle it."

Through the grin plastered on his face, Grafph replied, "Sure. Will do. I'm really enjoying the work you did here."

Neladith shot back, "What, you've never seen tits before? I'm a dedicated agent. I do whatever needs doing, however it needs doing, to get the job done. I deployed a tactic to exploit a subject's weakness and get him to talk."

Angry with Grafph's comment but actually more so with herself, Neladith took control, fully aware her state of undress gave her power over them. Brushing off her junior position within the unit, she issued orders to the two men outranking her. With authority in her tone, she demanded, "He's got nothing to say now. Get him out of here. Bury him or dump his body deep in the woods where wild animals can feast on it. I don't care, just make sure he's dead."

Neladith allowed her orders to settle in and enough time for the men's lizard brains to recede in order for their operative-trained gray matter to take back control. Quiet disappointment rolled off her tongue as she spoke to the security boys. "Just get him out of here."

"Will do."

Neladith was furious with herself for not directly securing the information from Arek. She thought, *Knowing Arek, it should've worked. The tease should've been enough for him to spill. Shit!* Arek had defeated her. He may have paid the ultimate price for victory, but he still won. It gnawed at her, yet she couldn't let it show to Tylus. She forced her face to comply.

Before the pair could act on her instructions, the sound of someone pounding on the door reverberated throughout the house. In unison, the three Evidar agents stiffened, and all heads snapped toward the unexpected acoustic intrusion.

Tylus whispered, "Who could that be? No one knows we're here. It's gotta be someone looking for the old couple."

Neladith again took control. "People have seen me around town. If either of you two answer the door, it'll raise suspicions. I'll throw my clothes back on and go see who it is. If they're looking for the dead geezers, I'll give them my sweet-girl persona and tell them I'm a long-lost cousin or some bullshit. Stay here. Stay quiet while I get rid of whoever it is."

Without waiting for Tylus's approval, intending to keep the unknown intruder from entering the house, she rushed up the stairs and shouted, "I'll be right there. Gotta throw on something presentable. Give me a minute." Fighting her own unwilling thighs, she raced back down to the basement sink and doused a bucket of water over her blood-soaked body.

"Help me, guys. Quick." The men eagerly helped Neladith rub blood off every inch of her body. They even helped where blood hadn't landed. She didn't care. But for failure gnawing her insides, she otherwise would have enjoyed the hands of two men, working together, rubbing her down, exploring her body.

Tylus finished by running his fingers through her hair, wiping it clean of blood. The trio worked quickly, and the entire process consumed only a dozen or so heartbeats.

Neladith, sans clothing, asked, "Everything gone? You see any blood?" She turned in a circle for her fellow agents to inspect the results.

Tylus smiled and replied, "You're good."

In no time, the remnants of Arek were washed away from both her body and her mind.

She dressed in seconds and bolted up from the cellar. Closing the basement door behind her, she yelled a second time, "COMING!" as she finished buttoning her blouse.

Neladith grabbed a hand towel, wiping water from her hands and face. Another loud knock demanded attention. Still wobbly and weak, her legs threatened to give out with each step. She kept herself upright and opened the door.

"Neladith?" Mithany stammered in a stunned voice. "I didn't expect to see you here. Anyway, I'm looking for my brother. Someone told me he came this way. Have you seen him?"

THAT IS THE QUESTION

TETH: 2ND DAY OF THE HARVEST MOON

Jerithan

With the time-honored ritual of sealing in the Council of Prudents, shutting them off from the outside world, the formal call for a Vote of Revocation had been invoked. Two majestic, enormous oak doors housing the conclave came together and resounded with the rattle of the locking metal latch. As the separate halves of the wooden portal kissed, a loud *kerplunk* echoed through the chamber. They gathered, infused with a solemn purpose, a single goal, to make a fateful decision: to keep or remove Jerithan Cree as First Lord of the Temple of Life.

Sequestered for hours, the Council of Prudents deliberated, cackled, debated, threatened, and quoted scripture, all in support of whatever position a particular speaker espoused in the heat of the moment. Hours of intense debate did little to move entrenched opinions or to sway a single mind.

Prudent Serco, a man in his fifties of average features that included a full head of hair peppered with graying temples and a large midsection earned from pampered years of overeating, decried of First Lord Jerithan, "Days. It's only been days. How could you let this happen? First, the Chancellor disavows the Covenant right under your nose, and then you lose control of the city. There's a mob outside the Palace as we speak." Pounding his fist on the table, spittle flung about as Jerithan's chief rival yelled out his rehearsed condemnations.

Jerithan fought back. "Where were you?" he demanded. "You dare to lay this at my feet. I ask again, where were you? You are our lead prudent in the Kingdom of Adelle. You've spent years in their capital city. You brag amongst your fellow prudents of your special relationship with Chancellor Tomelai. You were the closest amongst us to the man. You proudly brought his plans for electrics to this very Council. He played you. You failed to ferret out Chancellor Tomelai's real objective for that dark day, to end the Covenant. You, I'm sorry to say, failed all of us here in the room. No, even worse, you sealed our fate. You failed the Temple of Life. You failed! Not me."

Supporters of the First Lord slapped their open palms on the table repeatedly. Serco's faction sat back in unison with folded arms across their chests.

Serco tried to yell over the calamitous pounding. "Ten, I said ten of our fellow prudents are absent. Thirty-two of our brethren should be here today, but only twenty-two are. Senior prudents, Marvo, Hansel, Aquila, to name a few... each and every one of them capable of influencing us all with their insights and faith. The outcome of this sacred vote could have been swayed by any one of them." His arm flew across his body with an accusatory finger aimed at Jerithan. "You did this!" His eyes shot hatred. All the while Jerithan's supporters continued slapping their palms against the conference table to drown out Serco's accusations.

Battle lines were drawn even before the men and women of the Council of Prudents entered the room. The professed sacred gathering of holy prudents proved neither holy nor sacred, given the intransigent childish behaviors of the gathered and the self-interests underlying every utterance.

Jerithan lamented the Voice's absence: the mysterious, shrewd advisor who spoke into his mind from the time of adolescence. He'd long suspected the Voice originated from the mouth of God, who encouraged and guided him to become First Lord. It no longer mattered. The Voice fled him. Its departure coincided with Tomelai's call for the Covenant's dissolution only days before.

The Voice had told Jerithan he no longer held relevance in their shared quest to create the Empire of Tartica. Abandoned, Jerithan had been left to achieve his conquest alone. And now, instead of aggregating power across the continent as its emperor, Jerithan fought to hold on to his position as First Lord. His dreams of becoming Emperor of Tartica had gone up in the conflagration of chaos's grip on civilization. Glory was slipping through his fingers. Everything he was as a man depended on making it through Serco's attempt to unseat him.

Jerithan lashed out at Serco, "And what of our esteemed Second Lord Razoal? What have you done with him? Nothing in all the heavens would keep him from this unholy call for Revocation. Razoal is a deeply religious man who loves our faith, who supports my leadership. A man who would admonish you for your sinful power grab. You, Serco, and all of your lackeys, should be ashamed. To keep a fellow prudent of Razoal's standing from fulfilling his sacred duty to take part in this vote should disqualify all of you from casting a single ballot.

"Look at him. Guilt is written across his face," Jerithan said, pointing at the usurper. "The truth hits too close to home." Serco's slip of a smirk reinforced Jerithan's condemnation.

A staunch supporter of Serco, obviously intent on defending her leader, jumped out of her chair. Before she could say a word, Prudent O'Hurn cut her off. In a commanding bellow, he demanded, "Sit down! You are all prudents; dignity and respect for our faith demands you act like it. I will not have this."

Jerithan's appeal for his loyal Second Lord roused emotions, just not in the way he intended in those determined to depose him. Like in the realm of politics, words in the service of religious fervor played best to a friendly audience. Hypocrisy nor duplicity mattered much if the rhetoric supported the position du jour. While Jerithan decried Razoal's conspicuous absence, he'd prevented several key prudents who opposed his reign as First Lord from attending the conclave.

Conditions in Teth proved the ideal crucible for effecting delays. At Jerithan's hand, several of Serco's supporters struggled to successfully traverse the dangerous journey through the riots and the chaos to the Temple Palace. Paid Thuggery brigands successfully kept enough prudents from the Council meeting to give Jerithan a chance to defeat Serco's efforts to unseat him.

Serco, no doubt, did the same, but by Jerithan's head count, he had just enough votes to squeak by, but it was going to be close. Help from his Second Lord would have made a huge difference but in the here and now, alone, Jerithan forced Razoal's absence out of his mind and focused all his energy on saving himself.

Serco appealed to the conclave, "Second Lord Razoal is his own man. I've done nothing to prevent his attendance here today. I'm offended by your baseless accusations. Look around at the open seats at this table. His is not the only absence keenly felt. It's bedlam in the streets of our beloved city, all because you allowed Chancellor Tomelai to demand the end of the Covenant. In Greenlin, there are reports of riots. In Kantos, wild mobs have stormed the capital. You brought this on all of us. Your incompetence is to blame for those unable to be here. In a just world, each empty seat should be a statement demanding Revocation."

Prudent O'Hurn, a large, overweight, wise, and respected elder statesman, selected by those present to be the conclave's facilitator, attempted to return decorum to the assembly. "My fellow prudents, those fortunate enough to be here, we have been discussing the motion of Revocation for most of the day. And yes, it is our solemn duty, and we place no time limit on our deliberations. I offer the observation that we have been covering much of the same issues repeatedly, some by new voices, others by the same." O'Hurn paused, looking to both Serco and Jerithan.

The conclave's facilitator continued, "Let us offer any to speak on a new consideration, and if none are forthcoming, I would offer a motion to close off debate and move to a vote."

Jerithan's eyes bugged out, his ears burned, his mouth and tongue became as dry as a desert. The moment of decision loomed. Frantically, his focus darted from prudent to prudent. As he scanned his fellow holy officiates, those who he identified as enemies, Jerithan looked for any sign of a new speaker prepared to take center stage. He watched for a hesitant nod, an uneasy parting of lips, for a jaw muscle tighten, but he saw none of it. He observed heads turning from side to side as though each was expecting the other to speak. His heart raced against the fear of another verbal attack, one that threatened to change minds.

Stillness reigned in response to O'Hurn's challenge to end debate.

Under the table, Jerithan's fists clenched, digging his nails into the soft flesh of his delicate palms.

The First Lord ran the expected vote count in his head of the twenty-two prudents present. At best, he expected exactly half would vote for Revocation. A split vote, fifty-fifty, meant he would retain his position. Revocation required a one-vote majority to remove a sitting First Lord. Jerithan believed he'd secured the fifty percent he needed, yet with his count tenuous, he couldn't afford for even one vote to go differently than expected.

He offered much in exchange for their votes. Of the uncommitted prudents he'd swayed to his side, some demanded rank as compensation; others sought choice appointments; the truly greedy asked only for coin—a lot of it. Jerithan agreed to every request. He promised more than he could possibly deliver. A problem Jerithan left for another day. First, he had to get past the call to remove him from office.

As the seconds passed, Jerithan's heart beat madly in his chest. The vote could no longer be avoided. Anxiety stabbed fear into his brain, and each blistering jab compelled him to face an unthinkable future where power slipped through his fingers. His insides tormented him thinking of the life he'd face if he failed. Revocation would leave him humiliated and powerless. The removal of a First Lord had happened only twice in the history of the Third Age. One prudent took her own life as a result, if the written records were to be believed. The other, a senile old man, who outlived his ability to perform the duties. In an act of kindness, the Council quietly removed him from office. In his deluded thoughts, he still held the title. Jerithan believed himself too young to endure such degradation in the life of a dethroned ablegate. Senility would not hide his failure, and he didn't welcome the prospect of being murdered, not believing the party line that his long-dead predecessor took her own life.

If he lost the vote, his only solace—revenge.

With sharp, narrow eyes, one by one, Jerithan stared down each of the conspirators.

He marked them all.

—Just in case.

Serco, Jerithan decided, would pay most severely for his impudence once the Council got past the formality of the balloting: an outcome, Jerithan's tentative calculations suggested, skewed in his favor. But, win or lose, Serco's action sealed his fate—a different future than the usurper expected. Jerithan would see to it.

Prudent O'Hurn addressed the conclave, "Then, with no further issues, it falls to me to close off debate."

Jerithan considered challenging the motion, but thought better of it. It would make him appear weak, fearful, and while both may have been accurate, it could tip the vote against him. Instead, he said, "We've all said our peace. We now leave it to Teth to guide our hearts." Forced and unfelt, he smiled nonetheless.

Cloture proved the only issue the embattled prudents unanimously agreed on. The time for talk had ended.

Prudent O'Hurn announced, "Debate has concluded. You've all taken a solemn vow to do what you believe to be in the best interest of our faith and to vote your conscience. Let us then—"

The door to the sealed chamber swung open. The worn and tattered image of Prudent Hansel swept over the room's occupants. A collective gasp rang out. Out of breath, the man labored to explain, "... apologies... all of you..."

His ear dripped blood. His left eye was bruised, unable to open. "... waylaid... on... my way here..." He stopped and drew in a lungful of air. "... entourage fought them off..."

With each arm hanging on to one of the massive doors, as though bridging the chasm separating the conclave, he lifted his head.

Hansel's eyes met Jerithan's. "I pray I'm not too late."

Expectations & Answers

Hensdale: 2nd Day of the Harvest Moon

Mithany | Neladith

Mithany's eyes narrowed with suspicion. Finding Arek, her immediate goal, proved more important than the unlikely circumstance of Neladith being at the farmhouse.

Neladith said, "Mithany, I didn't expect to see you this far from home. How are you holding up?"

A pregnant pause followed before Mithany replied, "It's hard. I miss him so much."

She deliberately changed the direction of the conversation. "Can we put aside whatever it is between us? I'm worried about Arek. He promised to meet up with me. He and I are going on the road, looking for Daedyn. We were supposed to have left already, but I can't find him anywhere."

Neladith replied, "Nonsense, there ain't nothing bad between us. I liked you from the beginning, when we met back in Owls Neck. I just been trying to find a way for you to like me."

Mithany wanted to believe her, for Arek's sake. *It's in the eyes,* she told herself, an oft-repeated phrase her inner voice frequently reminded her of. But Mithany couldn't detect anything other than joy expressed in Neladith's eyes. Her attempt to read Neladith so far coming up empty, Mithany decided to study more of Neladith's facial tells and, for now, trust would have to wait.

"I've been asking around, and someone said they saw him and two guys heading off in this direction. This is the only house out here. Seeing you gives me hope he's here with you. Is he inside?"

"Well, I didn't tell you the truth, Mithany. Didn't tell Arek either. My real reason for stopping in Owls Neck. I was on my way here to visit family—my mother's cousin. Haven't seen them since I was a kid. This house always made me feel safe. They're getting older, and my mom thought it would be nice for me to see them before it's too late and they're in the ground. Nobody knows when Mother Earth will claim them."

"Is he here?"

"Oh, I'm sorry, I didn't answer you. No."

Mithany's posture sank at the pronouncement. The red-eyed, red-haired Neladith already towered over the diminutive Mithany. With hunched shoulders and with her head hanging down, Mithany shrank before her competitor for Arek's attention.

"He stopped by earlier in the day. You know your brother. We spent some private time together. I undoubtedly made everyone in the house blush with the noises we made. Heck, the dead probably rolled over in their graves. I thoroughly enjoyed my afternoon with him." She ended with a few quick eyebrow-judders up and down as though to emphasize her comment.

Mithany let it slide.

"I had to cut him loose. You get what it's like with family obligations. Anyway, he was beat. He said something about meeting up with you somewhere along the way tomorrow. I didn't know what that meant and, frankly, I had other things on my mind. From what you said, sounds like he planned to catch up with you after you set off."

Mithany studied Neladith with every phrase spoken. The playful delivery the taller young woman offered and her explanation of events all fit together nicely. Mithany had no cause not to believe Neladith, but every time Neladith spoke, alarm bells sounded off in her head.

Mithany said, "He does enjoy his time with you. I'm certain of that." She wanted to add more by way of defining the reason, but remained silent and moved on. "Did he say anything about where he planned on going?"

"I'm sorry, he didn't. To be honest, he may have, but sometimes I stop listening when he rambles on, talking about stuff you didn't even ask about. He's a great guy, but he does talk a lot."

"That he does."

"On the other hand, sometimes, when you ask him a direct question, he gets all quiet and stares back at you. I'm never sure if he's telling me the truth. He gets all tied up. I can't always figure him out. Then, out of nowhere, you discover a hidden quality about him you never suspected, and it gives you such pleasure to enjoy new things, new experiences with him."

As Neladith spoke, Mithany explored the woman's expressions and body language. She watched Neladith's eyes open wide, and they seemed to light up. Her mouth curled at its ends as though enjoying the moment or smiling at her recollections about Arek. Evident in her reading of Neladith, the wiry redhead had a pleasurable afternoon with Arek. Mithany read satisfaction flash large across Neladith's face, and her open body stance suggested she had nothing to hide. She concluded Neladith appeared to be telling the truth or, at least, not hiding anything Mithany could detect. *And besides*, she thought, *most liars can't hide universal tells. Unless she's a sociopath.*

Mithany said, "By the way, who were the two guys with Arek? Did you know them?"

"I really can't say. Not sure who your people saw. Maybe the guys with Arek faded into the shadows by the time I saw him."

"I'm going to head back. Maybe he returned home while I've been here talking with you. I'm glad Arek's safe, since you two spent the afternoon together. Who knows where he took off to? Thank you. You put my mind at ease. With or without Arek, I'm heading out in the morning."

"You know what, Mithany? I'll join you." Neladith didn't give Mithany time to rebut her offer. She poked her head inside the door and yelled, "Heading out to help a friend. Unless you need my help with that pig."

A faint, muffled voice floated to the porch, "We'll be fine, dear."

"Thanks. Don't wait up."

"Alright, dear. You have a nice time."

Mithany protested, "That's not necessary—"

"Nonsense. I insist." Neladith closed the front door. "On second thought, I'm going to grab a sweater. Be right back. Wait here."

Neladith left Mithany standing alone on the porch. Once inside, with her legs still unsteady, in awkward bounds she bolted for the basement. Muscle spasms gripped her left thigh before she took three steps and almost collapsed. Only her wobbly right leg kept her upright, with an assist from her hand on the wall.

She made her way to where Arek remained motionless—tied to a chair. She spoke without concern, or with any emotion, at the sight of his lifeless body and continued on as though he no longer existed. "Guys, Mithany is here. We can pull her in and see what she knows. But I think she can lead us to Reyne Brenton. You both okay with that?"

Grafph answered first. "I still think we got our man. Reyne's dead, and this is a waste of time."

Tylus added, "You didn't get it out of Arek just talking to him. We had to bring him in. Look at him now. What makes you think she'll be any different?"

Neladith responded, "Listen, you two. Quith said Dylla's skeptical that Reyne's the one we killed. She's back on our world as we speak, talking with the Devil's Blacksmith about it. If she's right that Reyne ain't dead and we find him, we'll be heroes."

Grafph said, "Better her than me. That guy scares the shit outta me."

Rolling her eyes, Neladith fired off one word after the other in rapid patter, "Let me explain. Reyne's fiancée just told me she's going out in search of Daedyn, the brother. What if Daedyn's the one we killed the other night, not Reyne? Quith's mistake, not mine. If Dylla's suspicions are right, Mithany isn't going after Daedyn. She's on the hunt for our man. Mithany just might lead us directly to Reyne Brenton."

Tylus and Grafph discussed it briefly and agreed to her approach. Tylus added, "Alright, but we don't have a lot of time. If you can get it done today, before Quith gets back, we'll be fine."

"Agreed." Neladith turned, ready to sprint back to Mithany, then stopped. "I'm not so sure we'll find him before nightfall. If it takes longer, I'm gonna stick with her. You two deal with Quith when he returns. Let him know what I'm up to if I'm not back. I'm betting Mithany's our best lead yet."

Several heartbeats later, Neladith popped her head back outside to find Mithany waiting just where she'd left her.

Mithany noted, "That thing wrapped around your butt looks more like a skirt than a sweater."

Neladith slid one arm under Mithany's in a gesture of friendship and started down the porch. "Lady's prerogative. I can keep it tied around my waist until I need it later."

Mithany reflected, *Thank the Goddess Teth, I didn't need to see her ass hanging out the whole time.*

Returning to the prior conversation, Mithany asked, "What's all that about a pig?"

"Oh, that's nothing. We were playing, having fun. I might've been a little rough. The thing up and died unexpectedly."

"Aren't you worried it will be too much for them? They're getting up there in years. We should help."

Neladith looked down at Mithany and smiled. "Those two? Nah. They know what they're doing. They've been doing this a long time."

"If you say so."

Neladith skipped a few steps, pulling Mithany along. "I do say so. And I might add, you remind me of someone I used to know. The similarity is stunning."

Mithany pulled back. "Slow down."

"Sure. Just as well. For some reason, my legs are so tight." Neladith stopped, bent over, and gave her thigh muscles a thorough rubdown.

Mithany offered Neladith a quizzical look. "This person who looks like me. Is that a good thing or a bad thing?"

With a grin from ear to ear, Neladith explained, "It's a very good thing. I noticed it immediately when I first met you standing at that couple's table back at the Inn in Owls Neck."

Mithany walked on. "Yeah, and the white-haired guy. What a dick. But, glad to hear it's a good association you have with my lookalike. Are you friends?"

"Oh, yes. We were close. You could say, more than close. You look just like her. You could be her twin." Neladith winked. "Maybe we'll get close too."

The wink put Mithany on alert, as did the past-tense reference to the relationship—which, she figured, required context. "You said you two *were* close. What happened?" Although Mithany's mouth formed words, her full attention was focused on Neladith's eyes. *It's always in the eyes. And there's something hiding behind them red peepers of hers. I just can't figure it out.*

Neladith shot back in a quick, matter-of-fact voice, "She died."

"Oh, I'm so sorry. That's horrible."

Mithany studied Neladith, who didn't respond for a moment, then Neladith suddenly snapped to attention. "The past is gone. Come on, let's go find your guy. We've had no girl time, just you and me. I hope to get a lot out of our little adventure."

Derr's Revenge

Derr

Derr strode into an isolated sitting room, secluded from prying eyes, inside the private residence and ancestral home of the appropriately named Chancellor's Mansion. Tomelai and First Lady Kaythlin had taken positions seated in two elaborate high-back chairs appearing more like soft-cushioned thrones. A similarly ornate round table, stationed before the pair, and a smaller, yet no less formal chair sat empty, awaiting Derr. Upon Derr's entrance, neither Chancellor nor First Lady stood, as formalities weren't part of the relationship between Derr and the Tomelais.

"My dear Druin, welcome. Please join us," First Lady Kaythlin said, sweet and welcoming. Charm and elegance rolled off her as though endowed at birth to it. The years of practiced refinement beginning at an early age, at the insistence of her wealthy family who had ingrained in her a captivating and intentionally created graceful persona. Kaythlin exuded culture and confidence with every spoken word. A stunning beauty in youth, middle age did little to alter her striking appearance. With large, round, upturned eyes a warm shade of lavender, a single look, married to a gentle, kind-hearted smile, stole away Derr's attention.

The otherwise stone-hearted Derr had fallen victim to her charms before quickly realizing he'd been captured. Shaking it off, he turned his attention to his Chancellor.

Cheerful, yet in tone and manner more direct than his wife, Tomelai threw in, "Drew, have a seat. We have a lot to discuss." While roughly the same age as both Kaythlin and Derr, Tomelai's youth had fled him. Graying temples that matched his steel-gray eyes gave away his years. Yet, he carried it well. A tall, muscled physique stood out compared to other men his age. Madrotti Tomelai exuded a refined confidence underlying a well-educated affectation in both sight and sound that commanded respect.

Derr, not a man known for his social graces, nor did those in attendance expect any, said, "Good day to you both. I'll dive right in. What'll it be? Good news or bad? Highlights or details?" His standard opening when the three gathered for an informal briefing.

Chancellor Tomelai held the honor of making the call, as he always did. "I am in a particularly good mood today." Derr watched him look over to his First Lady with a boyish, wicked grin flashing across his face. Derr surmised the reason behind it.

Tomelai had a formal speaking style, nothing of the sort to match the charm-laced delivery of his wife. The product of high society schooling, unlike Derr.

Derr saw past each of their outward demeanors. He knew them for what lay beneath: the good parts, the bad parts, and the truly ugly parts. The Tomelais, like all human beings, hid the worst of themselves from open society—just not buried deep enough from Druin Derr.

Chancellor Tomelai rubbed his palms together. His deep voice bore the sharp edge of command in his words as it always did, even in the setting with his lifelong friend and his wife. Derr picked up on the subtle, warmer side of Tomelai that few others would ever detect.

"Let us start with some good news. Give me the executive summary. If I want details, I will let you know. You can leave out the recap of our trip to Teth and events inside the Council of Nations. We have covered that ad nauseam."

News of Chancellor Tomelai's unthinkable proposal to abandon civilization's entrenched way of life, to end adherence to the founding principles of the Third

Age, to turn away from Nature, to break from the Covenant of Absolute Human Obligations had reached the capital of Adelle before he and his entourage had made it back from the Feast of Teth. Derr considered, *Information travels fastest when unencumbered.*

Derr, stoic in his reply to his friend and Chancellor, said, "Adelle is relatively quiet. You've fared much better than Greenlin, Kantos, or Teth in the way citizens within each of these countries reacted to killing off the Covenant. They're all in chaos. We've yet to taste her wrath."

Tomelai released the lower lip he'd been biting on. "Take credit, Drew. Your team, the KCG, and the guy you cannot tolerate, General Kiple, managing Adelle's peace officers have kept everything under control."

Derr pursed his lips and elected not to reply.

Kaythlin asked, her tone flittering across the room as a gentle caress, "Druin, is that the full extent of your summary of the good news?"

"You've witnessed the gray cloaks, my agents, a lot of them, providing constant updates to me over the course of our return trip from Teth. There's more to report."

Tomelai leaned forward, nodding in approval. "Yes, the trek from Teth to Tandure proved uneventful in the aftermath of the Council of Nations address I made. For which we are all thankful. Though, I will admit to being pleasantly surprised at the crowds of well-wishers lining the roadways, especially the throngs of Samers."

On their trip back to Tandure, in many of the small towns they passed through, crowds lined the roads. Samers—single-sex couples—cheered as Tomelai triumphantly passed. In village after village, they came out to greet him. Endless shouts proclaiming Chancellor Tomelai a hero, a visionary, a revolutionary, in recognition of his perceived bravery to kill the Covenant. Derr knew it for the deeper truth hidden beneath the flattery: not a true measure of love outpouring for Tomelai as much as for the promise of freedom from its draconian procreation mandate imposed on Samers and heterosexuals alike. The latter basked in the Covenant's breeding quota, while the former despised it. Derr reflected on one comment that brought Tomelai and consequently the entire Adelleian entourage to a momentary halt when a woman yelled out, "Tomelai, you are a god!"

As long as none presented a threat, Derr let them have their say. He wondered if the lack of Covenant advocates remained absent due to fear of reprisal from the KCG or had support within Tartican civilization for its principles waned in recent years. The utter lack of any support for the Covenant in the villages they passed through, Derr assessed, portended well for Adelle in the inevitable conflict amongst nations borne in Tomelai's withdrawal.

Kaythlin laid a gentle hand on Derr's arm. "Druin, dear, you said there is more to report. Concerning the matter of the assassination attempt on my beloved husband, what news do you have for us?"

Derr heard the soft delivery but understood the steel in her resolve. Over the years, Derr took every opportunity to study Kaythlin. While the affection of friendship existed between them, Derr knew Kaythlin to be a hardened political warrior. Accepting her at face value for the graceful and sweet First Lady of Adelle, a mistake too many made—not Druin Derr.

One corner of Derr's mouth moved upward ever so slightly, and he turned to Madrotti in response to Kaythlin's query. "Lieutenant Ferpratt and his unit did some good work with the dozen or so dead would-be assassins they gathered up from the failed attempt on your life. High level, we think the Temple of Life is the most likely culprit. I pin it on First Lord Jerithan and Second Lord Razoal. We still don't know who they farmed out the contract to or if the dead were Temple associates. I'm working on that."

Tomelai busted with delight. "Great news, Drew. Do I need details? Do they make a difference?"

Derr sat back and crossed his arms. "No. Details are still developing, but I think we've enough to conclude the orders came from First Lord Jerithan Cree. Razoal most likely carried out Cree's instructions."

Tomelai made the same body movements, mirroring Derr's. "You know my next question."

Derr leaned in towards the Chancellor and, in a low voice, offered, "What're we doing about it, I presume?"

Tomelai smiled back at Derr. "Exactly."

Leaning back, Derr said, "There's some good news to report there as well. I sent a request to Nails in Teth with one of my grays. I am expecting Nails to take either Jerithan or Razoal or both within days, if she hasn't already done so. Failing that, Plan B: Serco will initiate a Vote of Revocation."

Tomelai asked, "Remind me, Nails? There are hundreds of names I need at my fingertips every day. This one evades me. It's in there but slips my mind."

Kaythlin spoke up, "Remember, dear. She is like you, only her organization comprises everyone who is involved with crime in Teth. You might remember her as Wendolyn Trencher when she lived here in Tandure."

"Oh yes. She is the head of the Thuggery. Why her?"

Derr replied, "The city of Teth has become a battle zone. Provost Kwuinan has lost control. Vigilantes run the city. A Citizen's Committee—that's what they're calling themselves—has a firm grip on it. Not good for Teth. Good for us. Not much of a surprise, Nails appointed herself head of the Citizen's Committee. She owed me. I called in my marker."

"I am sure I do not want to know why she owes you."

"I'm sure you don't. Anyway, she also helped us secure several prudents' safe return to Teth, so they'll be able to support a Revocation against Jerithan, that is if she failed to snatch him up. In my message, I told her to make sure Prudents Hansel, Marvo, and Aquila get to the conclave, if there is one. She's been very helpful to our cause. I've arranged for her to be well paid should she succeed."

Tomelai slammed his fist on the small table. "Outstanding, Drew. But if she fails to capture either Jerithan or Razoal, tell me more of Plan B."

"The Citizen's Committee will be holding trials of those they accuse of crimes against the good citizens of Teth. I made sure Jerithan and Razoal are high on her list."

First Lady Kaythlin said, "Ironic. Does not sound like there are many good citizens of Teth on the Committee if Nails is its leader."

Derr added, "I've left boots on the ground under my top lieutenant. Ferpratt's got it under control. If Nails gets her hands on either Jerithan or Razoal, Ferpratt will question them in private. Followed by a public execution by Nails. If not, they'll help round up the prudents needed to vote him out."

Kaythlin observed, "How quickly the tide has turned. We have lived under the yoke of the Covenant, the commitment to protecting human life at all costs, and just as quickly, utopia can fade away."

Tomelai raised one eyebrow. "None of us ever believed the Covenant guided every life in Tartica. If only ten percent reject its principles, there will be over one hundred thousand ready to step in and put sword to neck without hesitation. I am not surprised. And that only accounts for the fervent. It is going to get a lot worse when everyone else gets involved. Chaos is in its infancy."

Derr bent forward in his chair to lean in closer to them both. "Let me continue then in that same vein. I met with Serco after your speech at the Council of Nations. He's irate. Angry. Furious. Mostly at you, Rotti. His words, 'I thought more of Tomelai than to do something as stupid as ending the Covenant.'"

Tomelai rolled his eyes. "I got to know the man during his time in our capital as the head of the Temple delegation. He's nothing more than a useful idiot."

"But as pissed off at you as he is, he's even more so at his First Lord Jerithan Cree for letting it happen. I worked Serco into a lather. If Nails doesn't snatch up the First Lord quickly, Serco will be calling for a Revocation as soon as he has the votes lined up."

Kaythlin said, half as a question, half as a statement, "But Serco does not know Nails is making a play to execute Jerithan Cree."

"Precisely. And if Plan B is needed, just to be sure Nails doesn't fail us I've dispatched some of my grays to meet up with prudents who left the city after the Grand Ball of the Feast of Teth. I also told Serco to send riders to recall the ones he's certain will support Revocation. I've arranged for the right prudents to get to the conclave in time to vote. Like I said earlier, Prudents Hansel, Marvo, and Aquila don't have a lot of love for the current First Lord."

Kaythlin offered Derr a warm smile. "Very well handled, Druin. All this planning just in case Nails is unsuccessful in capturing him. You are a thoughtful friend. Madrotti and I appreciate all you have done."

Tomelai jumped from his seat, pulled Kaythlin up from hers, and embraced her.

"Drew, this could not have been planned better. You have been playing puppet master. Why don't I know any of this? Why have you waited to tell me?"

"Rotti, it's taken some doing to make this happen. I wanted to make sure it'd all play out. Didn't want to promise more than I could deliver. Keep in mind we don't have results yet. This is only the foundation I've laid down. Plans within plans."

"A strong foundation at that." Tomelai beamed at his Captain, his friend. He grabbed his wife and planted a celebratory kiss. After releasing Kaythlin from their embrace, he said, "This has been a wonderful briefing. Thank you, Drew, for all you have done."

He looked at his Chancellor with stern, narrow eyes. "My update isn't over."

"Oh shit. I know that look. I am not going to like what comes next, am I?"

"Sorry, Rotti. No. You're not. It's the Hidden Hand. You should sit back down."

Derr watched Tomelai flop into his chair. Though subtle, the look on his face told Derr that his Chancellor's ebullient mood had soured. He also observed Kaythlin's reaction to her husband's change. Tomelai harbored a deep hatred for the Hidden Hand. He alone owned power in Adelle. Any person who challenged what he loved most had to be destroyed. The Hidden Hand proved itself an implacable adversary even for Derr and the KCG.

Kaythlin took her husband's hands in hers, like a mother consoling one of her own. "My love"—she paused—"unlike Teth, which welcomes every facet of humanity within its borders, here in Tandure we are both blessed and cursed with only wealthy elites."

The uber-wealthy, to the exclusion of all others, comprise Tandure's citizenry. As Adelle's seat of government, Tandure remained relatively well-behaved following the news of the Covenant's demise. Collective fear of Captain Druin Derr's KCG, the Kingdom's Chancellor's Guard, accounted for part of the city's tempered response. Although, the opposition had yet to reach a consensus on how best to implement their resistance. Careful planning had always been the hallmark of the secretive movers and shakers of Tandure's obstruction-minded aristocracy known as the Hidden Hand.

Many of Tandure's citizens served one or more tours of duty in a string of Tomelai administrations. The Chancellor was always mindful of denying any platform built on long service. Despite all of Derr's effort, and in spite of Tomelai's imposed turnover, the informal, secretive, loose confederation of the privileged class called the Hidden Hand had its say. At the very least, the Hidden Hand proved expert at extracting their share of coin from whatever policy Tomelai invoked.

With the ownership by Hidden Hand members of the major newspapers, they controlled the flow of information, manipulating public opinion to support their financial goals. Through the ownership by its members of Tandure's private banking houses, the Hidden Hand controlled both the legal and illegal flow of loans, rewarding those who played ball and monetarily starving those who did not. Graft payments to whomever held office enabled the Hidden Hand to impede whichever of Tomelai's policy stood in their way of raking in more coin. Payoffs to local civil enforcement officers and judges ensured its members freedom to operate in illicit transactions. Bankrolling of the Dust trade kept their hands clean of its day-to-day drug distribution, but profits from Dust flowed back freely. At all times, Hidden Hand affiliation remained in the shadows, while its members basked in the open as the well-to-do elites of Tandure society.

Derr's KCG made certain, when detected, those complicit with Hidden Hand activities paid dearly, but nothing corrupts with as much certainty as coin. With each replacement of those the KCG removed, new payoffs ensured continuity of the Hidden Hand's influence.

Derr hung his head. "It's an insidious beast. With its people, whether in or out of government, the Hidden Hand, the same wide circle of elites, siphons power, formal and informal, from any and every source not in firm control by you. In this one thing, I have failed you... but not for the lack of trying."

Tomelai pulled his hand free, as though rejecting Kaythlin's comfort, and rubbed his chin. "Drew, you keep striking at their core, but still, they persist. You eliminate one of theirs and two rise up in response."

Derr knew a reaction from the Hidden Hand to be forthcoming and understood it wasn't done cooking yet. A full buffet of opposition would be laid out soon enough. He committed to stop it before it could be served.

Stroking Tomelai's face, Kaythlin looked her husband in the eyes, and Derr saw sympathy and love in her offering and, lurking underneath, a will of steel. "My dearest husband, Tandure, your city, is beautiful because of you. But much like the city of Teth, a cesspool in its own unique way. Tandure's magnificence and its depravity are commensurate with the luxury and standing of its wealth. In many ways worse than Teth because of higher stakes defined by the amount of coin in play, and more deadly in spite of Covenant dictates. These are not your sins, my dear husband. It is human nature that fuels the Hidden Hand. It is they, not you, who have tainted Tandure in spite of all you have done and despite Druin's every effort to eradicate it."

Tomelai grabbed and squeezed Kaythlin's hand.

Her gentle strokes put to an end.

His nostrils flared.

His chest rose and fell.

Anger painted his words. "It is the pinnacle of hypocrisy. On the heels of my decree, the Hidden Hand prepares itself to oppose my call to withdraw from the Covenant. A set of laws and a way of life the privileged elite class would see maintained for the lesser masses, but not one they themselves considered bound to follow."

"Rotti," Derr began. Tomelai's head snapped to face off with Derr. Tomelai stared him down, but Derr stared right back, not giving an inch. "You and I both know Tandure gives off the appearance of a polite, refined society of wealthy patrons, yet, appearances aside, it is a cesspit of greed masked behind a facade of the well-dressed, well-to-do."

With narrow eyes Tomelai shot back, "Where the ultra-wealthy gather at well-mannered, polite society dinner parties that serve only as a pleasant gossamer veil covering the cutthroat grab for money and power roiling underneath."

Tomelai pounded his fist on the small table, knocking it over. He shot up from his seat and roared, "I will not have it! Adelle is mine!"

Tough as Nails

Teth: 2nd Day of the Harvest Moon

Reyne | Nails

Reyne, with Mera at his side and secured out of sight from the mob, scrutinized a thickset, middled-aged, beefy woman seated at the center of attention atop a platform stationed directly in front of the Temple of Life Palace.

Mera said, "That face of yours tells me you're confused about the woman in charge. Her name is Nails. Now be quiet. I need to figure out what's going on here."

As a matter of intrigue, Reyne studied Nails as she rose from a strategically placed chair at center stage. The rabble egging her on appeared dirty, unwashed, and Reyne imagined the opposite for those sequestered safely behind the Temple's protective embrace. The splendid greenery of the expansive Palace grounds as Nails's backdrop juxtaposed against the ashen grays, burnt blacks, and disheveled appearance of the destruction visited upon Teth sparked Reyne to consider the comparisons. The aromatic remains of the fire-ravaged wood that once held up the buildings of the city's market center wafted through the air, touching Reyne's awareness. In the aftermath of the city's destruction, rich Temple lords fared well. The lower classes, not so much. While chaos reached out across Teth, it just hadn't seized all of it yet.

Reyne's eyes darted across the wreckage, the angry mob, and the players on stage. A pang of sadness, starting in his chest, washed hopelessness through him. Despondent, not for Teth's namesake city, but for his own sense of loss. As he inspected the devastation, leaving hints of what Teth had once been but now reduced to a husk, epitomized the current state of his life. The formerly beautiful buildings in ruination, like the bond with his brother that meant so much to him, but that future with Daedyn was destroyed—a future they would never share. He saw an unmolested door set in its frame, standing alone, with the home it once opened into missing. He pondered how it still stood, much like the false hope of a life with Mithany—both represented doors to nowhere.

The stage Nails stood upon, like Mera, symbolized leadership capable of delivering hope to the forlorn, the dislodged, the homeless. Self-proclaimed leaders always pledging to the newly minted aimless—himself among them—to have the answers of what to do next, what to think, how to react. And the revelation sank into his core: he and this miserable city were one and the same—doomed. Even worse, both he and Teth's downtrodden were primed to accept the manipulations of others. What choice did he have? Lost, set adrift into an uncertain future, he, like the crowd anticipating Nails's oratory address, allowed themselves to be led.

He longed for Mithany more than ever.

The sound of Mera's tapping foot broke through his self-pity fueled thoughts and fed into Reyne's ever-present annoyance with the man. Mera, the embodiment of his canceled wedding plans with Mithany, hardened his resentment. He craved a family, a life with the woman he loved, but Mera forced him to turn his back on it. Disdain for Mera grew by the second.

With irritation surfacing at Mera's every action, Reyne complained, "Can you knock that off?"

"What?"

"That foot. Can you stop?" Reyne pointed at the culprit.

Mera's shoulders rose and fell. "Oh, sorry. Didn't know I was doing it."

"You figure out what's goin' on here?"

"My best guess, Nails selected this location for its ability to deliver the seething anger of the masses she requires for her purpose."

"And what purpose is that?"

Mera's eyebrows shot up, and he nodded towards the heavyset woman. "We're about to find out. Now be quiet."

While standing, Nails opened her arms wide to address the gathered. Reyne thought the woman not much to look at, yet was struck by the inconsistency of her unkept, bulbous physique, a mismatch to her captivating eyes. Almond-shaped, violet-colored eyes set off in contrast to long, disheveled strands of auburn-colored ropelike hair matted across a face claiming full jowls and more than one chin.

The woman commanding Reyne's attention, as well as everyone else's, began to wave her arms—bearing skin hanging loose—up and down to settle the boisterous rabble.

Grabbing Mera's elbow, Reyne asked, "What do you know about that lady?"

A quiet laugh escaped Mera. "She's no lady. Maybe once, but not anymore. In her younger days, a Junoesque debutant from Adelle's elite upper class. Well educated. Cultured. Refined. Nails left it all behind. The story goes, she did it to answer the call of freedom that youth often promises. Things didn't go so well, eventually leading her to a life of crime, and then, in the years that followed, she seized control of Teth's criminal class, and now she's its Thuggery's chieftain. That's the short version. She's about to talk, so shut up... please. I'm worried for the Temple lord up on that stage."

Arms crossed, Reyne's look soured, but he heeded Mera's request.

It seemed to Reyne that Nails waited for most of the voices to quiet before drawing a hearty breath into what he surmised as cavernous lungs, if her oversized chest provided any indication. She projected out a voluminous belch that, for those in the front rows beyond the platform's edges, delivered not only a vulgar attack to one's ears but also a rank odor. Amused, Reyne surveyed many arms waving off the offending smell, and he considered, like a circus barker, her voluminous burp did the job to get the front row's attention.

"Alright, you pissants," Nails called out. "That's right. You're all pissants."

Fists raised in defiance, pounded at the air. Every vile curse of the Third Age rang out in response to Nails' taunt. One louder than the next. Shouts stepped over the tops of each other, but all had at their core a war cry in one form or another. Pushing and shoving moved through the mass of people like an undulating wave that rose and fell.

Nails cupped her palm to her ear and listened, apparently delighted in what they were demanding.

Reyne eyed a man up and down, most likely in his twenties, as the man called out, "Pissants! Show him what these ants can do."

A woman of the same age, like many in the crowd but not all, screamed at the top of her lungs, "String him up!" Reyne saw her face when she turned to assess the crowd's reaction. Scrunched features clenched tight, her face looked as angry as any he'd ever seen.

They were all angry.

Reyne's head snapped around searching the source of harpylike rantings of a shouting young woman's voice. "Cut his balls off," she demanded, pounding her defiant fist into the air. Reyne caught sight of the Samer license tattooed on her and figured she wasn't a fan of balls to begin with.

He listened as best he could to one raucous call after the other.

A disheveled man, as most of the gathered appeared to be of the lower classes, cupped his hands to his mouth. "He should lose his tongue."

One of the older participants, a gray-haired man, threw in, "Where's his boss?"

But the one that stunned Reyne came from a young girl who couldn't have been any older than her late teens. With squinting eyes and fury written across her face, she screeched, "Kill the fucker!" She turned to accept the crowd's adulation, and, letting go of her girlfriend's hand, the teenager raised both arms high into the air triumphantly. One look, and Reyne understood her, a Samer license, absent from where it should have been, fueled her anger. The Covenant hadn't granted her the right, nor the dignity, to be with the woman whose hand she'd just released.

Reyne couldn't comprehend the level of hatred spewing from these impoverished people. A yearning to hold on to something only those he loved could deliver went unanswered and drove despair deeper into his damaged soul.

He missed Mithany.

He missed Daedyn.

Nails called out, "How you like my Citizen's Committee? Should I introduce you to all these well-to-do muckety-mucks?"

In unison, a thousand voices answered, "Fuck them!"

A broad grin crossed Nails's beaming face.

Mera turned to Reyne. "Nails appears to have commandeered the Citizen's Committee from the well-intentioned, civic-minded nobles of Teth. I wouldn't be surprised if she assumed control almost as soon as the committee took shape. My best guess is that those fifteen well-dressed people on that stage had the best of intentions of exerting control over the outpouring of people into the streets following the news of Tomelai's Covenant killing proposal."

Reyne rubbed his chin. "She's just one person. How's that happen?"

Mera shook his head. "She's more than that. She's a whirlwind of depravity wrapped in a woman's body. Nails must have infused her own brand of threats and violence to seize control. That's not hard to imagine or too difficult to piece together. There are good people up there. But Nails isn't one of them."

Nails pushed on. "I called you all pissants because that's what your masters on the hill think of you." She turned her face from the crowd to look behind her at the Temple of Life Palace seated on the knoll of which she spoke. Her arm shot out, pointing towards the Temple lords' domed basilica in an accusatory gesture.

A chant ignited. "Fuck 'em all." The mob repeated it over and over.

Nails had them worked up. She waddled back and forth along the front of the stage. At the end of each pass, she stopped, squatted, hands on knees, she pushed her chin out in front and shook her head back and forth repeatedly. Flesh waddled as she intended. Only to do it again at the opposite side of the stage.

Her followers loved it, as Reyne gauged their boisterous reaction.

Those on the platform with her, reluctant participants from the noble class whose committee Nails overtook in a bloodless coup—if Mera had the right of it—only had the view of her rotund backside. The symbolism Nails probably intended, Reyne thought, and the message not lost on anyone who thought about it longer than a few seconds.

Mera told Reyne, "Not a single member of the Thuggery's inner circle sits on that Citizen's Committee up there. That would have been too obvious, but they, and their subordinates, no doubt, are mingling throughout the crowd, egging them on with their leader orchestrating towards some crescendo. I'm fearful of where this is heading. Look over to the man in the green vestments. The one who's tied up."

Before Reyne could reply, Nails, all five foot six of her weighing in at over two hundred pounds, raised both fists above her head. "You see him standing over there?" she said, pointing to Second Lord Razoal. "He looks down on all of you. He thinks he's better than you. He lives in his fancy palace."

Spontaneous chanting erupted. "Fuck 'em! Hang 'em!"

She let it ride a few minutes, then waved them to quiet down.

Second Lord Razoal, his mouth gagged, with hands tied behind his back, precluded any verbalized defense. Reyne pitied the man, watching his pleading, bulging eyes crying out to be heard. Yet, Nails nor anyone else responded to the man's silent pleas.

Mera said under his breath, "Shit."

Reyne shot an elbow into Mera's side. "What's got you so worried?"

"Those fifteen wealthy private citizens who thought to control this unraveling city now find themselves hostage to their own machinations. None dare step down now unless they want to find themselves standing next to Razoal. No one can dare challenge Nails. She set this all up, and Razoal is her target."

Nails looked out over the crowd and then to Second Lord Razoal. She stared hard at his pathetic form and her face contorted into a menacing grin. Their eyes met, and she locked on him. As though he could understand her thoughts, her hatred bore down on him. *You and me gone toe-to-toe too many times, Razoal. Yeah, you filled my pockets with Temple coins, but that ain't gonna save you. You came down hard on my Thuggery, over and over. You used Samer licensing as an excuse to ship my people off to those fucking birthing farms. I hate you, always have. But that ain't what you're doin' here. You and me got a little secret no one can ever know. Yeah, that's right. The hit you and that pious asshole Jerithan arranged on Tomelai. True, you paid me to carry it out, and my crew failed. My bad. But now, that little fuckup puts me at risk. Derr can never know I had a hand in it. Can't leave you out there. That's the real reason you're here. And I'll get to your former boss soon enough. Hope you like your send-off, you mother-fucking arrogant prick... I did all this for you.*

Nails turned away from Razoal and threw both her arms high overhead. They roared, and Nails reveled in delight. She allowed the evil growing inside her to plaster its self-expression across her face. She'd primed the pump of the vengeful, hateful, demanding mob.

We're almost there.

Nails kept pushing, working the crowd into a wild frenzy. "And the Covenant. What did it do for you?"

"Nothing," they shouted back.

"Who amongst you have been sent to the breeding farms?" Nails asked.

"Too many," they cried out.

"Samers. I share your pain." She proudly raised her right arm displaying its sagging flesh to the crowd absent the mark of a Samer license. She shouted in defiance, "I fuck men... and I fuck women." The crowd exploded, cheering her on. "Show all of us the indignity they marked on you," Nails demanded.

A deafening pang moaned across the crowd as arm after arm, sleeve after sleeve, rolled up, displaying the licensed tattoo each Samer reluctantly had been forced to bear—those officially licensed, anyway. The only recognized proof of legal authorization to engage in sex with another of the same gender, the freedom-representing yet much dreaded license tattoo. With, at the very least, resentment, those so defaced showed their tattoo, commonly referred to as *The Mark*.

Reyne, puzzled at Nails change in direction, opened his mouth to question it but Mera spoke first. "Not every Samer gets Marked; some can't... failing to produce the prerequisite number of children. Instead, rolling the dice on a life choice that could put them as long-term residents of one of the forced procreation facilities, if caught in the act... literally."

"Never thought much about it."

"In case you don't know the history of it, the Covenant of Absolute Universal Obligations was set up to secure the continued existence of the human race when less than two thousand people survived in the entire world after the Great Destruction. The founders did what they had to do at the time to secure humanity's future. The Covenant demands procreation from all, no exceptions. Utopia had its price. These are the people who suffer the cost."

Reyne looked back at Mera. "Yeah, but everyone's gotta contribute to making babies."

"Not all see it that way. It's been a millennium and a half, and Tartica's population is now over one million. A lot of people question if the Covenant's demands are still needed."

"Ain't that for the Council of Nations to decide?"

Mera hung his head. "Fact is, most Samers do their legal duty. Most arranged procreation cohorts from someone of the opposite sex. But for those who resist, the consequence of government-imposed reproduction is traumatic. Tomelai's call to end the Covenant gave all of them hope for a better future... as they see it."

Nails yelled out and cut short the pair's conversation. Pointing at a silent, haggard Razoal, she screamed, spit flying away as she shouted, "He did this to you. He scarred you for life. He is one of the great enforcers of the Covenant."

A roar exploded across the scene.

Nails moved her hands up and down, demanding quiet, motioning for silence. This time she didn't shout, didn't yell, but spoke gently, and she asked, "What should we do with him?"

In unison, to a man, to a woman, they all cried out for mob justice, "Kill him!"

Nails turned from the crowd, looked back at one man standing on a stump behind Razoal, and gave him an almost imperceptible nod.

The man picked up a razor-sharp axe. In one smooth motion, he swung the blade to lop off the head of the Temple of Life's Second Lord, Razoal. Much to everyone's horror, the heavy axe made it only most of the way through Razoal's neck. A collective gasp rose spontaneously from the spectators. Then, awareness and delight grabbed the onlookers and as one, cheers, hoots, and hollers roared in approval at the horrific spectacle.

Razoal's eyes fluttered as his neck slowly pulled apart, like an open door secured only by the narrowest of a hinge. His arms hung at his side and although his knees buckled, Razoal remained standing. The axe blade withdrew and exposed the gap separating his neck from his head. Slowly, gravity pulled on the listing cranium, and the gap opened wider. A second blow to the same spot did the trick. Razoal's head, his eyes open, made a hollow *thunk* sound as it bounced off the floorboards. His body stood headless a few seconds before crumbling to the ground.

Shouts exploded in delight.

Reyne and Mera observed it all from the corner of a building, looking on in horror as Nails, with the crowd's encouragement, did the unthinkable.

With anger in his voice, Mera demanded, "Let's get out of here. This is a dangerous place to be right now and not the city I remember. You need to stay out of sight. There's a tavern, the Whispering Eye. Gina, the one who's going to train you, hangs there. We'll be safe there."

Reyne tried to hold back the contents of his stomach—but failed. After retching, he wiped his mouth, spit a few times, and said, "That was horrible." He leaned to his side to release more chunks of vomit. After wiping his mouth with his sleeve a second time, he said, "How can people do that to each other? The

Covenant demands never to harm anyone, never take a life. These people are animals."

Mera rubbed Reyne's back. "More than a hundred-fifty thousand people live in Teth. Can't be more than a thousand here. That's all it takes. A handful of people in a coordinated effort, while ten times as many cower behind closed doors. Razoal paid the price of civic cowardice. You and I have to stay out of their way."

"You don't have to tell me twice. This place you mentioned, the Whispering Eye. If we can slip in quietly, I'm in. Lead the way."

"Remember what I told you about chaos coming to Tartica? I think it's found a home in Teth."

Damus & Decoherence

Evidar

Emosh

The Devil's Blacksmith stood and approached an enormous table in the center of the near-lightless room of his underground compound. For Synja Emosh, accustomed to Evidar's crepuscular conditions, surviving a lifetime in a world forever in darkness, it was normal, except that he required an update from her. She had one to deliver—not all of it good. He loomed large over her. Decoherence was a word he didn't want to hear, and one she didn't want to utter.

The young, silvery-white-haired Damus, Synja Emosh, bit at her nails. She'd have to get around to telling him eventually. *He needs you*, she told herself. *What am I so afraid of? Still, better to ease into it. Breathe in... breathe out.* By a circuitous route she'd get to it, but first, she decided, he needed context, or maybe she was just fooling herself—putting off the inevitable.

The journey of her explanation started in the muck and mire of unpredictable human actions altering the density distribution within a Probability Wavefunction. They shifted and changed in reaction to spacetime coalescing from that-which-might-be into the never-changing solidity of the past: causing once-certain outcomes to veer off in new directions. What was once at the peak of a Probability Wave height, showing Synja Emosh it to be the likeliest of outcomes, was now nearer to the descending line of the trailing tale in its bell-curved wavelength—not so likely to happen.

He rolled out a long chart depicting the shape of Earth's Probability Wave—Evidar's version of Earth—plotted against years and events. Anchoring hand-sized bean bags at the corners and along the sides, he deposited a dozen of the devices to hold down the curling edges of the chart, which barely fit the confines of the twenty-foot-long table.

In through your nose... out through your mouth. Her chest rose and fell as she began with words one-hundred eighty degrees from the meaning of Decoherence. Before she left the room, she knew she'd have to travel back over those one-hundred eighty degrees eventually. "So, the concept of Coherence. Think of it like this. You have a gigantic pool of water." She spread her arms wide while speaking in her rapid-fire style of delivery: anxiety coursing through her heightened the effect. "Two lengths of string are pulled tight from one end of a pool of water to the other. Each line, starting far apart at one end, but pinned together at a single point at the other end. Now, slap the water near the beginning of the strings, starting a wave from each point rippling towards that one point. The two waves begin at the exact same time. They roll through the body of water at the same speed. Imagine the string, sitting on top of the water rise and fall as each respective wave ripples across the surface." She paused to bundle annoying, long strands of hair falling across her face into a bun tied neatly at the back of her head.

The two locked eyes. Every muscle in her body stiffened.

With one arm across his broad chest, he rested the elbow of the other on it. His free hand gracefully stroked his chin. "I understand, Miss Emosh. The height of each of the strings' wave crests are the same as the other, both heading towards that one place where they are to meet. If they stay in sync in crest height and speed, at the instant the two waves come together, they merge and flow forward as one wave."

Emosh motioned her arms and hands to mimic the rolling up-and-down movement of which she spoke. "Each wave remains unchanged, but now merged... combined into one wave. Voila, Convergence." The silver-haired mathematical genius slowly drew the undulating hands together, putting one palm atop the other hand as she continued her wave demonstration. "When the two waves are in sync and on target to become one, that's Coherence. When they meet, Convergence. But if, at any point, one moves faster or the crest heights become different, if they do meet up, it would be a jumbled, dissonant mess. And just as bad, if either drifts off course, veers to the left or to the right, they'll never meet up. That's our Reyne Brenton effect. The Randon Phase Offset impacting our wave. Slamming into it and changing it." She pulled her hands apart, wiggled her fingers, and let her arms drift away from each other in different directions.

Evidar's leader moved his hand from his chin and ran two fingers over his lips. "And when they move apart, Miss Emosh, that is Decoherence."

She twirled a strand of hair that had escaped the confines of her bun. "Sir, yes, sir." *In through the nose... out through the mouth. He uttered the word. Now comes the hard part.*

The Devil's Blacksmith added, "I understand. This has been the accumulated efforts of other Damus, since the time of The Great Destruction when the divergence of our Earth into two distinct worlds began, both now existing in different dimensions. Like the two separate waves in your pool example. You and I are going to bring these two dimensions together to merge both Earths into one, Miss Emosh."

Hesitation leaked out in her words. "There's one more thing."

"Then be out with it, Miss Emosh."

"When we succeed at Convergence and our dimensions meet up, the physical matter from both Earths will experience a blending effect. Like all the little water molecules from our pool example mixing together. There are Probability Waves I have experienced in the Void that lead to Convergence, but none after. I can't calculate the outcome." *Finish it. Say the words. Tell him the rest of it.* But she didn't.

"Miss Emosh, I accept the uncertainty of what will happen upon Convergence. There is no choice left to us given the current state of our planet and what will become of it if we do nothing. We have no choice. We plan and we execute on maintaining our course until the Convergence."

She let drop both arms at her side and hung her head. "All your efforts to ensure we remained in Coherence, or at least very close to it, has brought us to this point."

The Devil's Blacksmith stepped forward and placed one of his huge hands on her delicate shoulder. "My last Damus… sadly her time with me cut short. Ironically, Edruk of Tartica, who had her murdered, is the biological father to this Reyne Brenton. It has taken my people over twenty years to find Edruk's son." He paused and shook his head. "But before your predecessor died, she predicted that the two planetary wave functions would drift towards Decoherence. But she couldn't identify the cause. If her timing is correct from twenty years ago, our opportunity to prevent Decoherence is running out."

The Damus picked up her head to look him in the eye. *Tell him. Now's the right time.* She mustered her courage. "Correct, sir. We're in danger of becoming, for lack of a better word, out of sync with Tartica's Earth." *There, I said it.*

The Devil's Blacksmith nodded, pulling his hand from her shoulder. "Tartica's wave in your pool example is changing. If that happens, we can never merge the two realities and our world is lost to be in darkness until the Venus Greenhouse Effect overwhelms our entire planet and everything dies. Earth, in Tartica's reality, is the only thing that can save our world. If Tartica's tranquility gets destroyed in the merge, so be it. The death of their world will secure our future."

That went better than expected. Damus Synja Emosh opened her arms and spread her hands. "Agreed. I've been studying this problem for months, along with the Probability Wavefunction of Tartica. Can we roll that one out on top of ours?"

Pointing to Tartica's chart—derived from an equation and represented in the shape of a long, massive wave—the leader directed Damus Emosh to extract the tube that housed it and to roll it out.

Laying the mycelium-based, semi-transparent chart atop the other, Emosh looked over the married graphs and smiled. "This is exceptional work." She ran her finger over one section. "See here how the two began to drift from each other, and one growing taller compared to the other? But this event, right here…"

"Yes, Miss Emosh, I introduced a plague on Tartica, killing a portion of their population."

"It's genius. Losing all those lives may have been the event that impacted Tartica's falling wave amplitude and kept the two frequencies matched up." Her finger raced from point to point as she spoke. "Brilliant. And here. And again here. There're exactly one hundred forty-two separate occurrences just like this one. Either ours or Tartica's wave began growing out of phase, showing signs of developing a frequency different than that of the other, and you brought them back into harmony by intervening."

"All of it accomplished from the advice of others like yourself." He nodded in appreciation. "Unfortunate that a Damus such as you, similar to the mind of an Einstein, comes around only once in a generation, sometimes longer."

"Sir, you're too kind. But it's you." She pointed and wagged her finger in his direction. "You're behind the greatest achievement of all time. But like I said before, all of this should not be possible. This is quantum mechanics applied to planet-sized outcomes. Planets do not behave like quarks. Somehow, two Earths entangled in different dimensions are acting as though they were subatomic particles; the reality of it exists outside the laws of physics. I don't know if this is physics or magic."

Evidar's leader palmed the back of his head. "And as I told you before, it matters not, Miss Emosh. We must play the cards we have been dealt."

"Yes, sir. I just not possible."

"Enough. Let us move on."

His harsh tone crashed into her and stopped her from saying another word on the subject. She recovered, picking up in the middle on his ongoing discussion. "... over a millennium and a half. Your predecessors have recommended that I intervene with impactful global events, and I have done so one hundred forty-two times, trying to keep everything in sync."

Evidar's Damus extended her arms and, with down-turned palms, rolled her arms through the air as though moving like a wave. "You *have* kept the two realities in similar wave frequencies. In other words, our wave crests, our speeds, our headings, all in sync… because of you."

"Thank you, Miss Emosh. But there is a threat, a Random Phase Offset variable you mentioned. What I take from your warning is there is a high percentage that Reyne Brenton will alter our wave and kick us out of sync with Tartica's."

Damus Emosh set open palms on the table and looked down. "That's exactly what I'm saying. Look at the charts"—she pointed—"at this spot, here, we are still in a near-perfect, in-sync state, a minor drift."

The Devil's Blacksmith grabbed the third tube and pulled out another timeline. "I will overlay the other new chart you brought me."

"This third chart shows where Reyne Brenton comes into play. Let me explain," she said as the Devil's Blacksmith spread out the new chart over the other two. She continued, "See how it begins to change our wave crest? And look here, a little further along in time. Our wavelength is shortened because of one man's impact. And even worse, our course drifts away from the heading of the merge point."

"So, Miss Emosh, this chart says that from this point here"—he slammed his finger onto the chart—"Reyne Brenton is predicted to impact our future. And from this one point, our reality and Tartica's will no longer be in Coherence." He finished with closed fists, resting his knuckles along the bottom of the three overlaid charts. "This should never have been permitted to get this far, Miss Emosh."

Evidar's Damus rolled her head from side to side. "This man has to be stopped to prevent this outcome from taking shape."

"Miss Emosh, it is hard to fathom how one insignificant person can have that much of an impact on an entire planet. It should not be possible. Are you certain of your calculations?"

Evidar's Damus crossed one arm over the other and stepped back. "You've taught me Earth's history. Think about what one significant person could do: Jesus Christ, or Adolf Hitler, and even Genghis Khan. Each only one man, and the impact they had as individuals on humanity's trajectory is undeniable. And what of yourself, sir? What you've done for all of us. One man can change everything. History proves they have. You have."

"I thank you for the sentiment, but it is not about me."

"Yes, sir. Anyway, these new calculations have taken weeks." She spread her fingers and ran them over the timelines. "I've been over them time and time again. At one point, I put all my work aside and started over. Unfortunately, my calculations resulted in the same conclusions. My last time in the Void, I touched events along several Probability Waves that tasted like Reyne Brenton's existence. I can't explain it. When in the Void, I sometimes feel, other times smell, and occasionally taste different possible futures. He's got a particular flavor. Bitter notes, sour undertones, but there is a sweetness and a honey-like aftertaste."

"As I understand your process, the trick is determining which one of the untold numbers of Reyne Brenton's futures seen in his Probability Wave Density has the greatest likelihood of coming to pass. And that is the one you plugged into your calculations."

"That's true, sir. He has millions of possible futures, and I have to pick only one. In this case, in the one I think has the highest probability of becoming real, Reyne's flavor is strongest, meaning that one timeline is the most likely to happen. I've plugged that experience into my equations, and you are looking at the results." She poked her fingertip at the spot on the chart, pointing to the point of Reyne Brenton's impact.

The leader crossed his arms. "Recently, my Tartican contact told me he believes our people have already killed Reyne Brenton. But Dylla has reported he may not be dead. His death remains unconfirmed."

"Reyne Brenton is not dead, sir. If it were so, the Probability Wave Densities of his I've tasted would have no aftertaste. No lingering flavors on my palate. His flavor lingers. It means he is alive." She tapped the same spot over and over as she spoke. "In fact, almost at the opposite end of the spectrum from zero, highly likely. Full of rich flavor. It is has sweet tones lingering beneath."

"Dylla's report supports your conclusions and suggests Reyne Brenton has not been dealt with yet."

Damus Sanja Emosh slowed down her rapid-fire delivery. "I'm sorry to share these ill-fated tidings with you. He's definitely alive. And I'm working on two other outliers who may play similar roles in our quest for Convergence. These others are different: we need them alive, unlike Reyne, who's got to be terminated. I've been trying to get a fix on them and should know more about it soon. It's just that I see changes to Tartica being swayed in our direction where the outcome is derived from people other than Reyne Brenton."

"Your calculations can be interpreted fairly simply." The Devil's Blacksmith said as his eyes grew darker and drew in tight. "The first, most important, and immediate task that needs to be handled, in layman's terms, is Reyne Brenton's death." Anger spewed from him. "He is still breathing." He glared at his Damus. "My hopes of ending our dark period of suffering are slipping away."

Staggering back, she stuttered, "Yes."

He slammed his fist into the table. "Our agents on Tartica have failed me. I have assigned other assets to Tartica to do what we have been unable to achieve so far: Reyne Brenton's death." His nostrils flared. He slammed his fists into the table. His voice thundered, "I am surrounded by incompetence."

THE MONSTER WITHIN

TETH: 2ND DAY OF THE HARVEST MOON

Reyne

On Reyne's trek to the Whispering Eye, where he and Mera expected to meet up with some woman named Gina, not much conversation took place between them following Razoal's gruesome execution. Shaken by the callous public murder of a Temple leader, Reyne began to understand the stakes of Mera's call to arms. While he understood it, deciding to join in, well, that was an altogether different matter.

Obscuring a clear view from Reyne's thoughts—of the menacing threat Tartica faced—Mera had called him a naïve, country-raised tenderfoot, born and bred. The insult mulled about in his head as the two walked in silence, blocking out all other contemplations. Reyne resented the accusation and knew it to be wrong. Life in the remote setting of Hensdale lacked the excitement of densely populated cities, but, *I know people... Naïve, no way.*

His thoughts had their own objective: to prove to himself he was anything but a dewy-eyed country orchardist. *Would a simple-minded man recognize that property might've been the mob's first target, but people will be its next? I know people. I ain't some naïve yokel.*

The silence separating the two men didn't match the roaring argument playing out between them in Reyne's psyche. As they walked on through the burnt husk of building after building, the efforts of his inner voice to prove Mera's opinion of him wrong took a back seat to his memory of the life form born of fire. *The Firaché were the conflagration that consumed Teth.* In the eyes of those who witnessed the devastation to Teth as it went up in flames, the fire was a catastrophe. Yet, Reyne pondered, the pure joy the blazing buildings must have given the hedonistic Firaché as they fornicated, multiplied, and consumed everything that would burn.

Daedyn was taken from him the same evening Mera revealed the Firaché. Images of Daedyn's lifeless body and of the Firaché queen were seared into his brain, never to be forgotten, and the two forever linked. He lamented Daedyn's death and, to a much lesser degree, the city's ruination—at least what of it he'd seen so far.

What it all meant, and where the city-state of Teth was headed next, Reyne's countrified worldview began to piece together.

This utopia of ours is falling apart.

Chaos is taking hold.

A reign of terror is coming.

Reyne considered the insights of his inner voice, *Not bad for a country simpleton, huh, Mera.* Over and over, Mera's insult gnawed at Reyne and it fed into his distrust of the man. Suspicion bloomed of Mera's real intent in dragging him to Teth. Reyne wondered if it had as its purpose to sway his sympathies, to commit him to the cause. He recalled more of Mera's words: "You'll be going to Evidar, not as a hero but as a disruptor."

Reyne stopped dead in his tracks. "Why're we really here, Mera?"

"I told you. To meet up with Gina. She'll train you. Plus, we have to figure out who exposed you to Evidar. If it's one of my people, we've been betrayed, and we're in deep shit."

Reyne crossed his arms. "Bullshit. Gina could've met us outside the city."

"Who was going to tell her to do that?"

"What about one of your minions? Coulda sent this Gina person a message."

Mera tipped his head back, said nothing for a few heartbeats, brought it forward again, and replied, "Did you see any minions cutting through the mountains we trudged through to get here?"

Reyne squinted hard. "Did you bring me here to get me riled up? See all this destruction? Win me over to your cause? That's your plan? Riots, mobs, buildings in ruin? Make me see why I gotta do this?"

From the point Mera arrived in his life, Reyne's dream of marrying Mithany and raising a family had been ripped from him. Mera claimed to be Reyne's protector, but Reyne couldn't find a way to absolve Mera for the misery his noble cause had inflicted on his life. Every interaction with the man, Reyne filtered through suspicion and anger.

Mera stuck out his arms in a wide, sweeping gesture. "This all happened while you and I were on the road to get here. Did you see me talking to anyone?"

Reyne shook his head. "Who knows? You coulda done your mumbo-jumbo magic act. Like you did with the Firaché or when you whipped up the past for me to witness."

"You think instant thought communication is one of my tricks? If only, but alas, no. What you're seeing is hitting me the same as you. But one thing's for sure, it's not safe out here today. These people have tasted blood. They'll want more."

"They remind me of you. You just keep taking."

"Insult aside, you got a point. Too many from the mob we just left will make their way to the Whispering Eye now that the main attraction is over. A celebration is sure to follow. Drunken fools craving vengeance isn't a good place for you to be."

"But that's where we're goin' to find Gina."

"Not anymore. Not today, anyway."

"So now what? We're not hookin' up at this tavern with Gina?"

"Tomorrow will be better. Too dangerous today. Remember, we're here for two reasons. We can still do the other. I hope to find answers in the home where your parents once lived: to figure out how Evidar learned that you even exist. I'm going to use my mumbo-jumbo, as you say, to call up the past to see if I missed something at your birth."

Reyne thrust an accusatory finger at Mera. "You told me... nobody but you... knew I'm Edruk's son. You screwed up. You caused this mess." As the words escaped his lips, Reyne's resentment towards Mera dug deeper after hearing his own thoughts out loud.

"That's the problem. Someone else must have witnessed your birth. They put the two pieces together. The first, Edruk could travel to Evidar, and the second, his offspring should be able to as well. That's why they're after you now: they know you're his offspring. I hid you away in Hensdale with Pachelle and Gwerther. Took Evidar all these years to find you. But they did find you, and I need to know how."

Red-faced, Reyne screamed at Mera, "You put me in the middle of all this shit! You ruined my life."

Mera stepped forward, coming nose to nose with Reyne, and shouted into his face, "I'm saving you. You'd be dead already if not for me." Mera backed off and settled in, a few feet away. In a calm voice, he continued, "But we're going there to find out who. It's something you are going to want to see."

With puffed cheeks, Reyne exhaled slowly as though in surrender mode.

This is a waste of time. I just need to get away from him, off to Evidar, so I can get back to Mithany and take her away from this shit without this pain in the ass knowing. He offered half-truths to Mera. "Don't matter much to me where we head next, tavern or Edruk's home. Whatever gets me closer to this other reality of yours, Evidar, the better."

"Good. I like to hear that."

"Don't kid yourself. I aint doin' it for you. And dragging me through this mess of a city don't change anything. I'm doin' all this for Mithany's sake, not for your cause."

"Nonetheless."

"If we're not goin' to the Whispering Eye, where's this home you want to show me? Is it far?"

"No, your parents had a house on the edge of Teth proper. But it's on the other side of the Temple Palace. Could be dangerous getting through the city, but it'll be safer than the tavern."

Reyne snapped. "I never knew them. Stop calling them my parents."

"If you say so. Then let's head over to where Edruk, his wife Silia, and their daughter, an adorable three-year-old girl named Baide, once lived." He paused. "Before they were all murdered."

Reyne stopped walking and stared hard at Mera. "You're a funny guy. But it won't work. I never knew them, and they mean nothing to me. I'm sorry about the little girl. What *does* matter to me is Daedyn. He's family. And he's dead, remember?"

Three people, whose appearance told Reyne they were not from high society, came around the corner where Reyne and Mera were talking. Two men and a woman, all in ragged, torn, dirty clothing, made Reyne wonder why he hadn't smelled them before he saw them.

The woman asked her companions, "Aye, who're these jerk-offs?"

The tall one with muscles and no hair replied, "Don't know. Don't care. Their coin's gonna be ours soon enough."

The woman nodded in agreement.

Reyne reached for a hidden knife, sheathed in his side pant leg pocket.

Mera grabbed his arm. "No. It's only coin."

The third would-be assailant stepped forward, coming nose-to-nose with Reyne.

Although not a brawler, but at just over six feet, youthful and muscled from years of physical labor in the orchard, few men evoked fear in Reyne. With the death of his brother gnawing at him every minute of every day, and an imminent threat from the man in his face, Reyne welcomed as an opportunity to release the pain consuming him on someone—anyone.

The corners of his lips curled upward into a wicked grin. *This guy will do.* A smile born in the craving to release the misery of his broken heart. Exhilarated at the prospect of unleashing his anger into the world and excited at the opportunity to cut ties with the gentle businessman inside him, Reyne thrilled at the chance to emerge reborn as the man he needed to become.

His eyes lit up. In a calm voice, he provoked his attacker. "Take your best shot... asshole."

The man crashed his forehead into Reyne.

A devastating blow.

Reyne staggered back.

Pain exploded into his head.

Stars filled his vision.

Blinding, white-hot agony raced through his skull.

At that instant, Reyne snapped, or something inside him did. Awareness fled him. It was as though a wild beast, unleashed from deep in his soul, took control.

The pain existed, but it didn't.

Reyne's body belonged to him, but it didn't.

The face of who Reyne had become took on an evil visage.

Quickly recovering from the headbutt, he lunged at the startled man. He cuffed the big man's ears with a two-handed slap. The man yelled out. A powerful thrust from Reyne's knee shot up. The man moved to block it. But not fast enough. Bone and muscle connected with the man's balls.

The wide-eyed mugger writhed in pain. He doubled over, shooting his hands downward toward his enflamed gonads. His hands never made it. Reyne smashed his fist into the side of his temple. Eyes fluttering, withered-testicle man toppled to the ground.

Bald-and-muscular guy lunged at Reyne.

He lowered his shoulder, drove forward, and slammed into Reyne. They careened into the side of a half-burnt stud. The entwined men plowed through it. The pair tumbled to the ground. Reyne, or who he had become, looked over from the ground.

It happened fast.

A woman with open hands spread her fingers apart with long pointed nails at the end of each. She swiped at Mera, who deflected the strike aimed at his face.

With her other hand, four sharp, dagger-shaped fingernails whipped through his shirt. The razor-like nails drew blood across his torso. She paid the price of her lunge. It exposed her nape. Mera brought down his elbow with all his weight, connecting with the back of her neck. She went limp on impact. Unconsciousness took her even before she face-planted into the hard road.

Reyne sprang up from the charred, broken stud. Bald-and-muscular guy quickly followed. Reyne unleashed a barrage of endless blows in an incessant, animalistic attack. Reyne's eyes looked like that of a wild man, pent-up rage set free from its imprisonment. Bash after bash found its target. Bald-and-muscular guy tried to cover up, but Reyne's fists connected over and over. Bald-and-muscular fell to the ground.

Despite the man being unconscious, Reyne kept ferociously beating him. Blood covered his face.

Mera stepped behind Reyne and put a hand on his shoulder. Reyne sprung and began attacking him. The fury, freed from within, found no cause to cease just because it was Mera.

Something primeval inside Reyne had control of him. It delighted in inflicting pain on others. Released into the moment, it didn't want to stop. The monster within enjoyed it. He'd beat anyone and everyone who got in his way. Mindlessly cathartic—soul-cleansing—it drained the coffers of his stored misery, little by little, with every anger-fueled strike he delivered.

Mera jumped back. Reyne's eyes receded behind dark, narrow circles. Breathing heavily, he looked over Mera like a wolf salivating over its prey. Reyne's arms hung at his sides, clenched tight in threatening blood-covered fists. His nostrils flared like a bull readying to charge.

Unable to control himself, the body belonged to Reyne, but ownership of it was all he could claim. A part of his primal self emerged from deep within Reyne the moment the first headbutt struck. Neither freely nor knowingly, he surrendered control to some other part of himself, hidden away in his subconscious, but in recent days feeding off his anger, his misery, and his loss, growing stronger, defiant.

In measured steps, Mera backed away without turning, keeping his eyes locked on whatever Reyne had become. Reyne scrutinized Mera's every footfall. His chest rose and fell with labored breaths. Mera stopped. Neither man moved. Seconds passed. Reyne coiled, ready to strike.

Suddenly, the claw-armed woman, joined by Reyne's first victim, sprung up in unison and bolted. The third man remained unmoving, unconscious. Reyne's attention was diverted from Mera to the pair racing from the scene. The distraction broke the primitive, single-minded beast's hold on him.

Reyne, the man Mithany loved, regained self-control.

His breathing slowed. All at once, his dark, narrow, deep-set green eyes settled back to normal. He released the fury in his clenched fists, and his hands hung limp at his side.

Reyne's eyes followed the two would-be robbers disappear from view, and he looked down at the third. "Mera, you do all this?"

"Hmm. Not sure how to answer that. But I will. Truth of it is I didn't do this. You did."

Reyne looked confused at Mera. "Get outta here. You're crazy."

His breathing slowed, and Reyne stretched out his arms like he'd just woken from a good night's sleep. "I gotta tell you, for some reason, I feel better than I have for days." He reached up to feel a large bump on his forehead. "Head hurts like hell, though."

Mera's eyes drew in tight, staring at Reyne, and he opened his mouth to speak. It looked to Reyne as though Mera wanted to say something but didn't. Instead, Mera turned away. "We have a mile or so ahead of us to Edruk's and Silia's home. It'll be safer there than on the streets."

"You sure?" Reyne asked, rubbing the bruise on his forehead.

"Yeah, no one has any reason to expect you'd go there. They think you're dead. And even if anyone from Evidar suspects you're still alive, they'd expect you to be headed for their world. Edruk's old house is probably the safest place for us to go."

Feeling refreshed, Reyne slapped his hands together and vigorously rubbed his palms. "Okay then, off we go. We need to avoid running into others like these three."

Mera tilted his head to the side.

Reyne followed with his own quizzical look. "Why you lookin' at me like that?"

"It'll be getting dark in an hour or two. We should swing wide around the Temple Palace. We can make it before dark. If the place is empty, we can sleep there. If not, we can camp in the woods near their old house."

Reyne said nothing.

Mera kneeled over the one assailant left behind and checked the man's neck for a pulse. "Good. He'll live. He's going to have one hell of a headache."

Mera turned his head up towards Reyne. Concerned by the way Mera studied him, Reyne opined, "Again with that look? I'm fine. What is it?"

Mera brushed his hands on his pants and stood. "It's probably nothing... I hope."

Death, Soon Enough

Hensdale: 2nd Day of the Harvest Moon

Tylus | Arek

At the home of two dead apple farmers, in the dead of night—the way the two Evidar agents liked it—Arek was thrown into the back of a wagon, offering no resistance. His body unresponsive, Evidar agent Tylus concluded Arek had nearly completed his journey from the world of the living to the realm of the dead. He would be at his new setting, wherever death transported one, soon enough.

With Arek lying immobile under a canvas in the back of a wagon-cart, Tylus had an idea. "You know, Grafph, best place to dump him is far away in an isolated area of woods. Remember that side road we passed on the way back from Owls Neck?"

Grafph replied, "Yeah, what of it? It's a few miles from here. It's a bit on the cooler side tonight. You sure we got to go that far?"

"So what? The horse is doing all the work. That location is perfect."

"I guess that's as good a place as any to dump this useless lump of flesh." Admiration poured out in his tone when he said, "She really did a number on him."

Tylus's eyes lit up. "Yeah. You gotta admit, she put on quite a show, and she's got a great set of tits. I'm a tit man. How about you?"

"I love it all. What I wouldn't give…"

"Like you'd ever get a shot at that."

Grafph asked, "You ever think about taking a crack at hooking up with Dylla?"

Tylus laughed. "First, she'd eat you alive in the sack, and second, you'd never get close. She's too classy for the likes of you."

"Like you'd have a chance." Grafph smirked.

The pair hopped aboard the single spring-cushioned seat spanning the width of the buckboard. Tylus released the handbrake, grabbed the reins, and snapped them forward, giving an order to the horse to get moving.

A few moments of silence passed as Tylus played out fantasies of Dylla and Neladith rolling around in his head. By the smirk on Grafph's face, he figured his partner had similar notions.

Tylus broke the quiet. "This was our first assignment working with Neladith. She's done well so far. I'll make sure it gets passed up the line. The Devil's Blacksmith will be pleased."

Grafph gestured with a shiver, "I hate that guy."

"I'd be careful if I were you. Say that in the wrong company, and they'll be the last words you ever utter."

"It's just you and me. He gives me the creeps."

Tylus laughed. "He gives everybody the creeps."

The two men spent the journey describing Neladith's skills as an operative but devoted more time gushing admiration over the features she'd put on display, the acts she'd performed, and about as much of anything of Neladith they could recall. Her demonstrative behavior, her skill with the two-bow, and her utter lack of inhibition made a considerable impression on the two otherwise stone-hearted operatives.

"You know, Ty, these two worlds are so different. It isn't that this place is forever in the light, but the attitudes about sex and the lack of clothing are so nonchalant. I can get used to the sunshine, but not sure I'll ever get used to these attitudes."

"Well, my friend, you won't have to. After we dump this asshole, can't imagine we'll get too much more time in this place. Quith and Neladith are on track to either confirm Reyne Brenton's dead or they'll finish the job pretty quickly. Best guess, we're done soon. And I can't wait to get back."

Looking up, Grafph lamented, "I'm gonna miss the stars. Don't see them back home. You know, all the shit in the atmosphere."

Tylus gave a snap of his wrists and sent the wordless command through the reins to the horse that said, *Pick up the pace.* "Forget the stars. I just want to get back home."

The wagon rambled, bounced, and jostled along the bumpy road as the evening rolled on. The pair took turns reliving former glories to pass the time until the cart delivering Arek to his final resting place arrived at the turnoff.

Approaching the barely noticeable entrance to the side trail by the light of the moon, Tylus leaned back, pulling on the reins. The cart came to a stop. He stood up, looked around, and pointed off to his left. "That looks like the spot. We'll turn here."

Grafph remained seated and, crossing both arms over his chest, rubbed at his biceps. "Getting nippy. How far down do you think we need to go?"

"A mile should keep his stink from wafting back to the main road. Animals will still pick it up, but humans won't."

Grafph rolled his neck. The familiar successive snaps and pops—similar to cracking one's knuckles—sounded louder in the quiet of the forest. "Oh, that felt good."

With an elbow, Tylus jabbed his partner in his side. "Good. Get loose. We still got to bury the body."

Grafph dropped his head backward and let out a sigh. "Why bother? We're out in the middle of nowhere. Who's gonna know?"

Tylus gave a nod to the wagon behind him. "Shovel's in the back of the cart. We're digging a hole. That's the end of it."

"You win. You're the ranking agent. You bring one shovel or two?"

With upturned palms and a shrug of his shoulders, Tylus said, "Could only find the one. We'll take turns digging."

Tylus began in no hurry to complete the assignment, but the chill in the air had started him thinking of diminishing returns. His enjoyment of the outing began to wane, and soon enough he reached the end of the line. He missed the ever-present warmth of Evidar.

Tylus pulled back the brake handle and wrapped the reins around it. "We're here. I should have worn gloves; my hands are frozen."

Grafph jumped down, unwrapped the reins, released the brake, and led the horse with the cart in tow to a nearby tree, where he tied off the restraint. "Let's finish this and get back to the safe house. I'm liking the dark, but I ain't so familiar with the critters in these woods. Better they eat him than us."

Tylus blew hot air into his cupped hands. "Don't be a pussy."

The horse snorted and stamped one leg over and over, all the while tugging at the leather strap limiting its movement.

Grafph ignored his partner's jab. "What's got the horse spooked?"

Tylus's tone turned serious against the chill of the night air. "Let's just get this done and go home."

Grafph threw back the tarp, exposing the battered, unconscious Arek. "Help me get him out."

A tone of commanding annoyance rolled off Tylus. "Keep that accursed horse still. The cart's moving too much."

Grafph walked around to the front and grabbed the cheekpiece of the horse's bridle. The visibly anxious animal stopped juddering. "I'll keep the mare still; you pull him off."

Tylus grabbed Arek's foot and yanked. Arek slid out the back and flopped to the ground. A muffled *thunk* that didn't reach very far resounded against the rustling leaves of the forest floor.

In admiration of Neladith's handy work, the pair looked down at the bloody, beaten, and bruised Arek. Arek's exposed body on display, unlike that of Neladith's, drew out none of the pair's commentary. Tylus looked up. "I'll get the shovel."

Before Tylus took another step, his head snapped in the direction of a sudden low, rumbling growl. Arek gave no sign of having heard the wolves approach. Yellow teeth appeared through its drawn-back muzzle, and a pair of reflective eyes glowered at the men. The horse whinnied wildly, rose up on its hindquarters with its front legs flailing, ripped the reins loose from the branch, and bolted with the cart in tow.

Tylus took several steps back, keeping his body facing the menacing beast, now joined by several of its brethren. He spoke slowly in a whisper to his similarly concerned partner, "Let's get the hell outta here. Grafph, no sudden movements. Back away slow."

Grafph released the clasp covering his blade as he stepped back. "Ty, you're armed, right?"

Tylus rested one hand on the leather sheath housing his knife. "Always."

Each rested one hand on their weapon and held out the other with open palm, as if to say, "Stay." Step by step the men made their cautious withdrawal. Tylus didn't take his eyes off the creatures. Snarling, the beasts inched closer. "Grafph, I know what you're thinking. If there were only one or two of them, yeah, but there's too many."

"Okay, but what're we going to do about him?" Grafph nodded to Arek's body. "She said to make sure he's dead. He's only mostly dead. He's not *all* dead yet."

One foot followed the other in slow retreat. "She's not the ranking agent, I am. He ain't goin' nowhere. I'm guessing he's about to be their next meal. Better him than us. We're done here."

Grafph's reply came quickly, "You give the order. I'll peg him through the heart with a flick of the wrist. You know I'm more accurate than anyone throwing a blade."

Tylus gave Grafph a direct order. "You try that, and I'll kill you myself. Any sudden moves, they'll be on us before your knife hits the target. Let it go."

A loud snap of a twig from a backward-moving boot sent the wolves into a sudden crouch, as though ready to spring at the men.

Tylus froze. His free hand squeezed into a fist—the universal signal to stop. "Don't move. Don't... fuckin'... move."

In what sounded like a whisper, Grafph added, "No argument here."

In similar hushed tones Tylus spoke but didn't take his eyes off the pack. "We kill him, or they do. Doesn't matter to me."

With hard, squinting eyes, scrunched snout, and showing a full set of fangs, the leader of the pack snarled at the men. "I think that's our last warning," Grafph said as he began again stepping blindly backwards. "Screw this. There's four of them things. We ain't gonna win any fight with them over his body. They can have it."

Crouched, a second wolf barring its fangs, growled, slinking towards the men. In unison, Tylus and Grafph picked up the pace in surrender of their prey. When both men had crept far enough away, Tylus commanded, "Now!" and they broke into a sprint. Cart nor horse were anywhere to be found. Neither man looked back as they ran like hell.

Awareness came slowly to Arek.

His eyes were swollen shut.

The ringing in his ears denied all other sounds passage through them.

The coppery taste of blood filled his mouth, and the cool autumn air chilled him to the core.

Where he was, or how he got there, failed to register in his barely functioning brain. He felt the tarp covering him, the hard boards beneath him, and movement. Pain of every variety attacked his senses while the cold leaching into his frame did nothing to dull the agony hammering in his head. He would freeze to death soon enough.

He drifted off.

When awareness returned to him, how long he'd been out, he had no clue. Only blackness penetrated his shuttered eyelids. Confusion reigned, but the tarp was gone.

His consciousness floated in and out. Then, his body crashed into the hard ground of the forest. Pain screamed into his brain pulling him back to reality. He heard a man's muffled voice.

He couldn't make it out.

The voice faded away—or he did.

His mind fluttered in and out of consciousness.

When something cold, wet, and small pushed against his thigh, it pulled him back to reality. His eyes resisted his call to open. The fear of death poked out between muddled, sentient thoughts. Now, with something poking at him, the fear of dying raced across every synapse.

An image shot across his mind of Neladith, breasts bouncing up and down while she straddled him, pumping furiously, grinding into his crotch, all the while flailing, pounding, and ripping flesh from his face and body.

He remembered it all.

He hated her.

He hated himself.

His inner voice howled orders into his brain, *Open your eyes. Open, damn it!* But his eyelids didn't listen. What little reserves he still had—drained at the effort—and he drifted off into darkness.

Ripped from *the nowhere* his unconscious mind had been hiding, awake once more, pain demanded to be heard. Excruciating, intense agony tore through his thigh. His unresponsive, locked-closed eyes sprang open. Sorry his eyelids finally responded, terror washed over him the moment his brain registered what he saw. He looked down the length of his body at a large wolf with its teeth buried in his leg and two of its companions sniffing at his groin.

Everything faded to black.

Arek drifted from the world.

AND THE WINNER IS

TETH: 2ND DAY OF THE HARVEST MOON

Jerithan

Jerithan's heart pounded wildly. Pressure drummed behind his eyes. Tingling hot embers danced along the tips of his fingers. Sounds suffused, thumped at his eardrums. All the ballots had been cast. Prudent O'Hurn respectfully set the vessel holding the secret votes at his side near the podium. Jerithan's future had already been decided. It hid from him inside the small container, a jack-in-the-box coiled to explode into his world as a jester delivering a cruel joke and he, the butt.

Sunlight had long faded as the deliberation consumed most of the hours allotted to the day. Warm, glowing candlelight from the elaborate chandelier hanging overhead flickered against the elaborate mural, one of many scenes from the Book of Teth, encircling the room. Jerithan experienced none of the revery intended of its depiction. His position as First Lord—his life's ambition, his plans for a united Empire of Tartica under his rule as its emperor, his reason for living—hung on the mercy of the twenty-three white and black ancient stones sequestered inside a box.

Prudent O'Hurn cleared his throat standing before the silent prudents. Gravelly noise from O'Hurn's pharynx punched at Jerithan's ears. "Fellow prudents," O'Hurn began, "each of you has taken a solemn vow to cast your vote in all good conscience, with the future of our faith your only deciding factor. As the leaders of the Temple of Life, we do this for all who follow our path."

Jerithan's thoughts screamed, *Open the goddam box!*

O'Hurn continued, "By our ancient right, we here in this room—"

Jerithan cut off O'Hurn. He couldn't take it any longer. To keep his shaking hands from being exposed, Jerithan gripped them tightly together. Stilled and resting on a table he shared with assassins sent to terminate his reign armed only with ballots, Jerithan's palms dripped of sweat. He did his best to control the fear leaking out in his words. "My esteemed colleague, I respectfully ask that we move past formalities and embrace the future of our order as determined by the contents in that ceremonial vessel."

O'Hurn—his opportunity to shine stepped on—appeared to Jerithan to be anything but pleased at the interruption. Seeing his reaction, Jerithan spoke up before O'Hurn formatted a wounded reply, "I think we can all agree you have conducted yourself as an impartial facilitator with great skill and are an example for others on this Council to emulate. My request is made based on my own accord to know what the future holds. I ask for your understanding and compassion to move forward, with all haste, now that the period of debate and the vote is behind us."

Prudent Serco, not letting any opportunity pass to damage Jerithan, jumped in, believing he had succeeded in dislodging the sitting First Lord, which could not be revealed soon enough. "It's always all about you. Not of our tradition. Our time-honored ways. There is a mob at our gates. They occupy the plaza surrounding the Palace, this symbol of our faith, and all you can think about is your future."

"Enough!" O'Hurn roared. "I will not have any more of this. Silence."

Jerithan's eyes watched Prudent Serco shoot an angry look at O'Hurn, but the apprehensive First Lord barely registered any of it. His only thought burned at the outer layer of the vessel containing all his tomorrows, all his hopes, the stones inside collectively screaming at the room to be let out, the whims of fate demanding its freedom to pronounce judgment and its consequences unleashed on the world.

Prudent O'Hurn turned away from Prudent Serco and spoke to the Council. O'Hurn, not a man disposed to acquiescence, and the ballots had yet to speak, sacred tradition granted him unrequited authority over the conclave, at least until it made its prophetic determination. In control, wielding his authority, O'Hurn declared, "As Temple canons require of us, I ask for two prudents to join me to assist in the counting of the sacred stones. First Lord Jerithan, the esteemed Second Lord Razoal would be one of the two, and in his absence, I ask for your permission to name both."

As much as Second Lord Razoal's status amongst the missing concerned Jerithan, with the enormity of the Vote of Revocation the First Lord faced, the absence of Razoal represented only a minor inconvenience in the counting phase. Who counted the votes would be immaterial. Jerithan required Razoal for his vote, not his ability to count, but that prospect had died a silent death. "Please proceed, and I will respect whomever you choose."

Voices and visions rippled through Jerithan's faint awareness of the goings-on around him.

He couldn't breathe.

He couldn't think.

His eyes darted about wildly.

His body pulsed and pounded with every beat of his heart. The attendees, the room, the counting all seemed to transpire on a different plane of existence. As though he sat alone, separated from the world while he awaited the final tally.

Prudent O'Hurn pulled out a single stone with each vote cast, revealed it to the Council, holding it high for all to see, and passing it to his second. Jerithan tried to focus as stone by stone, black and white, were presented for the Council, one by one.

Jerithan vaguely registered O'Hurn when he paused.

"There are two remaining sacred stones. The Vote for Revocation stands at twelve white and eleven black. Twelve for revocation. Eleven against."

A greedy, eager Serco looked at First Lord Jerithan with a grin plastered from ear to ear.

O'Hurn announced, holding up the instrument of decision, and proclaimed, "White."

NO! Jerithan's mind screamed. *Hansel!*

Devastation flooded through him. Like a collapsing palace brought down in one fell swoop, his world crumbled. His life was now nothing but a pile of rubble, impossible to ever rise again to its former majestic glory.

Ruined.

Worse than ruined, destroyed.

O'Hurn announced, "With this stone, a majority of prudents have so declared support for the motion of Revocation. Jerithan Cree has been recalled from his position as First Lord. Effective immediately."

Payback, Not Always a Bitch

Wilderness: 3rd Day of the Harvest Moon

Brenal

Every living creature within miles froze where they stood at the fearsome, thunderous growl resonating through the forest. Four wolves lording over a human body were no exception. A second terrifying roar commenced as the last one faded, but this one, closer to the small wolf pack, forced each of them to raise their heads, sniff the air, and scan the forest for movement before letting fly a collective whimper as though in disgust of having to give up their found meal to the approaching danger. A third heart-stopping howl, louder and closer than the first two, sent the wolves scampering away at full speed.

The enormous beast standing at least nine feet tall, a Great Yetgnal, lumbered forward with its nose turned up, taking in every scent the forest offered. At the top of the food chain, the monster, humanoid in shape, covered in fur, did not know fear. Wolves posed no danger to the creature, whether alone or in a pack. Hell hounds, the Great Yetgnal's archenemy, while dangerous in large numbers to a Great Yetgnal, didn't elicit the slightest concern.

Following its nose, the gargantuan, hairy, man-like creature lumbered its way to Arek's bloody, naked body where the two Evidar agents left it. Bending down without kneeling, it took in another longer, introspective pull of the human scent through its dried snot-encrusted nostrils. Rising to its full height, with its head turned up, it cried out in pain. With its mouth raised to the black sky, it released a fourth call, this one different in tone. Sadness seeped through it.

The beast picked up Arek, threw him over its shoulder as one might slap a washcloth over it, and began sprinting from the site. Faster than any human, and familiar with every detail of the forest, the Great Yetgnal, almost silently, traversed its way through the dense woodland.

It ran for miles, dispersing the night fauna in its wake with only its appearance. The beast made its way to the home of Hollid Brenal in half the time Tylus and Grafph took to make it to Arek's would-be final resting place. Pausing at the steps of the front porch, the monster flopped Arek's body to the ground before making its way up the stairs. He or she let out a gentler, although no less frightening sound, which again brought silence to the night from the woodland's creatures.

Hollid Brenal, the kindly, old village doctor, safely tucked away under his sheets, snapped out of a deep sleep as a blood-curdling cry from just outside his front door reached his ears. The country doctor, although he'd never encountered one, quickly surmised the source.

Half asleep, his heart thundered in his chest. Adrenaline pushed through his body. His eyes bulged. Terror-induced fear held him tight to his bed.

For what seemed like several minutes, he clung to the sheets rolled up under his chin with one hand, the other hand over his heart. Unable to move, afraid to breathe or even think, Brenal remained planted in his bed.

A resounding *thud* bounced off the walls and rattled every floorboard and furniture leg set upon it.

Oh, my god. The door. Bug-eyed, his thoughts raced. The muscle inside his rib cage squeezed harder. *It's coming for me. Teth save me.*

Thud.

"I'm an old man, leave me alone," he shouted.

Thud.

"Go away!"

Thud.

He expected he would die of a heart attack if he heard it again. Before his prediction of cause and effect came to fruition, a sharp pain seized his chest. On instinct, he clutched at the tightness gripping his heart.

Awareness seeped through the mind-gripping terror; such a creature could tear down his door with little effort. But why the monstrous beast only pounded against it escaped his understanding. He wondered if the creature didn't intend his death. That thought fueled the bravery to move. One foot touched the frigid floor. Then the other.

Oh, that's cold.

He let go of the sheet up against his chest, protecting him.

Thud.

Realization struck him; something other than his imminent death lay ahead. Dread did not escape his thoughts totally, but he began a slow trek to the front door of his modest home. Short of breath, he fought through it.

Thud.

The cold floor sucked heat from his feet with each step, yet he pushed the uncomfortable feeling aside.

The pain in his chest continued, undiminished, reminding him of the consequences of a weak heart and of its immediate cause: the beast on his front porch. If one didn't kill him, the other would. Uncertain if he was doing the right thing, with his hands shaking, Brenal reached for the doorknob and gripped the handle.

Thud.

The *thud* from the Great Yetgnal pounding on his door, shot through his hand, up his arm, and reverberated through his frail old body. It rattled his bones. It rattled his teeth. But mostly, it rattled his determination. Yet, he closed his eyes, squeezed them tight, and flung open the door.

Seconds passed, and he was still alive. Gathering whatever passed for courage in an old man, Brenal forced open his unwilling eyelids, and he came face to face with a hunched over Great Yetgnal. His heart felt like it slammed into a wall and fluttered with irregular beats, stealing from him—momentarily—the ability to breathe in the ungodly smell. He stood, juddering, more scared than at any time in his life. An aging, weak bladder released its gathered contents. Urine dripped down his leg. With his sight fixed on the monstrous thing standing in his doorway, unable to even blink, terror had a firm grip on him—body and soul.

The hunched Great Yetgnal, visibly struggling to fit itself between the floorboards and the porch roof, stared at Brenal but didn't move. With a sudden jerk, it turned away, leaped off the porch, and disappeared into the night.

After a reactive flinch at the monster's movement, Brenal spied a human body at the base of his porch stairs. A naked body, unmoving, lying on the ground, had been delivered for Brenal to deal with. *How is that possible?*

Brenal waited for the beast to disappear into the night. It moved swiftly and quietly, much to the village doctor's surprise. The foul odor of rotting leaves, feces, and intense body sweat it left behind lingered. He held on tight to the handrail, descending the stairs as fast as his elderly muscles would allow. Bloody, cut up, motionless, and unconscious, Brenal wondered if whoever it was, was even alive. Fear shot through him as he recognized the bloody lump of flesh.

Arek!

Years of medical training and dealing with emergencies of every nature allowed him to push aside all other thoughts. Confirmation of whether Arek still clung to life was Brenal's immediate charge before rushing to any judgment of how best to treat him. He endured the growing pain gnawing at him from behind his sternum, doing his best to ignore it.

"Arek, what happened to you?" Brenal asked aloud, standing over the body, not expecting a reply. Arek had been flopped down on his side, showing deep cuts along his cheek, and a piece of his ear was missing. Squatting as best he could, his knee joints released a popping sound as he bent down, setting one hand on Arek to steady himself.

Brenal ignored the dried blood covering his neck and placed two fingers on Arek's carotid artery. His wrinkled, arthritic-misshapen fingers, having lost a degree of sensitivity to touch—another indignity of age and unfortunate for a person entrusted to the community's wellbeing—could not detect the requisite pulse of life. He inspected Arek's red, soaked chest, praying to capture its rise and fall. Intently he stared, but in the darkness just before dawn, his eyes, not the instruments they once were, failed to conclude any movement. With Arek lying on his side, Brenal thought better of it and rolled him onto his back and gave it another go. It rolled easily, and in the resulting reveal, Brenal caught sight of the damaged flesh of Arek's previously hidden inner thigh.

His hand raced to cover his mouth. "Oh my. You poor man. This is bad," Brenal said aloud. Talking to himself was a habit borne of isolation and loneliness since the death of his wife many years ago.

Unable to move Arek from the spot where he lay, Brenal bolted up the stairs, or what masqueraded as such for the country doctor, grabbed his medical bag from inside the house along with a blanket, moved back down the stairs, pulled out his stethoscope and returned to his prior position alongside Arek's body—knee joints sending a popping sound into the night once again.

Streaks of pink proclaiming the promise of dawn fought back the receding night against the horizon, but were not sufficient yet to assist Brenal in his visual assessment of Arek.

The forest was eerie in its silence since hearing the calls of the Great Yetgnal. The creatures of the night receded at the beast's arrival, and like the day fauna in and around Hensdale, neither had yet to venture out. Brenal's elderly, diminished ears welcome the woodland's relative quiet. With the stethoscope earpieces secured, Brenal placed the listening device over Arek's heart.

Relief washed over him with each *lub-dub, lub-dub* leaking through his stethoscope. The sound was faint at best, ever so dim, yet a heartbeat nonetheless—but for how much longer? Brenal's trained ears heard Arek's heart fight to maintain its rhythm, struggling against the injurious effects on the body. The chance for survival slipped further away with each weak contraction of the muscle, barely moving life-sustaining blood through his body. That is, what little of the red, life-giving fluid he still had.

Brenal put all his years of experience and medical skills to work at the base of his porch stairs, right there in the dirt. The environment was far from ideal, but

Brenal couldn't afford the time it would take to find a clean operating theater, and without help, he had no way to move Arek. If Arek could be saved, the effort would have to be here, and it would have to be now.

He was unable to adequately assess all the damages. There was too much blood, matted hair, and dirt all over Arek's broken frame to afford a proper visual inspection to determine where to begin his efforts to save the young man. Back up the stairs, Brenal rushed to find a clean cloth, fill a bucket, and without losing too much water on the return trip, he made his way back alongside Arek.

He worked quickly.

Time was his enemy.

Arek didn't have much of it left.

In the back of his mind, vague awareness of his own pain haunted him.

Brenal stood and looked over the many lacerations, gouges, and tears to Arek's flesh. He determined the facial damage, while significant, was not life-threatening. His torn eyelid would have to wait. Although his neck was another matter, seeping blood from three separate wounds, and two required immediate attention. His practiced fingers threaded suture line to needle, and he set about closing the wounds.

Many of the chest cuts were profound, as though someone drove short spikes into his chest, ripping through skin and muscle tissue. Some, Brenal figured, looked like an object bit into muscle and pulled down against it, extending the damage. The seepage at the incisions had to be stopped.

Brenal faced two major problems: Arek had lost too much blood, and his thigh had taken severe damage. If he lived, there would be long-term muscle impairment. He decided, like with the young man's chest wounds, to stop the loss of even more blood and to effect the non-life threatening repairs later—if Arek recovered. A tourniquet to the leg would stop the bleeding, but risked the possibility of exacerbating the damaged muscle. He decided that would have to be a concern for another time. Brenal ripped his shirt sleeve from its shoulder seam, grabbed a nearby stick from the ground, and did his best to stem further loss of blood from Arek's thigh.

While satisfied with his immediate efforts, much remained to be done. Arek needed blood. It couldn't wait any longer, and Brenal feared Arek would soon pass over the threshold into hypervolemic shock, with death close behind.

Brenal didn't store blood or plasma at his home. Neither could he leave Arek in his current state. Brenal had only one source—his own. If not a match, giving Arek his own could be the final straw pushing Arek toward death. He had to be certain. Ten minutes is all it would take to cross-type Arek's, but did Arek have that much time?

With the stethoscope once more placed to Arek's chest, his heartbeat sounded even weaker.

I'm losing him.

He's lost too much blood.

Cardiac arrest loomed ahead in Arek's immediate future.

Arek would perish without an immediate transfusion. If Brenal cross-matched types and if they weren't a match, Arek would die. If he took the time to cross-type, Arek would expire waiting for the results. And what if they didn't match? Every scenario led to the same conclusion—death.

Brenal made a fateful decision. Whether or not a match, Arek had only one chance to live. It would be a gamble, but he had no other choice.

Brenal rushed back up the stairs into his house, fumbled for his transfusion equipment, and scrambled back outside. The old doctor wheezed, out of breath but not out of determination. He tried to push through, but the pain in his chest seized him. He stopped dead in his tracks, clutching his chest at the acute discomfort his efforts up and down the stairs caused. Knowing well the symptoms, he reached into his bag and pulled out a bottle of willow-bark powder. Brenal quickly swallowed an undetermined amount of the dry dust and hoped for the best. Time did not afford him careful measurement, yet experience allowed him an adequate approximation. Along with constricting, breath-stealing chest pain, a thousand tiny, finger-like, minuscule tentacles flittered about his thorax, erasing all doubt he was having a heart attack. He'd had them before: mild, if any heart attack could be considered mild. This one felt different. Willow-bark powder had worked before. It had to, one more time.

He couldn't stop. He had to save Arek. But giving blood while in his condition would likely kill him. But if he didn't try, Arek would die, there, in the dirt.

Nobody would hear his calls for help, and he didn't have time to go for aid.

I'm Arek's last hope.

Brenal laid the blanket on top of Arek and left a good portion loose on the ground next to him. Inserting a needle into himself, Brenal kneeled over Arek, inserted a second needle into his patient's arm, and positioned himself to lie alongside. Pulling the plunger of the transfusion device, he pumped and pumped as the flow of red through the tubes began.

Fear the Beast

Hensdale: 3rd Day of the Harvest Moon

Quith

Furious with Neladith for creating doubt of Reyne Brenton's death, Quith's blood boiled as he hid in the tall grass outside Reyne's home, one hundred forty-two yards from where someone slumped over the front porch railing, dead, several nights ago.

That cocky, self-assured, backstabbing shitbag Neladith told Dylla that someone said, "You'll see him again." That's what kicked off this clusterfuck. Those four fucking words, "You'll see him again." It's bullshit. Reyne Brenton is dead. But no. Now I have to prove it.

She'll pay for her lies.

She probably started all this just to dick around with me.

Quith might not have feared Neladith, but he did the Devil's Blacksmith. A man not known for his compassion;, the Devil's Blacksmith didn't suffer incompetence. That's how it would be taken: Quith's incompetence. A solid operative for many years, he successfully completed a lot of dangerous wet work for *the cause.* None of that mattered. If Reyne lived, Quith was a dead man walking.

Dylla would be the instrument the Devil's Blacksmith unleashed against him. He feared her too, and with good reason. Before rising to the ranks of management, Dylla proved herself as good at killing as anyone Quith had ever worked with.

Only one of two truths would save him: proof of either a dead Reyne Brenton or a lying Neladith Karlis. The thought played over and over in his head. He had to fix this problem. He still had time, but not much. If Reyne was alive, he would have to find him, today, and kill the bastard himself.

Quith put it into perspective. Three possibilities existed, and whichever proved out, someone else would be dead within days. The answer to the question—who would be the next to die—hinged on the identity of who lay under all that dirt at the gravesite.

In scenario one, Quith figured the team had in fact killed Reyne as reported. All this bullshit would then blow over, but Neladith would pay with her life for her betrayal. He'd make sure of it.

In the second possibility, Daedyn took the arrow and Reyne would soon follow his brother into the grave. The third piggybacked off the second. If Reyne remained upright and walking, and Quith couldn't get to the live-and-breathing version of Reyne quickly, Quith himself would be Death's next victim. In all the versions a fatal ending hung over someone's head; it was going to be either Neladith's, Reyne's, or his own. Quith was determined that it wouldn't be him.

Quith believed Reyne was dead. He just had to prove it. *That would show them.*

Before departing the safe house earlier in the day, Quith tasked his team with abducting Arek to see if they could squeeze information out of him. He needed proof of who they put in the ground the night of the killing. Yet, he couldn't rely on others to save him. Years of experience in the field taught Quith not to trust anyone. To that end, he spent much of the afternoon hidden at Reyne's family orchard, in a field, at the exact location where Neladith let fly the arrow that started him down this journey. The arrow that perfectly struck its target in the back of the head.

From his sequestered location, he gathered intel.

Who came. Who left.

Was it Daedyn? Was it Reyne?

He needed to put eyes on one or the other.

Absent a visual confirmation, he planned to dig the body up himself as soon as he could, under the cover of dark. The way he—an agent of Evidar—liked it.

Throughout the day, several unfamiliar faces of those working in the orchard came and went. He observed only two people enter the house; a civil peace officer they called a Judjurex, someone named Tetrip who'd begun an investigation into Reyne's death, and another older guy who ran the farm. Quith remembered them from the team's advance briefings. The second man he identified as Santander. Both Hensdale men eventually departed, going their separate ways, and neither Reyne nor Daedyn were amongst any of the people Quith witnessed.

Day passed into night, and Quith spied no other activity over the long stretch. *Maybe I'll take a look around inside. Easier than digging up a body.*

Rising from his hideaway, he slipped out of his tan camo outfit, swapping it for his operational blacks underneath. Pulling a hooded mask of the same color from his pocket, he slipped it over his head, covering his white mane. In middle-age, Quith trained hard every day, and his physique bore proof of it. Wrinkles had yet to claim a home on his face. His pale skin, like most from his world, and his brown eyes had recovered from the symptomatic light sickness all Tweeners from Evidar experienced upon arrival in Tartica.

Stealthily, he made his way to the treestone structure of the Brenton homestead. Climbing over a railing onto the porch, he avoided the well-worn, creaky stairs. Inch by inch the front door gave way as he cautiously entered what appeared to be an empty dwelling. After searching every room for Reyne, he found nothing to help his cause. Moving back outside, he had one option left: to dig up the body.

Quith skirted the tree line and quietly found a shovel inside one of the utility barns. From out of nowhere, Quith heard the heavy barn door squeal. He dove behind a huge cart.

Santander.

Keeping careful watch on the big man's every move, Quith readied himself to strike. With a snap of his arm, he released the ever-present gravity knife—hidden up his sleeve—into his waiting palm. A dead Santander would bring more attention to his cause than he wanted, but Quith understood: if Santander had to die, so be it. When Santander moved towards the cart, Quith coiled—

"Hey boss, what are you doin'?" a voice called out from the open doorway. "It's late. Time to go home. Come on, let's get out of here."

"I was just about to get the cart ready for tomorrow morning. Give me a hand." Santander replied.

The voice. Could it be Reyne's? Like a mother finding a child who'd wandered off, hope shot through Quith. He inched his head out from behind the cart's rear wheel. *Shit, it's not him.* His excitement evaporated in a heartbeat.

"Boss, forget about it. I'll come in early and get the cart ready in the morning."

"Fine." Santander turned, walked away, and closed the barn door behind him.

After allowing enough time for the men to put distance between themselves and the orchard, Quith made his way to the gravesite. Finding the exact spot to dig came easy, since the grave gave away its location to Quith at the sight of recently upturned dirt. The Evidar agent worked with as much vigor as doing it quietly would allow.

On alert for Santander's reappearance, Quith scanned the area in between each bite of dirt the shovel extracted. Long into the night, he worked nonstop. Finally, his efforts revealed the dirt-stained shroud hiding his prize. Brushing aside the brown earth, Quith pulled back the cloth to reveal a torn-up face.

His mind raced.

FUCK! Not him.

His thoughts were cut short. From somewhere nearby, a horrific bellow pierced the night air and reverberated in waves of fear-inducing growls. The beastly roar penetrated through the trees, the ground, the creatures large and small, and it stabbed at Quith's dread. The experienced Evidar operative had never heard such a sound in his world or in all the time he'd spent on Tartica. His body movements locked in place with the first touch to his ears of the unforgettable, soul-piercing call. Nothing but a monstrous beast could project such compelling resonance from its body. It embodied the promise of eminent devastation, destruction, and nothing could stop whatever created it. Instinctively, Quith knew to fear whatever birthed such a cannonade.

He respected the way the creature projected demise to all in its path. He admired the intentional terror it induced. Mostly jealous, he longed to have such a talent to foreshadow his approach in a manner that gripped his target with terror in the knowledge of their own inescapable doom. Standing in the hole, leaning on his shovel, Quith considered his connection to the unseen, savage animal.

Jealousy sparked a thought, and his purpose changed in an instant. Reyne lived, and that meant his own life was forfeit. He'd ordered the wrong man killed. A mistake for certain, but his mistake. He gave the command to Neladith to release the arrow. He declared the target to be Reyne. Dylla would see to it that he was retired with prejudice.

But he wanted to live. Quith fancied himself the beast incarnate to those so unfortunate to pursue him. Extracting himself from the hole, he considered leaving the body exposed but thought it best to put everything back in the condition he found it.

No one would detect he'd ever been there.

No one would be on alert.

No one would see him coming.

He'd become the unknown danger lurking in the shadows.

For him to live, the men and women of Evidar, his team, would all have to die.

Death Unmasked

Teth: 3rd Day of the Harvest Moon

Reyne

Well after dusk, Reyne and Mera finally arrived at the forsaken home of the biological family Reyne never knew: Edruk, his wife Silia, and Baide, the couple's three-year-old daughter. Mera assured Reyne he'd find out how his life had been upended, how Evidar hunters discovered his existence as the progeny of Edruk. According to Mera, Reyne's self-proclaimed protector, the answer lay in the abandoned homestead—twenty-two years in the past.

Reyne's father by birth, two decades gone from the world, Edruk had been a thorn in the side of the Devil's Blacksmith, killing important people crucial for the dark-worlder's plan to succeed. Edruk, a Tweener capable of moving between Earth's two known dimensions, sired another who likely possessed similar talents, or so Evidar feared. Hidden from their clutches since birth, somehow Reyne's existence and his location as a Hensdale alphen nut purveyor came to Evidar's attention, marking him for death. Mera told him that figuring out how Evidar came to have that knowledge meant life or death.

The pair were now standing before Edruk's home, where Mera would pry the past held within the grips of the surrounding and seemingly inanimate objects to reveal the events surrounding Reyne's birth. Reyne had been witness to the impossible once before, when Mera conjured specters from the past, as though standing before him in real time, for Reyne to behold Neladith release the arrow that killed Daedyn. If all proceeded according to plan, Reyne would be an eyewitness to the moment his mother gave him life. Edruk, Silia, and Baide, according to Mera, were his biological family, and all had been murdered the night of his birth in the very building Reyne now stood before transfixed.

Excited, anxious, apprehensive, angry, and confused, Reyne didn't know what to think. Yet, he denied them a link to his heartstrings. *I know one thing. These people ain't my real family.* Gwerther and Pachelle, they were his parents, and Daedyn his brother. He didn't need any other family, no matter how hard Mera tried to force Edruk, Silia, or Baide on him. Reyne told himself they were only names. But despite his efforts to tamp down any sense of connection, a spark of "something lost" flared in his heart as he stared at the empty building: the place Silia, his biological mother according to Mera, gave him life—a place he might have called home.

He pushed it down before it germinated into affection. Daedyn and Mithany weighed heavily on his thoughts. He afforded no others room in his heart. It belonged to Mithany; it belonged to Daedyn.

Physically tired and emotionally drained, he'd face Silia's death and his own birth with weakened mental defenses. And he thought of Mera: *Is he trying to manipulate me? To make me care about these people so I'll be a good little soldier in his war?* And he wondered, *Does it really matter how Evidar found out about me?* Reyne considered why Mera even brought him to this place. *Maybe Mera needs to see this. I can buy that. But why do I have to witness it... he's trying to get to me. I know it. What a sneaky bastard.*

His eyes roamed over the one-story structure of rammed earth holding up a dilapidated thatched roof. Reyne gathered the building hadn't been in use recently. The earthen walls held up fine, but the hole-ridden, scraggly roof gave notice of its uselessness to protect anyone beneath it. Other similarly constructed nearby homes fared better, and all had candlelight pouring out closed windows.

Mera approached the one home—Edruk's—depleted of any inside lights. "Reyne, it doesn't look like it's occupied. Wait here, I'm going to make sure."

Distrustful of Mera's intentions, Reyne asked, "Are we safe here?"

"If Mithany and Arek did their job back in Hensdale, Evidar still thinks you're dead. We'll be alright for the night."

"Didn't you tell earlier today to keep out of sight? Someone could recognize me?"

Mera placed both hands on Reyne's shoulders. Face to face, he replied, "Two different things. Random recognition in a crowd versus trained assassins hunting you. It's dark, and we're kind of isolated, so I'm not too worried about being recognized this time of night. As for the team of hunters, fingers crossed they still think they succeeded in killing you. Either way, we'll be okay here for a while."

Mera released his hold on Reyne and headed off toward the abandoned homestead.

Reyne offered nothing in response and didn't follow.

Mera scampered to the front door and knocked on it several times. Pushing the door open, with the handle still in his hand, it broke from its hinges.

Before Daedyn's murder, Reyne would have found the sight amusing. His sense of humor died with Daedyn.

Setting aside the door, Mera turned to Reyne. "I'm pretty sure the place is empty." And he stepped inside.

Reyne's feet took over and mindlessly directed him to join Mera.

"Your parents' home," Mera said, sweeping an open arm over the scene. "You would have—"

Reyne cut him off, "Don't make me ask again. Stop calling them that. This ain't no stroll down memory lane. I don't know these people, and I don't give a shit about them. People die every day. We have a place to sleep and do whatever you brought me here for. Then we meet up with this Gina so you can get me to your fantasy world as soon as possible."

"My apologies. You did say that before. I forgot."

Reyne didn't believe Mera forgot. Clear to Reyne, Mera had his own agenda.

The furniture was gone, and spiderwebs along with garbage were strewn about by the nameless, untold number of probable indigent occupants that called it home over its many empty years. The wood floors were burned to charcoal in several places from the fires the unknown squatters likely set to stay warm. The roof looked better from the outside. From the inside, it provided a clear view of the stars above.

Mera suggested, "We can crack open a few alphen nuts and dig into the dried sausage, or we can get right to it. Reyne, what do you prefer?"

"Let's just do this already," Reyne said, tired and annoyed.

"If you don't mind, I'd like to grab a quick bite. This is going to take a lot out of me, and I'd rather fuel up. No fires nearby to siphon off Firaché energy."

Ignoring the Firaché reference, he said, "Then why did you ask me? What, you thought if I decided, it would make me feel like I'm in charge somehow?"

Shrugging, Mera said, "You got me. Guilty as charged. I took a shot. I had a fifty-fifty chance."

"You're really pissin' me off. It's one comment after another with you."

"Fair enough," Mera said, dropping his backpack to the floor. After a quick search through it, Mera extracted two six-inch, fat sausages. "Reyne, I think you have most of the alphens in your pack. Would you mind pulling us out a few?"

The two men shared the beef sticks and calorie-rich nuts between them. Every bite of the shell-less ovules flooded his memories with thoughts of Daedyn. Reyne stared down at the fragmented pieces in his palm and reflected on how they mirrored his own life—broken. In his imagination he saw the faces of Mithany, Pachelle, Gwerther, and Daedyn in the bits of broken alphens.

Reyne looked longingly into the fragments and tossed the bounty aside.

Neither man spoke through the sparse meal. When they were done, Mera got up and reset the once-useful front door across the opening it left behind.

"I need to prepare you for what I hope to show us."

Reyne's ever-present anger towards Mera rose to the surface as he spat out, "I remember." The words came out harsh. "We did this before. You showed me the red-eyed woman who pulled back the arrow. She released it and killed Daedyn."

"I'm going to remind you anyway. Like I said last time, life exists everywhere. It's in those tiny little quantum particles that make up everything in the universe. I'm going to open your Eye of Heaven so you can see what they have to show us.

The Eye of Heaven connects us to all of creation, which means access to what the quantum world remembers, where information can never be destroyed. Sadly, humanity abandoned it millennia ago. Your Eye of Heaven lies dormant in the frontal lobe of your brain. I'm going to wake it up." For emphasis, Mera tapped his own forehead.

"And then I'm going to reach out to the life residing in Baide's room because that's the place where Silia gave birth to you. I'm going to ask the quantum world to show me the night you were born. Since knowledge is never lost, whatever all those tiny quantum particles bore witness to that night, we're going to see. The slivers of data they hold, well, it's just random. I will try to find it and organize it in a way we can see it."

"I'm ready," Reyne told him, uncertain if he believed any of Mera's explanation.

"You're going to have to be on the lookout for any sign of someone other than Edruk, Silia, or Baide. That's what we're looking for. Who else witnessed your birth? You're going to see me as I was in the past as well. And you're going to see some horrific things. Can you handle it?"

Reyne girded himself and said, "If I can handle seeing my only brother murdered when you did this last time, I can handle this."

"Then we'll need to do this in your sister's, excuse me, Baide's room. Follow me. It's down the hall. The one on the right at the end, facing the street."

Reyne approached the room, its door long since removed, lying flat on the bedroom floor. The tiny bed's shredded mattress served as the foreground to a faded painting of kittens that hung askew above it. Jagged, broken glass outlined the frame of the window. A toy box, or what once had been, stood smashed in recognizable pieces with weathered, worn, and tattered children's playthings spilling out. A filthy, ripped stuffed animal caught Reyne's attention. The one missing button-eye gave it a morose look that meshed well with its overall tattered appearance. Reyne entered the chamber expecting to be unmoved. He was wrong. Death called to him from everywhere in the little girl's room. A sadness sank into his chest. His hands and jaw clenched tight.

Mera pulled him from his reverie with a tight grip on his shoulder. Shaken, Reyne said, "Let's just get this done."

"I can do this without you if you're not up to it."

"No. You're right... I was wrong. I gotta see this as much as you."

"I've got to find one moment in time amongst millions of slivers of memory the life in this room holds in all its little nooks and crannies. It'll look like a jumbled and disorienting mess until I can pull it together. You remember the way this goes?"

"Yes."

"Then kneel here with me and we'll get started."

The men took up their spots, with each folding one knee to the hard floor. Mera raised his hand, placing two fingers on Reyne's forehead.

"Ah, the eyeballs of heaven."

Pulling back his fingers from Reyne, Mera said, "The Eye of Heaven, yes. I need to access and open your Third Eye. We've done this before. No talking." Mera returned his fingers to Reyne and placed the palm of his other hand on the floor.

Mera's hand moved in slow, small circles at first. One arm anchored to Reyne's Eye of Heaven and the other to the floor, Mera's hand moved faster and faster, but his arm never did. It stayed planted in place. Reyne watched. A single finger rose from the back of Mera's blur of a hand, impossibly and firmly unnaturally pointed up, while the rest of his hand circled even faster, vibrating beyond Reyne's ability to make out its constantly shifting shape. Another stationary finger rose to join the other as the hand attached to it zipped along incredibly fast. The solid floor, without moving, undulated in wave after wave and rolled outward from Mera's palm like a stone dropped into still waters. The hand, only a blur of flesh with two protruding stationary digits, sent pulses of rippling reality wafting through the room.

The walls, the floor, the missing roof above swirled into a tornado of stretched, drawn-out elasticity. Wisps of images dripped from the whirlwind that was the bedroom to seep down the sides of the rapidly spinning funnel. Tiny little packets of images, each smaller than a pinhead, held pieces of scenes inside. Thousands, if not millions, of scenes from Baide's room within each of the slices whipped around him at impossible speeds. People struggled to take shape only as partially formed specters, unable to hold on long enough to coalesce. Or maybe Mera let them go as he slapped away one speck of reality after another.

A woman in her late twenties appeared over and over, hundreds of her, then thousands. Reyne could picture them all, scattered over every inch of the room. They rose and fell in fractions of a second, but somehow his mind had time with each. Her form pulled apart, swept away by the winds, over and over: forming, dissolving, reforming, dissolving.

Other people emerged, popping up in an instant before being whooshed away like a flag battling a storm. Reyne watched Mera brush aside hundreds in the blink of an eye.

In an instant, everything stopped spinning. Wave after wave pulsed out entire room-sized scenes, one after another. Ghostly bodies, translucent, then solid, disappearing, then reappearing as nonstop realities changed and shifted as they undulated out from Mera's palm flowing over the two men. Colors from the little girl's dress pulled on her like dripping lava. She existed everywhere in the room at once as the embodiment of a thousand of the same girl, in different outfits but with the same face. Reyne's mind jolted at the one view of her hugging tight to the stuffed animal he'd seen only minutes ago in the real bedroom. Both button-eyes joined the toddler's to look back at Reyne, haunting him. And like a person caught in a whiteout, dust-sized slices of reality pelted the three-year-old and her stuff animal until, piece by piece, as each blizzard-driven snowflake struck their apparitions, they frayed and were swept away. Reyne reeled, shaken in the half a heartbeat it took to transpire.

A man that looked a lot like him flowed through the bedroom doorway. His form appeared only partly whole as the force of pulsing waves blew back much of his body, stretching its cohesion as the front-facing surface of his form moved into the room and the back half of the man remained at the opening. In defiance of the forces stripping one reality into the next, the man moved forward with arms reaching out towards the little girl hugging the stuffed toy. In a massive gust of energy, the man's image peeled apart, bit by bit, before he could reach her.

Suddenly, a commanding wave radiated from Mera's palm and pushed aside everything in the room. An explosion of reality sent a shockwave out in every direction from the spot Mera's hand touched the floor. The force of it slammed into Reyne's mind. It struck nothing but his thoughts. His head snapped back, his knee buckled, and he was thrown back. His shoulder crashed into the floor. Pain screamed into his brain. He brought up his forearms to protect his face against the blast, but just then, everything blew apart and the scene cleared—like breaking through into the eye of a hurricane.

He understood: Mera had found that sliver in time, buried deep in the past, and coaxed or conjured the collected memories from the quantum realm for him to witness.

A young woman, not much older than him, with red hair that whipped high in the air and danced around her face, came floating into the room from the window. Bits and pieces of her body ebbed and flowed, chopped and changed, all the while flittering about. He struggled to keep his mind on her fading in and out. Realization struck him: it wasn't the same woman who fired the arrow that murdered Daedyn. Images of Daedyn's killer were seared into his brain. No, this one was different.

In horror, Reyne saw the red-haired apparition draw a knife along the sleeping child's throat.

Her little eyes sprung open.

Terror filled her last gasps for life.

Helpless, seething anger flooded Reyne's soul.

Red spilled across the scene, flowed and floated about the chamber while the red-haired woman slid along the wall. Fury washed over him. His jaw squeezed tight. His brain shrieked against his inability to save the little girl. From deep in his core, a monster inside him screamed to be released. Somehow, Reyne knew it craved vengeance. But just then, movement out of the corner of his eye stole his attention.

The bedroom door opened and closed. Like blowing sand atop a dune in a windstorm, forces stripped away the woman's hand on the knob. The woman he saw earlier, the thousand views of her, opened her mouth to scream. Reyne heard the woman's cries—decades old. The agony of the sound ripped open his heart. He witnessed the horror written across her face. She raced to the little girl, her pillow soaked in a pool of blood. The three-year-old's confused, pitiful face gave way to empty, lifeless eyes that stared out in no direction.

She was dead.

The anger in Reyne erupted. A deafening roar spewed out of him and reverberated throughout the little girl's bedroom. His fists squeezed tight, seeing the red-haired woman, hair whipping about, her body there one instant, gone the next, only to reappear where her walk projected her to be.

He seethed in anger.

His blood curdled.

The beast within howled into his soul for its freedom. But there was nothing he could do. From behind, the red-haired assassin wrapped her ghostly arm around the grieving mother's head and swiftly drew the same bloody knife across the front of her neck.

The little girl's mother fell to the ground.

Reyne's eyes bulged.

Unfathomable fury hammered inside his skull.

Helpless to save her.

Helpless to strike at her attacker.

Rage consumed him and fed the beast.

Nausea gripped him at the horrific sight; he retched. Vomit spewed out of him.

And then he saw his mother's stomach. *Pregnant!* Why didn't he notice before?

Crash.

A twenty-two-year-old sound wave slammed into his ear. Baide's bedroom door flew off its hinges and smashed into the floor.

A naked man, one shoulder out in front, plowed through the open space, and rushed the room. The man's image amazed Reyne. The man, it had to be Edruk, looked like an older version of himself. Reyne couldn't hold the image together; it slipped away. His thoughts fought against the specter from dissolving, and Reyne—or Mera—brought it back. The man had changed locations. Still half-formed, ghostly but there. The Reyne-like man, now lying against the wall, near the tiny bed with his dying wife and lifeless three-year-old, had a knife buried deep in his heart. The older-looking version of Reyne, the man who burst through the door, was dead.

As seconds ticked away, the red-haired woman slipped out the window almost the instant before Mera's own quantum-revealed-apparition appeared, rushing through the space of the broken-down door. A twenty-two-year-past version of Mera scanned the room and jumped to the pregnant woman. To Reyne's astonishment, Mera hadn't aged at all. The specter of Mera put his ear to his dying mother's mouth. He listened. He ripped her hips free of clothing faster than Reyne thought possible. Slipping a knife from his belt, Mera drew his blade across her torso, cutting the pregnant woman open. The grimaced reaction on her face told Reyne she registered the pain but was too close to death for it to matter. Mera's ghostly yet bloody hands pulled a small baby from Reyne's dying mother and placed the crying newborn on her red-soaked chest. Her mouth moved once and stopped. Her head flopped forward. She was dead.

The Mera apparition from the past quickly cut the umbilical cord.

Tears flowed freely down Reyne's cheeks. *The newborn, it's me. The dead woman, my mother.* He knew it. His heart felt it. More than he wanted, his soul cried out from his mother's death. In those few seconds she held him, love filled the room. He sensed it. How, he didn't know. Maybe that's part of what the quantum world shared, he wondered. But how didn't matter.

He looked away. Reyne's head flopped forward, unable to bear the loss of the love from a mother he never knew. Her love overwhelmed him. Her love touched his heart. Her loss, her sacrifice, bore deep into his soul. He wept openly for Silia, his mother; for Baide, his sister; for Edruk, his father—and for himself.

With the heels of his palms, he wiped tears from his eyes. Furious at the ghostly assassin, he burned to strike at her. He added her to his list of the soon-to-be-dead that included Daedyn's murderess. A plan formed in his mind: once he transfigured to Evidar, he'd immediately return to Tartica to embrace Mithany and to extract his revenge. A plan he'd hide from Mera. Mera wouldn't approve, wouldn't let him. But he'd do it anyway. As the plan took shape in his thoughts, the caged beast inside his soul roared in laughter.

He shifted attention to Mera in the present. His palm whirling against the floor, refusing to release the specters back into their quantum hosts. But when Reyne looked away from current-day Mera into the past, the same red-haired woman—pulsating in and out of focus, hair whipping wildly about her—looked in through the broken window. Shock gripped him. The face in the window was the woman who'd just murdered his family.

As quickly as she appeared, she slinked away. He understood. The woman who'd killed his biological family stayed around long enough to witness Mera pull him from his dying mother's womb. The apparition of Mera from the past, windswept, fading in and out, took newborn Reyne from his dead mother into his arms. Mera cradled him as a baby. It touched Reyne deeply. With Mera's caring for the newborn measured against the death all around him, his ever-present anger towards Mera drained from his soul.

At that exact moment, only seconds old, his life changed. Mera started him down a new path with Daedyn as his brother. Recognition of the monumental role Mera played in his life, delivering him as a babe into the arms of Pachelle and Gwerther to raise as their own, touched his soul. Almost more than he could bear, Reyne now understood he owed Mera more than he could ever repay.

As Mera from the past took baby Reyne into his arms, their bodies began to flitter away like a thousand butterflies heading off in different directions. Before dissolving into nothing, the specter of Mera jerked his head up to look around, but the assassin's apparition, already gone, left Mera to gaze out an empty window. Mera never knew. Never saw her.

A mental shockwave of tremendous force blasted through the room, blowing away the altered reality. The power of it struck hard against Reyne's mind. From his kneeling position, he fell back. The door Mera opened into his Eye of Heaven slammed shut in his brain, as though driving hot spikes through his eyes, nailing it closed. And just as suddenly, the pain in his mind fled, but the torment gripping his soul burned even hotter.

Reyne brushed himself off, settled in on his knees with his butt resting on his heels, and let out a sigh. He looked about the dilapidated, weather-worn, missing roof of a bedroom and knew it for the present, not the past—a place in time where his family was taken from him. The experience Mera provided left him broken-hearted and affected him in ways he hadn't thought possible.

A beautiful, innocent baby sister he never knew—murdered.

A dying mother's love, gone almost twenty-two years, reached across time to caress his soul.

A father's love for his family was denied to him by an assassin's dagger to the heart.

Apparitions from the past, conjured by a man he no longer resented, scorched his heart in the flames of regret.

From his knees, Reyne looked to the heavens through the sparse, tattered thatch. Torment and anguish were beyond his ability to keep restrained. With fists clenched at his side, he gave voice to the monster lurking in his soul as it howled in pain. Misery poured out of him and emptied into a world different from the one he knew before entering his sister's room. And when too hoarse to utter another sound, the wailing of his heart kept on.

Midnight Rendezvous

Mera

Mera left Reyne passed out in Baide's bedroom and set out to find Gina. Reyne's introduction to her would have to wait for another time. Concerns Mera had for Reyne's training—to prepare him for Evidar—needed to be hashed out without the Hensdale native present. Midnight approached, and Mera expected the physically exhausted and emotionally drained Reyne to remain out of it until he returned, which Mera thought would be sometime around dawn.

Mera targeted the Whispering Eye, a seedy tavern in Teth's underbelly. It served as a de facto marketplace, although not the only one, where buyers and sellers of every illegal transaction could be found. Mera figured, where else would an assassin-for-hire be?

Undaunted by the slippery nature of whatever business transpired within its walls, Mera eased his way into the Whispering Eye. He scanned the barroom for familiar faces of the troublemaking sort. Unconcerned for his own safety, he was confident in his fighting skills that matched well with his possession of the Soul Stone, which, together, put him out of reach of anyone in the crowd to do him any lasting harm. Not that Mera thought himself invulnerable—he'd been injured plenty. But the Soul Stone being bound to him, it had a vested interest in effecting his recovery from almost any wound. Fortunately for Mera, although injured many times, he'd not experienced anything beyond the Soul

Stone's limits—yet. He aimed to keep it that way, engaging in physical combat only when necessary—for his own safety as much as theirs.

More than usual, the tavern was packed with Thuggery associates: men and women from every level within the consociation, along with other, non-aligned drunkards. Events earlier in the day, the highlight being Razoal's beheading, had many worked up, no doubt.

The wide range of clothing choices from proper business attire to the barely dressed filled the space. He even noticed off in one corner two people fornicating, not an uncommon occurrence for the Whispering Eye. Nor uncommon were the spectators gathered around the fornicators shouting encouragement to one of the participants or the other. The demands of the Covenant to repopulate the world, Mera figured, didn't factor into the otherwise entwined couple's lustful motivations.

After untold years of either living in or visiting Teth, Mera held a deep familiarity with the city's black-market purveyors, a consequence of his dedication to the elimination of Evidar agents wherever they might be found on Tartica.

The musty aroma of the Whispering Eye hit him immediately. Its distinct bouquet, a mix of stale beer, sweat, mold, urine, and blood, attacked the otherwise resilient palate of his nostrils. In spite of the offense, Mera took it all in with a deep pull through his nose. Strangely, both off-putting yet compelling. *Who can ever forget that smell*, he thought.

The bar, set up in the center of the room, formed a horseshoe shape that opened in the back to the office. The dark wood wall paneling held the accumulation of smoke, liquor, and bloodstains from untold years of barroom brawls and other patron abuses.

Poor lighting, heavy smoke, and overcrowding made it a challenge for Mera to find Gina, if she was even there. After five unsuccessful minutes of searching, he recalled she had a favorite table, a place which offered a clear view of a good chunk of the establishment. Mera pushed his way through the unruly clientele, making his way to the second floor.

At the top of the stairs, Mera stopped and scanned the area. His eyes found her first. When she finally returned the glance, Gina's face lit up. Her hand waved from side to side and Mera's ears locked on to her voice as she yelled over the boisterous rabble. As Mera approached, Gina shouted but didn't get up, "It's been quite some time, old friend. Sit down, if you can find a spot."

There weren't many empty seats to be had. But Mera found one, although it was only *mostly empty*. He first asked politely for its use. After being ignored by the patron, Mera yanked the chair out from under the foot claiming it. Mera finally got a response from the half-drunk staking his claim to the seat. "Hey buddy, you do that again"—he flopped his foot back on the chair, reclaiming the prize—"I'll make you eat it."

Gina's eyes lit up. She smirked at Mera and put both hands to her cheeks. "Oh no, bar fight."

After a wink to Gina, Mera turned to face belligerent chair guy. Mera's eyes grew dark. His mouth offered the man a wide, evil grin while his body seemed to rise up, growing impossibly larger, towering over the man who threatened to make Mera eat the chair.

"Fuck it. You can have it." He kicked the contested chair towards Mera as he shot out of his seat and scurried away.

Gina applauded. "Seen you do that trick before. One of my faves."

"How about a hug, ole friend? It's been too long."

"I'm not the hugging type. You know that, but what the heck? For you, sure."

He towered over the much shorter woman. After the good-natured embrace, Mera spun the chair, sat, and rested his chin on the backward-facing chair rail. His eyebrows rose and fell quickly several times as he asked, "How you been?"

Gina leaned forward. "It's always good to see you, but I'm guessing this ain't a social visit. We can catch up later. Hit me with it. What do you need?" She hesitated. "Excuse my manners. How can I help my dear friend?"

Mera reached out to place his hand on hers. "You're always so agreeable. I miss you."

The thirty-something, dark-haired Tartican, athletically proportioned assassin for hire, dressed in skintight, all-black attire, plopped her elbows on the table and rested her face in her palms. "I can't ever say no to you."

"Big crowd tonight."

"Been this way ever since the Covenant went to shit."

"You heard about Razoal? What Nails did?"

Gina swept her hand across the room. "It's all these chuckleheads been talking about."

Mera changed subjects. "How's business lately?"

"Slow. Only got one contract in the hopper. Since the Covenant's practically dead, suddenly everyone thinks they have the balls to do it themselves. Most find out it ain't that simple killing another human being. Demand will pick back up. That's why I'm here tonight. Lookin' for business. Why you asking?"

"About your contract, do I know this person?"

"You know just about everybody, so yeah."

"Do I care who?"

"No. You never do unless they're helping your nemesis. This one's just your average every day Tartican loser. No one's gonna miss her."

"Then I've got one more for you to train. It's another Tweener I've got to send to Evidar."

Gina rolled her neck, similar to cracking her knuckles, and a series of popping noises followed. "Has this person been to Evidar before? They know how abhorrently awful it's supposed to be?"

"Haven't confirmed this one can actually transfigure to the other dimension, but factoring in his heritage, I'm ninety-nine percent sure we have a full-blown Tweener on our hands. So, I can pull you away from all this to help?"

"Of course. I can deliver on the contract later tonight. It'll be a little ahead of schedule. I've only done basic recon. But what the hell, it's a simple job. She's not too bright. Will be easy enough. Cut and run. No disposal included in the price. The dead body will be for the girlfriend to deal with. I'll get to it later after we're done here. We can meet up tomorrow afternoon."

"That's my girl."

"Now, now, Mera, you know I don't like any of that girl shit."

"Sorry, I forgot."

"There you go. So, tell me about your new Tweener. Woman? Man? How old? Give me all the details. Leave nothing out."

While downing several rounds, Mera detailed Reyne's situation, background, family history—both, and answered Gina's every question.

Gina listened, taking in every piece of information. An hour slipped by.

Mera said, "That's all of it."

Gina took a pull from her beer and asked, "You left out one important item. How long do I get?"

Mera pressed his lips together.

Gina drew her eyes in tight. "Every one of the others I prepped took at least ten weeks, minimum. You know the process. I gotta tear them down before I can reshape their self-image into a passable killer. And that's the bare minimum. You give me ten weeks; I give you a novice."

Mera shrugged.

Shaking her head, Gina pouted. "You know this takes time. You remember that one gal? Had her for training six months. She had me a few times, too." Gina laughed. "She even took on a few contracts I farmed out to her here in Teth. But it took half a year to get her ready. They're all different, but there's one constant. I. Need. Time."

Mera puffed his cheeks.

Gina tilted her head to the side, and with big round eyes, she complained. "Really? So how much time will I get with him? Keep in mind, I'm no miracle worker."

Mera released a gush of air he'd been holding. "A week. Ten days tops."

"What the hell, Mera? Can't train a dog to sit in a week. You want me to turn a farm-boy into a killer? Impossible in seven days."

Mera leaned back in his chair. "That's all the time we have. Do your best."

"You're sending him off to his death."

"Now, now. You're better at this than you think. You can give him the basics. When you get right down to it, the physical act of killing's not that hard. The roadblocks are all in the mind. And as far as mind-fucking goes, you're one of the best."

Gina hung her head. A few seconds later, lifting it to meet Mera's eyes, she said, "Only for you. I'm getting paid for this. Right?"

"I'll put something together. It'll be generous. It always is. But... I can't get to it until we're done."

"That's fine, but know this, I'll deliver just the basic level of *'I'm willing to kill somebody.'* Not that he'll be all that good at it after only seven days of prep."

Again, shrugging, Mera said, "I get it. It's asking a lot. What do you need?"

"Killing another human is beyond most people. Thankfully, otherwise what would I do?" Gina smirked.

"Yes, thankfully." Mera rolled his eyes.

"Even if they think they can, when it comes time, unless they're a psychopath or facing their own death, most can't. That's why I like to have my trainees do a trial run on one of my contract hits before turning them over to you. You know, making sure they can go through with it."

Mera nodded. "You'll have to hone in on the mental prep. Get him angry. Get his head out of the idyllic world of Hensdale. Basic knife work and technical fighting skills will be needed too. If he can't get past everything he believes in about the sanctity of life, teaching him how to kill won't matter."

"I'm gonna have to break him down fast. That means getting past whatever nonsense is in there now. More times than not, all that inner self, who-I-am bullshit gets in the way. Means getting verbally aggressive with him... nonstop."

Mera drained the remains of his mug and clunked his stein on the table with a thud. "If anyone can do it, you can." He ran his sleeve over his mouth. "I believe in you, Gina. There's no one better at killing, and there's no one better at mind games."

"Yeah, well, don't believe in me too much. What you're asking is impossible in the time frame you're giving me."

"Not going to work, kiddo. I'm counting on you. Again, what do you need?"

"I'm gonna have to go for the jugular. Gotta be aggressive on steroids. Pushing him and pushing him. Even *I* don't like myself when I'm being that annoying."

"Not an issue. Do what you have to. He doesn't have to like you. But he does have to be ready. This would be so much easier if I could send you instead."

Gina shook her head. "We tried that before. I can't even get into the Void. That leaves us Reyne. Gonna have to hit him hard right out of the gate. Tell me, what's he care about most? What's at his core that I can hammer away at, strip from him?"

"Like in the background info I gave you. For starters, his wedding never happened. I pulled him away from her. Had to leave her behind. Reyne's heartbroken over it. And don't forget, Evidar agents killed his brother. They mistook Daedyn for Reyne. That mistake, while fortunate for us, is now a problem. It means I've got to get him into Evidar before they realize they botched the operation and come after him, full force."

"You don't think they know he's alive at this point?"

"Maybe. It's been a week, give or take, since Daedyn's murder. If they haven't already figured it out, they will soon. Then it'll be another few days to a week to pick up our trail. If we stay in one place, they'll find us in days. That gives us a week to ten days. If we keep moving, we'll have a better chance."

Gina slapped her palms together. "This Reyne fellow's had one shitty week. I'll give him that. But silver lining, it's left some nasty scabs for me to pick at. Can use it to get the anger in him working for us... rage, acrimony, hatred, it all helps the process along."

"He's been a mope since we left. He's lost himself over his brother, and he misses the woman he loves. He's got his head up his ass. In that state of mind, on Evidar, he's dead meat."

Gina rubbed her forehead and huffed. "At the very least, he's gotta get his head outta his ass. I'll have to get him focused in another direction. I'm pretty sure I can distract him," she proclaimed, running both hands over the contours of her body.

Mera offered her a smile. "I've seen you put that body to work. Deadly as any blade."

Her tone, serious. "It's not a game. The stakes are life or death. His."

"My coin's always on you, no matter the odds. Stakes, though, are a lot higher than just his life. All of Tartica is in play. I wish we had more time to prep him, but we don't."

"As for getting his mind off his problems, I'll keep pushing him in any way I can. Works best when I react to what they give me. Sit back, let them speak. Then pounce on what they say. Twist it all up. That'll keep his emotions tied up in anger, aimed at me. It's one of those things I'll have to play by ear. Whatever he says, I'll find a way to turn it against him. Get him riled up, over and over. It's the quickest way to get him out of his slump."

"Constant agitation. Don't give him five minutes' peace. He's got Mithany on the brain. You've got to change that mindset."

"My first goal will be to get his mind off this Mithany woman in that fairytale Hensdale life of his."

With both arms outstretched, palms up, as though addressing a congregation at Temple services, Mera said, "That could work. Your biggest obstacle is going to be cracking the nut of lost love. His heart won't let go easily. It's a shame it's got to be done this way. I need Evidar's Damus taken out, and quick. Reyne's all I have left to do it. The future of Tartica depends on him, whatever the cost."

Gina stared at the ceiling. After a minute passed in silence, she lowered her eyes to meet Mera's. "Reyne's in love." She puckered a few mocking air kisses. "He won't be when I'm done with him."

An Unlikely Alliance

Hensdale: 3rd Day of the Harvest Moon

Mithany

Daybreak brought with it a new hope in Mithany's broken heart. After spending the night at her family home, with Neladith imposing herself, the pair woke at dawn. They set out to meet up with others of the impromptu search party, minus Arek, who still hadn't returned home.

Crisp, cool fall air battled the warmth of the sun to dominate the day as the two women exited the house. Colorful leaves in shades of red, orange, and yellow had begun to turn. Mithany pulled in the aroma of autumn dawn, and the smell of decaying foliage carried memories of Harvest Moon's past. She closed the door behind her without waking her father. She loved the man, yet momentarily stared at the knob in her hand, contemplating—and not for the first time—how such a caring, compassionate father ever saw anything in her mother to love.

Mithany smirked, knowing she never again had to endure her mother's rage. The fateful accident ending her mother's life proved the only answer that stopped the frequent beatings she and Arek endured from an early age. Thinking of her mother, dead, brought a smile to her face in ways her mother wouldn't have appreciated.

Her father's lack of a backbone—evidenced by his failure to even once intervene—didn't evade Mithany's notice, though it did escape her scorn. Although she kept it buried and well hidden, even from Reyne, Mithany didn't kid herself: she believed she was damaged goods—affording her mother all the blame.

She considered her physical well-being the fortunate benefactor of her mother's passing, yet lamented the residue it left and the scars it inflicted on her emotional stability. Living with the insidious, persistent psychological aftereffects, Mithany struggled, forever affected by the woman who lived in her head every minute of every day. But when buoyed by Reyne at her side, thoughts of her mother, the cause of her inner turmoil, simply faded away. His presence, his love, a salve to her wounded self-esteem, shut out her mother's voice. But he was gone.

When Reyne's hand slipped through hers the night Daedyn died and Mera took him from her life, it proved more than her damaged inner self was capable of handling. She broke that night in ways her own self-awareness couldn't comprehend. The damage rippled through her, reaching to break outward in search of relief. She carried it in her head and in her heart, both the pain she recognized, and even more so its hidden ghosts, and carried it into each new day, including the one she now faced with Neladith at her side.

With a pleasant grin, borne in the hope of a better day than yesterday, she turned to Neladith. "Thank you for offering to come along and for staying with me last night. My dad didn't mind. I know we didn't get off on the right foot in Owls Neck, but without Arek, Spetzer might've been more than I could handle by myself on some isolated forest trail. Thank you for doing this."

Mithany's responsibility to stand vigil at the Ceremony of Return held for Reyne's false death where Daedyn had actually been buried was now many days behind her, and she wouldn't be denied from venturing out to find Reyne.

Screw what Mera said. Who's he to order me to stay put? "Make everyone believe Daedyn was killed," he said. "Stay safe in Hensdale,'"he said. *Sorry Mera, that just won't do.*

Mithany didn't consider Mera's instructions or his warnings of any importance, nor did it much matter. Her one and only desire: find Reyne. *Just because I agreed to Mera's plan that night doesn't mean I can't change my mind. It's a girl's prerogative.*

Mera had no influence over the wounded half of Mithany's heart, which cared little for Mera's orders to stay put in the face of her growing need for Reyne at her side. Maybe if Daedyn hadn't been murdered, she could have pushed through. Daedyn's death hit her hard, and with Reyne ripped from her life, it all proved too much for her damaged psyche to handle.

I'm a grown woman and will make my own decisions. Some guy's not gonna tell me what to do. I don't think so.

She set Mera's concerns aside, ignoring the call to present a united front in the deception of Reyne's feigned death in favor of her own unrequited emotions for what she'd lost—Reyne's affections, anchoring her against the inner forces threatening to unbalance her.

Clues to Reyne's whereabouts or of his destination, though denied to her by Mera, pointed towards the men having set a course due north that night. *You went north, my love, and so will I.*

An internal voice, an uncertain feeling, poked at her, nagged her. A single thought played over and again, *Reyne's not safe.* Mithany could neither accept it nor live with it. Her frayed inner self could never be sated until she reunited with him. Mithany understood the extensive damage her mother caused held greater sway under the emotionally stressful situation. Gone from her life, Reyne's influence to drive the presence of her mother's voice into the shadows diminished by the day.

As tough as most folks thought her to be—having known only the outer shell Mithany allowed others to see—she never believed them. She'd tried to convince herself on the night Reyne departed she could handle his absence. In the days since, she came face to face with the reality of being wrong. She needed him. He was her salvation for a life free of the past. Without him, she feared depression's reemergence, or worse. The early warning signs of her broken psyche had already begun to show.

Mithany and Neladith talked a lot through the prior evening. The effects were cathartic for Mithany, sharing her loss with another. It soothed her to unbridle the remorse building inside her, although Mithany remained careful not to let slip the deception of Daedyn's death. She cried more than once, and on one occasion in Neladith's arms. The comfort she took in Neladith's embrace scared her. The pair parted for the evening with Mithany in her own bed and Neladith on the couch.

Morning air delivered a refreshing, brisk autumn kiss to her cheeks and a familiar scent on the gentle breeze. Mithany looked up through the trees and spied the sunlight dancing through the thicket of branches and leaves.

Mithany thought she saw Neladith look away from the beaming morning rays just before saying, "Oh, that's alright. Like you said, only until Arek joins up with you. I'm happy to fill in for him. You did say last night that we could swing by your shoppe this morning and grab me some traveling clothes for the trip. This short skirt and tied-off blouse aren't gonna cut it." Neladith playfully flipped her skirt's back panel up and down a few times, wiggling her ass at each reveal.

Mithany wanted to look away, but curiosity didn't allow it.

During their time together the night before, Neladith opened up about the young girl who passed away and how seeing the physical similarities in Mithany stirred up forgotten feelings. Although, unlike herself, Neladith's tale of loss did not end in tears. Their unplanned night together did result in a shift in perception; Neladith wasn't the she-demon Mithany made her out to be when they first met. She seemed nothing more than a forever horny, carefree young woman setting out in the world, enjoying whatever came her way and hopeful of taking advantage of every opportunity life offered. Mithany wondered if Neladith's peek-a-boo ass display had been motivated with intent, with her being one of Neladith's hopeful opportunities.

One girl to another, gotta admit, that is a nice booty.

Mithany realized she was staring and quickly blurted, "Your outfit is kinda cute, but you're right, not suitable for travel. My shoppe is nearby the Forest Maiden Inn, and that's where Spetzer said he'd meet up with me a little after dawn. We'd better get a move on."

"I feel like we bonded last night. It's got me thinking about your little village in a whole new way. Brought up feelings for a life like this I never knew I had."

Before last night, Mithany cared little for Neladith, although, if honesty held sway, jealousy played a part. Mithany welcomed their girl-time bonding as it paved the way for a more friendly, productive trip.

As an afterthought, she realized she'd made a big mistake asking Spetzer, but she couldn't head out alone on open trails as a solo female traveler. Neither did she trust the currently missing Arek to remain by her side throughout the journey. Any pretty young thing could steal him away at a moment's notice.

The Covenant of Absolute Human Obligations didn't offer her protection in the isolated environs her search might take her. Sure, the Covenant stood for protecting human life and precluded the commission of harm, but alone and isolated in the middle of the nowhere her journey might take her, she didn't trust the Covenant's security blanket to hold up to human nature. The Gift of Flesh had a greater hold on some men than even the sexually free norms of Tartican society considered healthy or safe. The seeds of suspicion, wondering if Spetzer were such a man, only took root after she'd asked him to join her.

With Neladith along for the ride, at least until Arek caught up with her, Spetzer would be held in check and have someone else to focus his devious, disgusting, perverted thoughts on.

"The Forest Maiden Inn's tavern isn't open, but where else would Spetzer be?" Mithany laughed as she told Neladith all about the ever-present tavern regulars, Spetzer's crush on her, and his self-proclaimed position as the Forest Maiden's leader of the pack. The pack comprised five angry losers who buried their resentment of their shared lot in life in a constant state of inebriation. Mithany told Neladith, "Trell isn't too bad once you get him away from the others. Not sure how he's gonna do on this trip. He's not built for walking. You'll see when you meet him."

The tall, red-haired woman asked, changing the subject, "Did you hear that thing last night? Had to be one of those Great Yetgnal creatures we heard that day when Arek shit his pants. You remember, on our way from Owls Neck?"

"Sure did. Almost got outta bed to join you on the couch," Mithany confessed.

Neladith asked, "Does it worry you that Arek isn't here, and it sounded like one of those Yetgnals last night?"

"No. Arek saved the life of one of those things. If a Great Yetgnal intended to do anything to him, it would have been back near Owls Neck. You remember, you were there when Arek freed one of them that had its foot stuck. After Arek freed it, the creature let him live. Guess they, or it, owes him one."

Yet Mithany couldn't resist the opportunity to sow dissension between her brother and Neladith. It might've been out of jealousy, but whatever the reason, Mithany seized the opportunity. "Knowing my brother, the more likely scenario is he met up with someone last night. He does love variety. He's forever on the hunt for strange. Don't get me wrong, he'll take all the familiar he can get. In our little village, not much strange out there he hasn't tapped already."

The two women giggled.

"You don't have to tell me. It's a struggle to keep his hands off me. Sometimes I think I just should tie him up."

"That's probably the only way."

"Your brother has some peculiar tastes. You can't beat the surprises out of him. Anything's possible with that boy."

Neladith offered what Mithany read as a knowing smile. *It's always in the eyes,* she told herself. *Something's going on inside that head of hers.* Mithany suspected more hid behind that smile, but movement off in the distance stole her attention. She slapped Neladith lightly on the arm and pointed. "Look, on the steps of the Maiden, Spetzer and Trell."

Spetzer popped up and waved both arms high above his head. Trell's large butt remained plastered on the steps.

Neladith stopped and turned to face Mithany. "Everything you told me about this Spetzer suggests he's an asshole."

"He can be, but when no one's around, just him and me, he's a different guy. That doesn't mean I trust him. He's the only one I got to agree to this. Trell, well, he does whatever Spetzer tells him to do. I thought Trell would be security from Spetzer trying anything stupid. Now that you're here, I'm sure Spetzer will behave. But he's still gonna be an asshole most of the time."

Neladith threw an arm around Mithany's shoulder, and the two women laughed. Mithany shrugged her arm away. "Don't let him see that; it doesn't take much to get him sexed up." The giggles continued. Mithany played along, her own laughter half-felt.

Neladith hopped and skipped along. "Oh, this is going to be fun," she said, and continued towards the men. "That guy Trell fits your description to the tee. Kinda short. A bit overweight, and that sourpuss of a face says it all."

Mithany poked her elbow into Neladith's side. "Don't leave out Spetz. He'd be almost good looking, and he's got nice brown hair, blue eyes, decent build and is a wee bit taller than most, but his personality trumps all the gifts Mother Earth handed him."

Mithany snapped her head towards Neladith as she felt the taller woman slide an arm under her own. Neladith smiled at her and said, "Huh, gotta say, might be an asshole, but he's kinda cute."

"Don't let him hear you say that. You'll never get him off your back."

With a smirk, Neladith said, "Something I could be open to, if he isn't a total dick. Then again, maybe he's got a big dick and giant balls." More girlish giggles before Neladith continued. "Who says we can't have fun on this trip? Anyway, you want me to carry your pack for a while? Looks heavy on you. I've got some inches on you and might handle it better."

"Thanks, no. I got it. We should get you one of your own. I have more of these in my shoppe."

Surprised she let herself slip half-heartedly into the schoolgirl giggle-fest with Neladith, Mithany considered, *Neladith appears to be a few years younger. Everything about the male anatomy or sex must be new, exciting to someone that age.* However, Mithany thought herself beyond such notions, "tee-heeing" along with Neladith over talk of genitalia. But she mused, *Okay, giant balls... that is funny.*

Yet, the realization she'd unintentionally mirrored Neladith's behavior, upon reflection, astounded her. It revealed something about herself; she harbored a desire for Neladith to like her. Two of the last things she ever thought she'd do: picture an image of Spetzer's testicles in her head or that she'd seek a friendship with Neladith.

Mithany stood motionless in contemplation while Neladith eyed her up and down before cheerfully announcing, "We gotta get me into an outfit like yours. You look so nice in those tight brown leather pants. Makes your ass look great. It's like a journeyman's outfit. And I just love the matching vest. Your boobs just pop. You look so..."

Mithany waited to hear the rest, but Neladith didn't finish the thought. She held back her concern for Neladith's lip curl and wicked smile and said, "Sure, but it might be a different shade. I'm out of stock in that color for your size but have plenty of inventory in a tan outfit just like the one I'm wearing."

The sinful grin morphed into a broad, friendly look across Neladith's face, lighting up delighted eyes as Mithany read them. Excitement dominated the tone of Neladith's reply. "I just love that idea. I'm looking forward to spending time with you. I can pick your brain about Arek and so many things about this place. Who knows, I might stick around at my cousin's house longer than I first expected. This quaint little village of yours is so much nicer than where I come from. It's starting to grow on me."

Mithany examined Neladith. *It's in the eyes,* she reminded herself. Mithany saw joy in Neladith's eyes and on her face, but something lurked beneath it. Deception? Lust? She would have to study Neladith more to figure it out. And then she considered, *If that tone, those words, and that look came from Spetzer, I'd know what's behind it. Hum.* Mithany let it go and said, "Great. Daedyn told me he intended to head north. So that's where we'll start. We'll head off towards Topak."

Neladith wrapped her arm around Mithany's shoulder and pulled her in tight. "Well then. That's settled. Let's get into your shoppe and get me outfitted for this trip. You can watch me try on a few things"—she paused—"and after that, off we go. We have a man to find."

WAKE UP

HENSDALE: 3RD DAY OF THE HARVEST MOON

Arek

How long Arek had been out, he had no clue.

He awoke on the ground, lying next to Doc Brenal. The sun hung in the sky, and a vague awareness of its warmth gently touched his face. Every part of his body hurt. He turned his head to face Brenal, who looked to be enjoying a peaceful nap. Awareness seeped in; a blanket placed over his naked body kept in what little warmth he could claim.

"Hey, Doc," Arek squeaked out in a hoarse whisper.

He tried again. "Brenal. Wake up."

No reply.

Arek felt a sharp pain in his arm. His thigh screamed for attention, and his chest and face felt like a hellhound chewed him up and spat him out. His body hurt worse than anything he'd ever experienced. He lifted his head only inches before deciding the effort didn't measure up to the prize it promised.

With one arm from under his cover, he fumbled it about and felt something affixed in the other. Probing its shape, Arek found a hose with a needle at the end inserted in his forearm. Extracting the needle, he groaned through the effort. The minor struggle to remove the transfusion apparatus exhausted him.

Nausea gripped him.

His eyes fluttered and closed.

He faded away.

Again, he woke, unsure of how much time had passed. The sun, still in the sky, had moved. He remembered Brenal being nearby when he last awoke, and he turned to face the village doctor. Brenal, still at his side, still fast asleep.

Raspy and weak, Arek said, "Doc, wake up."

Brenal, face turned towards the sun, didn't reply.

Arek put more words together, though they flowed in nothing more than a whisper. "Wake up, damn you."

With what little reserves Arek could muster through the gripping pain everywhere, he flailed an arm at Brenal to jar him from his dreams. Arek's arm flopped on Brenal's chest.

Brenal didn't move.

"Doc?"

No reply.

Arek gathered his strength, and, working through the agony with every movement, he pushed against the sleeping doctor several times.

No response.

He tried to rise but fell short. Able to pull himself close to Brenal, Arek turned the doctor's face to his own. Alarms rang out in Arek's head, and his heart sank. His friend, the village doctor, with eyes wide open—empty as though staring at nothing—was dead.

Breakfast with the Tomelais

Tandure: 3rd Day of the Harvest Moon

Derr

Derr's official invitation for breakfast at the Chancellor's Mansion, set for seven o'clock sharp, was more formal than his relationship with the Tomelais required, but First Lady Kaythlin wanted it to be special. A simple, private, yet important event intent on blending family bonding with important state business that included the promise of elevating one of their own.

If all went as expected.

Derr's counsel proved ineffective in dissuading the Chancellor. He did however secure a concession from Tomelai to allow conversation at the morning meal to proceed before deciding. While there remained the slim chance the preferment died on the table, Derr believed the Chancellor had already made up his mind.

Derr, called to the Tomelais' breakfast table for more than a social event, had been tasked with advising the Chancellor in real-time, on the spot if called to, over eggs and toast. A familiar role: observe, gather, and assess from the available information, even if it included one of Tomelai's own family members as the subject of evaluation. Of personal interest to Derr included his Chancellor's willingness, although reluctant as necessitated by circumstance, to share power, even a small piece of it. The parsing of his Chancellor's authority, a quality Madrotti Tomelai didn't normally possess, but the likelihood of war loomed, and choices were limited.

Derr, clad in his formal attire of a hon-silk suit jacket that included almost imperceptible epaulets of his captain's rank, hated wearing it. The Feast of Teth had been the last time he'd worn his KCG dress uniform, yet for Kaythlin, he begrudgingly donned the costume for the second time in a week.

Derr arrived, and the formally clad doorman announced him as per protocol. He'd been to the palatial estate an untold number of times going back to his childhood, yet aggravation bloomed at being announced with every visit. The only people in earshot included himself and the attendant answering the door.

Led to the family's private dining room, not the formal dining area where the Chancellor and First Lady entertained guests, another attendant moved swiftly to pull out a chair for Derr. Derr held up one hand to halt the process, pulled out the chair himself, and sat. The same scene played out a thousand times, yet in spite of his being the second most powerful man in the Kingdom of Adelle, he couldn't make them stop. Derr's authority proved impotent against the house staff's silly rituals.

The table had been set with seating for five.

Derr tipped his head back, let out a sigh of resignation, and folded his arms across his chest.

Within seconds, Kaythlin swept into the room. At seven in the morning, Kaythlin's radiance, although not a surprise to Derr, still stole his attention. A stunning beauty in youth, middle age did little to alter her appearance. With large, round, upturned, welcoming eyes a warm shade of lavender, a single look, married to a smile, stole away anyone's attention—even the stone-hearted Derr.

Out of respect, Derr stood. "Good morning, Kaythlin. How you do it, I'll never know. Can't say in all these years I've ever seen you anything less than stunning. Even at this hour."

"Good morning to you as well, Druin. Thank you for accepting my invitation. And I might add, you look handsome in your dress formals."

"Only for you," Derr said, offering a rare smile.

"It's so nice to see you smile. I welcome any opportunity to see it. Even at seven in the morning. Perhaps I will have to invite you to breakfast regularly."

"Please don't if I have to wear this every time. By the way, something smells great."

"Why, thank you, Druin. Made it myself. Tane and Loseff will be dining with us, and Madrotti will be in soon. His Chief of Staff roused him early this morning with some pressing matter. I am sure he will fill you in later."

Tane, the heir-apparent to the Tomelai family's firm grip on the chancellorship of Adelle, and her younger brother Loseff were late.

First Lady Kaythlin turned to her own master-steward. Her tone was sweet and graceful yet left little doubt that her request was a command to be carried out exactly as directed. "Eztra, would you mind dismissing the staff on my behalf for the remainder of the morning? Gather them back for nine o'clock, please. That will be all, thank you."

Eztra nodded his acceptance in a manner more like a formal bow and headed out just as both Loseff and Tane poked through the kitchen doorway.

Loseff grumbled, "Mother. Seven. Why seven?" He pressed the heels of his palms into sleepy-looking eyes.

Derr scanned them both up and down as the siblings moved towards the table.

Absent her mother's natural beauty, Tane resembled her father in both looks and body. She had a square, flat face, a pronounced jawline that cut along the sides of her sharply angled cheeks, and stood taller than her brother. Tane also possessed Madrotti Tomelai's steel-gray eyes. A product of them both, hard and determined like her father, yet notably skilled, like her mother, at all the social graces.

The Tomelais' son featured more like his mother in appearance and mannerisms, minus any of her respect for proper etiquette. With slight feminine contours notwithstanding, his rebellious behavior, an outgrowth of his resentment of his position as second-in-line, matched more with his father's approach in life.

Both gave Derr nothing of note. Loseff projected an air of insolence, as usual, while Tane maintained her default facial expression, one that mirrored her father's customary stoicism.

Kaythlin offered her son a motherly explanation to his question concerning the early call to breakfast. "Because, my dear, your father has very important issues to discuss this morning, and you are of an age now to understand your next lesson in the complexities of governing."

Loseff kept his objection going. "I'm just a spare. She's the next in line," he said, looking over at his older sister, Tane.

In his mind, Derr smirked. His face failed to follow its lead. *Young Loseff, you missed the first clue. Disappointing.*

"My dears, you are, in my heart, both equals. It is your father's and my intention to prepare you both to rule. The future is not ours to know. A mother's love knows no bounds and holds no favorites. Tane has a formal role now, and you will take a position in your father's administration soon as well." Kaythlin extended her arms and pulled her children in tight to her bosom.

Loseff brushed her off. "Suppose I don't want to," he pouted.

"Don't want to do what, son?" Madrotti Tomelai entered the room.

Kaythlin jumped in. "Nothing, dear." With both hands on his shoulders and rising on her tiptoes, she kissed Madrotti on the cheek.

Madrotti walked to Tane, then Loseff, and kissed each on their foreheads.

"Drew, you want one too?" Madrotti Tomelai joked, puckering his lips.

Derr replied holding up one hand, "I'm good, Rotti."

Derr used Tomelai's entrance to offer his appreciation, a formality even for him. "And good morning to you, Rotti, and to you, Tane and Loseff. Kaythlin, thank you once again for asking me to join your family this morning."

Loseff, showing no self-control, blurted, "So he's the reason I had to get up this early."

Derr offered a nod and raised eyebrows to Tomelai. *His resentment of authority on display. Could be good in what's coming. Could be bad.*

Friends from the time of early childhood, both understood each other's unspoken communications in the squint of an eye, the lift of a brow, an upturned grin, and so much more.

Tomelai showed signs of a rebuke aimed at his son building, but looks from both Derr and Kaythlin silence the pending fatherly retort.

Kaythlin spoke to everyone in the room, "Come. Let us sit. I have sent the staff away, and I prepared a simple meal of scrambled quail eggs, thifarian toast, and pan-fried hog's bladder sausages. I have put out an assortment of fruits, but I know you all too well and expect much of the fruit to go uneaten. A mother has to try."

Tane slid her hand over Kaythlin's. "Thank you, Mother. You'll have to teach me how to cook like you. You've taught me so much else."

Always ready with just the right words. It'll serve you well. If only you could get some of that to rub off on your brother.

Loseff sneered at his sister. "Suck-up."

Tomelai said, "You get used to it, Drew. The teenage years are the most challenging."

Again, Derr aimed advice at Tomelai. His raised eyebrows said, *He's a pain in the ass, but he's not a lapdog. That's a plus.* Derr watched Tomelai offer an almost imperceptible head bob. A knowing reply to Derr, he understood.

"We have a guest," Kaythlin noted in a gentle tone for her adult children.

Tomelai followed, "You are all my family. I include Drew in that which I am certain you already know." He gave a look toward Derr. "Kaythlin and I wanted you all here to talk about what we are about to face."

Derr took in Tane's widening eyes, focused firmly on her father. Loseff wanted to appear unconcerned, but Derr spied the slightest clench to his jawline. *He cares more than he wants to show. Caring is good. We can work with that.*

"With my call for the end of Adelle's participation in the Covenant of Absolute Human Obligations, it is going to be a rough ride. As a family, we are going to get through it."

Derr, not accustomed to family gatherings other than those he attended with the Tomelais, not having one of his own, had to factor in domestic relationships in uncovering Tane's and Loseff's reactions.

Kaythlin stood. "Tane, Loseff, please help me." The First Lady headed into the kitchen, returning with her young adult children close behind, all carrying platters of the meal Kaythlin promised.

Setting down a common clay-fired tray, glazed in scenes of autumn in Adelle, Kaythlin announced, "Dig in."

Derr didn't move while Tane, Loseff, and Tomelai attacked the morning offerings.

Kaythlin gently scolded him. "My dear Druin. You are family. We do not stand on ceremony for family. Please help yourself."

"Old habits die hard. It's from a time when I sat here as a boy. Rotti would agree. His father—your grandfather Tane, Loseff—ruled with an iron fist. Sitting at this table, just a kid, the man scared the shit out of me."

Tane tilted her head to the side. "Imagine that. Captain Druin Derr afraid of something. You're human, after all," she said and laughed.

Tomelai put down his fork. "Drew, you got that right. As a boy, he scared me too. Anyway, keep eating while I talk. Just leave me a few of those sausages. Like I said before, we are headed into a tempest. Drew reported to me the other day that while Teth, Greenlin, and Kantos are in a shit storm, an even bigger one is percolating in Adelle."

Tane looked up. Loseff ignored his father.

Both reactions interested Derr. *Tane, attentive and in the moment. As you should be. Loseff, you're much too determined to present yourself aloof and uncaring for the affairs of state that don't involve you. But they will. Maybe.*

Tomelai continued, "What do you two know of the Hidden Hand?"

Neither replied, but Derr spied recognition in Tane.

"They are the faceless, powerful people who try to steer the ship of state in ways that benefit themselves, sometimes in the direction that I, the head of our nation, do not agree with. It is a constant battle and is going to get worse. They have signaled their opposition to this move."

Derr searched both Tane and Loseff for their depth of understanding. He noticed Kaythlin observing her offspring in much the same manner.

Tomelai went on, "We are about to face chaos on two fronts. From external forces out of Teth, Greenlin, and Kantos, and from internal Hidden Hand efforts to fight us every inch of the way as we break free of the Covenant. The internal pressure will come from secretive and powerful Adelleian frenemies. Traitors, if you will. They have too much tied up in the coin they generate, and they want to keep it that way. Tane, what are your thoughts?"

The heir apparent to Adelle's chancellorship didn't immediately answer. After a dozen or so seconds, she said, "There are a few thousand bureaucrats entrusted in carrying out our laws and implementing programs in the way we want it done. There's a lot of wiggle room for them to operate and untold opportunities to rake from the pot."

Derr watched the father in Tomelai, proud of his daughter's insight, nod in approval.

Loseff's pouted lips came together and offered air kisses in his sister's direction. The non-verbal response Derr thought: *Disappointing*. Derr offered a look to Tomelai. In the unspoken language, the men who shared a lifetime of understanding between them, said, *You sure about this?*

Before Tomelai could reply, "Loseff," Kaythlin said in a kind, motherly voice, "This is for you as well, my darling. It is our hope that you take this opportunity to step into a role of authority for the good of Adelle and your family."

Derr looked on as Loseff rolled his eyes. *This might be tougher than Rotti expects.* He considered and then observed Madrotti's and Kaythlin's eyes meet. She subtly nodded her head. A signal to go ahead as planned.

Tomelai had not gestured to him for his input in the moment. *This is a family decision. I can buy that. But it's not without risk.*

Derr understood his friend when Tomelai moved forward in spite of his son's insubordination. But it only reinforced Derr's opposition to the move.

Derr's ear detected a father's hope for the future in Tomelai's voice when he said, "Son, you are a man now. I cannot change your order of birth, and it would not be fair to your sister who has been with me this past year, even if I could. But I think I can offer you something that matches well with your talents. Your interests. You are an excellent swordsman, a superb athlete, you recall everything you read, you think quickly on your feet, and any young man or woman your age would not want to go toe-to-toe with you in a fight. I need your help, son."

Tomelai paused, and Derr's interest spiked. Tomelai held Loseff's eyes in his. *He's searching for an answer before continuing. Last chance to back out? You won't. He's your son.*

Tomelai looked away to Kaythlin. Derr watched the tips at the end of her lips curl upward, offering her husband reassurance.

Tomelai puffed his chest.

Here it comes.

"Adelle will establish a standing army for the first time in our history. Loseff, I want you to be part of its leadership, and I want you heavily involved in training the new men and women who will fill its ranks. I want you on my war council."

Loseff smiled but held back voicing a reply.

Derr studied Loseff's expression. The young man's eyes narrowed, and his lips pressed tightly together. And Derr saw him sucking in the air. His nostrils drew in at the effort. *Surprised, are you? Of course you are. Your heart's pounding. Breath's tight but you're playing it cool, are you? Taking the seconds you have to settle yourself. Thinking it through. Good, you're a discerning man. Now, let's hear what you have to say.*

Nodding towards Derr, yet facing his father, Loseff said his peace, "What about this guy? He's your right-hand man. Why me? Why not have him do it?"

Tomelai exploded, jumping out of his chair, "Yes! Exactly. This is why you are the best man for the position. You did not accept it. You did not say 'yes, sir' or 'no, sir.' You want to know why. You want to know more before you commit. You have made me proud. Son, if there are battles to be fought in our future, we need a man who does not just go along but someone who can think on his feet, and who can react appropriately to the circumstances. I need someone who will look behind the curtain. I will need advice, honest advice, not ass-licking generals telling me what I want to hear."

Loseff broke half a smile.

Tomelai continued, "And, to answer your question, Drew is going to have his hands full with the KCG keeping as much of the Hidden Hand in line as humanly possible. If it comes to war, he will also have his hands full with an army of spies and intel analysis. With both of you at my side and Tane helping on the domestic front, Adelle could not be in better hands."

Loseff hadn't finished. "Tell me, Father, how have you wielded power so far? Don't lie to me. We live by the Covenant. Have you ever broken it? Have you ever ordered anyone killed?"

He's got balls. Big ones. I like that. Useful in the face of an enemy.

Kaythlin, uncharacteristically, exploded, "Loseff!"

Tomelai reached for his wife's hand. "Kay, it is alright. He needs to know what the world is like and what it takes to run a country."

Kaythlin pushed back. "No, Madrotti. I raised him... we raised him to be better than this."

"Yes. You are right, Kay."

The father in you is soft, my friend.

Tomelai turned to Loseff. "On the trip we just returned from in Teth, people tried to assassinate me inside The Stand."

Although a close family, the assassination attempt was withheld from the world, including both Tane and Loseff, at Kaythlin's insistence, until now.

Tane dropped her forkful of scrambled eggs. Her hands shot over her mouth. Loseff's eyes squeezed tight as though offering an inspection of his father.

Kaythlin sat back slowly.

Derr watched, taking in the full scope of reactions.

"If not for the man I call my brother sitting here with us, I would be dead. And this last attempt... not the first time people have tried to kill me or that Drew stopped them."

Loseff ran his fingers over his mouth. "Father, I am happy you are still here. But it really doesn't answer my question." To Derr, it sounded colder than Loseff probably intended.

Kaythlin left behind any pretense of decorum. "Loseff!"

Unlike his wife, Tomelai's facial expression melted into something gentle. "Son, I wish I could tell you I have not, but I will not lie to you or your sister. What I will tell you: the few occasions I have had to resort to that harshest of solutions, I did so only to protect our family. So yes. I have ordered people to die. I also will tell you I killed one of the would-be assassins myself. The Covenant has many blind spots and has not delivered the utopia it has promised."

Tomelai's words Derr knew to be lies, except, of course, those concerning the Covenant. Tomelai lied as well as any and more often than most. Derr understood it to be a requirement of being Chancellor and of being a parent—to protect his children, both those he sired and those he ruled. But Derr spoke in half-truths just as often, and neither his nor Tomelai's lying ways presented any reason for concern. More died in the effort to keep his friend in power than just a few and not at all for the good of the family. Every death the Chancellor ordered was for the good of the Chancellor.

Loseff leaned in. "And the man you call a brother? He do most of the killing for you?"

Kaythlin apparently had heard all from her son she cared to. "Loseff, that is quite enough from you, young man."

Tomelai gripped her hand. "It is fine, Kay."

She shot a firm look to Tomelai, while her tone retreated into her genteel persona. "No, it is not. The three of us will talk more about this later."

Derr understood her irritation took aim at both Tomelai men. But what interested Derr most resided in Loseff's lack of response to his mother's protests. They had no effect on him. He shot another knowing glance to Tomelai. *That's a problem.*

Tomelai accepted the dressing down from his wife but offered nothing to Derr in return. Derr had seen Kaythlin command the Chancellor before but, like the intimate setting of the morning's breakfast, only in private. Derr considered this a family issue, and family, everyone at the table understood to be Kaythlin's domain. Tomelai might be Chancellor, but Kaythlin, the mother of two, ruled in this environ.

"The KCG, son, carries out my orders, and Captain Derr is its leader. So, yes, they have done what I commanded when death is required as the only solution."

Loseff locked eyes with Derr. Derr understood Loseff, trying to act like his father, but the young man blinked first.

Tomelai's nod at Derr, he understood to be a question from his Chancellor. *"And what do you make of that?"* As though Loseff's harsh gaze at the hardened Derr proved some point that Tomelai wanted Derr to take note of. But in Derr's smirk to Tomelai, he replied, *"Nothing to see here. You've lost enough of these stare-downs yourself."*

Tomelai smiled and slapped his hand on the table, telling Derr he acknowledged his reply and that it amused him.

Derr watched Kaythlin eye them both as he and Tomelai engaged in their silent, exclusionary conversation. She'd been around them long enough to understand their ways.

Loseff spoke, clearly aware of more than Derr expected, "Now I understand why you're here, Captain Derr. You're here to assess me and report to the old man later today. You're going to give him your thoughts on how I did. He's my father; he should know me well enough without your two coins thrown into the pot. I don't like it, but I can accept it."

Derr rubbed his chin. "That's astute of you. You're right, I'm going to give the Chancellor an assessment of a man he's appointing to his war council. Son or no son, it has major implications for Adelle. Giving that much power to one so young, it comes with problems. Power corrupts even family." His tone changed, and sarcasm dripped from his words when he said, "And, I'm so glad to hear you can accept it."

Loseff gave an accepting nod and turned from Derr to face Tomelai. "Alright, Father. You treated me like a man. Took me into your confidence. If that's how it's going to be, I'm in."

Derr watched Tomelai's pride in his son rise as the young man spoke. Loseff's potential, which had been buried under jealousy spiced with a lack of purpose, broke free over the simple setting of a breakfast table.

Derr concluded, *The young man of nineteen came to breakfast still a boy. He's leaving a man. But will he be a man who can be trusted, I wonder?*

The young man dug into what remained of the scrambled quail eggs on his plate and, without looking up, said, "When do we build this army of mine?" and grinned.

Derr didn't like the smug features taking root across Loseff's face.

DEEP CUTS, DEEP WOUNDS

TETH: 3RD DAY OF THE HARVEST MOON

Reyne

Light streamed in from the empty window frame in the house that Edruk, Reyne's father who he never knew, once called home. Reyne woke to the cold morning air gnawing at his cheeks. A musty odor poked at his nostrils. He sucked in loose mucus and ran his sleeve over his face. He sat up from the hard floor where his baby sister's life ended before she had any chance to experience the world.

Waking up with Reyne, in his head, in his heart, and in his soul, torment and anger burning away his love of life. Flooding his mind, remembering all he had witnessed the night before, he prepared to battle in the long war ahead, but first, he had to face another miserable day. A deep yearning to get to Evidar reenforced in the ruination of his genetic family, further amplified by newly acquired feelings towards those same people.

Reyne looked around and wondered at the absence of Mera. On the floor of Baide's room, where he collapsed the night before, he sat up, still shaken by specters from the past Mera conjured. The men hadn't the chance to discuss what they saw, Reyne having passed out from a cocktail of physical and emotional exhaustion and shock, waking only now to find Mera gone. Reyne, anxious to discuss the prior evening's revelations, called out for the man who he realized, after witnessing the life-saving heroics almost twenty-two years in the past, was, in fact, his protector.

Absent a reply, Reyne got to his feet. As he did, the sounds of boots on the hardwood floor alerted him of another's presence. Heavy footsteps grew closer. Reyne girded himself for an attack but settled back when Mera popped his head through the barren bedroom doorframe.

Annoyed, Reyne said, "Why didn't you answer me?"

"Sorry, been preoccupied. I'm here now. We've got to talk about last night."

"What, now you read minds, too?" Reyne's ears gathered in his own harsh tone. *Mera deserves better. If not for him, I'd of died in this room before even being born.* But knowing it and controlling it were not the same.

A half-sideways head tilt from Mera. "Only the dead's."

"What's that supposed to mean?" Reyne asked. On separate occasions, he'd witnessed Mera first pull a Firaché flame-being life form from a small fire pit and later whip up specters from the past out of thin air. *What else is he capable of?*

Crossing his arms, Mera said, "That's for another time."

"Always riddles with you." And again, annoyance sparked at Mera. *Let it go,* Reyne told himself. *Last night changed things. Because of him, you got twenty-two years with Daedyn. Found Mithany. None of it woulda happened if not for Mera.*

"Last evening, we answered one of those riddles. You saw an Evidar agent murdered your biological family. If I had seen the killer looking in through the window that night, we wouldn't be here now. The woman, Dylla Weisner, would be dead, and you'd still be hidden away. If I had seen her that night, I would have immediately gone after her. I'm sorry I let her slip past me unnoticed."

"From what I witnessed, you doin' what you did, I can't be mad at you. I wanted to be, for Daedyn's death and for pulling me away from Mithany. But not for what I saw you do last night, all those years ago. Can't let myself be angry with you anymore. I'm sorry too."

"Appreciate the thought. I only want to help. All I ever got from you since that Evidar agent hit you with the spiderworm poison is one ornery, prickly, son of a bitch Reyne Brenton."

"I blamed you. From the moment you appeared, everything turned to shit."

"Does that mean the pleasant, respectful, polite young businessman's coming back?"

"What I saw last night made me realize, if not for you, I'd never have been born. Woulda never got all those years with Daedyn, Pachelle, or Gwerther. Woulda never met Mithany. I owe you for that. As for gettin' the old Reyne back, don't see that happenin' anytime soon. Anger's still eatin' my insides. Daedyn's still dead. Mithany's still gone. Carrying a lot of it, lot a hate too, just not aimed at you no longer."

"Sorry for what you're going through. And I feel guilty, but you had to see those events from twenty-two years ago."

A clenched jaw tamped down quivering lips. Reyne pulled himself away from the abyss of losing Daedyn and Mithany that rubbed his soul raw and asked, "Tell me, what did my mother say to you that made you spring so quickly to cut me out of her?"

"She said, '... baby... save...' and her strength gave out."

"And the one word on her lips I saw when you handed the baby, I mean me, to her?"

"I barely heard it. She whispered your name, Reyne. And almost immediately after your name slipped off her tongue, she died, happy, with you in her arms."

"So close to dying, the physical pain... How could you know she was happy?"

Mera crouched down on his haunches and came face to face with Reyne. He put one hand on Reyne's shoulder. "Knew Silia for years. I saw it in her eyes just as the light of life faded from them. You were saved. That's all she cared about. Love filled her heart when she passed."

"Gotta be honest, didn't expect it to hit me so hard. I'm beyond furious. That poor little girl. That bitch just slashed her throat. Can't wait to get my hands on her. And the naked guy. He looked like an older version of me. He plowed through the door too late to save them. The things you showed me... Thank you."

"That guy, your father, had just transfigured from Evidar. Sadly, too late. Cost him his life. As for the assassin, we'll get her all in due time, my young friend."

Reyne let the friend comment pass. "What about that woman, the red-haired bitch who killed them all? The one you pulled up out of the past. Why didn't you ever come back here and look into the past before last night? Figure out who did this and kill them?"

"I know of her. Seen her once, years ago. Couldn't take her out. Had too many people around her. Her name's Dylla Weisner. Haven't seen her since, but I've been aware of her."

"She still around?"

"Yes. Leads the team from Evidar that's here now. From people I spoke to in Jarouhar soon after the murder of another Tweener like yourself, a woman named Lorique, someone spotted a person fitting Dylla's description at a café that same day. I'm guessing she and her team were responsible for the attempt on you and for slaying your brother."

Reyne closed his eyes, tipped his head back, and sucked in a deep breath. Opening them, he said, "Okay. I get what you're saying, but you still didn't answer the question. Why didn't you figure it out in all these years? Why didn't you come back here? Why didn't you go after this Dylla? Doesn't make sense waiting this long."

"Until they came after you, I didn't even suspect anyone from Evidar knew you existed. When Silia died, you, the unborn child she carried, would have been presumed dead as well. That's what I thought all these years. I was wrong. It took them almost twenty-two years to find where I hid you. A week ago, they found you. I'm sorry my mistake cost you so much."

"Alright, I can buy that, but what about Edruk? Why didn't you go after them to avenge his death? You needed him."

"Because I didn't have to, based on what I thought. At the time, it didn't matter who did this terrible thing. If they were from Evidar or worked for those bastards, I targeted every one of them for elimination. I had helpers, but lost many of them in the effort. We did considerable damage. I'm still after anyone and everyone from Evidar, but now I needed to understand how you got exposed. Had to make sure one of my people didn't give you away. Different issue. Now solved."

Reyne felt compelled to make his own position clear. "Alright, I can accept what you did in the past, but this is now. No more bullshit going forward. Be straight with me. Get me trained and off to Evidar. Teach me this Tweener stuff."

"Good to hear."

"You said we're meeting up with someone named Gina. When?"

"In a few hours. I left for the Whispering Eye last night while you were out of it. I just got back when I heard you call me."

A startled frown responded to Mera's confession of a midnight excursion. *Let it go*, Reyne's inner voice commanded.

"We eat. Then we go," Reyne said, determined to control events instead of reacting. Love for him from a mother he never knew overwhelmed him. Baide's horrific death had affected him in the same way as Daedyn's. Done with plodding forward, being led like a dog on a leash, Reyne grabbed the reins of life.

Evidar agents were stalking him. He accepted his fate. On his own terms, Reyne resolved to face the enemy head-on.

THE WHISPERING EYE

Reyne

A few hours after another cold meal, leaving Edruk's home as they found it, Reyne and Mera stood outside the only structure to escape ruination along a side street off Teth's Grand Protisium: a popular hole-in-the-wall, a tavern named the Whispering Eye.

Mera scanned the front of the building. "My guess is that a lot of the same people who rioted through Teth causing all this destruction are regulars of this place. Needed somewhere safe to revel in their achievements afterward. Voila, saved from destruction."

Reyne eyed the structure up and down. "It doesn't look like much from the outside."

"I'm sure you'll appreciate it more once you're inside. Come, let's go in. I don't need to tell you, keep a low profile. We don't need anyone recognizing you or getting into another brawl like yesterday."

Reyne slapped Mera on the back, his resentment towards the man having given way. "Like you said before, Evidar thinks I'm dead. Doubt anyone's lookin' for me here."

Mera added. "They're not hunting for you—yet. Don't get cocky."

Passing through the small opening of a doorway, purposefully crafted to grant access one at a time, Reyne slipped inside. There existed another service entry, a back door, but private and rarely used—access through it reserved for only the truly special patrons. Three steps into the dark, musty room, Mera stuck out his arm, halting Reyne in his tracks.

"Look up at the second floor near the alcove. She's sitting alone. You go up. She's expecting us. You need me to hold your hand, or are you okay on your own?"

His one foot rested on the first step of the staircase, and his hand plopped onto the newel post. "I'll be fine."

"Alright then, I'm going to walk around and check out the rabble. See if there's anything or anyone for us to worry about."

Mera walked away, and Reyne made it up the stairs. At the top, Reyne's eyes located Gina. She nodded to someone down below at the bar. Reyne followed her line of sight to see Mera return the gesture. He snapped his head back to whom he understood to be Gina in time to catch the residuals of a one-eyed wink aimed at his traveling companion.

Apprehensive, Reyne sauntered up to the woman Mera acknowledged. "You Gina?"

The woman nodded and replied, "You Reyne?"

Reyne couldn't get a full measure with her seated. His immediate take on her from just two words and from the look on her average face: *She's sure of herself.* Short black hair, large, round, purplish-colored eyes, and a small angular nose—she would easily blend into any crowd. But when she smiled at him, he noted she had a great smile.

She kicked out an empty chair. "Sit."

Reyne's face soured. "We've just met, and I get the impression you're a woman of few words."

"We'll see," Gina said, meeting all Reyne's newly formed expectations.

A confident voice, delivered slowly and mixed with a sweet feminine tone, didn't match the projected tough-gal attitude. Reyne guessed her to be in her late twenties or early thirties. A dark top matched with dim lighting gave nothing of her away. All he had to go on was her face, her attitude, and her limited use of words.

Reyne sat and looked around. The pair had a small, square table between them. The dark room offered dim lighting for the few patrons of early afternoon. While scanning his second-floor surroundings, not directly facing his soon-to-be instructor, Reyne said, "Mera tells me you're gonna train me. I gotta be twice your size."

"So?"

"You don't say much. Do you?" He did his best to get her to talk. She reminded him of similar difficulties cracking the husk of a green alphen nut not ready to give up its prize. *Difficult. Not impossible.* He accepted her unspoken challenge.

Gina responded with the longest string of words she'd put together to that point. "When I have something to say, I will. Like, look at me when you're talking to me."

"Point taken."

Gina furrowed her brow and gestured two fingers at her own eyes as though to command Reyne, *Look at me.*

"We're gonna be spending a lot of time together. I need to know all about you. And all the closeness sometimes gives trainees the wrong idea, so any thoughts you have about getting into my pants, you can put those to rest. Unless, of course, I change my mind, but at this point, from what I have seen so far, I doubt it."

Reyne threw up his hands. "Where'd that come from? Not even thinking about it. You want to know about me? I'm your average small business owner running a nut orchard, and I'm engaged to a wonderful woman named Mithany. My brother got murdered, and I don't care how close we get, your pants can stay on."

"I know all about your brother. I'm sorry for your loss. Partly why you're here. And I thank you. You're a gentleman leaving my pants untouched. Imagine that, I'm gonna train a gentleman to kill people... We'll see."

In only two minutes, Reyne decided he didn't like her much, but that didn't matter. He surprised himself by briefly addressing Daedyn's murder, but then he didn't know this woman and didn't care to share his depth of loss. All he wanted from her was to get him ready for Evidar as soon as possible.

Reyne's puzzled look said as much as his words. "Good, we have that settled. You don't want me, and I don't want you. How did this conversation go so bad, so fast? I don't care about any of that sex stuff."

Gina offered him an obvious fake grin.

Reyne shook it off. "Maybe everyone else on Tartica is lookin' to meet their Covenant obligation, shagging anything that moves, like it's always rutting season, but not me. I'm getting married when this is over, so I plan on staying faithful. Just want to train. What about the training?"

Gina's pretend grin morphed into a genuine smile, and Reyne wondered, *What did I say that's got her all pleased with herself?*

"I need to know more about you so I can figure out how best to train you."

Reyne thought to say, 'That explains what we're doin' here but not your face,' but didn't. He'd had enough. "Listen, I don't know your story and don't really care. I had a shitty week, and life's dealt me an awful hand. My future's been pulled out from under me. So let's just do the training, and we can move on from each other."

Gina mocked him, rocking her head side to side in unison with her fake cries. "Whaaa—whaaa. You got it rough. Grow up. Life's hard, farm boy."

Reyne wanted to explode, but he needed her. Tamped it all down and said, "Yeah, it's been pretty bad lately. What do you know about having it tough? You're a fairly attractive woman and can get what you want almost without trying. I'm gonna guess life's been pretty easy for you."

Reyne knew his words for the misstep they were as soon as they left his mouth. He understood nothing of her and presumed too much.

She shot up from her chair, squatted to meet his gaze, eye to eye, and came to rest just inches from his face. She shouted, "Lately? How about every day? And you think being a woman makes it easier to get through life. Are you an idiot?"

Reyne, recoiled at her explosive reaction, stuttered out, "N—no."

Standing, Gina said, "You know how hard it is having one of these things?" pointing at her crotch over her short skirt. "It comes with baggage from morons like you. Easier, I don't think so."

Reyne's attempted recovery didn't help. "It's a compliment. You're attractive. I only meant attractive women can get better treatment in life. That's all."

Anger bloomed across her face, and in her tone as well. "Better treatment? How about more scrutiny? You walk into any room filled with men like you, and you're the only one with one of these," she said, still pointing. Her eye roll finished the thought. She paused for a few seconds. "Almost to a man, they eye you up and down. There's always one who thinks he can go in for the kill."

Reyne sat back, crossing his arms. "We're not all rutting beasts."

Gina sat, planted one foot against the table's edge, and tilted her chair back on only two legs. Her short skirt rode up and stole Reyne's attention.

"What're you looking at, farm boy?"

Reyne turned away quickly. Red-faced, caught in the act, he steered the conversation in another direction, "I don't like the farm boy comment. Businessman, not a farm boy."

"Whatever. Back to your girlfriend. Keep in mind, this is Tartica. The fucking is free and easy. It's the way of life around here. You know, the Covenant. Obligation to make babies and all that nonsense. Wherever Mithany goes, there's gonna be at least one guy who's going to take a shot at her. Like you just did, trying to peek up my skirt. How's that woman of yours gonna handle it without you around to protect her?"

Reyne pushed down the bile her comments about Mithany brought up, and slammed his open palm on the table with a *bang*. He leaned in, and his neck shot forward like a turtle stretching out of its shell. "I'm gonna tell you this only once. Leave Mithany out of this."

The table rattled, but she didn't. She replied, "Perhaps," and settled her chair back down.

Not sure if *perhaps* meant she might leave Mithany alone or that *perhaps* men weren't all the same, but before he had time to figure it out, she continued. Gina looked down at her lap. "It's a shame you can't walk around with one of these for just one day. You'd see the world differently. How about Mithany? She pretty? You know, she has one of these too."

Reyne's face flared red against the heat racing through him. If he could have spit venom, she'd have felt his wrath. He hated Gina in that moment. Mithany, his soul mate, meant so much more to him than the sum total of mating material.

Gina's laugh sounded dismissive. "Someone's always judging us as women. Mithany knows what I'm talking about. Do you?"

"No. Not really."

"It's a primeval ballet playing out, and you can't ever get off the dancefloor. It can be exhausting if you let it. Takes a lot of strength. Makes me think women are tougher than men having to deal with your constant idiocy."

Her finger pointed and waved incessantly in his face. "At an instinctive level, we all know what's going on. It's the dance of men pursuing, and women calculating how to respond. It lives just below the surface."

"How did we get on this topic? I'm here to talk about getting the training I need."

But Gina didn't relent. She kept egging him on, pushing him closer to the edge. "Women are the ones entrusted as the keepers of this gift. The thing is, we vagina owners are all different. Does Mithany embrace its power? Or is she one of those who doesn't want anything to do with it? Wants to deny the role Mother Nature forced on her?"

His jaw clenched. *Don't take the bait.* But he couldn't resist. Anger flared in his response—"I said keep her out of this"—as he pounded his fist on the small piece of furniture that proved barely able to withstand the blow.

But Gina kept up her attack. "The very survival of the human race ever since the Great Destruction depends on every woman putting theirs in play if you buy into the Covenant."

Reyne snapped at her. "Covenant demands the same of men."

A flippant sneer preceded an air spit and flapping lips. "Guys have a part in this procreation dance of nature, I'll give you that." Her voice rose louder, bleeding anger in her tone. "But you're not the gatekeepers of Nature's golden egg. What about your Mithany, think she'll put hers to good use while you're away? Or is that thing going into moth balls until you return... If you return at all."

Take deep breaths. Mithany would never cheat. Deep breaths. The comfort he took in the certainty Mithany would remain faithful did not waver in the face of Gina's efforts to cast doubt into his resolve. Reyne turned from thinking of his fiancée's unlikely infidelity to focus on the annoying person in front of him.

"Please, I'm asking you nicely. Stop."

Gina followed by another roll of her eyes. "Why? Afraid all this talk about your gal's resolve hits too close to home?"

Relentless, her words wormed into his thoughts. He wanted to, he needed to put it out of his mind. "I came here to talk about you helping me get ready for a trip to Evidar. That's all."

"If she can't hold out and wait for her man to come back to her, she'll be taking a big gamble. Picture it, each time Mithany spreads her legs for an eager lover, there's the chance she's gonna be left to care for a screaming brat nine months later, after some guy drops his load and disappears, never to be seen again. We women have different calculations to make each time the prospect of fucking comes up. If you cheat, not so many consequences, but if Mithany does, she rolls the dice... Protection's illegal, with society's constant push for more humans. But you can get them. Your gal carry condoms with her? She got that all figured out?"

Reyne squashed the images in his head of Mithany, pictured as Gina described her, as soon as they popped up. With Mithany stowed away in his heart, reassuring himself of her fidelity to their love, he calmly addressed Gina, "You're not at all what I expected," intending in his reply not to play this game with her any longer.

His observation fell on deaf ears, and she kept driving, pushing. "And don't get me started on bouncing or swaying breasts. How are your girl's? They attract attention?"

What is it with this woman? But he found himself thinking of Mithany's chest as though compelled to address Gina's every question, if only to himself.

Head games. She's playin' head games with me.

Gina stood up in front of him. "I see that dumb look on your face. We all know guys love looking at tits. It's buried in your primeval brains no law can root out."

Guilt grabbed him by the balls as he knowingly lied to her—and himself. "I'm not like that."

Gina smirked. "You think you're better than that? Few guys are. Wherever I go, there's always someone gawking at my ass or my breasts. Someone's eyeing up your gal as we speak. Could even be another woman. Some of us aren't much better. I'm sure of it. As sure as I am that one of you is going to cheat on the other."

"I'm positive Mithany can handle herself, and as sure as you think you are, I'm more. She won't cheat on me," he proudly replied.

"You think so, or you hope so?"

Reyne shot back, his face contorted with every muscle clenched tight. He leaned in. "I know so."

Gina aimed her eyes at his crotch. "Those things need to be fed regularly. You know I speak the truth, cause you own one."

Reyne's foot tapped wildly under the table.

"Don't get me wrong, I get it. But what you got dangling between your legs doesn't compare to the prize me and your gal walk around with every minute of every day." She laughed. "Not enough of the minge out there. Demand exceeds supply. Your woman is part of the supply chain."

Reyne craved an end to Gina's unending challenge to his resolve or faith in fidelity. He was already unsure he could even implement his goal to return to Mithany quickly—he didn't know anything of transfiguration, jumping between dimensions, or getting into or out of Evidar. He didn't need doubt rattling in his mind of either his own commitment to self-imposed, temporary celibacy or Mithany's until his return. He took a deep breath, closed his eyes, opened them, and said, "Maybe what you say is true, but I'm not like everyone. Mithany is the only woman I think about. I don't want or desire anyone else. So yeah, I'll hold out until I get back to her."

Gina tilted her head to the side, looking at Reyne. "Is that a fact? Your big head runs things? The little one's got no say? You gonna hold out in all the time you're away? How long? Weeks? Months? A year? What about her? She gonna hold out that long? Temptation's a hard bitch to deny."

She'd gotten under his skin, into his head. The number of days or weeks they'd spend apart remained uncertain. And even if he planned a quick round trip, just thinking of Mithany with another in her arms muddled around in his brain, in his gut, squeezing his inside. He tried to deny it a hold on him, but somehow the images Gina planted in his thoughts fought against eviction.

She would never, he reassured himself over and over, finally pushing the offending thought from his mind. He replied in the only words he could put together through the fog of emotional outrage. The words came out as harsh as he intended. "Fuck you."

Gina grinned. It held a sinister quality behind her façade, and it appeared to Reyne she took his reply as surrender. She'd declared victory. Victory in what, he wondered.

Her eyes softened, and she ran her fingers over her mouth. "Now, now. Fuck you, you say? There's no need for that. Peace offering. I want another beer. Can I get you one?"

Reyne looked away and stole a moment to settle his nerves. He offered her a wounded reply, "Yeah."

Reyne accepted the change in the conversation's direction as a positive turn. Glad to move on and glad to get free from her, if only for a short breather.

Gina stepped back from the table and sauntered towards the bar. Her short skirt hugged her form. Where on the incredibly tight garment she'd kept the coins to pay for it, his close inspection failed to determine. Her exposed legs accentuated her features as she skillfully placed each gentle step.

She knows how to work it. That's for sure.

Reyne observed a silent alarm go off across the room, screaming out "Gina." Heads turned, some slowly, others noticeably quicker.

Well, she made her point.

He hadn't noticed when his own eyes drifted from the onlookers and came to rest on her buttocks. She'd set him up and he failed.

"Shit," he muttered out loud, if only to himself.

In much the same manner and with the same results, Gina returned to their table, clutching two overflowing steins. "How'd you do?"

Playing dumb he said, "How'd I do with what?"

"My ass. How'd it look?" Gina smiled and set their drinks on the table.

Reyne lied. "Like I said, only got eyes for Mithany. Just watchin' everyone else, I do admit, you garnered some attention. I'm sure you got a fine derriere, but I didn't study it."

"Hmm, must be losing my touch," Gina's reply hinted at her skepticism of his denial. She remained unmoving for a few seconds, giving Reyne the impression calculations were going on in her head and she had more cards to play.

She spun a chair around and set it directly in front of him, with the open back of the chair facing him. She settled onto her newly arranged seat with legs positioned on the outside of each of the chair's stiles. Her pushed up skirt barely covered what hid behind it. Both arms came to rest across the top rail where she settled her chin. She positioned her bottom away from him along the back of the seat.

Gina beamed at Reyne. He didn't care for her one bit, but she had a great smile. He had to give her that. It made her look warm, friendly, not the combative person she projected.

He gulped down a good portion of the stein's contents and wondered, *What's her game?*

Reluctantly, he accepted Gina controlled the conversation from the moment he introduced himself. His thoughts were interrupted when she said, "What's going through that little brain of yours? Are you wondering if I'm wearing anything under my skirt? Didn't you figure that out from the last time you peeked?" She leaned forward and whispered, "I'm not."

Reyne turned his head and spit out his drink. "What're you doin'? You tryin' to prove a point? Not gonna happen. Like I said, Mithany." Reyne looked away. *This ain't over yet. Shit, shoulda spit it in her face.*

"Look at me," she said soft and sweet.

As Reyne turned to meet her gaze, she slid her butt forward from the back of the chair to the open front with only a top rail and a thin mid rail between them. The fabric of her short skirt clung to the wood of the seat and, as she moved her ass forward with open legs and disappearing dress, she teased, exposing herself to him.

What he couldn't figure out was, *Here's this woman complaining about men only to pull this stunt. Not consistent. She's up to something. But what?* Yet for all the want of understanding, he couldn't piece it together.

In spite of nudity being ever-present across all of Tartica, instinct took hold of him as he gazed down at her. He knew himself to be a better man than that. For all the want of decency, propriety, and respect for women, his inner compass compelled him to look away—but his eyes had their own agenda.

With her gentle tone gone, Gina laughed in his face. "Thought you only had eyes for Mithany?"

Reyne missed her warning; she'd stopped toying with him. His stated commitment to only having eyes for Mithany failed him: she had her victory.

Before he could wrench free his thoughts, or from what lay in his line of sight, both focused on the same thing, Gina moved impossibly faster than a shadow flows from its maker. In less than half the blink of an eye, she came to stand behind Reyne with a blade pressed against his throat.

The Dylla Effect

Hensdale: 3rd Day of the Harvest Moon

Quith

Quith arrived at the secluded Hensdale apple farm shortly after dawn following a long night of grave digging. The sweet smell of apples infused over decades competed with the dank, musty odor of the cellar in the safe house where he hid awaiting an opportunity to secure his future. His continued existence would cost the others from Evidar in the room above his head their lives. Well, that was his plan anyway.

Sunrise broke over Hensdale, welcoming Quith to his new home—the world of Tartica. For a man born to darkness, he considered the irony. His thoughts didn't linger; he had carnage to attend to. That part of his new reality hadn't changed, just who he had to kill did.

When Quith arrived, he discovered Tylus and Grafph sitting up, asleep on the living room sofa. He considered slaughtering them then and there, but the risk of waking either or both in the approach warned him off. *Saved by squeaky floors... for now.*

Before entering the basement, he'd completed a thorough reconnoiter. Coupled with his existing knowledge of the inside and surroundings of the farmhouse, Quith sketched out the foundation of a plan in his head. However, Dylla and Neladith were missing, and he'd also need to extract intel from one or the other of his soon-to-be captives, Tylus or Grafph.

Quith had entered the structure through a basement hopper-style window. He visually assessed every inch of the space, checked his sleeve for the thin gravity knife he always carried, and moved extra carefully without making a sound. A chair in the center of the room above the bloodstained floor gave him no cause for concern, as he understood its meaning, *Arek.*

Time passed as Quith waited for the right opportunity.

The familiar squeal of the front door hinges locked Quith in place. Someone had arrived. *And so we begin.* Tilting his head, tuning into the flow of sounds creaking along the floorboards above, he thought, *Dylla. I'd know those footsteps anywhere.*

In silence, Quith made his way to a spot along the basement headroom riser, pressed his forehead just above a narrow crack in the unfinished lathe-and-plaster exposed on his side of the wall, and peeked through. Grafph's snoring provided Quith a helpful bit of information. *Thin walls.*

From his sequestered hiding spot, Quith watched Dylla approached the two sleeping men. His counterespionage campaign began with one eyeball spying on his own unit. The goal, to eliminate them all—with prejudice. His fingertips tingled. His heart rate increased. He slowed his breathing to prepare for listening, watching, and gathering intel. Quith took joy in spying on others.

There stood Dylla, in Quith's clear line of sight. With a lateral hip tilt to the right, Dylla's confident management style on display, Quith heard her say, "Good morning, gentlemen. Don't get up."

Startled out of slumber, both grumbled, jerked their heads in unison, reacting to Dylla's voice. Tylus cleared his throat. Grafph rubbed his eyes.

Almost comical.

Dylla—dressed in a forest-green, knee-length skirt, still wrapped in a medium-weight, waist cropped field jacket to keep out the unaccustomed Tartican autumn chill—said, "Good, you're awake."

From years of working together, Quith knew Dylla well and picked up on the annoyance in her tone.

The senior agent, Tylus, pleaded, "We got back from an assignment around dawn and were just catching a few zees. Spent a long night getting shit done. This isn't how it looks."

Dylla raised her hand, giving notice for the two men to stop talking. Her reputation for polite manners included an unspoken threat. The more civil she appeared, the more dangerous were her intentions. With her civility turned up about halfway, Quith understood her meaning, *Shut up and listen.* The lack of a reply from either Tylus or Grafph told Quith they got the message.

"Then tell me how it is, boys. Please fill me in on why you two are sitting on your asses when there is a monumental problem to be solved." Her soft, calm, confident tone a cause for concern.

Quith, standing on the chair he'd previously moved, pressed his eye to the basement wall. From there he gathered intel, soaking up Dylla's, Grafph's, and Tylus's every gesture. Their body language gave much away to Quith, who fancied himself astute at reading it.

Looking over at his idle partner, Grafph nudged Tylus. Dylla's expression told Quith her bullshit alarm fired off before Tylus opened his mouth. Quith worked under her for too long not to understand her tells.

"Speak up, boys. I'd like an answer. And where are Quith and Neladith?"

I'm right here, Dylla. I'll be coming for you.

Dylla looked over the interior. She waited. No reply. The men, or "boys" as Dylla called them, faced each other. Not getting an answer to her question, Dylla headed straight for the cellar door. "Are they down here?" Placing one hand on the knob, Dylla looked back to the men for a response.

Quith coiled, released the knife from his sleeve to drop into his waiting palm, and prepared for battle. Surprise would be his, giving him the advantage, but Dylla posed a formidable opponent. The distance between his position and the stairs, too far to make in one leap, he considered how best to attack. He ran through the many options he'd previously considered when he first took up his position. Something he'd learned early: always plan for the unexpected. More than once, it saved his life.

The likelihood of noise in his movements worked against him. Quith lifted his foot, but immediately stopped when he heard Tylus speak. "Well, Quith took off yesterday, sometime after midday. He's after confirmation that Reyne Brenton's dead. He didn't return last night, and we haven't seen him since we got back. As for Neladith, she's pursuing info from Reyne Brenton's fiancée. She left with the woman yesterday... hasn't been back either."

Letting go of the basement doorknob, Dylla walked back to stand before her subordinates. "I'm pleased to hear our team is taking steps to develop the much-needed intel, but what have *you* two been up to?"

Quith released his body from its battle-ready stance, settled back into observance mode, and repositioned the knife back up his sleeve for safekeeping.

Grafph gulped, and Tylus fidgeted, sliding his hands under his butt. Quith delighted in watching his underlings squirm.

Tylus added to the update, "We've been busy too, ma'am. Yesterday, we snapped up the guy named Arek. I gave Neladith the interrogation. She did good, tortured him, but he died in the middle of questioning."

Dylla stopped him. "Did you get any useful intel before he expired?"

Yeah boys, did you get anything out of him? Or maybe it was just a waste of time? The interrogators are now the ones being interrogated. Priceless.

"Sort of, ma'am. He stuck with his story that Reyne's the one buried at the family plot. Could be true, but Neladith, Grafph, and me figured he's hiding something."

While looking down, Dylla rubbed her fingertips over her forehead. "Grafph. Do you have anything to add?"

Quith heard Grafph's foot tapping even faster than the words that spewed from his mouth. "After Arek expired, Neladith met up with the dead guy's sister. She's the fiancée of Reyne Brenton."

Dylla, one arm across her chest, held the elbow of the other. Her free hand in a curl, nestled on her cheek, one gentle finger slowly rapping against it, "No need to rehash what is already established. Just the executive summary."

With his foot moving wildly, Grafph continued. His words shot out in rapid fire. "Neladith's working on the theory that Reyne's alive and this Mithany will lead us right to him. After she left, Ty and I took the dead body out into a deep wooded area during the night and dumped him for the animals to feed on. So you see, we've been busy with the cause too."

Dylla transitioned to chin rubbing while the men sat without speaking. Quith thought they looked like little kids staring up at their mom, waiting for her to praise or scold them. She'd reduced powerful men, trained killers, people to be feared, to toothless pets. *That's the Dylla effect.*

She broke the silence. "I get the sense you're leaving a few things out."

Tylus spoke slowly, as would a respectful subordinate intent on carefully choosing his words. "Her methods were unusual but effective. Do you want specifics on the interrogation tactics?" He stood. "Come on"—he waved his hand in an obvious gesture for Dylla to follow him—"I'll show you the basement. There's blood everywhere." He raced to the basement door. Pulled it open. And looked back to Dylla.

She took a step in the cellar's direction. Quith's head snapped around to make certain the underground room's window remained open for a quick getaway. But could he get to it in time? Would Tylus see him slip out? That is, if he slipped out before someone pulled him back in.

Damn. Waited too long.

Fearful of making a sound, he froze. He considered just walking upstairs announcing his return then thought better of it. *Can't risk it. If she knows Reyne's still alive, it'll be three against one. Down here my odds are slightly better. One at a time.*

At just the right angle, his legs on the chair were exposed. He could see Tylus's foot at the top of the stairs on the sole plate. Quith locked his vision on that foot. If it moved in his direction, he'd strike first. Certain he could take out one, maybe two of the men in the confusion, but three trained agents and one being Dylla, he considered his chances of survival *not good.*

The sound of Dylla's footsteps stopped. Quith gambled, turning his eye back to the exposed crack in the wall. Dylla rubbed the back of her neck. "No. That's fine. We won't need this Arek fellow any further. I wanted all of you here for my update. Since it's just you two, I'll get word to the others later."

As she spoke, Tylus slammed the door closed and walked away. He took up his spot on the sofa. Dylla once again stood before the two seated subordinates.

Relief washed over Quith.

Dylla held up one finger. "Turns out, suspicions were well founded. Reyne Brenton still breathes."

The news Quith dreaded. Not that it surprised him—he already knew as much—but now it hung out there in the open. Biting his lower lip, he mouthed the word, *Fuck!* as his head angrily snapped up and down at the pronouncement. *Now they all know.*

His heart raced. His temples throbbed. Hoping to face each one-on-one in his plan to eliminate them, Neladith, Tylus, and Grafph were of little concern. The real problem, Dylla, wasn't to be taken lightly.

Tylus gaped. "What the—"

Grafph grunted. "You sure?"

She crossed her arms over her chest and projected one foot forward. "This isn't to be questioned or challenged. Reyne Brenton remains amongst the living. It is the basis of our next action steps. I don't want to hear any more about it. The Dev... Architect and his Damus have confirmed it regardless of what you, Quith, or anyone wants to believe."

To Quith, and Dylla as well, he had always been the Devil's Blacksmith, but never in front of the troops. Rules were rules—always show respect to the man by using his preferred title, the Architect. Their leader's self-image focused on his good intention of saving their version of Earth, not of the death, devastation, and ruined lives he left in his wake. Much of it at the hands of Quith and his associates, including Dylla, carrying out his orders. Quith knew Dylla always gave the man's preference for being addressed the proper weight it deserved. She enjoyed living too much to consider anything less. Quith smirked. *She caught herself—just not soon enough.*

"I've been back home, and I met with *him*, the Architect. I transfigured back here as quick as I could. I do so hate this world. Anyway, he's sending us additional operatives. The few remaining capable of transitioning here, in an all-out effort to terminate Reyne Brenton. Our orders are to hunt him down. Even if he is surrounded by Meratoruc and twenty other people. It's a kill-on-sight order, regardless of the consequences to any of us."

"Yes, ma'am," both men said in unison.

"We expect he's traveling with Meratoruc. From prior briefings, you'll recall he's known on this world as Mera. Keep your eyes and ears open for either Reyne or Mera. Where there's one, we'll find the other."

Like proper schoolboys attending a meeting with their principal, the men sat attentive, hands folded in their laps.

"Are we clear?"

"Yes."

"Since Quith's not here, I'll update him myself. If you hear from Neladith or if she returns, please share all this information, but leave Quith to me."

The message was clear enough to Quith. The Devil's Blacksmith had given Dylla a direct order to eliminate the source of the problem—him. He'd made the call. He identified the kill target that night—wrongly. Reyne was still alive because he made a mistake.

His fuck up.

Dylla continued in her clear spoken and well-mannered delivery, "I'm going to be part of the implementation phase as well. Putting on my assassin's garbs once more. I'm still a highly regarded operative. Back in the day..."

Tylus bobbed his head up and down. "Nice. It'll be great teaming up in the field with you."

You always were a kiss-ass, Ty.

Dylla's expression reminded Quith: *She always did enjoy killing Tarticans.*

"*He* wants it done quickly. So here is how it's going to be. Tylus, see if you can pick up a trail on where Reyne may have headed that night. More than likely, as I said, he'll have been joined by Mera, so be careful. Trail's going to be cold. Do your best. I have confidence in you."

"Yes, ma'am."

"Grafph, see if you can gather any information from the locals. You know, the Forest Maiden, the village square, that leather shoppe the fiancée owns, maybe this Mithany confided in one of her employees where she's headed. Don't be obvious. Be thorough yet discrete. I'm going to see if I can track down Quith and Neladith."

"Will do, ma'am."

"And Grafph, once you're done here, I want you in Teth as soon as possible. Reach out to my contact in the Thuggery, Nails. Tell her you're representing my interests. We need more help. I want a contract out on this Reyne Brenton. Tell her to go wide with it. It's an open contract. I'll pay double her rates. And double it again if he's dead in two days of the contract date."

Grafph pointed a firm finger at Dylla. "Yes, ma'am. It'll be done."

She pulled a scroll from her waistcoat. "Here's a likeness of Reyne from his dossier. Make sure Nails has her people copy it exactly. Post thousands of these images in every country, in every city, and in every little village. Get her people on it immediately. Cost is no object."

Grafph took the drawing and, without unrolling it, set it down on the nearby end table. "Yes, ma'am."

"Good. I need to be in Owls Neck tomorrow night to welcome our additional support staff. Agents Harvin and Kebra will be joining us. Both of you get back to me before either of you departs. Am I clear?"

Grafph added, "Sure thing."

Tylus vigorously nodded his understanding.

"Good. I'll track down Neladith with an update. Maybe we'll get lucky, and this Mithany plans to meet up with Reyne. If that happens, with Neladith in position, we'll bring this to an end quickly. Good thinking hooking those two together."

Tylus asked, "Anything else, ma'am?"

"Yes, and this is very important. If either of you run into Quith, I want to know immediately."

"Yes, ma'am."

With her index finger, Dylla motioned wrap-it-up circles in the air. "Gather what you need, and we're out of here. This safe house is no longer needed."

Quith listened intently to every word of Dylla's revelations. She would find him, pretend to brief him, and when he let down his guard, Dylla would kill him. That part of her plan she hadn't shared with the men on the sofa. Quith knew her well and surmised why Dylla withheld her assignment to kill him from the boys. *No need to expose the low-level operatives to the fact we eat our own. Might scare the regulars and kill the recruiting efforts if word got around.*

Quith knew the plan. He would quietly disappear, never to be heard from again. Presumed killed in action. He knew it to be true because he'd done most of the self-imposed eliminations himself the past few years—on Dylla's orders. This time, she'd make certain to be the one to kill him. He committed to never let that happen—whatever it took.

Quith prepared himself for this eventuality given the alarming discovery at the bottom of the grave the night before: Daedyn's body—not Reyne's. He recalled the howling of the Great Yetgnal, the fear it evoked, the jealousy he felt at how easily it delivered fear, the connection he made to its terror-inducing howl, and how it called to him. He'd have to become like that beast and a monster to the team he had once led.

Reyne Brenton's life no longer mattered to Quith. His own survival encompassed all that he cared about. If it meant killing his own people and, by his own actions, he enabled Reyne to live, so what? Reyne Brenton could live forever, for all Quith cared. Quith's existence transformed from hunter to hunted with the unearthing of Reyne's status.

With both hands, Dylla pulled down at the bottom hem of her waistcoat. "Gentlemen, you have your assignments." She clapped her hands together and held them there, out in front. "Now would be the time to get up and get started." Her eyes opened wide, as though putting an exclamation point on her orders. "And don't forget, leave Quith to me."

His heart pounded, and beads of sweat squeezed out along the furrowed ridges along his brow. The threat of dying in the field was ever-present in his line of work, but never really gave him cause for concern. He thought too much of himself to be worried. The Dylla effect, however, did evoke a level of fear in Quith. She was an accomplished and highly skilled operative, better than him in many ways. On several occasions he'd witnessed her take down skilled Tarticans and even agents from his own world. Quith slowed his breathing like he'd been trained and flooded his mind with images of her lying dead in a field—at his hand.

See it in your mind. Make it happen.

Transforming those thoughts into reality was not going to be easy.

Quith spied her walk away and with each foot placed on the old floorboards, they creaked and screamed at him, "Dylla's coming for you." Another step forward, "Dylla's coming for you." On and on it rumbled. Although only a few short feet, it seemed like an eternity.

When she paused, reaching for the door, he took relief in the silence, however brief. Moments later, the rusty hinges squealed as though complaining at the interruption, but hidden in the noise held the promise of her departure. Dylla turned, nodded to the now standing men, and closed the door behind her. Quith let out a whoosh from his lungs. He didn't recall when he'd stopped breathing. Relief eased through him, seeing her leave.

After gathering supplies, Tylus soon followed her out the door on his mission to pick up Reyne's trail.

That left one man alone—Grafph.

Quith gave himself a few minutes. He calmed his rattled nerves, but he told himself the respite he allowed was cautionary, just in case either Dylla or Tylus circled back. Absent either's return, he slipped out a cellar window, checked the horizon for any movement, and rushed to the front door.

Quith entered the soon-to-be-abandoned Evidar meeting place. Nonchalant, he called out, "Anybody home?"

Grafph replied from the kitchen, "Quith. That you?"

"Yeah, just me. Anyone else here?"

"No. You just missed Dylla and Ty."

Grafph entered the living room, where Quith had taken up a spot on the sofa. With his back to the kitchen, Quith said, "Come. Sit down with me. Give me an update. Tell me about what Dylla had to say."

Grafph put down his glass of water on a nearby end table and plopped onto the couch.

Quith gave his teammate a pat on the shoulder. "Nice to see you."

"She just left. If you hurry, you can probably catch up with her."

Quith smiled. "Sure. I'll meet up with her soon enough. So, tell me what I missed."

"You're special. Dylla wants to fill you in herself."

Quith pushed, "Come on, it's just us two. You can tell me."

"Sorry, Quith. Got my orders."

Quith had his answer. Grafph took the side of management. Quith couldn't blame him. *Nobody wants to cross Dylla. I get it. Too bad, though, you just made the wrong choice.* In their short exchange, Quith made a life-and-death decision. His life. Grafph's death.

Quith slapped both thighs. "Going to grab a cup of water from the kitchen. You want anything?"

"No. I'm good."

Quith rose from his seat, walked around behind the sofa, and headed towards the kitchen. On his return, he slipped a dagger, hidden in his sleeve, into his waiting hand. Moving normally so as not to give away his intentions, he passed directly behind Grafph. In one smooth motion, Quith slid the blade out of its protective casement and into the base of Grafph's neck, where the space between the cervical vertebrae of the atlas and the axis left the spinal cord vulnerable. An expert operator, Quith caught it perfectly, severing Grafph's brain from its stem before the victim ever knew what killed him.

Grafph's hands flopped down, cut off from any further instructions. His chin dropped to his chest, bringing his head down with it.

A rolled-up document on an end table near Grafph's dead body caught Quith's attention. *Huh, must be the Brenton image from Dylla.* After unraveling it, he stared at the drawing for several seconds. *Not a bad likeness*, he thought, before crumbling it up and tossing it over his shoulder.

Quith then walked around to stand before the lifeless Grafph. "Can't say I'm sorry. It was you or me. You picked the wrong side." Devoid of remorse for the deceased, he wiped the blood from his blade along the corpse's pant leg. Satisfied, Quith snapped the gravity knife into its base and returned it to its familiar hiding spot up his sleeve.

He said out loud, as though Grafph might understand, "I'm thinking Tylus should be next. Then Neladith. I'll save Dylla for last."

Is That the Best You Got

Mera | Reyne

Mera snapped, "Gina!" and stepped out from the shadows not far from where she held a blade to Reyne's neck.

With the threat of death in her hands, she cracked, "What?"

Mera demanded, "Let him go."

Gina replied without removing the knife. "Why? He's a waste of my time. He'll be dead within hours of stepping foot on Evidar." She winked at Mera behind Reyne's back as if to say, *"We're on track. I'm not really gonna kill him."*

Mera offered her a barely perceptible head nod he hoped Reyne wouldn't notice and, even if he had, wouldn't understand it to mean anything. But what he did mean to say to Gina with his gesture, *"You're breaking him down, as we discussed."*

With one arm holding Reyne across the chest, the other remaining anchored to her hand gripping the knife to his throat, Gina flashed a quick thumbs-up out of Reyne's field of vision.

Mera dropped his aggressive tone and playing into the charade as reinforcement to bolster Reyne's belief in himself, he ordered Gina, "He's my last hope. Let him go."

Without moving his head, Reyne's eyes rolled up to look Mera in the face. Mera spied concern and a touch of fear on Reyne. He also noted the defiance Reyne carried was absent. Mera hoped Reyne turned a corner just as the young man promised he had only hours ago.

Mera pointed at Gina, then moved his finger and aimed his eyes to direct her to a nearby chair.

Gina acquiesced. She pulled back the blade from Reyne's gullet, moved away, and returned to her seat. "If he's what you're banking our future on, I gotta say, we're in trouble."

Reyne rubbed his Adam's apple. He looked down at his hand, inspecting a tiny smear of red along his fingertips. His head rose, and his eyes narrowed at Gina. He spat out, "Cunt."

"Ouch, that hurt so much," she mocked. "If that's all you got, farm boy—"

Gina hadn't finished her sentence when Reyne shot up from his chair, lunging at her.

Mera remained still.

Gina moved fast, her body only a blur in motion, easily evading Reyne's attack. The dark outline of her moving shape blended into one solid-looking stretched out human form, beginning from the spot where she started to where she stopped. The visual effect lasted less than half a second. It challenged the mind to follow, much less to make sense of it.

Gina stood, solid and unmoving behind Reyne. Her blade's edge pressed once again to the flesh of his exposed neck.

Reyne stuttered, "How? What the—"

Mera interrupted, "Enough already."

With sharp steel threatening to open Reyne's throat, Gina leaned forward. She spoke slowly and clearly into his ear, "Don't ever call me a cunt again. Mera nor anybody else will be quick enough to stop me from what I'll do to you. I'll assume we understand each other, farm boy." She gently nibbled at his earlobe, stepped away, and sat down. She scooched back, forcing her skirt up, taunting him.

Reyne spun an empty chair around and plopped himself down, facing his tormentor.

"Gina," Mera pleaded, "are you done?"

Gina snapped her legs closed and crossed her arms. "Yep."

While standing, Mera loomed over the two and looked down at them. "I need you both to play nice. We've got a lot to do together."

Gina retreated to her feline ways and said, in a soft voice, "Just as long as farm boy over there understands."

Reyne turned his face up to Mera's. "I'm a little worried if she's the best you got."

Mera shook his head from side to side. "She's not only the best *I have*, as you say. She's the best there is... on this world or the other."

Reyne asked, "Then why don't you send her there?"

Mera cupped his hands in front of his chest and rested his chin there. "I wish it were possible. She's never been able to even enter the Void."

Gina curled the ends of her lips up, clearly offering Reyne a fake smile.

Mera rolled his eyes. "Can we get on with this, you two? Please."

Reyne considered Gina's evaluation of his chances and concluded she was probably right about his prospects for surviving Evidar. He didn't know how to fight properly. Other than a few barroom brawls and brotherly scuffles with Daedyn, all he had were his instincts.

The need to learn from her proved more important than victory in their verbal jousting if he expected to survive his time in the dark world and return to Mithany. He settled back, accepted his subservient status, and committed to playing along until the moment training ended. But he had to know: "How'd you move so fast?"

"That's my secret, farm boy. Maybe I'll tell you one day. If you live long enough."

"If you're half as good as you think you are, and some of it can rub off on me, I'll live long enough, and then some."

Gina ran fanned out fingers through her hair. "Great to hear. Who knows, if you're a good boy, there might be other rewards for you."

Mera tipped his head back. "Gina, please stop."

With an evil grin, she responded, "Eyes only for Mithany... my ass."

Voices from outside grew louder and louder. The ever-increasing clatter from the streets reached into the Whispering Eye, almost drowning out Gina's last reply. Shouts, screams, and the sound of breaking glass flooded the tavern.

Mera ran to the nearest window facing the street. "Dammit, we don't need this now. It looks like a riot is about to break loose."

Gina jumped up. "What's going on? What do you see?"

Mera turned back to the two of them. "Looks like a battle between anti- and pro-Covenant supporters. My guess, Temple loyalists know why the Thuggery left the Whispering Eye unmolested. Bet your last coin on the fact they're here to violate it in the worst way."

Gina shook her head. "Makes sense. Deny the opposition its favorite honey hole."

Reyne stood. "Should we help?"

Mera rubbed at his facial stubble. "No, we're not staying and doubt we're ever coming back here. We need to put Teth behind us. I've always enjoyed whatever time I could spend in the Whispering Eye, but its days are numbered. There's a back door. Let's get out of here while we still can."

With Mera in the lead, the three made their way down the stairs to the first floor. At the bottom of the stairs, he shot out his arm to halt Reyne where he stood. Before them, crazed men and women, shouting, waving clubs, whipping chains about, streamed in through the door in rapid single file. Twenty or more Thuggery supporters launched themselves from their bar stools and charged at the brigands bursting through the small portal.

Bar regulars, called to action, punched and sliced at each of the destruction-minded party-crashers. More and more intruders kept coming. Interlopers quickly outnumbered patrons. Men and women struggled in close hand-to-hand street fighting. Several tumbled down and were buried underfoot. Blood flowed, covering the dirty wooden floors. The brawlers skidded and slid at each other through the red discharge covering the Whispering Eye's walls and floorboards. Invaders and defenders crammed into the room, wildly attacking each other. Arms flailed in every direction. Screams of pain, shouts of anger, and life-ending threats from both sides bounced off the walls. The din of battle spilled out the broken windows, the slit of a door, and filled every inch inside the violated, tightly packed Whispering Eye. Inside the constricted space, none had room to maneuver.

Reyne, Mera, and Gina pushed and shoved their way to the rear entrance. Other would-be rats fleeing the sinking ship overwhelmed the tight area around the back door, blocking the trio's escape and preventing anyone access to the rear exit.

From over his shoulder, Reyne caught sight of a torch. Its arc in flight carried it sailing over the melee. Then another. When a third torch flew over the heads of the embattled and hit a shelf full of rotgut, flames exploded. The fire raced across spilled accelerant, biting into the wood, climbing up the walls. The smell of burnt wood filled his nostrils as the fire spread quickly. Dark smoke threatened to overtake the room.

For a brief second, Reyne imagined, hidden in flames, the hedonistic Firaché unleashed inside the Whispering Eye: cavorting, fornicating, and destroying whatever they needed to consume in their collective quest to hang on to life. The thought swiftly passed.

Reyne, following Mera's lead, tried to push his way out the door. "Please," Reyne shouted, "I need to get through." Nobody reacted.

Packed in front and being pushed from behind, someone shoved Reyne into Gina, shouting, "Back off, dickhead. We're all tryin' to get out."

Reyne said nothing in response to the anonymous voice. His and every other body pressed closer and closer together. Panic spread as quickly as the flames. Attackers and defenders abandoned their causes. They all shared a new goal: to get out before the fire enveloped everyone.

"Enough of this," Gina yelled and blurred through those in her way, dropping each in quick succession. Reyne's sight could barely keep up with her movements. Like a shadow, with substance and force, Gina whipped through the obstructive crowd with dire consequences to anyone in her way. A path to safety created, Gina shouted through the noise and the smoke, "Come on, we need to get out of here! Now!"

Reyne felt Gina grab his hand. She pulled him along, stepping over the unconscious she'd disposed of. Reyne followed her and Mera, when suddenly he stopped. He yanked his hand free from hers and gripped Gina's shoulder, spinning her around. "Those people you knocked out, we leave 'em here, they're gonna die."

She turned back around and yelled over her shoulder, "They will. But you won't."

Mera called out, "Gina, get one and pull him into the alley."

"What, now I'm saving lives?" and she grabbed onto the collar of one of her unconscious victims. Reyne and Mera had already done the same, backing out through the rear of the Whispering Eye, each with their quarry in tow as bodies flooded past them.

Three bodies standing and three unceremoniously unaware of their position on the ground made it into the back alley, escaping the life-threatening blaze spreading rapidly. Everyone else was racing away as quickly as possible.

Reyne, Mera, and Gina looked at each other through the expansive smolder filling the alley. Reyne turned to watch smoke billow through the doorway while a constant flow of frantic escapees continued rushing out, appearing like a magic trick of people materializing from out of nowhere through the dense smoke. With his embedded concern for others, Reyne looked through the opening, trying to spot anybody close enough to yank out of danger, but the heat, the blackened fumes, and the rush of bodies pushed him back. A return trip to save the unconscious lying on the floor, if not yet trampled to death, was all but impossible. The others Gina had removed from his path to freedom by rendering them temporarily senseless would all die. Three would live. Reyne thought these semi-innocent people didn't deserve death at his expense.

Dark smoke rise over the tops of the canyon-like walls of the alley, filling the sky where the Whispering Eye once satisfied all who entered. Some entered the unique watering hole to escape; others to revel in its companionship; some for the pleasures it offered; and still others came to bury their sorrows. Regardless of the reason—they came. *Not anymore.* Reyne lamented its demise, and those still inside condemned to death. The agonizing and harrowing screams of those trapped inside billowed into the alley with ever-decreasing volume. It was a haunting sound Reyne expected to live in his thoughts until the day of his own demise.

The flow of hopeful escapees stopped.

Teth's infamous hole-in-the-wall reminded Reyne of the Forest Maiden Inn. A similar place in Hensdale he loved and hoped to see again. At first, it brought a smile to his thoughts, but almost immediately transformed into sorrow, remembering the nights spent there with Daedyn.

The Night of the Three Sisters came to mind, and Reyne reflected how it began at Hensdale's own Forest Maiden Inn. A special evening he and Daedyn experienced together, as three sisters shared two brothers between them through the night. Daedyn frequently reminisced how perfect that night had been and how special it was to have shared it as brothers. The reverie of that wondrous night no longer held its edge without Daedyn to share the memory with. Bitter, he tasted the black bile of sadness at the realization the Forest Maiden Inn, absent Daedyn, would hold memories as dark as its dimly lit walls and would forever deliver to his heart a burning emptiness reminiscent of the flames engulfing the Whispering Eye. With the fiery destruction of Teth's favored gathering place for criminals—never to be enjoyed again—as inspiration, his mind burned memories of the Forest Maiden to the ground.

He pulled himself out of his thoughts and prepared to lash out at Gina. Behind Mera and Gina, a dozen or so Temple faithful were rushing towards him. In the narrow alley, Reyne shot out his arm, pointing and gesturing for Mera and Gina to turn around.

One of the onrushing attackers yelled out, "Get them! Don't let them escape."

Mera turned, lifted both arms high, and yelled out, "Wait!"

But they kept coming.

Reyne wondered how a religious person dedicated to the Covenant of Absolute Human Obligations, founded on doing no harm to another human being, could throw it all away in a misbegotten effort to preserve that very way of life.

Gina, there one instant, gone before his eyes the next, stole his attention. She charged at the incoming rabble. At blinding speeds, Gina quickly disposed of the presumed leader and two others.

A rock flew past her, striking Reyne in the side of the head.

Triggered by the blow, or perhaps the pain it caused, the doors to the cage holding back Reyne's inner rage snapped open. His eyes drew in tight. A murderous sneer escaped from his monster within, lighting up his face. Without thinking, having ceded control of his actions, Reyne's inner beast lunged into battle.

A malevolence, born of the agony tormenting him, had been unbridled with the blow to his head. Unquenchable, emotional pain had been building, roiling beneath the surface like a volcano under pressure, ready to explode. Now, it had been set free. He'd lost all sense of himself in the moment and lacked any control over what he'd unleashed. It had been feeding off feelings molesting his soul.

Furious at Daedyn's murder—it fed.

Angry Mithany had been torn from him—it fed.

Incensed at Baide's brutal slaying—it fed.

Crazed from watching his biological mother ripped from his life—it fed.

The malevolence inside Reyne born of recent events grew strong, nourished by pain, yet all the while restrained from acting by his love of a simple life. A life with Daedyn at his side. A life with Mithany as his bride. A mother he never knew that loved him. But now, with its jailer weakened, the monster within escaped to freedom.

Whatever part of Reyne seized control, his body charged at a large man waving a cudgel. Wild, Reyne lunged at the man. A club struck hard against Reyne's arm. Pain shot through him, but whatever now controlled him pushed it aside. At full speed, he rammed his head into the man's chest, knocking the wind out of the large attacker. Without hesitating, Reyne pummeled the man's face. He beat him down to the ground as the man collapsed.

Absent any thought or plan, like a rabid dog, Reyne raced to his next victim. A woman with hatred and fury in her eyes swiped at Reyne. Claws attached at the end of her fingers aimed to eviscerate him. He easily batted them away. Reyne punched her hard in the center of her face. With a crunching sound, she dropped.

Breathing heavily, his eye shot from side to side. Crazed, he took off after the only man still standing—the first to appear in his sights.

The monster he'd let out wanted blood.

It didn't matter whose.

Just another body to taste the fury his psyche demanded of release.

The beast within howled for vengeance to quench its pain.

With curled fists ready to strike, he pulled his arm back to deliver a powerful blow running at the target, when Gina plowed into Reyne from the side, knocking him off his feet.

The force of the blow brought him back to his senses. Laying on the ground, Reyne shook his head. "What'd you do that for?" he asked Gina, standing over him.

"You were about to hit Mera. What's wrong with you?"

Scrunchy-faced and confused, Reyne didn't believe Gina's account. "Mera? What? Me hit him? You're crazy."

Gina looked away from Reyne and over to Mera. "What's up with him?"

Mera leaned in close to Gina, "Not sure. He did this once before."

She brushed it off. "Well, not sure about all that, but he fights better than I thought. Took out a big guy in no time. We just might have something to work with."

Mera told her, "We'll have to be careful. I'm not sure what's going on with him. One minute he's worried about innocent people dying, and the next, he's wildly attacking anyone he lays eyes on. Seems we have two different Reynes."

A Call for Justice

Hensdale: 3rd Day of the Harvest Moon

Arek

Arek woke to darkness.

Cricket chirps, croaking frogs, and the occasional rustle from off in the forest filled the air. A chill pulled at the exposed parts of his legs, peeking out from under the blanket. Brenal's cold corpse robbed his own body of heat under the woolen covering. He looked into Brenal's empty, lifeless, open eyes. Arek's head jerked back sharply from the near cheek-to-cheek encounter.

Cold, weak, tired but mostly heartbroken, Arek struggled to sit up, wrapping the covering around his shoulders. One hand extended out from under the protection to gently pull on Brenal's eyelids, closing them for the last time.

The strange-looking device at Brenal's side, a tube attached to a needle in the dead man's arm and the one Arek previously pulled from his own, told the story. How he arrived at the country doctor's doorstep for that series of events, he hadn't a clue. But from what he gathered, the scene hinted at Brenal saving him at the cost of his own life. He couldn't be certain, but it sure looked that way.

Sadness gave way to anger as Arek recalled being tied to a chair. He recalled two men before being rendered unconscious. He recalled Neladith admitting to him she killed Daedyn. He recalled being stripped naked—tortured—abused—bleeding—left for dead. The terror of the wolf pack crept into his memory.

Every inch of his frame induced messages of pain carried on ravaged nerves. He endured, offering a prayer to the gods, not for somehow surviving Neladith's efforts to kill him, but for Brenal, that his friend would be welcome into the Community of Souls. Not a religious man, yet in confronting death, Arek discovered a part of himself that believed. As though Brenal might hear him, out loud, he prayed. But sorrow invaded his soul and closed his throat. He pushed through it, and enduring both physical and emotional pain, Arek rasped out:

> *Father of Light.*
> *Mother of Earth.*
> *You are divine.*
> *Hollid Brenal is but a transient vessel*
> *For your holy gifts.*
> *Grant him freedom in death,*
> *To forever and for all time*
> *Be welcome into the Community of Souls,*
> *In the never-ending Circle of Life.*

Arek's state of dehydration denied him an offering of tears to his friend. He concluded with the traditional Signum Circulus of the Temple faith by circling his thumb around his heart, finishing with his palm pressed against the center of his chest.

When Arek last evoked the Signum Circulus, the Sign of the Circle, his mother had passed away. Tears evaded him then too, but for altogether different reasons. He took solace standing at the family's burial site at the time in offering his mother the religious farewell gesture. His sister, Mithany, did not. Mithany never forgave their mother, but he did, long ago. It fell to him to send the soul of the much-loved country doctor, his friend, into the hands of Mother Earth and hopefully onto the Community of Souls.

Wrapped in the blanket Brenal thoughtfully left to him, Arek contemplated the meaning of death, Hollid Brenal's and his own. Arek gave in to the demands of the aches calling out to him and let slip the blanket, exposing himself to the air's chilling effects.

With his eyes, he probed the damage.

With his fingertips, he explored the repairs Brenal attempted.

In horror, he saw blood caked everywhere on his body.

Pain pulsing with each heartbeat ached across his face and drove into his legs.

Fingers probed his cheeks. His once smooth skin, torn and ripped. A thin layer of dried blood cracked and gave way to the force of pressure everywhere he touched.

Unable or unwilling to continue, his arms flopped to his side.

He pitied himself. He pitied Brenal's death.

And then he thought of Neladith.

She gave birth to his will. She fueled his desire to go on.

Anger surged through him. He had to survive. Not for his own sake, but for Brenal's. Arek burned for justice. It consumed him. He had to survive to see justice administered to the self-proclaimed murderess. He now had two reasons to live: Mithany the other.

Arek tried to stand, but collapsed at the point of putting pressure on his right leg. Deep in his thigh, agony screamed into his mind. Brenal had sutured the wounds, but it bit deep into the muscle. With his battle against the pain lost—awareness slipped away.

The More the Merrier

Quith

Selundra Quith arrived in Owls Neck later than he wanted to in order that he might observe the influx of new Evidar agents to Tartica. To see their faces. To know who to add to his kill list. Dylla mentioned Harvin and Kebra, but he had to be certain.

Light reflected off the waxing Harvest Moon hanging over Tartica, providing magnitudes of illumination more than the ever-present darkness Quith's home world ever afforded him.

He settled near the inn, a place he shared breakfast with Dylla several times. From the safety of the tree line nearby, Quith sequestered himself within hearing range only a few dozen yards from his prey—Dylla and the extra agents she promised.

They had arrived before him. He risked a quick peek, lifting his head just above the limits of the forest undergrowth. *Good, the newcomers are still naked. Means they must have just transfigured. I only missed the arrival by minutes.*

Dylla made up the entire newly-arriving-agents welcoming committee. "You've both been to this world before and nothing about it has changed. Yes, there is upheaval in the cities, not as much in the outlying areas. That both helps, and hurts, with our efforts. It will be easier for you to blend in, but harder because of your target's ability to fade into the crowds."

Quith knew them both. The woman, Kebra, took the folded pile Dylla handed her and began to dress. The man, named Harvin, did the same.

Kebra raised the black top over her head, stretched her arms through the sleeves, popped her face through the neck hole and slid the skin-hugging fabric over her breasts.

Harvin pulled up his undergarments over his exposed buttocks and guided one leg then the other into his pants.

Quith was acquainted with them both from several previous assignments, most recently in the town of Dead Horse only a few months ago, where they worked as a team to take out an older man thought to be a Tartican Tweener like Reyne Brenton.

Her pants secured, Kebra stood up straight, crossed her hands behind her back, and directed her question to Dylla. "We've been briefed before we left. Any changes? We've been told the primary target is this Reyne Brenton, and the secondary is Selundra Quith. One of our own."

Quith's gut clenched. To hear it out loud, his own people aiming to kill him angered him. *I must've really pissed off the Devil's Blacksmith pretty good. He gave them my termination papers before sending them here. Dylla kept it from my crew, but the Devil's Blacksmith put it out there. He must want me dead, real bad. You can kiss my ass, Blacksmith.*

The constant struggle for survival defined life on his world. In the end, Dylla Weisner and the Devil's Blacksmith made sure Tartica's version of Earth proved much the same to Quith.

All my accomplishments. All I've done in the name of altering Earths two time-lines. All I've done for you, Dylla, for the Devil's Blacksmith, and what, no reprieve? Sure Dylla, you got your orders. Yeah, I botched Reyne's execution. Yeah, I made the call. Yeah, I made a mistake. Now you're going to make me pay. I don't think so, Dylla. I got other plans.

Dylla vigorously rubbed her hands together, addressing the new arrivals.

Not nice and warm like it is at home. Good, hope you freeze.

"You two are exceptionally skilled hunters, both known for your tracking abilities. You're going to need those skills. Including myself, Grafph, Neladith, and Tylus, we now have six experienced agents after Reyne Brenton. I've pulled in Nails and her Thuggery with an open contract on him as well. Grafph should be on his way to deliver the contract to Nails as we speak. But going after Quith, it's only us three. Even with his situational operations training and real-world experience, his chances of surviving the three of us are slim."

Harvin, lacing up his boot, looked up at Dylla. "Understood, ma'am, but just to be sure, Reyne Brenton's the primary target."

"Yes. Reyne is who we're after. We'll get to Quith soon enough. But, if the opportunity presents itself, while you're pursuing the primary, take Quith out if you can. Don't waste time on him. If it's an easy kill, take it. I don't need to remind you how important Reyne is to our leader's operation. He has to be eliminated with all due haste. Quith screwed up. He ordered the wrong man killed. Then compounded the problem by reporting Reyne dead. His mistake sent reverberations through the Damus's calculations."

Quith accepted it as a compliment to see the disbelief written on Kebra's face. "That's a surprise. In all the times I've worked with him, I would have never thought he would be so careless."

But when the leader replied, Quith heard resolve in Dylla's voice. "Is it going to be a problem, Agent Kebra?"

Quith knew the threat behind Dylla's words and assumed Kebra did as well.

"Not at all, ma'am. Just making an observation,"

Dylla's eyes pulled in tight. "You two have slept together more than a few times. If there is going to be any hesitancy, I need to know now."

Quith's mind drifted back to the times they spent naked together in an outpost village on Tartica the locals called Dead Horse. Kebra's pale, smooth skin, sharp, pleasant facial features, and lithe body brought a smile to him as he watched her. *What a waste I've got to kill you.*

Kebra snapped to attention and Quith heard in her reply the serious, military cadence reminiscent of their training days of long ago. "No, ma'am. Plenty of good lays out there. Easy enough to find another."

"Good. And what about you, Harvin?"

Harvin, having finished tying his bootlaces, stood. "Who me, ma'am? No. I never slept with him."

"Not what I meant, but good to know. Now, is your past association with Quith going to be a problem?"

"No, ma'am. Not going to be an issue. Never liked the guy much. He's a self-assured, arrogant prick. It'll be a pleasure to be the one to finish him."

Fuck you too, Harvin. Maybe you'll be next.

Dylla's voice interrupted Quith's thoughts. "There are more than enough of us to complete a simple assignment. The target is an unassuming businessman running a nut farm. It shouldn't be all that hard. You just have to find him. That's the challenge. I'll assume you've been shown the image of him I created for the Architect during your pre-transfiguration briefing."

Harvin nodded his understanding while Kebra gave Dylla verbal confirmation.

Dylla wagged a finger. "But beware of Meratoruc—they call him Mera here, and he's almost certainly traveling with our target, so that will complicate matters. That's why I'm changing things up from what you've been briefed on. You two stay together. Work as a team. Watch each other's backs. Harvin, you take lead. Kebra, that means you do everything he says."

In unison, they replied, "Yes, ma'am."

Harvin's eyes moved with his head making it clear to Quith that the muscled, tall, hulking specimen looked Kebra up and down. *Dylla, putting that guy in charge, big mistake.* Based on Kebra's reaction, it seemed obvious to Quith she didn't care for Harvin's plans for applying his authority.

"Don't think that's what Dylla means, dickhead," Kebra said, and punched Harvin in the stomach. While much smaller than her partner, she put everything her sinewy arm could generate into the blow. All five foot two of her stepped back and smiled.

Harvin broke a grin without otherwise reacting. He neither looked Kebra's way nor moved a single muscle in response or acknowledged in any manner he'd been struck.

The Kebra I knew would have crushed his ball sack. That torso jab barely registered. He could snap you in half in a heartbeat. Kebra, either you're slipping or I'm guessing you're doing him, and you need his balls intact to deliver the goods. Ha!

Dylla stepped forward, her face inches from Harvin's chest. Her voice dropped and Quith heard the soft words that told anyone who knew Dylla her tone offered a command: listen carefully if you value your life. "I don't care what consenting adults do, but your authority doesn't go that far, Harvin. Maybe on past operations I turned my back to such things, but this isn't that kind of assignment. What we do here is dead serious. Am I clear?"

Quith heard Harvin's deep, testosterone-fueled voice. "Only joking, ma'am. My apologies to you both."

In Quith's assessment, Harvin demonstrated intelligence higher than most, but observed that the man's cocky attitude often led him to take liberties both personally and in the field of operations. *It will be your undoing one day, Harvin.*

Dylla began to pace. "I'm going to join the effort in two days if Reyne is still breathing. I'll set up at the inn behind us. I expect results before that. Do we understand each other?"

"Yes, ma'am."

"Tylus has gone north. Neladith is following another lead. Grafph is headed to meet with Nails in Teth. I'm sending you two on a southeastern path. You pick anything up, use a local and get word back to me. But first, we've got to be sure the Thuggery has a contract out on Reyne Brenton. Stop in with Nails and take this image of Reyne with you. If Grafph beat you to it, great. If not, you two are insurance. Then head towards Tandure. From there, on to Jarouhar. Check out every town, village and city along the way, but stay out of the melee. There's a lot of chaos in the cities."

Quith heard enough. They had their plans, he had his—kill them all before they get the chance to do the same to him.

Having learned where each of them would be traveling, Quith formulated a new strategy.

Tylus, you'll be next. I can't say you'll be first; Grafph's already dead. Then back to Owls Neck for Dylla and after that, southeast for Kebra and Harvin. Neladith I'll save for last.

Like a snake, he crawled silently along the ground and once safely out of the trio's earshot and out of their line of sight, Quith stood, brushed himself off, and set off north to hunt down his next victim.

SHAME & DETERMINATION

Hensdale: 4th Day of the Harvest Moon

Arek

Arek woke outside the home of the deceased Hollid Brenal. How long he'd been out, a few minutes, the next evening, Arek had no way of knowing. His body shaking from both the cold and being pushed beyond its limits, he rested a spell before turning his attention and his dwindling physical resources to Brenal's corpse.

As best he could accommodate the Circle of Life rites, Arek sacrificed the blanket left to him by Brenal and settled it over the body as an impromptu burial shroud. Not traditional by any means, but the best Arek could manage. It meant a lot to the now freezing, exhausted Arek to provide his friend at least a small measure of the religious traditions Brenal followed in life.

With determination, he crawled up over the porch's four stairs. In his current condition, it might as well have been the same as summitting the Razors. Triumphant, he reached the wooden floorboards of the front porch. He rolled onto his back. Agony and a biting chill pulled him away from accepting respite's embrace. His right thigh thundered misery with every beating pulse. He wanted to scream. To release the pain. Yet he feared he couldn't waste the energy.

The mental capacity to withstand pain had been the only gift his mother bequeath him. He pulled, crawled, wiggled, fought back misery, torment, excruciating hot barbs driven deep into both his thigh and his mind, to cross over the threshold of the front door and with one hand, gripped the latch. Expending all his reserves, Arek made it to Brenal's bed. He crawled under the old doctor's sheets and almost gave out.

After resting a bit, still weak and burning up, Arek began shaking with chills. The bedsheets had become soaked in sweat. Fever pulled every ounce of moisture from him. His mouth was dry, his lips parched and cracked; he needed water.

While his legs objected to his efforts to move them, his arms, although bruised, worked perfectly fine. He grabbed a corner of the bedspread and used it to wipe the beads from his forehead. In so doing, Arek's fingers discovered the dents, cuts, and gouges of the once-smooth skin his youthful face formerly displayed. Coagulated, pasty, sticky clumps of blood—scabs in the making—pooled over many of the cuts, punctures, and gashes. Several other open wounds oozed blood, or worse. Nauseated at the finding, Arek fought against the demand to wretch.

Dried blood patches caked on his flesh. Pain emanated from his shoulders and face. His thigh throbbed with each contraction the life-giving muscle in his chest pulsed out. He pulled back the covering to expose his body. The damage inflicted upon it horrified him. Arek ran his fingers over the threads Brenal used to close the wounds. Revulsion filled his eyes. Disgust rose at the sight of his thigh, missing a chunk ripped from him. An orange-red discoloration surrounding the wound rose on his flesh. Similar bruises covered much of his body.

His thigh throbbed, warm to the touch. He pressed on the slightly raised, discolored area around the wound. A thin, milky liquid escaped between the sutures as he exerted pressure. As much as it hurt, he struggled to force newly accumulating pus from the site as best he could bear. Several nearby deep punctures in his thigh gave up their hidden, dead blood cells sacrificed fighting off the apparent infection. He wondered, *Brenal must have medications somewhere in his house for this sort of thing. Where?*

Again, chills shot through him. He began to shake vigorously. Covered in sweat, exposed to the air, he was freezing and burning up at the same time. In his current condition he knew he wouldn't survive long without proper medication, food, or water.

Arek sat up with the help of his arms. He swung both legs over the side of the bed. The leg missing a slice of thigh muscle reached for the floor. With two hands on the mattress, he tried to stand. Instantly, agony shot up his leg. Pain exploded in his brain. *"FUCK!"*

Fighting through the misery, he placed his other foot on the floor. Tested its response to just a little pressure. It hurt like hell. But he discovered it could bear weight. Palms flat on the bed, he pushed off, coming to stand on one leg. *Yes!* It proved a momentary victory. An instant later, he collapsed. Pain reduced him to a heap, like a pile of discarded sheets.

Arek fought back the pain and dragged himself to where Brenal kept his clothes. The last thing he needed—another injury. He worried about the only part of his body to escape physical harm, his manhood. At the thought of Neladith riding him, her eyes fluttering, her head thrown back, pumping up and down in his lap, against his will, he raged against the floor. "AGHHH!" he screamed, pounding his fists on the treestone woodblocks.

He hated himself for being unable to control his primeval response.

He hated himself for giving her pleasure.

He hated himself as she rode him up and down.

He hated himself when she climaxed because of him.

But more than anything, he hated himself because he took pleasure from her abuse.

The beating, the pain, the arousal, and at the instant she slid him inside her—so warm, so wet, so tight—he wanted to explode in ecstasy. Only his unyielding love for Mithany kept him from letting himself release it. He forgave his mother years ago, although, in the here and now, he hated her for doing this to him. For making him, as a child, forever crave her love only to be given physical abuse and anger as her only attention. The saving grace he took away from the abuse he suffered at Neladith's hands: he never gave away information about Mithany or Reyne. With iron willpower, he swallowed his anger at Neladith, but self-hatred refused to give up its firm grip on him.

Through the day he searched and gathered the items within the confines of Brenal's home he needed for survival. Agony remained his constant companion. Wherever his damaged flesh pressed against the surface, hot spikes drilled into him. With determination as his intransigent ally, he found water and bread, a bottle of alcohol, and medication, but crutches were nowhere to be found.

In small doses at first, he drizzled alcohol on the sutured area of his thigh. The alcohol burned, bubbled, and foamed as the healing liquid's induced pain shot blinding light through his brain. As it washed over his skin, screams fled his throat. Wherever his lacerations exposed him to infection, he repeated the procedure. He repeated the screams.

Following a short rest, Arek swallowed a measure of powder from a jar marked 'For Infections,' washing it down with the water he had left. Exhausted, Arek flopped into bed, pulling several layers of covers over his ravaged body.

Images of his time tied to a chair in the basement with Neladith swept through his mind. He ran through several scenarios of how to capture Neladith. How to bring her to justice. A bigger problem than he could tackle just yet. He drifted off, not knowing if he'd ever find a way.

WHAT THE HEART WANTS

Mithany

Spetzer and Trell trailed behind Mithany and Neladith by a good twenty paces. Mithany hadn't given the two men much attention over the past few days since the four began their trek north to find Daedyn. Neladith, Spetzer, and Trell searched for Daedyn. Mithany kept her secret from the others, her heart set on finding Reyne.

The Salmon Moon had waxed and waned, giving birth to the Harvest Moon and the onset of autumn across Tartica. A mist born of the tiniest of droplets began to fall, stealing the sun and its warmth from the four travelers along a barren stretch of road between Hensdale and Topak—a large town in the center of the Peoples Republic of Kantos.

Mithany set a leisurely pace. Neladith asked, "I know you said it before, but are you sure Daedyn headed north? We've been walking for days and we've barely come across anybody."

Mithany, more cheerful than a grieving fiancée should have been, replied, "That's what he said. He probably just wanted to be alone with his thoughts. If we don't catch up with him by Topak, we'll figure something else out or go back. There's not really too many places he could have gone if he came this way. There're a few smaller villages we can check out."

"If you say so."

Mithany ran her fingers through her dark brown long strands and inclined her head back. "You know, I'm more concerned we haven't seen Arek yet. He should have caught up with us by now. Those two chuckleheads behind us have been marking trees for Arek to follow."

With a tease in her tone, Neladith patted Mithany on the back. "I've known your brother only a short time, but my guess is he's holed up somewhere with a pretty, young plaything keeping him all tied up."

Mithany stopped combing her hair with her fingers. "Doesn't it bother you he might be with another woman?"

Neladith waved both palms forward through empty air. "Oh, no. He doesn't have a hold on me. It's just sex. I hope you don't mind me saying. He's your brother and all."

Mithany placed her hand over her heart. "If it doesn't bother you, it doesn't bother me. But I'm a little worried about him. Sometimes people take advantage of his good nature."

"Mithany, I'm sorry to admit I've taken advantage of him, too. But it was so satisfying I couldn't help myself," she said offering Mithany a knowing, one-eyed wink. "Let's not talk about that. I'm sure you don't want to hear about your brother's sexual proclivities."

"Yep, we can definitely skip that part." Mithany had no desire to hear the details of her brother in the arms of another woman.

"You've been in such a positive place these past few days. Don't let Arek bring you down. You know, I've been surprised. You're more upbeat than I would have guessed. Losing Reyne and all that you've had to endure."

"He's in my heart," Mithany said, her hand still resting on the center of her chest. "I think of him all the time. Thinkin' of him makes me happy. I don't focus on losing him. I have him here. The heart wants what it wants, to be happy."

From the point Reyne's hand slipped through hers, loss and depression gripped her heart. She broke that night when he walked out of her life. The uncertainty of when or if he'd ever return played on her thoughts. Reyne promised he'd return. A promise based on nothing but wishes and even if he did keep it, when he'd come back remained open-ended—a week, a month, a year, longer. With his life in danger, Mera took him from her. She needed reassurance he'd return, and no one existed to give it to her. Her inner voice never spoke the words, but her soul understood what needed to be done—she had to find him or forever exist, absent the man she loved, a broken woman.

The subliminal processes in her brain began protecting Mithany from the deep morass threatening to consume her by finding a pathway to deal with the intense loss. Not a mindful effort, given the unawareness of her own subconscious rebuilding her psyche in order to secure a means of surviving without Reyne's presence in her life. The consequence of a broken mind brought on by frequent childhood beatings from the one person who should have showered her in unconditional love. Her child's heart, body, and soul damaged beyond a youngster's ability to comprehend or handle, all those years ago created its own subconscious mechanisms to cope. And now, losing Reyne, Mithany, unaware of her own mind's efforts to protect herself, sought relief in forcing a more cheerful persona to the surface.

If absent the childhood beatings and if she'd grown up in a healthy, loving environment, she might have been able to deal with losing Daedyn and Reyne in the same night. She wasn't that lucky.

The sorrow-filled, empty husk of a woman who stood vigil at the Brenton family gravesite had, in the past few days, shed her morose chrysalis. She emerged a cheerful, optimistic, forward-focused, adult female feeding off the hope of tracking down Reyne, much to the credit of a process she didn't control, understand, or even have any awareness of—her subconscious protecting itself.

Neladith gave Mithany a knowing nod. "You are an exceptional young woman, a petite powerhouse. Stronger than I would be at losing the man I loved. You surprise me."

Mithany watched Neladith's face shift to a suspicious-looking grin when Neladith said, "I have to know your secret."

"I'm just happy you and I have become friends these past few days. We didn't get off on the right foot. As for those pieces of ourselves we hide from the world, I'm sure you have a few of your own."

"We all have skeletons in the closet, I suppose."

Mithany wondered if Neladith might share one of hers. "Like those red eyes of yours? I've never seen that color eyes in all my years. Is there some story behind them?"

"It would be nice if I had a special something I could share with you to bond over. I got nothing. As for my eyes, well, I have a condition. There are others like me, but we're rare. These peepers of mine won't stay red. I've been told they'll go back to their natural color soon enough."

"They're very pretty."

"That's so nice. The iris of my eyes is usually black. The redness in the white part will fade and go back to white. For people like me, this red-eye thing comes on under certain conditions."

Mithany blushed and admitted, "I like them this way. They look just a wee bit less red than when I first met you back in Owls Neck."

"It's the first time mine have popped red, so I'm not sure how long they'll take to go back. Arek didn't tell you? I explained it all to him."

"No, he never said a thing. Then again, we haven't had too much time together lately."

Neladith patted Mithany's shoulder and in a cheery voice said, "Sorry about that. I've kept him from you. It's like he's gone too."

"We do spend a lot of time together at the shoppe, but things changed after I fell in love with Reyne. I will always love my brother with all my heart. It's just that things were different between me and Arek, before Reyne." Thinking of her fiancé warmed her heart, confident she would find him. Memories of her life before Reyne, much of it spent with Arek, remained hidden away inside the broken half of her fractured mind.

With a happy face Mithany rambled on, "What about you? Ever lose anyone close?"

Neladith didn't answer for a few seconds, then said, "I can't say I've lost anyone that I cared about other than the one who I told you about that looks just like you. Other than her, haven't been many people in my life I've been close to. I've had a few in my sights, but they're gone now."

"That's kinda sad. I'm not judging... just saying."

"Not at all. I enjoy my life. Love what I do. The places it takes me. For me, up to this point, it's been great. Though, I have to say, I'm surprised how much I've grown to like this little world you live in. Hensdale is nice. Owls Neck too. It's so peaceful around here. Not like where I come from. Maybe when this is all over, I'll stick around. Get to know you better. I think we'd be very good together."

"You mind if I ask you something, Neladith? How old are you?"

"Really can't say. Nobody ever told me. But, if I had to guess, younger than you."

Mithany, always curious of the childhood experiences of others, given her own, shrugged. "You don't have a birthday? That means you never had a birthday party. That makes me sad. Did you have any fun as a kid?"

"Yeah. Of course. But I spent a lot of time practicing stuff. Grownups always worried about making sure you're ready to be an adult someday. Preparing you to do adult things."

Shaking her head from side to side, Mithany observed, "I can't get over how cheery you are... all the time. You want to know my secrets; I'd sure like to know yours. You're always so happy. Is it all fun and games?"

Neladith kept walking alongside Mithany and gave a backwards-angled head nod. "Speaking of fun and games, what about those two behind us? You know them well. What would you think if I hooked up with one of them?"

Mithany didn't think anything unusual about the question. The way of life under the Covenant's yoke of rebuilding Earth's population—a founding principle of civilization—sex always ever-present across Tartica, especially to those in their early twenties or in their last years as teens having to deal with raging hormones and new to the copulation game. Mithany gave it some thought and considered Neladith's suggestion an open invitation to get Spetzer off her back.

"Actually, you'd be doing me a huge favor. I think Spetzer stays behind us so he can look at my ass all day." Mithany laughed.

Neladith raised and lowered her eyebrows in quick succession and chuckled. "I've admired it myself. You got a great ass. As for Spetzer, consider it done. He might be an asshole like you said, but he's kinda cute." In a sing-song way, her head swaying from side to side, she skipped alongside of Mithany and chanted, "Neladith's gonna get lucky tonight."

Mithany, watching Neladith prance around, pondered, *That girl's always so cheery. How can anybody be like that all the time? She's either the happiest person I ever met or she's a psychopath... And why is she looking at my butt?*

KILLERS JUST THE SAME

Mera | Reyne

For several days, Mera guided the trio through uncharted backwoods trails, determined to prevent Reyne from realizing their intended destination. The trio made several stops along the way, setting up camp each night and engaging Reyne in training exercises by the day. Mera set out every morning, scouting ahead and gathering intelligence. Of paramount concern to Mera: Had Evidar agents discovered the ruse of Reyne's death? For Reyne's protection, Mera desperately needed to find out just how well the deception held. How much time Reyne had left on Tartica depended on how well Mithany and the others maintained the sham of a dead Reyne. Only one place gave Mera the opportunity to access the much-needed information. They'd arrived at a spot not far from Hensdale. Dangerous for certain if Reyne realized where they were, but a necessary risk nonetheless.

Along an isolated forest clearing in the middle of a remote area of Kantos, twenty-five miles from Reyne's orchard and a mile in from the commonly traveled road between Hensdale and Topak, Mera selected the day's training location to meet his purpose. With every extra hour of skills-building, Reyne's chances of surviving Evidar improved.

At Mera's insistence, Gina pushed Reyne constantly through combat preparedness exercises. The head games continued unabated, keeping Reyne angry with Gina and his mind off Mithany. In the open glade near where they'd set up separate sleeping tents, instructor and apprentice progressed through their paces.

Mera left the pair to drill while he attended to other pressing issues—issues which he failed to share with Reyne. Known to Gina, but withheld from Reyne, Mera strategically located the training site near enough to afford him access to Mithany, Arek, and Brenal.

Mera had engaged Evidar agents in a game of chicken. Holding Reyne on course, training, improving his skills, pressing Reyne's mind to deliver death to another—in spite of the young man's core belief in the sanctity of life—training for as long as possible before Evidar agents came after him. Sooner or later, operatives from the dark world would figure out Reyne lived, and then, and only then, would Mera ship Reyne off to Evidar in whatever state of preparedness he'd achieved.

Bird calls died on the damp breeze. Mist, the tiniest of droplets, kept Reyne's hair matted to his head. Over time, his clothes became soaked, and the cool, cloudy autumn day drove away any capacity of his body to generate sufficient warmth. Gina appeared to withstand the weather's plodding attack much better than Reyne.

Wet leaves released a scent reminiscent of early fall in Hensdale, and it tugged at Reyne's unconscious thoughts as he drilled.

The instructor snapped into her I'm-ready-for-an-attack stance and said, "Again." Gina demanded louder, "Come at me again."

He dropped his arms to hang limp at his sides. "I'm freezing. I'm gonna start a fire."

Before Reyne took two steps towards the pit between their tents, Gina stuck out one leg in his path. "You're not done, farm boy."

Reyne tried to step over the obtrusive limb. "Get outta my way. Enough for today. I'm cold. I'm wet. I'm tired."

She mocked, "Whaaa whaaa. Baby needs his mommy. He's chilly. Maybe you want mommy to wrap you in a warm blanket where you can suckle on her teat?"

"Screw you."

"I'm sure you'd like to." She stayed poised for his advance. "Take me down. If you do, I'm yours." One finger at the end of her extended arm reached out, motioned back and forth, taunting him, as if to say, "Come on."

"Not this again," Reyne said and flopped his head to his chest. "Can we just stop for the day?"

Gina changed personas in Reyne's hearing of her words. A serious, dedicated teacher emerged. The mocking and teasing, gone. She eased from her state of preparedness to assume an at-ease stance. "You don't know much about me. I've kept it that way, so let's clear things up." With her hands on her hips, one hip tilted out, she asked, "What do you think I do?"

Reyne had thought about that very thing several times since meeting her. "Best I can figure, you work with Mera defending Tartica against the shady world of Evidar." He ended it with arms apart as though announcing, "Ta dah!"

Reyne studied Gina's face, but she didn't bite at the gibe. She simply said, "I kill people."

"That's what I said."

"Not exactly."

"Killin' is killin'. What's 'not exactly'?"

"Who do you think I kill?"

"Like I said, the bad people from the dark world who make it to Tartica"—he assumed all her targets to be Evidarian hunters—"but I don't know. Lots I suppose."

"Think about it." Gina tapped the side of her temple with her index finger several times. "Evidar has the same problem we do. Few can move from their world or their reality, whatever Mera calls it, into ours. If the bad people from Evidar find ones who can, how many want to be assassins, hunters, and even if they are willing, how many are good at it? It's been a small number. They trickle in. And that's if we even know they're here. Not enough to keep me busy. And you think Mera pays me enough to live off, for the services I provide taking out Evidar targets?" Her mocking slipped back in, "Think again, farm boy," she said, repeating the taps to the side of her head.

The revelation caught Reyne off guard. "What? You murder Tartican people for coin? That's messed up. The Covenant and all."

Gina's voice remained calm. "You're a naïve businessman who runs a nut farm. You know so little about the real world. You been sheltered away in your little village, and you think all of Tartica is like bucolic Hensdale. All the folks, all over the continent, so nice to each other? The rest of the world isn't like that. Tartican utopia is a mirage."

"Leave those folks alone. They're just livin' their lives, religious, faithful Covenant followers. What's wrong with that?"

"Nothing except you all been suckered. The Covenant is for those who have something to protect."

"I might be a wee bit naïve. Maybe. But it's the Covenant. You don't get to pick and choose when you want to follow it. It's the law."

A gust of exasperation blew through her lips. "Yeah, you do." Gina crossed her eyes and, with a head slant to the right, offered Reyne a lighthearted jest. She straightened up, slapped her palms together, and rubbed them vigorously. "Here's your civics lesson for the day. Consider it part of your training."

"Lucky me."

"Shut up and listen. All laws benefit those who need rules to keep others away from their valuable stuff. They make the laws to hold on to what they have. The rest of us just gotta live under them, well, most of the time. Everybody breaks them one way or another. Some like me, rather egregious, others in little bitty ways, but we all do it. By the way, how'd you like the word *egregious*, farm boy? Another one I haven't used in some time."

"Yes, you're very smart. But I don't agree. Sure, there are lots of people who break the law all the time, like the Thuggery, but most of us don't."

"Think again, farm boy. Even the holy and the faithful pay me for my services... to kill. That's the game of politics, finance, and love gone wrong. I don't play those games and I don't pretend there aren't lots of bad people living in our utopian world, just like Evidar has good people and bad people in theirs. I make a very good living ignoring the Covenant right here on Tartica."

He didn't want to come off an inexperienced bumpkin but didn't accept killing based on the immorality of it. "I can't say I support takin' a life. I'm not judging you. But I'm not you."

He didn't want the world to be as dark as Gina portrayed it, instead wanting to hold on to his belief that there are good people everywhere. Reyne needed to embrace a kinder, gentler worldview. He strove to be one of the good people as the foundation of the life he so desired with Mithany.

She threw her head back. "Then what are you doing here?"

He offered Gina the easy answer as he understood it. "Helping to save Tartica from Evidar."

Gina didn't let him off the hook. "Don't think the Covenant of Absolute Universal Obligations says anything about an exception to the no-killing rule if it's for bad guys from an evil reality. If you do this, if you go to Evidar and take the life of just one person, you're going to become another killer... just like me. Can you do that, farm boy? Can you become that guy?"

He shook his head in the universal sign for *no* and said, "It's not the same."

"Sure it is." The confidence in her reply unnerved him.

They stared at one another. He thought himself as just an average fellow, fighting to save the girl, while in Gina's version, he would become nothing more than a cold-blooded killer. In Gina's version, he couldn't be both. Not that he desired to think of himself as another Gina, yet why did it have to be one or the other?

Gina patted him on his upper arm. "You do this, you'll be operating outside the law. Breaking the Covenant. Like me."

He told Gina, "I'm doin' it for the good of Tartica." And in his inner voice, he reassured himself, *That's why I can be both*. He could be the good guy, and if he had to end an Evidarian's life, so be it.

"Are you telling me your reasons are justified and mine aren't? Who gets to decide that? You, farm boy? Once you go down that road, you're putting yourself above your precious Covenant."

Reyne protested, "You're wrong. When I get to Evidar, and I take out this Damus person, I'm doin' it to save our way of life."

"So you know better than the lawgivers. You take that position, that old piece of paper is worthless. You're not special. Nobody gets to have their carve-outs. You claim I don't get to have mine. I'm depraved 'cause I do it for coin and you're not, because my reasons for breaking the law aren't as good as yours. Sorry, farm boy, it doesn't work that way."

Reyne stayed silent.

A smile broke across her face. "The Covenant has that one problematic word in its title—*Absolute*. You like that big word, *problematic*, huh, farm boy? Haven't used that one in a while."

Even so, terminating the two red-haired women seemed justified. Reyne ignore the scoff mocking his rural vocabulary and wondered, *Is she right? Absolute means no exceptions. What about all the other people with good reason?* Either the Covenant had flaws, or he did. Just as quickly, he pushed it from his thoughts. They murdered his brother Daedyn, his biological family, Edruk, Silia, and Baide. Justice had not been meted out. He didn't want to think about it any longer; it hurt too much. Cold and exhausted, as well as intellectually backed into a corner, Reyne pouted, "I just want to start a fire. Why is everything so hard with you?"

Gina flashed him two thumbs up. "Good move. Change the subject. Did I make a point you can't wiggle out of? *Absolute* means no exceptions."

Reyne pulled in a deep breath through his nose. The wet leaves on the air smelled like Hensdale in autumn. "What's that got to do with Evidar? There's no Covenant there. And I'm tired, cold, and soaked to the bone."

Her answer came swiftly, and it came from the serious side of Gina. "You go to Evidar and kill someone there, then you and I are the same. As far as being tired, in the killing game, you don't get to decide when you've had enough. When to call it a day and pick up your toys. Evidar isn't any place for a hero and certainly not for a good man. You can't just go home when events conspire against you and the going gets too difficult for you. You absolutely have to accept who you are, or who you're going to be, before you set foot on that dark world, or you're a dead man walking. Sure, you're cold. Yeah, you're soaked to the bone and yes, you've had enough. But know this; I don't care."

"What's your point?"

"If you're on Evidar, on a day like today. You're drained. But it's the only chance you have to do what you're sent there to do: kill their Damus to save all of Tartica. But you're tired, so you figure, the heck with whatever happens to Tartica, too bad, you're taking a nap. Or maybe they're tracking you and you're exhausted. If they catch you, you're dead. Are you going to pack it in for the day? Give up? Or are you going to be a man, bite down, push through, and get it done?"

"Bite me."

Ignoring his protests, she continued, "This is the best time to train. When you're worn out. When you hit your limit. This tells me whether you're ready, mentally and physically. So, what are we going to do, curl up in a ball and stay safe and warm, or are you going to go out and get what you want?"

Reyne thought this wasn't the Gina who constantly taunted him, teased him, made him angry all the time. She revealed herself to be a serious mentor making an effort to mentally prepare him for a world he couldn't even contemplate. This side of Gina, he wanted, he needed.

Gina's words, "to get what you want," hit home. A yearning burned in his soul to get back to the life he had been promised with Mithany. Nothing would stand in its way. Not even who he had to become. He told himself he would do whatever it took to get back to her. To keep her safe from the Evidar hunters. Yet, up to this point, he didn't want to accept Gina's assessment; he had to become a killer, just like her. He didn't care what she called him, killer or hero. It only mattered what he thought of himself.

Gina nailed the truth of it: he had to be tougher.

Exhausted. Cold. Wet. He pushed aside the signals racing around his brain demanding rest. Fueled by his desire to reunite with the woman he loved, girding his will into iron he said, "Alright. We keep going."

Reyne told himself, *I'll never become another Gina. But I know what I gotta do... whatever it takes to save Mithany. I can live with that... but I can't live without her.*

Reyne hadn't put it all together before Gina challenged him to see who he had to become. He'd spent too much time being angry, first at Mera, then at Gina. It all seemed clear to him now. He'd committed himself to the noble pursuit of protecting love—protecting Mithany, and if that meant Gina called him a killer, so what. *I know who I am and what I gotta do. There's no going back.* His body language shifted. He stood up straight and tall.

A smile bloomed on Gina's face. She snapped into her ready-for-assault body stance. "Good. Back to where we left off. Now, come at me again. Take me down... If you can."

He lurched into an attack position.

And with that, Reyne changed.

Over a Barrel

Derr

Derr intended to extricate the truth from Jerithan Cree about his involvement in the failed assassination attempt on Chancellor Tomelai. With Jerithan their captive, the KCG's efforts to that end had yet to bear fruit. Although Derr never enjoyed torturing prisoners, he held torture in high esteem. In his experience, nothing proved as effective, aside from threatening the lives of loved ones. The latter proved challenging when the only loved ones to threaten were small children. While Derr had resorted to promising death to a beloved son or daughter, he had never carried through on killing a young child. Although most believed him capable of such a heinous act, he had his limits. Few, but limits just the same.

Jerithan, a father of three by way of several prearranged Coupling Cohorts—fulfilling his Covenant Obligation of procreation—proved unresponsive to KCG threats made against his grown children that, as adults, were fair game. Not that Derr expected the tactic to succeed with the former First Lord. Jerithan Cree cared only for himself.

Forcing scores of detainees to face the rack over the years, Derr accepted the procedure as a necessary consequence of keeping Tomelai in power. While the raw act of torture held little interest to Derr, viewed as a psychological game to ascertain the limits of an individual's ability to withstand either physical or mental abuse—or both—appealed to him. The downside to a pain-induced confession,

Derr fully understood, amounted to a certain weakness inherent to the human condition: at some point, most people will do or say anything to make the pain stop. The trick, one that Derr well appreciated, was knowing just how hard to push before reaching the I'll-confess-to-anything threshold.

Bloodied and beaten, the deposed First Lord remained unrepentant, sequestered inside KCG headquarters. Prudent Serco, now First Lord, made good on his promise to deliver Jerithan to Derr soon after the Council of Prudents elected him the Temple of Life's new leader—the price Serco paid for Derr's behind-the-scenes support in deposing Jerithan.

However, Serco failed to deliver the Second Lord as promised, but only because Razoal had been beheaded before the new First Lord could secure him for delivery.

Lieutenant Wilem Ferpratt had taken the lead on the KCG's efforts to elicit a confession from Jerithan. With Jerithan naked and bent over a table, his buttocks propped in the air, blood mixed with shit dripped down his thigh. The sight of Jerithan's hands and legs splayed apart and tied to the four corners of the table welcomed Derr as he entered through the heavy wooden door. Another KCG officer, standing directly behind Jerithan, was getting dressed, pulling up his britches just as Derr entered.

Derr ignored the offensive fecal odor and the KCG underling stuffing his privates back into his pants. "Ferpratt, what do you have so far?"

"Jerithan Cree's proven he's a stubborn son-of-a-bitch. In the last two days, he's been whipped, racked, hobbled, and, well, you can see for yourself today's efforts. But so far, he refuses to admit he ordered the assassination attempt on the Chancellor."

Soft whimpering escaped Jerithan.

Derr paid it no heed. "Keep at it. Report to me as soon as you get anything," Derr said to the senior lieutenant, turned, and marched towards the door. The menacing sound of heavy footsteps bounced off the walls filling the void of the room's threatening silence.

In a weak voice, Jerithan pleaded, "Wait."

The KCG Captain stopped, walked back to Jerithan, and crouched down on his haunches to face the man tied to the table. Jerithan's exposed buttocks on one side, his head hung over the edge of the other. Derr grabbed a smattering of disheveled hair, lifting Jerithan's head to look him straight in the eyes. "Tell me you did this thing."

Tears, sweat, blood, a missing tooth, a split lip, and puffy eyes stared back at Derr.

In a weak, hoarse voice, Jerithan croaked, "I can be of use to you."

Derr let go of the thin strands of gray hairs entwined between his fingers, dropping Jerithan's head. Only limp, sinuous neck tissue kept the prisoner's head from falling to the floor.

Struggling to lift his face, Jerithan begged, "Wait, please."

Calm, lacking any emotion, Derr studied Jerithan's expression, evaluating his state of mind. Neither said anything. If eyes could offer a plea for relief, Jerithan's did. Absent a feeling heart, Derr neither felt pity nor anything else towards the suspected assassination mastermind: he only considered how close he'd taken Jerithan to breaking. He concluded, *Not there yet.*

"Unless you can tell me about how you planned and executed the failed attempt on Tomelai's life, I have nothing left to say to you." He paused, searching Jerithan for any sign of weakness he could exploit. But Jerithan was still holding back. *There's more in there. Let's see if we can't nudge it out of you.* "Except to tell you there are others in the KCG who will enjoy a man much like yourself. Ferpratt here is going to gather them up. They're going to take turns with you."

Defiant, Jerithan said, "I just endured your first. What makes you think anymore will have any effect?"

Derr shook his head from side to side. "You have no idea the agony you're in for."

Silence filled the room for a dozen heartbeats.

Meek, barely loud enough for another ear to collect, Jerithan whimpered, "It wasn't me. It was Razoal. I swear, it was all his doing."

"Convenient, blaming the dead."

"He's what?" Jerithan squeaked. "I didn't know."

More than fear leaked through Jerithan's feeble voice. Concern for Razoal absent in Jerithan's reply, but what Derr did hear, apprehension, told him instantly the process had taken a turn. Derr understood Jerithan's journey. Experience told Derr the former First Lord inched towards acceptance, trying to hold back. Not wanting to reveal everything, but offering just enough to save his own life. Intent on holding on to some piece of himself he could live with. Testing Derr's boundaries.

Through his KCG surrogates, Derr took part in torture too many times not to understand the patterns of transition from defiance to acceptance and, finally, to submission. In his experience, the prisoners didn't know the path they were on or even that they had arrived at a point of decision—reveal the truth or die. And some did die. But Derr understood Jerithan at that moment, and he moved his prisoner closer to the endgame, where he expected Jerithan's choice included an alternative to death.

Derr placed a hand on Jerithan's shoulder as though offering sympathy, although he lacked any. "You may think the worst is over with your first, but after the third or fourth, your anus is going to get very sore. Rectal burn is like nothing you've ever experienced... and you're going to wish you hadn't. By your tenth or twelfth, you'll be in agonizing pain. Nothing like you've ever experienced. And Ferpratt isn't going to stop the process even if you decide to talk when you've hit your limit to endure the anguish. Your only chance is to talk to me. Right here. Right now."

Jerithan tried to raise his head, but obvious to Derr, he didn't have the strength. Facing Derr's boots, labored breaths escaping in between his words, he said, "I found out that morning. Razoal confided in me. He thought he would stop Tomelai's push for electrics in the Council. I didn't have time to stop him."

Like two old buddies chatting over morning coffee, Derr spoke slowly and almost friendly. His deep baritone voice carried in its message a dire threat. "I simply don't believe you."

"You need me," Jerithan begged in a whisper.

"What would I need you for? You tried to kill my Chancellor once. How could I either need you or trust you?"

Out of breath, frail, apparently exhausted, and without the strength to lift his head, Jerithan kept facing down. "Because everything has changed. Serco plans to oppose Adelle. He'll never agree to ending the Covenant. I can be your inside man at the Temple."

Derr wiped his hands on his thighs. "You opposed electrics. You opposed Adelle. How is Serco's opposition any different from yours? It doesn't matter what the Temple leader does. Adelle has already pulled out of the Covenant. What good are you to me?"

Derr denied Jerithan what he proffered in exchange for his life. However, he was pleased the process had entered the negotiation stage, with Jerithan probing what bare minimum he had to give away to secure an end to his misery and, more than that, avoiding the promise of Ferpratt's men. Derr wouldn't accept the minimum. He wanted everything from his captive.

Information.

A confession.

And most of all, his dignity.

Derr had done this dance with many others. Buried behind Jerithan's pathetic offering hid Derr's real prize. Derr's confidence in reading Jerithan correctly, coupled with his captive's mental state, hinted at Jerithan's imminent surrender. The process had taken another turn.

Jerithan's words pleaded for the value of his offer. "There's been talk... Teth aligning with Kantos and Greenlin... A preemptive attack on Adelle... Forcing you..." He stopped mid-thought. The ex-First Lord appeared too fatigued to continue.

Derr stood, slipped both hands behind his back, and paced before Jerithan. He had expected the possibility of an alliance against Tomelai. Adelle had started gathering its own military force in preparation. Derr considered Jerithan's offer. Knowing detailed plans of their opponents would be helpful. Derr put it aside. These were only tidbits. He wanted everything from Jerithan.

His opponent had been primed through Ferpratt's efforts. The signals were out in the open for Derr to read. The time had come to plant his flag. Negotiations with Jerithan ended here.

Derr stopped pacing. Standing directly before Jerithan, he offered him a clear view of his footwear. As a concerned father might gently counsel his misguided son, Derr explained, "I'm going to ask you one question and one question only. Fail to answer, or if I think you're lying, Ferpratt will continue. And don't think I buy that bullshit about Razoal ordering the attack on Tomelai. You pulled the strings. Maybe your Second carried it out, but you ordered it. He's dead and you're here. Now, there's one more person you involved in your little scheme. Who did you pay to carry it out? Before you answer me, I expect to hear one thing. No other words. A name."

Jerithan remained silent.

Derr's boots stayed planted where they were at first. Derr lifted one foot, initiating his exit, and stepped towards the door and Jerithan's certain death. After several paces, he stopped. He spoke to Jerithan without turning around to face him. "Give me your accomplice, and I'll consider putting you to use as my spy. When I walk out that door, this offer, unlike you, will be off the table. If you choose not to tell me, once you've satisfied my men, you'll be dead before the sun comes up tomorrow."

The sound of Derr's footsteps again filled the chamber.

Derr stopped at the exit.

Silence hung in the air.

Derr gripped the deadbolt.

The rusty iron lock squealed in surrender.

Derr pulled on the door.

It swung open.

The hinges creaked, pronouncing Jerithan's coming death.

Suddenly, Jerithan spat out one word.

"Nails."

As Ready as I'll Ever Be

Reyne | Mera

Reyne stood defiantly with his hands on his hips. As though offering a command, his boot slapped against the hard ground. "Days. I've been doing this shit for days. Enough already."

Mera sat on a nearby boulder, with one foot propped on its smaller cousin, like a headmaster observing teacher and pupil plodding through the day's routine. "I get it. You think you're ready."

Like a petulant child protesting to a parent, Reyne demanded, "I *am*."

"You're getting there. It's a judgement call, pitting a need to get you over into Evidar as soon as possible measured against my assessment of your skills. I've got to be certain you're prepared to handle the danger."

"I'll never be free of risk. From what you've been spouting off about this place, there isn't any amount of combat training to keep me outta harm's way. I'm as ready as I'll ever be."

Reyne considered the plan he'd been keeping to himself to return to Tartica the minute he set foot on Evidar. Yet, it didn't sit well with him since that night he witnessed Mera save his life as a newborn. He owed Mera more than he could ever repay, but he worried about the threat Evidar held out to Mithany. *Maybe I can do both. If I can locate this Damus quickly, I can still get back to Hensdale fast. What to do?*

Yet he did have solid motivation driving him to improve his tactical skills. Two faces burned in his mind's eye, pushing himself even harder than Gina had: the windblown face of Dylla, the ghostly apparition of Neladith.

The images Mera's magic act revealed haunted him.

... when he trained.

... when he ate.

... when he slept.

Like a shank at the end of a rope dangling before a rabid beast, forever out of reach but never neglected out of a lack of trying, desire pushed him. He trained hard every minute of every day. But, he'd had enough. The time had come to let down the rope. To attack the shank. His problem: Mera didn't think he was ready.

Maybe Mera's right. If I do go after the Damus and I'm not as ready as I should be, I'm screwed. But I can't wait any longer. Gotta get back to Mithany. Every day I waste here puts her at risk. Shit... what to do?

Overcast, the autumn air failed to warm the forest glade where he practiced fighting. Dressed in tight leather pants, a vest, and long-sleeved shirt, mud from the wet ground clung to him, chilling his bones. Puddles left behind by the overnight rain welcomed Reyne frequently, thanks to Gina's eagerness to educate him on his need for further practice. Time and time again, Reyne tasted the cold waters of the small pools, face-diving into one or another over and over at Gina's hand and much to her delight.

Gina offered Mera, "All things considered, he's not really too bad. In that last exchange, with anybody else but me, he would have taken them down."

Mera, his arm outstretched, rolled his index finger in a circling motion. "Gina, can you show me again? Slow it down to normal speed this time. What I've seen so far, when it looks like he might have you, you call on that special ability of yours and dump him in another wet patch. He's not going to face anyone like you, ever. So, slow it down."

"Remember, he called me a cunt."

"Yes. We all remember. If you're done extracting payment, perhaps you can get on with it. I need to know what he can do. Is this what you've been doing while I've been gone?"

Reyne answered for them both. "More or less. But, think about this. I'm never gonna face anyone as fast as her. Sure, stronger, but not quicker. It's been good."

Mera stuck out his neck, shrugged his shoulders, and with upturned palms, asked, "What has she taught you other than don't ever call her that?"

"I learned a few things, like getting out of a neck hold, evading punches by deflecting the incoming arm, using an opponent's forward momentum to my advantage. A few ways to throw a charging body. I end up on my ass a lot. She didn't make it easy. Not saying I do these things perfect, but got the basics down. Might not be what she intended, but I'm better for it. And she knows I haven't changed my opinion of her, so I end up on my ass a lot."

Gina teased, "You'll pay for that farm boy."

Ignoring the threat, knowing she'd make him pay anyway, Reyne asked Mera, "You've been comin' and goin'. Barely seen you much around here. So, what've you been up to?"

Mera's face turned serious. His deep voice added to his warning. "It's a cluster fuck out there. Good thing we're in the middle of nowhere, away from everyone. People I talked to said in just about every town, village, or city, folks are going at each other... who's in favor of the Covenant... who's opposed. Tomelai opened a deep divide. I heard Topak almost burned to the ground. The anti-Covenant crowd isn't giving an inch. One of the birthing farms erupted in violence. The people inside got their chance to tear it down, and they didn't waste it. The Kantonese Prime Minister, Larsed, he's out. Government didn't have any confidence in him to handle this mess. In Greenlin, President Dimenk is holding on by a thread. Riots across Greenlin are making it tough for her."

Gina asked, "And Teth?"

"It's gotten worse since we were there. Word is Jerithan Cree is out as First Lord; Serco's taken over. He's always been a Temple zealot. He'll never let go of the Covenant. Nails and the Thuggery own the streets and her people do battle with Temple faithful flocking into the city by the day. The Citizen's Committee, which is a smokescreen for Nails to exact revenge, has taken prisoners, a couple of prudents in the mix. There's going to be more trials. Serco can't stop her."

Reyne, eager for news of Mithany, asked, "What about Hensdale? What do you hear? Did you go there?"

"No. Didn't want to risk it. Evidar hunters or their lackeys are most likely watching. But, I asked about it. A few minor protests, but it's been lucky so far to avoid any strong opposition. No news on Mithany. I'm sure she's safe."

Reyne raised his hand to his chin, looked over to Mera, and rubbed the stubble on his cheeks. "How close did you get?"

"I've got a few contacts who had been there. I trust them," Mera replied.

Not satisfied, Reyne politely pointed out, "You didn't answer me. How close did you get to Hensdale?"

"You know the road to Topak. I got about halfway between there and Hensdale."

Reyne stared at Mera and Gina. Thoughts of Mithany tugged at his heart. He had enough talk. He had enough training. Desire to take action burned inside him. He'd hadn't decided: go after the Damus—he owed Mera—or protect Mithany. Either way, it started with him in Evidar, not sitting in the middle of nowhere. Reyne walked away. He made for the tents set up forty paces from the center of the glade.

Mera waited for Reyne to be out of earshot. His eyes followed Reyne into his tent and immediately snapped his head towards Gina. "I've got to know, all bullshit aside. How long before I can send him? I know he can't possibly be one hundred percent. Hell, I'd settle for fifty."

Gina mimed her hands as though weighing some imaginary load. "He can fight. He still needs more practice with knives. Can't throw a blade for shit. But he's a fair shot with a bow. Building a functional one when he gets there needs work. A few more weeks and he'll be ready. On the plus side, something's changed about him. He's shown himself to be more committed and less belligerent. We had a breakthrough. My assessment, he'll do what it takes, and by that, I mean his mind has accepted he has to become a killer. I just gotta get his skills to the point where his technique catches up to his mindset."

Concern crossed his face. "Good to hear. Sounds like our strategy and your head games had some success, but I'm afraid we don't have weeks. And what about those episodes of his? When you've done hand-to-hand with him, any wild-eyed, out-of-control, mindless attacks?"

"No. I've seen none of that, and I need more time with him. I get it, I can't have ten weeks, but one or two more will make a big difference."

"I started out on my way to Hensdale but didn't make it. Wanted to check in with Mithany and Doc Brenal. Couldn't tell Reyne I intended to go there. Saw Mithany and Neladith walking together on the road not far from here. Looked like a pleasant conversation. Couldn't make out what they were saying. They were being followed by two Hensdale local guys, not Evidar agents. Mithany didn't stay put like I told her. Reyne can't know she's close."

"That's going to be a problem. Is the girl safe?"

"From what I could make out, she's not in immediate danger, but that could change in an instant."

"What game is Neladith playing? Evidar agents don't take friendly strolls with pretty little Tartican women for fun. There's always a purpose."

Mera scratched at his scalp. "A question I keep asking myself... have they figured it out? Seems like they know he's alive. They're back to going after Reyne. Is this Neladith hoping Mithany leads her to him? Why else is she traveling with her?"

"So, good news, bad news. You're thinking Evidar knows he's not dead, but the fiancée is safe for now."

"For now, but Arek, her brother... nowhere to be seen. That concerns me even more. It gets worse. I picked up signs that suggest we're being tracked but didn't see anyone. It's possible they're on our trail already. I don't like it, and I need you to scout out the area."

"Yeah. I can do that."

"Reyne can't find out we're being followed, or that Mithany left Hensdale, or that she's with Neladith. Our grip on him is fragile, and he's holding in a lot of hatred for the murderess of his brother... and she's the one with his fiancée."

"Fragile, sure, but that bitch Neladith definitely's got him motivated."

"The two women are headed in our direction and a hunter from Evidar is likely pointed our way. Reyne will take off if he finds out about any of this before you or I uttered the word, 'No.' The best thing we can do is to get him off Tartica."

"How soon?" Gina asked.

"Soon. Very soon."

Gina reacted more forcefully than Mera expected. "You can't do that to him. You'll be condemning him to death. He's... not... ready."

Mera held up both hands as if to say, stop. "Whoa, where did that come from? Didn't think you cared one way or the other about him."

Projected louder than their private conversation warranted, Gina shot back, "I don't." Closing her eyes and shaking her head, she continued in a softer tone, "Well, maybe just a little. He kinda grows on you. I simply can't stand by and let you send him off to die."

Mera moved his hands up and down. "Quiet. You want him to hear you?"

Not heeding Mera's advice, she shouted, "Yeah, maybe he should know." Her volume grew louder with each syllable uttered. "He's a dead man walking."

Mera looked over to see Reyne pop his head out of his tent. Mera yelled to him. "Go back inside! It's just Gina being a twat."

Reyne shouted, "Got it." And he escaped back into his tent.

Gina's nostrils flared. "Fuck you, Mera. I do all this for you and that's how you treat me?"

"Calm down, just needed some way to get him to go away. You get it, give them the easiest explanation they won't question. Of course I didn't mean it. I'm sorry."

Gina folded her arms over her chest. "He doesn't know that, so... again... fuck you."

"Listen. I don't like it either, but our options are limited. If Evidar comes after him, and they're more than likely already on the hunt, there'll be no more training. We'll be on the run from moment to moment."

"Then I'll train him tracking techniques and evasion methods. I'm begging you. Don't do this."

"And what if they call in Tartican contractors like yourself? You and I can only do so much to protect him. His chances here won't be any better."

Gina closed her eyes and angled her head back. To Mera, it appeared she considered his assessment.

Gina turned the volume down in her reply. "Depends on whether they put the contract out for wide distribution or offer it up to only a few of the most dependable hitters. I can handle the one-offs. That'll give me more time to prepare him. Could buy us another week."

Mera locked his fingers together behind his head and leaned back. "Can we take that risk? You know as well as anyone it only takes one slip up in a protection detail. You and I are good, not perfect."

Gina took in a deep breath and let it out slowly through puffed-out cheeks. "Oh, this sucks. The poor bastard's screwed either way. I like his chances here better, but I get your point. It's a toss-up. How soon?"

Pleased that Gina accepted the bitter reality, Reyne was as ready as he was ever going to be, Mera stated in a firm tone, "Time's up."

REBELLION OF THE RICH

TANDURE: 7TH DAY OF THE HARVEST MOON

Tomelai

Madrotti Tomelai and his wife Kaythlin sat on a chaise lounge at the foot of their bed, discussing the resistance from Adelle's elites. First Lady Kaythlin offered her husband, "My love, you have made it clear; the Kingdom of Adelle has withdrawn from the Covenant. There can be no going back and no debate. You have delivered freedom to all civilization. Only first to Adelle."

Madrotti Tomelai looked down at the hand she rested on his. "I know. It breaks my heart, though, our own people pushing back... if only the very rich."

Kaythlin stroked his hand. "We are facing a battle on two fronts. I fear the one at home will prove the most difficult to overcome." She settled her head on his shoulder.

Kaythlin spoke as Tomelai ran the fingers of one hand gently through her long, chestnut-brown hair, while the other pulled her in tight against him. "Madrotti, you and I know it goes deeper. Tandure is a swamp disguised in beautiful homes, wealthy elites, judges, lawyers, business owners, and the idle rich who hold garish parties with the purpose of planning, plotting, and disseminating instructions to the bureaucrats doing their bidding."

Tomelai's muscled chest rose and fell as he pulled in, then released, a deep breath. "I swap out administrative leadership often enough to keep the bastards at bay, but it is like digging in sand."

With her head still on his shoulder, Kaythlin rested an open palm on his chest. Her warm, gentle touch calmed him. "It is the thousands of underlings who have held key positions for years who need to be controlled or removed."

Tomelai issued his decree to the people of Adelle, withdrawing from the Covenant soon after returning from the Feast of Teth. General Kiple, head of Adelle's National Police, proved loyal in tamping down open rebellion throughout Adelle amongst the common folk. Although, more than twenty local constables allowed pro-Covenant rallies in the towns and villages under their civil enforcement jurisdiction. Kiple had each of them summarily dismissed upon receiving reports of their heresy. Their replacements, loyalists committed to the Tomelai family.

The capital city of Tandure, the wealth center of the Kingdom of Adelle, boasted a population of the country's most affluent families, to the exclusion of most in the upper class. While an asset threshold didn't exist as a prerequisite to live in Tandure, the exorbitant cost of housing ensured only the nation's preeminent rich were welcome in the city. Like the reduction process of a demi-glaze, burning off everything but for the concentrated wealth of the most powerful.

Open rebellion took on a completely different appearance amongst the financially endowed. Controlling the powerful, not as easily assuaged as replacing a disgruntled constable or breaking up a gathered crowd of commoners, presented its own set of obstacles for Chancellor Tomelai.

With her long delicate index finger, her palm motionless, Kaythlin daintily outlined small circles repeatedly on his chest. Tomelai closed his eyes, enjoying her attention, and tipped his head back. "Kay, I would like to hear your thoughts on how best to manage Tandure's privileged behind-the-scenes movers and shakers. The Hidden Hand is a thorn in my craw."

Kaythlin lifted her head from its nestled position. Tomelai looked into her inviting violet eyes and felt like he could escape into them and never return. Kaythlin spoke and the caress of her voice swept into his ears. "They have so much tied up in maintaining the status quo."

More than the meaning of her words, a message hidden in her tone, he understood Kaythlin promised him sanctuary from the daily struggles of ruling Adelle—in the love she held for him in her heart. But the sound jilted his concentration and broke her hold over him. Tempted in the moment to give everything away, his true love of power pulled him back from the abyss.

Only slightly distracted, Tomelai, still in full command, replied, "Our move to withdraw from the Covenant they take as a threat to each of their self-imagined fiefdoms. Their only concern is how it will impact the flow of coin into their pockets."

The melodic sound of her words, soft yet powerful, played on as they continued tugging at his will. "My love, we have sat through many briefings by Druin and his people. There cannot be more than a few hundred shadow primes pulling the strings behind the curtain. It would take time for the KCG to deal with them all and I do not believe we have that much time."

Through pursed lips he went on. "And, even if we did, others would pop up to fill the vacuum like they always have. Taking the Hidden Hand on, one by one, is a failed strategy."

Kaythlin paused, squinted as though in concentration, tapped one finger against her forehead and made an observation. "A few, like Charmet, have the conviction to attempt a preemptive strike. Even if you took him out first, there are too many of his kind. I do not see letting loose the KCG on the entirety of the Hidden Hand as a plausible approach. Too much risk with an uncertain outcome."

Tomelai squeezed his fists tight as though ready for battle. "It would be much easier if it were only a few."

Kaythlin got up and rested both knees on the bedroom carpeting, setting herself between his legs. She eased both her palms over his hands of whitening knuckles, hovering just above his lap. He looked down at her into her eyes and his anger at the Hidden Hand melted. Her feminine touch consoled him as only an intimate partner could. Her voice soothed him, it didn't matter the words, when she said, "Druin has done well disposing of Hidden Hand one-offs over all these years."

They spoke to the business of ruling and the problems of the day, but so much more communication played out between them in their looks, their tone, their expressions, and in the nuances only explained by the years they'd spent together. Tomelai knew himself to be the lesser of the two in that regard, but appreciated Kaythlin for never manipulating him—without his consent.

Tomelai pondered Kaythlin's input. "You know me too well. I agree. The KCG is not the correct tool this time. We need a different approach. Not a lead pipe. Well, perhaps just a few of them should taste the pipe." His chortle at the end punctuated his remarks.

Kaythlin rose and came to stand before him. Tomelai ran his eyes up and down her body, but closed them when she slowly ran the back of her hand down his cheek. "Facing an insurmountable problem with a laugh. That is the man I love."

Tomelai popped open his eyes, looked up at Kaythlin, and said, "I could cut the puppet master's strings by terminating the entire bureaucracy. No outlet to give their orders to. Could you imagine the bedlam?"

Tomelai wrapped his arms around Kaythlin's waist and, with hands gripping her buttocks, pulled her in.

"Just one problem, dear. All of governing would come to a halt," she said and kissed the top of his head.

He settled the side of his head against her chest. "I know. It is only wishful thinking." Her heart beat in his ear and he thought, *Ah, the music of love*, but kept it to himself.

She reached behind her waist and lovingly unlocked his arms. Tomelai's eyes followed her step back and take a seat once again by his side. She steepled her hands together, her chin coming to rest on her upward pointing index fingers. "There is always treason. A show trial of one or two, as an example to the others. Reputations destroyed in the press before the trials ever begin. I am certain Druin would discover or provide whatever evidence we would require. Seize their estates, their property, their entire accumulated stockpile of wealth. It would put their families in the streets and others of the Hidden Hand on notice."

Tomelai wrapped his big strong arm around her shoulder and pulled Kaythlin in tight. "You always know how to cheer me up."

They both laughed.

Tomelai's arm slid down to her waist. "It would be effective, yet I fear those in the shadows would declare war on our supporters most visible in the public eye. Their contacts in the press are as dedicated as ours. It could be done at a very high cost. I would have to shut down the press first."

Kaythlin rested her hand on his thigh and ran the tip of her long, thin middle finger back and forth. "It is an option but only of last resort."

Electricity tingled along the traces of where her fingertip caressed his skin. They bantered back and forth about the affairs of state, but both felt the tug of what prowled underneath.

When he and Kaythlin were alone and engaged in political analysis, she aroused him. Her mind captivated him; he thought it even more breathtaking than her stunning physical beauty. And when the combination of both came to bear, he knowingly fell under her spell. Much to his delight, Kaythlin usually reacted in the same manner.

The search for a solution would play on but both understood the crescendo promised at the end of talking, as it did more often than not. He knew she used it as a way into his heart, to get back to the way they were in the early years of their marriage. He never resisted her efforts.

Tomelai followed his wife's lead and settled one of his own hands on her exposed thigh just below the hem of her bedroom attire. He looked her in the eye. "Power is a blood sport. And I have on my team one of the best."

Kaythlin hopped into Tomelai's lap. "You are too kind, my love." Gentle, she leaned in and kissed him. Her voice lyrical, her natural charm laced every word, yet her message for Adelle's opponents, harsh. "To undermine your base of support, I suspect they are calculating whose reputation to destroy as we speak. We should be prepared to act, even if you decide not to strike first."

They stared deeply into each other's eyes. He looked for answers and reassurance in hers. "It all seemed so clear when I proposed to withdraw from the Covenant in the Council." He recognized her gaze, searching for love in his. He wondered if she grasped the truth of it. His heart held power as his first love. Tomelai, too afraid of what she might say, never asked Kaythlin what she saw when he looked back at her.

Kaythlin leaned in again, this time kissing Tomelai on the cheek. "You did the right thing, my love. Now, we have to find a way to navigate the ship of state to a safe harbor without the Covenant to moor us."

Tomelai combed his finger through her hair. "You are so very beautiful. And yet, it is that mind of yours." Tomelai understood his wife. She prided herself on maintaining her natural features as the years rolled on, but truly appreciated him when her intellect took center stage.

Her smile radiated love and connected the two. "Madrotti, the reason we withdrew from the Covenant was to eliminate threats on your life. If we turn back, we return to where we started. We need to keep going forward. We will find a way."

Tomelai wrapped both his huge hands over hers. "Kay, one of my advisors has suggested I let them have what they want. Publicly, we maintain our position. Adelle no longer adheres to the Covenant's terms, but privately, we allow the Hidden Hand to have their sway. What do you think of that idea?"

Kaythlin smiled. "My dear husband, are you waiting for my reply? I know you too well to think you are serious about surrendering to the shadow people. After hearing that kind of advice, such an advisor must be on their payroll."

"You see through me. Of course, you are right. Even the lowest peasant would see me as a weak leader. It is not in my nature. I keep him around as a mouthpiece of the shadow-policy position makers. I like to stay informed of what the other side is thinking." Tomelai gave Kaythlin a peck on the lips.

Kaythlin ran her fingers through the hair along the sides of his temples. He experienced the excitement of the foreplay. Her strokes slid down along his cheeks to hold his face in her hands. "My love, I think there is a way to combine a lot of these ideas into one sweeping approach. If you can accept holding back for a month or so, and from personal experience, I know you can hold out until the time is right, for which I am always grateful. Loseff may hold the key. Once our army is in place, we send them out, drilling through the streets of Tandure."

Tomelai nodded. "Seeing a military force at our disposal will send a powerful message to the Hidden Hand. With Loseff out in front, someone they cannot corrupt would give our behind-the-scenes opponents pause to think twice. It would not stop them, but it will slow them down."

"Consider this as well: under our son's direction, we can seize an entire department or two, putting our army at the helm of key administrative functions. One by one, you can bring the entire apparatus of bureaucracy to heel."

Tomelai's chest rose and fell. "The Third Age has not known war. It is intuitive to see while the costs are high, there is a lot of money to be made by war's suppliers. We have contracts to hand out."

Excitement filled her voice. "Weapons. Boots. Clothes. Food. Barracks to be built. My dear, you hold the purse strings. Like ravenous suckling piglets to a sow, I think we can make a dent in the Hidden Hand's pushback."

"There is much to consider. At the very least, the framework of an approach that needs more details to be fleshed out. You are not only the smartest person I know, you hold advantage over all others who provide me input." Tomelai clasped the hands of his wife and moved them to his lap. An impish grin bloomed. "You are, in a word, compelling. I am overcome with the desire to explore all of you."

Tomelai wondered, had she led him here with a trail of teasing breadcrumbs? What came next, all her idea? Had he been played? He didn't care. Even if she had, it excited him all the more.

"I know that look." Kaythlin offered him her own devilish beam in return.

With one finger, he slipped the thin, challenged strap of Kaythlin's chemise from her shoulder and said, "Yes, you do. And now, with business out of the way..."

Are You Kidding Me

Reyne

Reyne planted himself on a boulder, Mera at his side, with Gina seated on a nearby smaller pile of rocks in the open field where he trained. The trio discussed several obstacles facing his inevitable journey to Evidar. One such complication he alone bore the weight of—Mithany.

For Reyne, facing the actuality of transfiguring to Evidar, decision time fast approached. As much as he owed Mera for saving him at birth, Reyne still leaned towards infidelity to Mera's cause with an immediate return to Tartica, forgoing Mera's plan for him to hunt down and kill Evidar's Damus. Reyne revealed nothing of his intent to either Mera or Gina, but guilt at the ongoing deception gnawed at him and grew heavier by the day. Love moved him in one direction, obligation in the other.

Mera slapped Reyne on the back. "The first thing about transfiguring into another dimension is it's a lot easier with a partner to guide you through the Void. There's always a danger of ending up somewhere other than the place you're shooting for. In the Void, the realm of possible futures, the biggest problem is they can all look so much alike with only the tiniest of differences."

Reyne tilted his head, confused. "Since I'm the last Tweener you got, there's nobody else to partner with. How we gonna do it? I mean, who's gonna make sure I don't end up hundreds or thousands of miles from my intended destination?"

Mera pursed his lips. "That's going to be a problem."

"So you want me to, what, close my eyes, snap my fingers, pop up in Evidar, and hope for the best?"

"Let's talk about the process. How to get from here to there."

Reyne, no longer holding a grudge towards Mera, but still unable to commit one hundred percent trust in the man, said, "You know, you never just answer my questions."

"I don't always have the answer. Sorry."

Reyne's reply lacked the irritation for Mera he'd put behind him and, in its place, he stated matter-of-factly, "That's bullshit."

"Believe what you want. I'm doing my best to prepare you for your trip."

Reyne slapped his hands together and rubbed them to generate a small ration of warmth against the cool fall air.

Mera's holding something back.

"There's one important thing about this Tweener stuff you still haven't told me. How does it work? I mean, what do I do, dance around a fire, howling to the moon?"

Gina laughed. "Mera, you never told me Reyne's such a funny guy."

Reyne glared at Gina. Their shared venture into building a trusting relationship hit a stumbling block the moment he met her inside the Whispering Eye. From their first encounter, she rubbed him the wrong way, and he put little effort into forging a connection. Aside from the skills she could impart, whether she liked him held no importance to the Hensdale businessman. He had another person to worry about—Mithany. Converting Gina to a friend wasted energy. He put it to better use: preparing himself for survival in the dark world of Evidar.

"I tell you what, Gina. You share with me the way you can move so fast, and maybe I can help you improve that belligerent personality of yours."

Gina slapped her thigh. "Mera, see what I mean? He's hilarious."

Reyne turned his focus to Mera, ignoring her gibe. He didn't plan on sticking around long enough with Gina on Tartica for her opinion of him to matter. Reyne threw up his hands. "So, Mera, you gonna enlighten me about how I get to Evidar, or we gonna sit around all day?"

Mera glanced towards Gina. Her eyes darted back and forth across the changing expressions on his face. Reyne wondered about their obvious silent conversation. He waved his arms to get Mera's attention. "Forget about her. You need to explain to me how to do this transfiguring stuff."

Mera spun to face Reyne. "To start with, your body is all that gets into Evidar."

"You mean, no knives, no bow and arrow? Just me?"

"Just you."

"That sucks. All the training we've done with blades. Why? It just wasted time."

"Not really. We have allies on Evidar. Once you get there, your first task will be to find them. They'll get you outfitted with everything you're going to need, provide you with maps, and they'll have current information about the primary targets. Your contacts will be a guy named Aderlee and a woman named Siandra. I'll get you more info on them before you depart."

"Wait, go back. Only my body. What about clothes? I pop in naked?"

"As the day you were born. I don't make the rules. Remember when you saw your father Edruk plow through Baide's bedroom door the night they died? He didn't have a stitch of clothing on because he'd just transfigured from Evidar."

"No way, I'll freeze my balls off."

Gina piped up, "Something tells me it won't be a big loss," obviously amused.

Reyne ignored her. "Mera, tell me you have a plan. Or am I gonna prance around Evidar, flopping and bouncing my privates as I murder my way through our enemies?"

Gina laughed. "I'm just running that image through my mind. It's a riot."

Reyne shook his head. "Oh, this is getting better and better."

A broad satisfied grin from Gina grew slowly, and she threw in, "Strip down. Let's practice your arrival on Evidar. Show us what that looks like. Running around, your dick flapping in the wind. Mera, promise me I can be there when he makes it back to Tartica. I got to see this."

Mera lined up his sight along his pointed finger, aimed directly at the amused woman. "Gina. Please. This is serious."

Her faced changed—amusement gone. "Not really, Mera. You made your decision. You know my opinion. You've already disregarded it."

Reyne offered, "Gina, why don't you go? I'll stay right here and go after those two redheads myself."

"Wish I could. Can't. Plus, the naked arrival dance with your bouncing balls around, I can't miss that." Amusing herself once again at Reyne's expense, she rolled off the boulder, laughing.

Reyne turned to Mera. "And that's another thing. You've never explained to me why I'm the only one. Send that... her."

Gina stopped laughing, "Ah, farm boy, you caught yourself. Learned your lesson once. There's hope for you."

Mera's cheeks puffed and he let loose a long, drawn-out, exasperated breath. "You two have got to stop. I'm begging you."

Gina flicked her eyebrows up and down. "I will if he will."

"I will if he will," Reyne mocked. "What are you, six years old? Mera, do we still need her here?"

"Yes."

"Fine. Then explain to me how I make this magical journey."

Mera paused. "You know when you have those dreams when you're floating around out of your body—"

"Who told you about those? Nobody knows about them."

"The morning we broke camp, the day you ate your first meal after we left Hensdale. You had an episode, standing, frozen in place. You couldn't move. Couldn't talk. I had to yank you back. Couldn't believe my eyes. I witnessed you in a lucid dream state while awake. Amazing."

"Never happened to me before, you know, while awake. Only happens when I'm sleeping... until that day. Scared the shit outta myself."

"I knew you've had out-of-body events while you slept."

"Awake, asleep, doesn't matter. I hate when it happens."

"Lucid dreaming while asleep is something all Tweeners can do. But if you can access the astral plane from a non-sleep consciousness, wow! Not even your birth father Edruk could enter the Void without first being asleep. Wish we had more time to explore and develop that talent of yours. We'll look into it when you return. You'd be unstoppable moving between dimensions at will."

"Who told you about me? About those night terrors. Only two people knew: Mithany and my mom, and I asked them not to tell anyone."

"Mithany didn't betray your secret. Pachelle shared it with me when you were very young. Before you asked her not to tell. Please forgive her."

Reyne's mood soured. His mother, Pachelle, the person who raised him and who he loved more than anyone other than Mithany, shared his secret. It ached like betrayal and burrowed sadness into his heart. Gone from his life, dead seven years, he'd never have the chance to confront her. Mera's explanation made sense; it happened before he told her not to share. Irrational or not, it hurt. Reyne buried his pain and listened to Mera's continuing explanation.

"The medical-psychological term for them is vestibular-motor hallucinations, but most people just call it sleep paralysis, astral projecting, or night terrors. People who don't understand call them hallucinations, but they're not. They're real. The state of sleep paralysis, when your mind is free of its body, is the first step in the transfiguration process."

"That surprises me. Go on."

"It's a rare thing for a person's consciousness to leave its body. When it happens, your mind feels like it's floating, and you look down at your own sleeping-self. You hover close, out of instinct. For your own safety, you believe your untethered consciousness has to remain near its physical host. Awareness of the periphery fades into the background of your perception. Beyond the fuzzy outskirts that you're vaguely aware of is the Void. My guess, you never even knew it existed."

"Nope."

"Of course not. What reason did you have? You were in sleep paralysis, experiencing what people call night terrors. Your mind wanted to remain anchored, to get back into your head. It's frightening being outside your physical form. You don't know how to get back. Your body can't move a single muscle. You're scared, you try to move just a finger. You can't. You try but can't speak. You struggled to call out. Your vocal cords don't respond to your command, but you somehow manage to squeeze out a guttural noise. When you're lucky, either Pachelle or Mithany hears your pleading grunt and is there to wake you—to pull you out of sleep, back to the safety of body and mind as one. Did I get it right?"

"That's the part I hate the most. Can't move. Can't make words. I always feel helpless."

"That helpless feeling makes you frantic. You're crazed, trying to get your mind back into your body. I'm pretty sure that's what it's been like for you."

"Every time."

"But next time, let go. Stop fighting the instinct to get back. Let yourself drift. Push through the worldly environment your consciousness is in. Then, when you're looking down at your own body, ignore it. Turn away. The Void is just beyond the fuzzy periphery."

"Easy for you to say."

The excitement in Mera's eyes spoke louder to Reyne than his words.

Mera continued. "Inside the Void, it's like a hub to every possible future of every life. If there are other realities, and if the membrane of our dimension, our Earth, touches the membrane of another dimension, all that other world's futures for every life are there in the Void. And we already know there is at least one other reality, one other dimensional membrane touching ours—Evidar."

He didn't want to believe in Mera's fantasy world, but if he sought any chance to return to Mithany, Reyne had to swallow all of it.

Gina threw in, "See, you have a special skill just like me, only different. I'm a little jealous. Wish I could go. Me and Mera tried to get me there but couldn't. Be better for all of us if I could."

Reyne gave Gina an appreciative nod. "I wish you could too. I wouldn't have to do any of this."

Reyne turned from Gina and told Mera, "Since that ain't gonna happen, Mera, go on."

"Gina," Mera began, "When we're done here, can you do a wide sweep of the area like we talked about? Make sure no visitors. I'll stay with Reyne tonight. Reyne and I will talk more about all this."

Gina nodded. "Sure, Mera. Can do."

Turning back to Reyne, Mera continued where he'd left off, "Your thoughts have to punch through a metaphysical barrier based on nothing but mental will. Once you pierce it, you enter the Void. Here's the tricky part. Probability Waves of every living thing across the universe exist in there. You'll experience uncountable numbers of Probability Waves, like a vast, endless ocean jouncing all around, interacting, interfering with each other. The Void starts out black, but as you focus your thoughts on that single consciousness you want to touch, a light grows all around you. Some Probability Waves hold a more likely future than others. Each wave represents one possible future of one consciousness. Each life force holds thousands, if not millions, of possible alternative futures. Instinct will help you find the one you seek. If you're wrong, you can get lost in them."

"What the hell. Suppose I do get lost. What then?"

"Stay focused on that one life force. Your thoughts must stay locked on the one point you hold firm in your mind: your target. What you focus on will find you. It will sense your presence in the thoughts you send out into the Void. Reach out to it. You might see it, touch it, smell it, taste it, or just hear it. Everyone has a different experience. Some get only one sense in there. Maybe you'll access all five, maybe just one, but once you sense any in any way, you're connected to it. When I sent Gina, she couldn't even get past the astral plane into the Void."

"Sounds like mumbo jumbo. How will I know it's the right one?"

"You'll feel it. Some people have the rare ability to interact and communicate with a single person's thoughts. Doesn't matter what dimension they're from. These are usually people who can get into the Void, but not beyond it. Remember what I told you: everything is alive, rocks, trees, land, not just people, every piece of matter teems with life. Quantum particles make up everything, and those particles are the basis of all life."

Reyne smirked. "Yeah, I remember. The little quantum whaticles. The basis of all life. See, sometimes I listen when you talk."

"Yes. Good. Anyway, moving on. Find it and hold on to that connection, the one point in the Void where the consciousness of your target flows. And if you can, you ride its wave crest back to where it resides in the physical world. Once you do that, your own corporeal body will follow. Some have failed to ride the Probability Wave crest of their target's consciousness back through the other reality's metaphysical barrier into the other world. My suspicion is they've locked onto a Probability Wave with a likely outcome close to zero. But you can never know what happened to them in there. They're lost."

"And if I ride a wave with the zero outcome?"

"I'm not going to lie to you. You'd be fucked. You'll be lost forever."

Reyne blurted, "Oh, this is just GGGREAT! Either I land balls-ass naked, no weapons, somewhere I've never been, looking for people I don't know who don't know me. And that's if I'm lucky. Or I just disappear into the Void, never to be seen again."

Mera nodded to the side. "Yeah, that sounds about right."

"You gotta be kiddin' me."

"Sorry. It is one of the reasons so few people exist who can do it."

Reyne contemplated the Void as Mera described it. Tried to picture it. He struggled to believe. *How can any of it exist the way Mera explains it? Voids? Different dimensions? It's all impossible. But he did show me the Firaché and that Firaché queen. Seemed impossible. He conjured the past. Seemed impossible too. Showed me a different biological family. And Daedyn's not my twin, I'm adopted. Showed me those two red-haired women who stole so much from me. Hard to believe, but if I'm gonna get back to Mithany, I gotta accept it. Got no choice.* But Reyne had one more question. "Mera, how do you know all this?"

"I've been around long enough and have sent others into the Void. Some have returned to tell me their experiences. I can help you get there but, like Gina, can't go myself."

"You sure about that, Mera? When you spoke of what it's like in the Void, it struck me a little more than just secondhand information. Heard passion in your voice. Saw a gleam in your eye. You may've gotten some secondhand accounts, I'll give you that, but seems there's more to your story."

"Wish it were so. But let me be even more honest with you, Reyne. You're deflecting. I think you're conflicted. You're dealing with an internal battle pitting the reality of what you think you understand about the world against one that you have to accept if you want to return to Mithany."

Mera had it right. What couldn't be real, the Void, pitted against what he absolutely needed to go on, Mithany's love. Mera's tale of the Void, although incomprehensible, had to be accepted. With pure will, Reyne shut down the engulfing conflict between his mind and his heart. He embraced the impossible in order to have a remote chance of reclaiming his reason for living—Mithany. His needs dispatched his doubts. But in pushing past his reservation, fear emerged as a residual casualty of acceptance. He dreaded what came next.

"It's a bit tough to chew. I'll buy your story only because I have to... if I want to save Mithany. But I would be lying if I said I wasn't at least a little afraid to put myself in the Void. What if I get lost in there like you said? I'll lose everything."

"There's good news and bad news. I can wake you up if your body is still in our world. Waking will pull you out of the Void. If I think it's taking too long, or I sense you're lost, I can rouse you."

"Okay, what's the bad news?"

"Once your physical body flows out of Tartica's reality, there's nothing I can do. You'll be on your own."

Resigned to do whatever it took, Reyne's voice escaped in a whisper. "So what comes next?"

"You're going on a test flight into the astral plane, and you are going to touch the Void."

FIRST DAY OF A NEW LIFE

TETH: 8TH DAY OF THE HARVEST MOON

Jerithan

The KCG dumped the once First Lord Jerithan, without food, without water, and absent of coin, along a back alley somewhere in the slums of Teth. Jerithan purchased more time on Earth with a promise to Derr to be his inside man: to provide information of First Lord Serco's plans in the fomenting confrontation between the Kingdom of Adelle and Teth's governing authority, the Temple of Life.

Dressed in commoners' clothes and provided a backpack containing only his holy vestments, Jerithan groaned, face down in gutter wastewater near a dilapidated hovel.

In every direction, single-storied, decrepit structures adjoined to each other by common walls delivered the bare necessities to be considered housing. Shack after shack lined both sides of the dirt road passing between them. The gloomy gray clouds of the overcast morning matched both his surroundings and his mood.

Small fragments of pea gravel pushed from the center of the unkept lane accumulated along the base of the ramshackled homes. The scattered pebbles embedded in the hardened dirt surface hinted at a roadway once covered by the tiny rocks, but had long ago surrendered to the forces of indifference.

His eyes darted from side to side. Uncertainty and fear told him to avoid body movements until he understood the risks. Jerithan scanned his surroundings to discover others like himself scattered about the narrow alley and, much like him, presumed homeless. Cold and wet, he thought, *At least my ass no longer burns.* The physical pain had subsided, but the mental anguish of the ordeal would never heal.

Were the lumps of tattered clothes bearing people underneath, spread over the limits of his sights, reaching out in every direction, threats to him? How could he not assume otherwise?

Jerithan had grown accustomed to the finery and trappings of his station as First Lord. He considered how far he'd fallen. The filth of the alley, the rundown condition of the buildings, the stench rising from the gutters—all seemed an adequate metaphor to him for his new life. His life's work, his burning ambition to wrest control over all of Tartica as its emperor was dashed against a wall of betrayal by his fellow prudents. His dreams of triumph had morphed into the nightmare of the decrepit alleyway. The Council of Prudents stripped him of everything. Their actions set off a chain of events that put him in this dirty, filthy, miserable alley.

They will pay.

Hatred consumed him for the one man behind his precipitous down-fall—Prudent Garragent Serco.

He will pay.

Abandoned by his secret ally, the Voice, and lying in a gutter, Jerithan tasted the bile of resentment. His predicament forced him to realize the Voice couldn't have been his God. God would have protected him. God wouldn't have left him destitute, a man without a home, without a means to survive. The Voice wasn't even his friend. The fate of his one true friend, Prudent Razoal, was death. He had new friends, hatred and anger, to keep him company.

Retention of his Prudent status, yet without a portfolio, meant nothing to Jerithan. Although not defrocked, Serco certainly wouldn't welcome him into the Temple Palace compound. And even if permitted, he wouldn't go; he held on to what little had been left of his pride.

The Temple of Life's newly elected First Lord Serco had turned him over to Derr, the soulless bastard who had his people do unthinkable things to him. Jerithan despised Derr as if he did the evil deed himself.

Derr will pay.

In time, they all will.

…Just not today.

First, he had to put his life back together, except he didn't know how.

Agents of Derr are everywhere. If I don't deliver, Derr will find me. I have nowhere to hide. There is the one exception. The one place I cannot go and the one place where Derr needs me to be—First Lord Serco's inner sanctum.

Derr lacked direct access to Serco's closest advisors. The blind spot in Adelle's clandestine, intel-gathering operations earned Jerithan his reprieve. But if Derr lacked access, so did Jerithan. Serco's hatred of Jerithan left him little chance of delivering on the lifesaving bargain he'd struck with Derr.

No worse rock. No worse hard place.

He yearned to scream.

He burned to lash out.

He craved the release of pent-up resentment at what had been done to him, throbbing beneath the shabby, worn garments scarcely holding off the chill of the morning air. It had barely begun, yet he hated his new life as much as he hated the people who forced it on him.

Jerithan's butt was parked on gravel-encrusted dirt, while his back rested against a run-down shack. With bent knees to his chest, he rested his head between them.

A squeak of rusty hinges, *creaaaak,* yanked Jerithan's attention from the contemplation of his miserable existence. A heavy-set older woman emerged through the door and threw piss-pot water into the street. The night's-long accumulation of human waste landed a few feet away. A splash of urine found Jerithan's leg, and he looked up at her.

"Get away! Get out of here you bum, or next time it will land on your head." She cupped the empty chamber pot under her bulbous arm and slammed the door behind her. The force of it threatened to render the building into a pile of rubble while the clatter roused a few of Jerithan's new brethren. His eyes bulged as a new understanding of his predicament gripped him: *What if any of them recognize me?*

A voice rang out. "Hey you there. Who're you?" It came from under a pile of ragged clothes with two eyes peering out.

The threatening sound of angry words sent panic racing through Jerithan.

His head shot down between his knees, hiding his face. He pulled his body in tight. Dread pounded inside his skull. One thought flooded his mind: he would be found out.

"I'm talkin' to you," the man yelled.

Jerithan didn't move. Yet with each squeeze of the muscle in his chest, pressure pulsed through his veins, sending deafening drumbeats to his ears.

"Hey, hey! Guys, wake up. We gots company."

The once pampered First Lord inside Jerithan didn't know the rules. Instinct took hold.

I'm not welcome.

This is enemy turf.

Suddenly, abandoned memories of his childhood flooded through him. Those difficult years taught him the harsh realities of survival on the streets. The coddled prudent in him had consigned to oblivion the guttersnipe way of life, but the boy in him remembered. His gut tightened, never wanting to ever think of those days again. Memories from his younger self played in his head and screamed warnings into his thoughts.

I am their hope.

Hope for better boots.

Hope for better clothes.

Hope for whatever I have that will soon be theirs.

He knew of their hopes. He too once held on to them.

Jerithan sprang up, heeding the warnings from his long-buried youth. Before any of the homeless roused to action, he bolted from the alley, turned a corner, and entered the unknown dangers of Teth's shantytown.

Hunting the Hunters

The Woodlands of Kantos: 8th Day of the Harvest Moon

Quith

Quith's concentration broke the instant a knife point pressed into his back. Blood leaked from where the sharp tip bit into his flesh. Pushed into him just deep enough to release a small amount of the red, life-giving fluid and to alert him that either Tylus, the fellow agent Quith now hunted, had improved beyond all expectations, or he was fucked.

Exactly where in an isolated midwestern forest in the Tartican nation of Kantos Quith had been compromised, he couldn't be sure. One thing he knew with absolute certainty, he never heard a sound from whomever now held a knife to him nor did he witness anyone approach. With an unknown assailant poised to kill him, years of field experience kicked in. He'd been in situations like this before and lived.

Keep your head. You'll live through this.

Assess first. Then act.

Not dead… they want something.

Myriad options raced through his mind searching for a life-sustaining way out. Moves he'd executed hundreds if not thousands of times, in both preparedness exercises and during firsthand deadly encounters, came to mind. He rejected them all. Someone skilled enough to get the jump on him wasn't anyone to be taking chance with; better to play it safe.

I'm still alive. If they intended to kill me, I'd be dead already. Stay put. Wait for an opening.

Quith hoped his attacker to be Tylus playing games. Tylus, or whoever held the blade, would make a mistake. An opening would appear. One always appeared. Survival hinged on whether you were good enough to recognize it when it came and skilled enough to take advantage of the opportunity. Quith considered himself good enough at both. In the end, his best move—no move.

Experience and training taught him not to feel. Not to fear. But to think. To assess. To survive. Emotions—especially fear—in moments like these only got you killed. And Quith had years of experience burying his feelings.

His assailant remained silent. Not a sound. Not a single movement. Only the blade, drawing just enough blood, alerting Quith to the peril.

He offered a friendly tone, hoping to ease his attacker from thoughts that might put him in further danger. "Well, I'm not dead. What do you want from me?"

A voice replied. "You'll be dead soon enough."

The voice caught him off guard. Yet the intonation surprised him.

A woman.

The voice, not Dylla. Not Neladith. Not Kebra.

He expected Tylus.

Concern leaked in as blood leaked out.

Running through his options, he concluded, *No sudden moves... for now.*

Not as friendly this time, Quith said, "You have me at a disadvantage. I'd like to turn around so I can face who holds my life in their hands."

"No."

"Alright then. What's next?" He considered making a snap move to free himself. Just as he coiled to strike, he felt the tip slide in a few millimeters deeper, as though she read his thoughts. A caution he heeded and remained still.

The female holding him motionless with her blade said, "Tell me why I shouldn't put a quick end to you."

The metal's sting wanted to leech pain into Quith. He denied its purchase. Little doses of blood and discomfort were easy enough for Quith to manage. The flow of his bio-fluid, while minimal so far, held little concern, but only if it stayed that way. The liberation of more of it would harbor bigger worries.

With a goal to escape the encounter with his life intact, Quith fed her an explanation she might accept. "I'm trying to find a friend. He wandered off somewhere around here."

"We both know that isn't true. You should have played it differently. Your nonchalant attitude gave you away. Any of the locals would have shit their pants. You didn't. You gave me the clear impression you've been in situations like this before."

"Maybe I'm just brave."

"Maybe you're just stupid."

Dammit. She's right. I expected Tylus. Played it off too light. Shit.

After reflecting on his mistake, he said, "I'm that kinda guy. You know, warm and fuzzy." Not expecting her to buy it, but it didn't hurt to get her to let her guard down.

"Dressed in black. Skulking around in the dark of night. A dagger in your left boot. Another attached to the side of your right pant leg along with the one up your sleeve. Then there's the way you stepped into each of the footprints Tylus left behind. We both saw they were still fresh. He came through here a little over an hour ago."

Only another trained agent could have picked up on all that. Did I miss a third recruit of Dylla's? And how does she know Tylus, or that they were his tracks? Not good.

Quith's muscles tensed.

Is this woman one of Dylla's locals, or one of Mera's contracted hitters?

Quith realized, while she had him figured out, he remained at a disadvantage knowing nothing of her. His mind grasped for a solution—one keeping him alive.

I got only one shot at this. It's now or never. Might die in the effort, but better to try than to die doing nothing.

Now!

Quith shot forward several feet from his would-be executioner. He drew a knife secured along his pant leg. He spun around. With blade in hand, Quith faced off with his assailant jumping into his battle-ready stance. Her hand and the knife hung in the air where his back had been. The woman hadn't moved. She tilted her head and offered him a quizzical look.

Quith kept his gaze fixed on the woman dressed like him in operational black. Her eyes were all she left exposed. He reached down to extract a second weapon hidden in his boot. Each hand armed with killing metal, he said, "Time to die."

She smiled at him.

He sprung his attack.

Only feet apart, he lunged at her. But assaulted only empty space. His target, gone from where she stood, Quith snapped his head around. She'd moved to the spot where he began his attack. Not allowing a second's reprieve, Quith charged again. She'd disappeared before he reached her. He turned around only to find her back where she started.

She said, "You're smart enough to know I could've killed you already. Do you want to know why you're still breathing?"

"That's impossible... Who the fuck are *you*?"

The woman pulled back the black hood covering her head and obscuring her face. "You can call me Gina. And I'm going to guess you're either Quith or Grafph. You're definitely not a local. Those eyes of yours reflecting in the moonlight gives you away, for those of us who know what they mean. I once had a cat. Your eyes remind me of his. I've known others of your kind. Not for long, mind you. They're all dead now."

"You seem to know a bit about me. Guess you know more than just names."

"Yes, I do. And where you're from. And what you're doing here. I can't allow that."

"Then why am I not dead like the rest of them? That is, if you think you're man enough to kill me."

Quith watched Gina's face change. "I don't like that. Why would you think it takes a man? You must not respect women. Makes me want to end you right now. But before you die, there's a few things I want to know."

"What makes you think I'm going to tell you anything?"

Gina chuckled. "Those exact words were spoken by your buddy Tylus less than an hour ago. Oh, he won't be joining us. Or anyone, for that matter. Ever again."

He'd known Tylus for years. Even liked him. Respected him as a solid operator. A bit of an ass-kisser, but now his death brought Quith one step closer to a reprieve from his own Evidarian death sentence. *Fuck him,* Quith thought, lacking any remorse for the man. *I'd of killed him myself.*

Quith put it together quickly: *She's hunting the hunters.*

A grin took hold of Quith's face; born in an idea, a vestige of hope—one slim chance to survive the encounter.

Will she believe it?

Laying the foundation of his reclamation, Quith began, "Tylus is gone. I'm good with that. In fact, I planned to kill him myself. That's why I'm here. If you didn't do it, I would have."

Gina walked up to Quith. She leaned in close and said, "Wow. That one's a whopper."

Quith contemplated slicing her throat but wasn't sure he could pull it off, given the speed she'd shown herself capable of. He wondered if she gave him the opportunity as a test.

Stay put. Don't take the bait.

He didn't move.

Gina remained close, turning her back on him, just feet away.

Still, he didn't move.

"You have me curious, Grafph or Quith, whatever your name is. I would have figured you to attack a helpless woman with her guard down. I gave you the opening."

She turned to face him.

"You don't give me enough credit. You're neither helpless nor was your guard down. But, that's not why. My name is Selundra Quith, and Grafph is dead."

Quith heard Gina's reply come back at him with a playful lilt. "Oh my. Tell me more."

Quith's efforts at a reprieve continued. "We can help each other."

"What could an agent of Evidar, sent to my world to exterminate a helpless young businessman whose life revolves around running a nut farm, do to help me?"

"You know, we don't call it Evidar. We just call it Earth."

"Who gives a shit what you call it."

"Just saying. Anyway, I slipped a dagger into the base of Grafph's skull. He won't be joining in the effort to find Reyne Brenton. I did that."

"Am I to believe you betrayed your kind?"

"You seem like a smart girl. Figure it out."

Gina frowned. "There you go again. Girl? Do I look like a girl? This woman is going to kill you in the next few minutes, and based on your attitude about women, I'm going to enjoy it."

"I betrayed my people because I'm a wanted man."

In front of Quith, dressed in skintight black, Gina said, "I extracted some useful information from your associate. He said nothing about going after you. I'm fairly certain he told me everything he knew about your little operation... although reluctantly. If you'd gotten here sooner, you might've heard him screaming."

Calm, Quith pleaded his case. "Reyne Brenton isn't the only one on their list. So am I. They blame me for fucking it up. The other Brenton brother took the arrow meant for Reyne. I confirmed the target. I made the call. Now they want me to pay for letting Reyne slip away. The guy who runs the show, some call him the Devil's Blacksmith, isn't all that forgiving."

"He doesn't sound very magnanimous. The moniker gives it away, wouldn't you say? You like that big word... magnanimous?"

He watched her pace, deep in thought. But what stood out as she strode back and forth, not a sound escaped under her feet. *How is that possible?*

While pacing, she said, "There were a few things I didn't understand. I watched you place your footsteps on top of the tracks he left behind. And that's what got me curious. Who are you hiding from? Not me."

"So, curiosity kept me alive."

"Yes, it has. You had no clue I'd be looking for your kind. Who did you expect to be stalking you? That's the question that's kept you alive. That's why I didn't slide my dagger through your back, into your heart, yet." She held out the blade. "It's a long one."

Gina, a woman exceptionally skilled, artfully playful and, without a doubt, deadly, piqued his interest. The kind of woman he'd always been drawn to. His life hung on his next words, yet he gambled with a playful quip. "I got a big one too. Want to see it?"

In small movements, she shook her head. Disgust and disappointment colored her words, "Ugh, just answer my question."

"Suppose I don't want to?"

"Don't. No reason then for you to keep breathing." Gina took one step in his direction.

"Stop." He shot back, holding up one hand. "Thought we had some frisky banter going there. Guess I got that wrong. I'll tell you everything you want to know."

Halting her forward movement, Gina said, "Go on. I'm listening. And by the way, you were w-a-a-a-y-y-y off base."

Quith shrugged. "I'm assuming you know who Dylla Weisner is. I didn't want her or anyone else to know someone hunted Tylus. She'd figure it could've been me. I did what I did to buy more time for myself."

Gina held out her arm and rolled her finger over and over. "And?"

"Dylla is going to find Grafph dead soon enough. I think she made a tactical error not sharing with Tylus or Grafph that she wanted me dead. Wanted them to focus on getting rid of Reyne Brenton. She didn't want to distract them with thoughts of having to take out their boss I suppose."

"And what about Grafph?"

"There's an isolated apple farm in Hensdale. On the outskirts. We eliminated the older couple and had been using it as our base of operations. Go there, you'll find him sitting on the sofa. He can't get up. Probably smells a bit ripe by now. Should prove to you I'm telling the truth."

Quith had little choice betraying his own. In all his years spent killing others, he'd always loved the thrill of the action. The single-minded devotion of the Devil's Blacksmith to the cause of dimensional reunification never meant as much to Quith as the excitement of the hunt. Leaving Evidar behind was a minor sacrifice he was willing to accept; dying in the backwoods of Tartica, that was an altogether different matter.

Gina rubbed her chin. "Why would you do that?"

Protecting secrets no longer meant anything to Quith. A way forward, saving himself from his own people and from the enticing woman before him, that's all he cared about. Quith made his final pitch to Gina, and the more he shared, the better his chances. "Like I said, if I want to live, even if it has to be in this place. I no longer give a shit if Reyne Brenton lives or dies. I need to eliminate everyone from my world who's here now, before they do it to me. I tracked Tylus so he'd join his buddy Grafph. Dylla Weisner is next on my list. I can also tell you Dylla's brought over two more agents. A woman named Kebra and a big brute called Harvin. They're heading south to Teth, together, looking for Reyne Brenton... and me. Both are exceptional trackers and deadly. Of the two, he's virtually impossible to take down, and she's as smart as, and more cunning than, anyone I've ever known."

"Good to know."

Quith asked, seeking a pronouncement of life or death, "Are we going to go back to our battle-ready positions or are you going to accept the fact that, while I'm not on your side, I'm going to kill everyone from what you call Evidar who is here, now, on my new home world?"

"Battle stances. Nah, it would've never come to that. I'd just slit your throat before your brain even knew I moved. Don't assume I won't do it at some point in the future."

Quith exhaled. Relieved. Yet, uncertain he could believe her. In a show of feigned trust, he bent down to slip a dagger back into his boot. His gaze darted at the hidden, miniature scabbard inside his footwear only for a second. He looked up and started to say, "Do we have a—"

But Gina was gone.

At the Threshold

The Woodlands of Kantos: 9th Day of the Harvest Moon

Reyne | Dylla | Gina

In a glade isolated in the Woodlands of Kantos where Reyne trained, Gina walked into camp, returning from her nighttime scouting excursion. Reyne offered her a wave hello. Mera announced, "Great. You're back. We can get started. Time's arrived for Reyne to enter the astral plane and touch the Void."

"What, Mera, no hello?"

"Hello, Gina. Welcome back. Sorry, I want to do this straight away. You and I'll talk after. I'm anxious to hear of your scouting results of last night."

Mera orchestrated where he wanted everyone. Reyne took up a position, prostrate on the ground face up with Mera kneeling over him, both men at the base of two large boulders. Gina sat off to the side at her regular spot on a pile of large rocks.

The improbable transition kicked off with Mera's two fingers placed on the apprehensive nut farmer's forehead. "Reyne," Mera began. "We've done this now three times. I'm going to open your Eye of Heaven. Once you can access your Eye of Heaven on your own—some call it your Third Eye—you won't need me anymore to transfigure. But, for now, you require assistance."

Each time the enigmatic older man opened Reyne's Eye of Heaven, another secret of the universe revealed itself to Reyne. First to expose the fire-beings Mera call the Firaché, and later, on two occasions, to call forth the past to appear before him as an apparition in the present.

The Eye of Heaven, buried in the frontal lobe of the human brain, powerful yet rarely accessed because of the neglect and ignorance mankind fostered of it over the ages. Mera had told Reyne of books in the Temple of Life's secret library that spoke of ancient cultures, shamans and others skilled at accessing the Third Eye. All dismissed by the civilized world of the Second Age as hokum. How Mera knew anything of the Second Age he never explained, yet Reyne bore witness to the power of the Third Eye. With Mera as his guide, Reyne's fourth undertaking into the unknown awaited him.

Trepidation gnawed at Reyne. "Mera, I gotta admit, I'm a little concerned 'cause of what you told me about the Void."

Gina added, "You can do this."

"I never been hypnotized," Reyne told Mera. "You sure you gotta put me under?"

On one bent leg, Mera kneeled alongside Reyne. "Hypnosis solves two problems: first, you'll achieve a sleep-like state fast, and second, remember what I told you? I'll place you under and give you a suggestion for your mind to leave your body while you sleep. You ready?"

Reyne called to mind the life-changing events stirring him to risk everything. His heart raced.

Lub-dub, the image of Daedyn's murdered body flashed in his mind.

Lub-dub, Mithany's hand slipped through his, gone.

Lub-dub, his mother gave him life, cradled him in her arms, then died.

Lub-dub, his little sister's lifeless body, soaked in a pool of blood.

Lub-dub. Lub-dub. Lub-dub... His ears, his head, burned with each pulse.

Mera said something. The deep commanding tones pulled Reyne from his thoughts. He heard Mera call out. "Reyne?"

"I'm ready. Let's do this."

"Good."

Reyne reached up. Grabbed Mera by the collar. "Promise me, Mera, if this goes wrong, you'll yank me back. If you can't, if I don't make it, you watch over Mithany for as long as she lives."

"Of course."

From off to the side, he heard Gina say, "I'll be there for her too."

Gina's offer caught Reyne off guard. He let go Mera's collar. "Thank you both. Your offers mean a lot."

Still kneeling alongside Reyne, Mera said, "Nice to see you two getting along."

Gina picked up her head to face Mera. "Don't get ahead of yourself, old friend. None of it will be necessary. He's gonna do great."

"As much as I appreciate both offers, fingers crossed it won't come to that."

Gina cupped her hand along the side of her mouth and aimed a whisper at Mera, "We could've used another couple of weeks."

On the ground, motionless, Reyne shot back, "I heard that."

Mera cut in, "Never mind her. I wouldn't be sending you if you weren't ready. Remember, today you're just going to look into the Void. If it goes well, tomorrow you go in."

"You're going to do great," Gina repeated. "You're a natural." Not watching her face, Reyne imagined she rolled her eyes.

Mera continued, "You've studied the image I gave you. That's the landscape you focus on. One exact spot on Evidar. It's an open field teaming with quantum life forces and the Probability Waves coming off that place are what you're looking for. Search through them for the one you want. Next time you go into the Void, you'll grab hold to just the right wave crest. But not today."

Reyne's disposition changed. He buried his anxiety, clenched his fists at his side, mustered his resolve, and said, "Enough talk. Mera, do your magic."

"One thing before we start. I see your hands balled up tight. That's a problem. I need you relaxed for hypnosis to work. I can get you there once you're in a peaceful state of mind. Open your hands, shake them out, and let me know when you're ready. Take a couple of slow, deep breaths."

Reyne did as Mera asked and felt two fingers on his forehead.

"Relax. Focus on my voice. Feel the peace flowing into your mind. Coming into your head. Flowing into the Eye of Heaven, your Third Eye." Reyne heard Mera's slow patter and to his surprise, he sensed calmness, serenity seeping in, spreading throughout his body from the very spot of Mera's touch.

Reyne continue to concentrate on the soothing tones as Mera slowly directed him, "From your Eye of Heaven into your brain, fill your thoughts with relaxation. It moves into your ears, your eyes, your lips..."

Waves of calm washed over Reyne.

Mera kept going, "Feel the peace reach your neck, into your spine, and let it flow. Feel total relaxation in your shoulders. It carries peace down your back, into your chest, down your arms. Your fingers are at ease."

Reyne, committed to the process, followed Mera's every word. His voice was melodic, calm and soothing, Mera guided peace through each of Reyne's bodily features. Reyne's mind followed and at what point he'd fallen under Mera's spell, Reyne didn't know. He thought he heard something about releasing his mind from his body.

Dylla Weisner moved through the forest in silence. Searching for Neladith, who headed towards Topak, brought Dylla north, somewhere in the Tartican midwestern forest of the Peoples Republic of Kantos that the locals called the Woodlands.

Earlier that morning, Dylla spotted the telltale signs of off-road travelers, always worth exploring to an experienced tracker tasked with hunting down unsuspecting Tarticans. A few patches of trampled grass leading away from the main roadway set off alarms to her trained eye. The repeating pockets of crushed turf might have amounted to nothing, but she had to check it out. Similar signs over the past day or so all led to dead ends. These footprints, however, continued well off the road. As the tracks led into an open field, she moved to the edge of the forest tree line, remaining out of sight. Almost two miles in, instead of finding her own agent, Dylla looked out over the open field to the hiding place of Reyne

Brenton. However, Reyne was not alone in the isolated glade surrounded by trees. Two others accompanied the problematic Tweener.

She recognized her target, Reyne Brenton, lying on the ground, Mera kneeling at his side, but also present was an unfamiliar woman sitting on rocks. The woman didn't matter. Dylla considered her of little consequence, easily disposed of. Mera, an altogether other concern, represented a more serious threat, one she wouldn't let stand in her way.

Caution demanded, because of Mera's presence, Dylla remain absolutely still until the moment of her attack. Mera's extraordinary skills could lead to her detection. He'd proven himself a thorn in Evidar's side too many times not to afford him a wide berth. And facing off against all three at once would even challenge her skill set.

Flushed with excitement, she assessed her options. Dylla scoped out the setting, the players, weather conditions, all directed at guiding her to the best approach—to kill Reyne.

The Devil's Blacksmith will be pleased when I finally put this bastard down.

The distance from the forest edge to Reyne's location made it impossible for Dylla to hear them talking. Words turned out to be irrelevant. Dylla's mind reeled when Mera placed two fingers to Reyne's forehead.

Shit, it's beginning.

Dylla recalled when, years earlier, during her first time transfiguring to Tartica, her supervisor, a Mr. Lesni, placed his two fingers on her brow, opening her Eye of Heaven.

Reyne has to be eliminated at all costs.

My entire world depends on me. Here. Now.

He can't be allowed into the Void.

I might never get another chance.

She reveled in the opportunity to be Evidar's savior.

Secured behind a large tree trunk, remaining out of sight and without making a sound, Dylla strung her bow. She silently slipped an arrow from her quiver, nocked it, and prepared to strike.

Determined to fulfill her mission, a command from the Devil's Blacksmith himself, she would kill Reyne. If Mera exacted revenge in the aftermath, so be it. Dylla accepted her pending sacrifice if it came to that, but she wouldn't go down easily.

It's now or never.

She drew back her bow.

Terror gripped Reyne.

Sleep paralysis always scared the shit out of him. Without warning, his mind escaped the confines of its physical form. Reyne looked down on the glade from above. The sight of his body lying on the ground, Mera on one knee at his side and Gina sitting on her familiar perch atop a nearby boulder, sparked fear surging through him.

He caught movement in the tree line. From above, his view offered him a perspective Mera nor Gina could access. But it vanished as quickly as it appeared.

Ignore it.

Mera said turn away.

No distractions.

Focus on the fading edges.

Fight the fear.

He struggled to swallow the anxiety, to permit the peace Mera had instilled in him, to embrace his mind, now free of its corporeal home.

Mera's lips were moving, yet not a single sound from the material world touched Reyne's free-floating, untethered awareness. Mera had delivered sleep as promised and his hypnotic suggestion gave birth to Reyne's current existence in the astral plane. Mera's efforts delivered him to this point. The rest of his journey, accessing the Void, would be up to him. Before he ventured further, he had to get past the unsettling terror of being two separate entities, one of mind, the other of body, a single being unconnected from its constituent parts.

Instinct told him to flee back to the safety of flesh and bone. Desire and determination to hold Mithany in his arms demanded he not.

He existed as a thought. No beating heart or pulsating adrenaline warning him of danger. Panic from somewhere in his non-physical awareness tugged at him. Reyne had to defeat it with the only tools he had: whatever made up his soul, his core, his very being absent the flesh that housed him. There were no eyes to close, no arms to flail, no voice to shout at the dread, and no legs to propel him forward. He had only his will.

Reyne existed without form, without shape, and with no physical boundaries imposed on his out-of-body self, as though inside a very real dream. He forced his attention away from the open field where his body rested. Nothing of him moved, yet he achieved his goal. The physical world held fuzzy edges beyond his ability to perceive into the distance.

Must be the barrier at the edge, leading to the Void.

Uncertainty bore with it the return of fear seeping into whatever he'd become. Gloom fought against will, to turn him from his desired path. Drifting backwards towards his body... *No, Mithany*, he called out, but without voice. From somewhere deep inside, he heard, *Go back*. Clutching at the love he held for her, Reyne pushed down the panic, the uncertainty, the dread of being without physical substance.

You're afraid. You're scared. Too bad. You gotta do this.

Before courage failed him, Reyne raced towards the undefined barrier separating his world from the Void. But movement in the tree line again tried to steal away his focus. A moment's hesitation redirected his eyeless sight to the suspected distraction. He watched for only a second, but nothing moved.

Ignore it.

He pushed forward, slamming into a barrier, a point of convergence of empty space, yet impossibly dense, solid, and impenetrable to his mind.

Reyne wouldn't be denied. His will drilled into the transparent block preventing his advancement. How long he'd been stuck in the molasses that defined the barrier, the edge between the astral plane and the Void, Reyne didn't know.

In spite of whatever force defied him, he moved forward at a glacial pace. Stuck in the grips of nothing, his perception sought the cause of resistance. Disappointed and confused, he discovered only emptiness at its source. He tried to look back to where Mera and Gina should be. But the enwrapping barrier denied him access to the physical world. With no choice left to him, Reyne turned everything he had to breaking the barrier's hold on him. Mera told him only to touch the Void, but he sensed the need to go beyond mere touch. He crept forward slowly towards the Void. Thoughts of Tartica's physical existence faded inch by inch as he plowed forward.

A force pulled at him from behind, trying to deny his progress.

No, he exclaimed, *no.*

He pushed himself ever harder, forcing whatever tried to hold back his consciousness to release him. With all his desire for Mithany in his non-corporeal heart, Reyne concentrated on moving forward, yet the grip of nothing held him even tighter in place.

He pushed forward.

It pulled back.

He shoved.

It constrained.

A day, a week, a second, he didn't know how long he fought against it but kept trying.

A spark. A thought. A realization. To be released of the barrier's grip, he had to break the connection of his mind to the material world he left behind. With only pure will to drive him, Reyne propelled himself forward leaving everything surrounding his prostrate, sleep-induced, body behind—Mera—Gina—and Tartica. Slowly, reluctantly, he sensed it give way. At the instant he expelled all such thoughts from his awareness, the iron grip, the force denying him, shattered.

Freedom.

His momentum expelled him onward, aided by an explosive force at his rear. His mind crashed through a compelling, non-existent, conundrum of the impossible barrier.

Reyne left the world that anchored him. He entered—or as his mind perceived it, he experienced—pure nothingness. He'd broken through, only to be instantly enveloped.

The absence of everything, everywhere, emptiness in every direction.

Infinite nothing, impaling him beyond the limits of his thoughts to grasp.

Completely, utterly alone.

His mind existed as pure thought, the only thing in all the universe of the reality encircling him.

Awareness seeped in of terror's efforts to take hold of him and with it, the untainted darkness of oblivion encased him.

Mera sat back. Neither he nor Gina took their eyes off Reyne lying on the ground as the young man's mind existed somewhere between a simple dream and the impossibility of the Void.

Gina fanned her fingers through her hair. "Reyne looks peaceful lying there. I wouldn't tell him this, but he's not so bad. You know the process. You asked me to break him down. Play mind games. I rode him pretty hard with lots of sex talk. Glad that part's over."

"Appears you've had some success messing with his head."

"Keeping my fingers crossed he survives today. When he returns from the Void, his combat skills need more time. He's not ready to take on your nemesis on Evidar."

"We can only hope he's ready enough," Mera said.

"All the others you had me train, the Tweeners you sent over there to take out the Damus, failed. They're all probably dead. You never shared that with him."

"Not important. He's got something they don't, or they didn't have. He's doing this for the woman he loves. They were only doing it to save our world. Love's a powerful motivator. I wouldn't count him out."

"Could be he wants both. To save Tartica and save the woman he loves. From what I've seen of him, he's got heart. Sure, he's annoying, but he just might be the hero Tartica needs. But, he's not ready for heroics yet."

"You keep beating that drum. I've heard you. It's out of my hands. Hunters are after him. They'll kill him sure enough if he stays here. On Evidar, if he sneaks in undetected, he has a chance."

Gina huffed. "Saving Tartica can wait. First, he's got to get his mind through the barrier and into the Void. Something I've never been able to do myself. Hard to tell if he's there yet."

"Be patient. Not everyone can make it through the barrier. Even if he reaches the Void, might be as far as he gets. This could take some time. The Void's a big, scary place."

Gina interlocked her fingers behind her head and leaned back. "I should tell you I caught up with the guy named Quith. Says his team is after him for botching the Reyne assassination. Claims there's a kill order on his head. Says he already took out one of his own and is going after the rest."

Mera returned a look that spoke of skepticism. "Never trust a word any of them say."

"I don't."

"Good girl."

"Mera..."

"Sorry, go on."

"Anyway, Quith told me more of them have landed on Tartica to go after both Reyne and himself. Maybe you've heard of them—Kebra and Harvin. Quith says he isn't after Reyne any longer. He knows his team killed Daedyn instead of Reyne by mistake. Quith doesn't care about anything but staying alive. You know, saving his own ass."

"You didn't kill him? Your face tells me you let him go on his supposed quest to terminate the others from Evidar. Not what I would have done," Mera said with his back to Gina, again kneeling over Reyne, this time to grab a few alphens from the young man's pocket.

Just as Gina stood, she spotted an arrow take flight, emerging through the tree line sixty yards away. The small, deadly wooden missile headed straight for Reyne.

A Hurricane in a Whisper

Outskirts of Topak: 9th Day of the Harvest Moon

Mithany

Topak, an average midwestern city in the People's Republic of Kantos, lay in ruin.

The closer Mithany, Neladith, Spetzer, and Trell got to the population center, the more they heard constant warnings of danger from the flood of people seeking its escape.

The foursome traveled a course due north from Hensdale. Mithany set out to locate the man she loved, Reyne, while Neladith, Spetzer, and Trell were looking for a dead man they would never find—Daedyn. She couldn't share with them her true objective without betraying Mera's plan for Reyne's safety. How it would play out when the troop found Reyne, Mithany's fractured mind hadn't reconciled. Her duplicitous treatment towards those who gave of themselves to help her caused her no remorse as she struggled for control of her own conflicted persona.

Her search brought her to the outskirts of Topak, where she never expected to encounter a horde of dispossessed. Tales of destruction, burnings, and insurgents seizing control of the city from its duly elected leaders did little to impact Mithany's newly gained positive outlook. She felt for them, yet burned with a singular purpose of her own that nothing could impact.

Within the past few days, Mithany transitioned from her remorseful, self-pitying disposition at Reyne's departure from her life to the joyful wanderer with her heart set on finding him. While Reyne lived, she would walk the four corners of Tartica to find him. Although the sounds of hopeless cries and the lamentations of the recently fashioned homeless battered against the mental shell protecting her psyche, her positive inner voice persevered.

In her hopeful state of mind, Mithany scanned every face, hungry to find Reyne or Mera amongst the tsunami of Topak deserters.

Neladith sidled up to Mithany, slipping her arm under her traveling companion's.

"You're in an especially cheerful mood, Nel."

"Nel? That's new. Your brother called me Nel."

"Called?"

"Calls."

"Of course..." Mithany rested her head on Neladith's shoulder. "I feel like we've gotten closer. Hope you don't mind. I like the name Nel."

"Nah. I kinda like it. And yeah, I am in a good mood. The last couple of nights with Spetzer have made me a happy girl. He's a bit odd, a little self-centered, but he knows his way around the female body. What else can a gal ask for?"

Mithany shook her head and shoulders in a feigned shiver. "Just glad it's not me. No offense. I'm happy for you."

"None taken. It's not like I give a shit about him." Neladith gestured her hand through the air like an actor on stage. "He's but a pleasant distraction."

With a laugh, Mithany said, "The Covenant does encourage that sort of thing."

"Covenant, smuvenant, he helped me on my way to four 'Big-O's' last night. He knows how to hold out. He's quick to reload and he's got other talents too."

Mithany looked up at the broad smile on Neladith. Her thoughts wandered to the nights she'd spent with Reyne in his arms.

A man, his head down as he walked, plowed into the entwined arms of Neladith and Mithany. Neladith pushed back against the intruder. "Hey, asshole. Watch where you're going."

Without looking up, the man mumbled, "Sorry," and kept walking.

Neladith reached out to grab the man's shoulder as he passed. Mithany reacted quickly and stuck out her hand. "Let him go. Can't imagine losing your home. These people are going through a lot. Look around: smoke clouds, burned out homes, and all the clutter we seen in the streets. Let it go."

"Sure. Why not? Not gonna let him shit on my glorious mood. Fuck him."

"Certainly one way to put it."

Neladith stopped, halting Mithany in her tracks. She turned around, cupped her hands aside her mouth, and yelled, "Hey, boys. Get up here."

Mithany dropped her head. "Did you have to? We're doing just fine without them. What do you have in mind?"

"You'll see."

Answering Neladith's call, Trell and Spetzer joined the two women standing in the center of the road. The mass of Topak's newly minted homeless flowed around them like an island standing fast against a deluge.

Spetzer, having raced forward at Neladith's command, breathed hard. "Nel, what's up?"

Mithany spied a knowing smile from Neladith, proud of her control over Spetzer.

Neladith dropped the smirk and said, "Topak's a shithole. Fire's destroyed so much. Can't imagine anyone would want to stay here. If Daedyn's trying to heal his soul over his brother's death, this place would make him feel worse, not better."

Normally a second fiddle to Spetzer, Trell piped up. "So what're you saying? We leave? Look for him somewhere else?"

"If it's okay with Mithany and you two guys, let's head back to Hensdale. We've been out looking for him more than a week. We got nothing. Maybe he's back home by now."

Mithany watched Neladith's expression. The woman's face offered only joy. Mithany wondered of its cause—the residual satisfaction of a night with Spetzer, however revolting? Or if Neladith's mood reflected the friendship born on their journey? Either way, Mithany took it as a sincere offering of helpful advice.

Unfortunately, not the advice Mithany wanted to hear nor take, in spite of its good intentions.

Spetzer offered input. "I don't know about the rest of you, but I could spend another couple of weeks of my life wandering about with this crew." He finished by slapping Neladith hard on her ass.

A girlish squeal of delight escaped Neladith.

Mithany considered, *Better her than me,* before speaking up. "Guess we could. You're probably right about Topak. Not the place to look for Daedyn. But shouldn't we go in and do a quick check? Maybe something happened to him in there."

"Wherever she goes," Spetzer said nodding towards Neladith, "I'm coming."

"Said those same two words a few times myself last night," Neladith laughed.

Mithany pretended to laugh and scanned their faces for reactions. *It's in the eyes.*

Trell's look caught her attention. His eyebrows pointed up while his lids drooped at the corners, which Mithany read as a forlorn puppy. *Seen that look before. He's a bit jealous of Spetz. Can't blame him. Trell, you're always on the outside looking in.*

An unknown woman approached the foursome to stand directly in Mithany's path. "I'm sorry, miss," a stranger said to Mithany and the others. "Overheard you saying you're thinking about going into the city. Don't."

Mithany replied, "May I ask what happened? Others we spoke to only said it's dangerous."

Dressed in fine attire, suggesting her station rose above the Hensdale contingent, the woman explained, "Topak is a mess. Not much of it is left. I have lived here my entire life. My family home's been wiped away. It stood for more than a hundred years. Now it's gone." Water pooled on the lower lids of her bronze-colored eyes.

A man, attired in a fine overcoat, slipped his arm around the woman's shoulder. "Come, dear. Let them be."

The woman spun her upper torso, disposing of the comforting arm of her apparent husband. "No. These young people need to know what they face if they go in."

"Thank you for your kindness," Mithany offered in a gentle tone. "There's four of us. If we stick together, we'll be safe... no?"

The woman appeared to Mithany to be of the upper class and in her late forties. A refined woman of means, now one of many nameless, faceless indigents.

"My dear, don't go into Topak. You may know of the birthing farm just a few miles north. Many in Topak worked there. It is not a pleasant place for either the workers or those forced to procreate. A few go to the farms by choice to have children, but not many. It is what our Covenant asks of all of us, so we, in Topak, supported the farm over all the decades it's been here."

Six people stood in the center of the street on the outskirts of a dying town. Mithany and her friends listened to the rich lady's tale. The exodus from Topak continued to drift past them as she spoke. "It started at the procreation center. Word spread quickly, the Chancellor of Adelle had called for the end of the Covenant of Absolute Universal Obligations. The proverbial spark to the dry tinder, those who were the forced to breed."

"How'd it start?"

"Just words... The Chancellor's words... Simple sounds, with such little physical force to even blow a petal off a flower. But that's all it took. A harmless breath formed a sound, and it reached eager, waiting ears."

The high-society teller of the tale held her palm in front of her mouth as she spoke. "I can barely feel the air pushed out from speaking. And all this destruction followed."

Neladith gave Mithany a look that said, "What the fuck is she talking about?"

The woman dropped her hand to her side. "It is impossible to comprehend how such a shallow force contains within it such immense power. A tiny resonance, the waves of sound in the Chancellor's words, unleashed hell on us. A hurricane in a whisper." The lady stared at her hands and her husband tried to pull her along to rejoin the fleeing hoard. She ripped her arm free of his tug.

Mithany looked to Neladith with sympathetic eyes at the lady's plight. Neladith seemed to offer only a mocking retort when she scrunched her face.

Spetzer held out his arms, shrugged his shoulders, and asked, "So what happened?"

The man continued the woman's story, "The hundred or so consigned to the farm rose up. Such things have happened over the years, but they never amounted to much. But the power behind the Chancellor's call must have fueled their burning desire to be free once and for all."

"Mithany? Trell?" Spetzer asked. "You remember the guy? Big fellow. Worked at the old geezer's apple orchard. Oh, what's his name? Anyway, not licensed, he got caught too many times hooking up with other dudes. Judjurex Tetrip sent him to one of those baby-making farms."

Trell scratched the top of his head. "Yeah. About three or four years ago. He never came back. Remember, everyone in Hensdale talked about it for months after Tetrip's decision."

Mithany joined in. "Maybe he's still there. I heard some of them have kids right away and get out. Others are in there a long time before they meet their baby quota."

The wealthy, homeless woman frowned. "Mostly Samers, I suppose, destroyed the compound. We even heard of multiple indignities forced upon the farm's officials before the Samers turned their anger on the town who supported the birthing facility all these years."

As if to say "Wait," Mithany held up one hand. "So, they run the town. That's why it's not safe?"

"Yes. And they are an angry lot. You absolutely cannot go in to Topak. I beg you, don't go there."

Spetzer squinted. "How many days ago?"

"The riots started two days past. I've been a faithful follower of the Temple my whole life. I held no ill will to the Samers until they did all this. I can't imagine how the Goddess Teth allowed this to fall upon her people."

Neladith tilted her head to the side. "As much as I like the sound of a place dedicated to fucking all day... guys or women, I'm game either way... these birthing farms sound pretty messed up. Surprised it didn't happen sooner."

Mithany shot Neladith a look that said, "Be nice."

The woman's husband added, "Our Prime Minister, Larsed, I heard is helpless getting it under control, if he's even still in power. What happened to Topak is happening all over Kantos. I never expected so many people of our community to join in the destruction. Samers didn't do this by themselves."

Mithany noticed the man give Neladith a harsh stare as he spoke.

"They're tearing down the Covenant. I'm heartbroken." The woman buried her head in her husband's chest and wailed.

Mithany, her own emotions raw at hearing Topak's and the woman's plight, felt a tear run down her face. "Where will you go?"

The husband spoke for them both, "We have family in Port Royal in the capital. We hear it's still relatively safe. Hope it still is when we get there. Will be a long walk, but we are better off than most of these people. I don't know what they are all going to do. They can't go back. Everything's been burned or broken."

With a pang in her heart, Mithany offered, "Here, take my pack. There's a bed roll and still quite a few alphen nuts. The nuts alone should keep you fed for the next week. I wish I could do more."

The man extended his arm to accept the offering while cradling his wife with the other. "Thank you."

It made Mithany feel good to help. *They might be destitute; at least now they got enough food for a week.*

Mithany's heart sank as her eyes followed the man and the woman shuffle away. She lost sight of them as the pair faded into the sea of Topak's homeless hoard. *Wish I could do more. Just look at 'em all.*

Neladith interrupted Mithany's chain of thought. "You're an exceptional woman. A petite powerhouse. Where I come from, can't say I ever seen anyone give away all their food... willingly."

"One of these days, you're gonna have to tell me more about this place you come from. Where you come from sounds sad."

Neladith rolled her eyes. "You have no idea... But, you know, I'm getting to like it here. Been thinking, I've got one or two things I have to finish off. And, after that's dead and buried, I might just stick around."

Spetzer grew an evil grin, and Mithany concluded it grew out of the prospect of spending more time with Neladith.

Mithany continued to eye the mass of people, heads down, distraught, empty, and to a person, hopeless. Without looking at Neladith, Mithany said, "I think I'm going to take you up on your idea to head back to Hensdale."

Neladith slapped Mithany on the back. "Splendid."

"When we get back, I'm gonna do more for these folks, somehow."

Reyne sacrificed his love for me, his passion for us to be married, his reason for living. He's endured the loss of his brother. Sacrificed it all for the good of others. That's love.

Yet here before her own eyes were untold scores of folks in dire need. *What am I doing to save them? Nothing. One pack filled with alphen nuts and a bedroll. Pathetic.*

Mithany recognized her own selfishness in her desires to hunt down Reyne while so many helpless, homeless, cried out in need of food, housing, and hope. She considered the Covenant's Third Universal Absolute Obligation and what it demanded of her as an absolute duty, not a personal choice—Promote the General Welfare. She considered Reyne's sacrifice, and she considered the uncertain plight of thousands of homeless people.

Mithany stood in the middle of the roadway. Lost inside her fractured thoughts, caught somewhere between her love for Reyne and the silent cries for help from the suffering mob, in her indecision, she froze. An idea bloomed, *A hurricane in a whisper.*

Not Fast Enough

Gina

In the bright morning sun, scintillations danced along the arrow's metal tip, ripping Gina's attention from her conversation with Mera. She caught sight of the projectile, now at the height of its parabolic arc less than one hundred fifty feet from its apparent target—Reyne. An assassin's arrow carried the promise of death as it flew through the crisp autumn air.

Fifteen feet away from Gina, Reyne lay in a state of sleep paralysis on his first attempt into the Void. Mera, his back to the threat, searched through Reyne's pockets for alphens. Gina, Reyne's only hope for survival, sprang into action.

The assassin in her understood Reyne's peril instinctively. The long, narrow missilette hurled through the air at two hundred feet per second. Gina had only a single heartbeat to stop the killing strike, let alone warn Mera.

Frantic, she leapt. The arrow streaked towards Reyne. She closed the gap between herself and Reyne quicker than an eye blink. Nothing could stop it, save Gina's abnormal speed—Reyne's last hope.

The deadly barb threatened to reach Reyne before her. *Almost there.* Gina's arm shot out. Her hand stretched open. Fingers only inches from the deadly projectile as it screamed toward Reyne. With every scintilla of effort, Gina strained forward. The speeding bolt brushed against her fingertips. Her fist curled around it. Desperate to grab it. Halt it. Snatch it out of the air. The shaft's fletching grazed her palm. Her hand snapped closed, and the arrow sailed through her empty grip.

Shlush. A soft, whisper-like, hollow squishing sound skimmed across Gina's ears. Her head turned in a snapped to its source. Horror gripped her at the sight. Her eyes shot open wide. The shock of it stole her breath away.

The airborne spike buried itself deep into flesh.

Mera's flesh.

Piercing through Mera's flank, the arrow poked out his other side. Blood seeped into his clothes. Mera's eyes fluttered. On his knees, he seemed to hang in the air. A second later, his body wilted. He slumped forward, landing on his face. His fallen limp frame and protruding arrow missed Reyne only by inches.

Gina froze. She watched the shaft push up from his back when his body hit the ground.

She'd seen death many times. She dealt in death. Delivered it to so many for a price. But for the first time, the threat of death touched her soul.

She kneeled at his side. "Mera!" she cried out, but no reply. Gina, terrified at the blood spilling from him, gingerly placed two shaking fingers to his neck. *Faint pulse.*

Her heart longed to help. To comfort Mera. To do whatever she could. To save him.

Gina gently stroked the back of Mera's head. She had a choice to make and no time to make it—go after the shooter or help Mera. She faced a life-or-death decision: Tartica's life, Mera's death. The future of Tartica demanded the unthinkable of her.

She knew he couldn't hear her, but she needed to explain her decision to him anyway, "By your own words, Mera, Reyne is Tartica's only chance to stop the Devil's Blacksmith. An Evidar agent out there, free to attack again, at any moment... too great a risk to Reyne. I can't attend to you and watch over him at the same time. By luck I caught sight of that arrow. Might not see the next one. I gotta stop whoever's out there. Reyne's our last hope. Mera, I'm sorry...

With a heavy heart, she gazed into his unresponsive face. "Don't you die on me. I'm coming back for you."

Gina dashed from Mera's limp form to the trees where the shot originated. As she ran, she scanned the area for signs of movement.

Nothing stirred.

She arrived at the spot and stopped.

She listened.

A stick snapped somewhere off in the distance. She darted in the sound's direction.

Revealed in the undergrowth Gina found a single telltale sign: the light-colored wood of a freshly broken twig poking up through a pierced leaf.

Gina called out, "You're here somewhere. There's no hiding."

In a grid pattern, Gina raced from where the sound initiated. With operational precision Gina crisscrossed the wooded area. She covered a lot of ground in less than a minute.

Gina stopped, certain she'd located her prey. *Someone's behind that boulder.*

Silently, step by step, she drew near. Ten feet away, a large upright slab stood between her and the shooter. She was confident that whoever hid from her view didn't detect her approach. With Mera dead or dying and Reyne helpless in an unconscious state, Gina didn't have time to play games. An amalgam of fear, anger, and love born of friendship for her dying mentor drove her to find the shooter, kill them, and return to Mera with all due haste.

Death will come quick.

Slowly, red hair from the top of a head began to rise from behind the enormous stone. *You just made the last mistake you'll ever make.*

Gina watched and assessed her best method of attack. *I have to end this fast.*

Two eyes peeked out over the top. Gina locked on her target. The target locked on Gina.

A woman, the shooter, sprang up. She bolted. Gina raced after her. In a heartbeat, Gina plowed into her from behind. Knocked off her feet, the woman sailed through the air. Her body tumbled forward. It rolled over several times. The woman came to a sudden stop against a large tree trunk—and sprang into a battle-ready crouch.

A middled-aged woman's angry face looked back at Gina.

Gina said, "And who might you be?"

"The person who is going to kill you. That's who." The Evidar assassin couldn't have known of Gina's capacity to command her mind-body-muscle response beyond the accepted norm of humanly possible—a boon granted her by Mera on her eighteenth birthday. The woman charged at Gina. Blades in each hand. Hatred in her eyes.

Gina raced forward at eye-blurring speed. She pulled free a dagger of her own. Gina held her knife in empty air, neck high. It happened so fast. Too quick for the woman's brain to register. Gina waited less than a half second, stepped to the side as the woman rushed at her. The Evidar assassin's throat crossed paths with Gina's razor-sharp knife. It sliced through her carotid artery in one smooth motion. The stroke cut deep. Blood spurted out instantly. And didn't stop. But the woman did, two steps later.

As blood spewed out, spurt after spurt, her knives fell from her grip. Surprise lit up her face as one hand reached for her neck. In the moments she had left, confusion in the woman's eyes seemed to scream out, "How?" The skills of the bleeding-out attacker might have been sufficient, or even better than most, but against Gina, they made little difference to the all-but-certain outcome.

The red-haired woman flopped forward on her face. Blood continued to ooze from underneath the soon-to-be-dead, unknown attacker. Liquid red spread out from her opened throat, mixing with the colorful autumn leaves of the forest floor.

With her foot, Gina rolled the body over and gave it a quick once-over. *Huh, no bow.* She wondered where it could be and if the dead woman could be the Evidar operations manager Mera spoke of, Dylla Weisner. Satisfied the woman was dead or would be soon, Gina sprinted back to Mera. The whereabouts of the assassin's tools mattered little. Mera, if he still lived, consumed her thoughts.

Gina pulled up. Neither Reyne nor Mera moved.

Gina kneeled beside the older man and leaned in close. Faint breaths escaped the wounded Mera. He was alive, but for how much longer? She had no way of knowing what damage he'd suffered inside the lower right quadrant of his abdomen or the injury the arrow inflicted upon his internal organs.

Aware of the Soul Stone Mera bore, she remained reluctant to pull the bolt from his flank. The full extent of the Soul Stone's capacity eluded her, details she thought she'd never need to know. She rolled him onto his side. The partial shaft poking through. Mera, unresponsive, eyes closed, his breathing grew shallower. Gina lightly slapped Mera across the face several times, hoping to wake him. No response. She struck him harder. Nothing.

Gina dealt in death; saving lives eluded her. She'd fixed herself up many times, attending to cuts and bruises, but those were minor compared to the complexity of Mera's injury. If she took the wrong approach, it would kill him. His clothes were soaked red, front and back. Her heart hammered in her chest. Instinct told her to extract the foreign element from his body, but she feared doing so might cause him to bleed out. If the arrow pressed against a pierced artery, removing it would release even more blood: a death sentence.

Indecision gripped her. She feared she'd lose her only friend. She couldn't leave him like this and couldn't pull the arrow out, either. The conundrum paralyzed her mind. *Options... I need options.*

Looking over at Reyne, she wondered if he had any training with injuries and considered his occupation. *Surely you dealt with impalement-type injuries on a farm.*

Minutes ago, she went after the attacker to leave the men unattended. The Evidar agent no longer posed a danger. Conditions on the ground changed. If Reyne could help save Mera, they'd redo his hypnosis and send Reyne back into the Void another day. Mera didn't have the same do-over opportunities. She looked at Reyne. "Either you and I save Mera, here and now, or he's gonna die."

Gina shot over to Reyne. She nudged his shoulder.

No response.

She shook him.

He remained motionless.

She jabbed and poked at his body.

Nothing.

Gina straddled her legs across his chest. Holding his head between her palms, she pleaded, "Please, please."

Reyne's eyes remained closed to the world.

Gina wailed, the forest flinched, and anger rang through her voice as she screamed. "Wake up, you bastard!"

But he didn't.

Tears welled up in Gina, ran down her cheeks, and dripped onto Reyne. With his face held gently in her hands, she pulled his forehead towards her own.

Softly, she begged, "Please. I need you."

And as her forehead touched Reyne's forehead, her body and his vanished from the face of Tartica.

Devil's Blacksmith

Seated on a familiar couch in his familiar den, ten meters below where the familiar yellow door announced to interested inhabitants of the version of Earth forever in darkness, the methodical Evidarian patriarch, the Devil's Blacksmith, held court.

He expected to receive an update from his Damus on revised calculations of the Probability Wave's trajectory of his world's future. Its purpose: to confirm the state of Coherence between the two separate versions of Earth had been maintained. Wavefunctions representing bodies the size of planets, the Damus previously told him, are an impossibility within the laws of physics as defined by General Relativity, but real nonetheless.

The Devil's Blacksmith, preferring the title "The Architect," said to his Damus, "Miss Emosh, please come in. Tell me what you have for me today."

"Sir, I know you prefer the bottom line first, but would you permit me an indulgence, just this once?"

Damus Synja Emosh, the only such person of her generation capable of the seemingly insurmountable contradistinctions of a future mathematically represented in a single, almost infinitely complex calculated outcome, made a big ask to evade the line delivering the grand finale up front.

Of paramount concern to the Devil's Blacksmith, seated on the couch was whether the Earth of Tartica and the Earth of Evidar remained on track to merge into one. Reunification constituted the only way to save his planet from the disastrous effects delivered in perpetuity to the Earth he knew from the time of the Great Destruction more than fifteen hundred years ago. Whether unification destroyed the reality of Tartica in the process presented no concern to the Devil's Blacksmith.

"Yes, Miss Emosh, we can do that. However, it suggests to me I may not be happy with your calculations or that you've not completed them. Please share at least that much with me before we begin."

In the ever-present glow of light-stealing black flames dancing in the hearth, Evidar's Damus said, "Sir, it's more complex than that." Her voice cracked as she spoke. She looked away from the powerful leader, her face aimed down at her shoes.

Polite, composed, holding back the annoyance taking hold, the Devil's Blacksmith folded his hands in his lap. "Then, please, Miss Emosh, make me understand, if you could be so kind. I am a patient man to a point."

Synja Emosh remained standing. She fidgeted. One hand folded over the other while fingers picked at her nails. "My recent exploration in the Void resulted in extremely complicated permutations of our future for me to consider."

In silence, rising from the sofa, the dull ebony pale of the room painted him in ominous gloom as he poured an alcoholic beverage from the bar. Without offering one to his Damus, he turned to face her. Through the darkness his hard, threatening eyes reflecting in the flickering deep purple and black lightless flames, he said to the nervous underling, "Miss Emosh, I respect what you do, yet please know your equivocations are approaching the limits of my patience. Now, let's hear what you are so obviously afraid to tell me."

The Devil's Blacksmith heard a loud gulp and then his Damus spoke. "From what I've gathered from my time in the Void, Probability Waves of several key players affecting Tartica's and our own world's futures have taken on new, higher likelihoods of coalescing into a timeline that does not suit our purpose." One finger slowly twirled several long strands of her silver hair.

"You need not play with your hair. Look at me," the Devil's Blacksmith commanded.

Miss Emosh lifted her view from her footwear to meet his gaze.

"Better. You are a brilliant and attractive young woman. Show me more of the confidence in yourself I am used to seeing. Now, go on."

Her words shot out in rapid succession. "Yes, sir, I will. Where once I understood the probability of those outcomes to be very small, several have completely transformed." She shook her head and waved her arms. "They've become almost future certainties. Probable outcomes that were once near zero are now each over eighty-nine percent likely, some near ninety-seven. Please, I beg you, understand I didn't make a mistake in my past projections. It's all changed."

Throwing back the entire contents of his drink, the Architect of Evidar's planned recovery from its dark, dismal existence slammed the empty tumbler down on the bar, but said nothing. The sound rang out cutting through the gloom hanging in the room. He didn't need to be prescient to gather the level of fear his actions produced in the one person who could not be replaced. A *capable* Damus came to the forefront perhaps no more than once every generation.

The question the Devil's Blacksmith had to ask: Had he himself mistakenly pegged Miss Sanja Emosh a *capable* Damus? A worthy Damus proved invaluable to his cause, but one who made mistakes could inflict more damage to his plans than a dozen Reyne Brentons, and couldn't be tolerated. Whether Sanja Emosh exited the meeting with her life depended on the answer.

Emosh pleaded her case. "An event that previously traveled along a Probability Wave into the future held little likelihood of collapsing this particular Wavefunction. What I mean is that it had an infinitesimal chance of actually happening, but something occurred, and it's changed everything."

"And you did not foresee this? The Void did not hint of such a future?"

"I've ridden thousands of waves into thousands of probable futures of thousands of people, and there has been a shift. Yes, I got a sense of it, but it previously showed itself as a likely zero outcome."

The Devil's Blacksmith sipped from his empty glass. He pulled it back and stared into its absent contents. "It is no secret the Void does not reveal so much to me. I touch but one Tartican's Probability Wave. I have been blessed and cursed needing the experiences of a Damus in the Void."

"I would not lie to you, sir. What appeared once an unlikely future for so many, a very tiny fraction of one percent, is now probably going to happen with a confidence level over eighty-nine percent. The net impact threatens to send Tartica on a path towards Decoherence between our two realities."

Calm yet menacing, the Devil's Blacksmith replied, "You and I are both capable of entering the Void, yet each of us cannot punch through into the reality of Tartica. We rely on what we experience while in it."

"Sir, if I could serve you on Tartica, I would. But it is denied me."

"Like you, the Void does not permit me into their reality. Yet, I have the exceptional ability to connect with the mind of only one individual. I am fortunate to have molded that one man, Jerithan Cree. I have guided him throughout his life to be of consequence to our efforts. I do not have command of the Void's full array, and so I cannot know whether you missed or misread what you have seen in the Void. However, here in this room, I can determine with certainty the life paths of individuals such as yourself and know how they end when they do not serve me truthfully."

Miss Emosh, flushed and turning red, pleaded, "Sir, I've never lied to you. I've made no mistakes. Certain unlikely events happened, and they've coalesced to change everything. You need me." With her concluding words, she hung her head.

"Look at me."

"Yes, sir," Miss Emosh replied, lifting her eyes to meet his and crossing her hands in front of her waist like an admonished school student.

"While true, I need a qualified Damus. I do not need one incapable of figuring out the math or one who sets me on a future course with no chance of success. Regardless of how impossibly complicated your calculations might be, what you have explained sounds dangerously like a mistake at best, incompetence at worst.

Am I wrong? Did you sense the outcome of this meeting on your most recent journey into the Void?"

A dangerous question to answer—telling the Devil's Blacksmith he was wrong.

Emosh replied to the latter first, "Funny thing is, I can't explore my own Probability Wave and therefore cannot see the alternate paths that lie ahead of me."

The Devil's Blacksmith poured another drink, gulped down its contents, and returned to his acting throne, the sofa. "Go on." He looked into his glass, running one finger around its edge.

Sweat poured off the Damus. "My purpose is to deliver to you the most accurate projections. If left unchanged, Tartica will drift along this new path and Decoherence is certain. In other words, she's begun a trajectory that will put her out of alignment with us. On her new timeline, we'll never reunite."

"If it is so, our world, like you, will die."

The Damus held out both arms, as if to say, "Wait." "But, I've started new calculations and I think I've come up with a solution to adjust Tartica to return to the correct course. This course-correction has a seventy-two percent confidence level of success."

"Miss Emosh, I don't accept prevarication. Seventy-two percent is insufficient. Because you are our only Damus and have come to me with a correction from your mistake, you will be permitted to continue in your role. Be more careful in the future, and in so doing, you will be more cautious with your own. There can be no next time."

"Thank you, sir. And may I say—"

A hand rose, cutting Emosh off mid-sentence. "I will hear your seventy-two percent remedy as a temporary plug in our leaking dike until a one hundred percent effective countermeasure is calculated. If I am to accept there has been a disruption and not a mistake—and I have not, yet I will ask—have you determined what event caused this supposed disruption?"

"No, sir. I haven't. It appears to be a series of unlikely events that, although independent of each other, have combined their impact into one massive distortion of Tartica's future timeline. I can't be certain until I unravel all I've compiled."

"Time allotted us is not endless, Miss Emosh. A state of eternal Coherence between us and Tartica is not our goal. Earth's two dimensions exist side by side, and one day soon, these two dimensions will occupy the same space at the same time. When they do, our two worlds will not collide but will blend together, morphing into one, like the two waves in your pool example the other day, effectively ending Coherence in reunification. I believe you named it Convergence. We will become one world out of two."

"Sir, it is as you say, and all I've done has been to achieve Convergence."

"Perhaps, Miss Emosh. Let us consider, alternatively, because the dimensions are growing out of sync with each other, as you have reported here today, in the future, at that one moment in time when Earth's dimensions cross along a similar path, we miss each other. One arrives later than the other, or one is at a higher point in its wave crest. Our two worlds in separate dimensions then will not occupy the same space at the same time. Our realities will not meet up and flow into one. We will not morph into one reunited Earth. We will be lost forever as two worlds fated never to join into one."

"I will not let you down, sir. I can assist you effectively."

"Our world cannot survive if the latter comes to pass. These two dimensions will cross paths one day soon. Ours must be in perfect sync with theirs when it happens. Are you capable of offering me a plan of how we can correct Tartica's current trajectory, Miss Emosh?"

"Yes, sir," she exclaimed.

"I am pleased to hear a hint of confidence in your voice, Miss Emosh."

"Thank you, sir. You mentioned Jerithan Cree. It fits. He looks to be the key of getting back on track. If we can reestablish him as First Lord of that silly religion, and there are a few specific actions you can get him to do that will affect their entire known world, we can achieve a correction that has a seventy-two percent chance of nudging Tartica's path back to where we need it to be." With silver hair matted to her head, Miss Emosh wiped the sweat dripping from her forehead and looked away.

"I'll need to hear more about these things Jerithan has to do. If I read you correctly, there is more you're not telling me."

"Oh, I'm sorry, sir. I just haven't gotten to it yet."

"Then, out with it, Miss Emosh. More bad news I suspect."

"Well, it's just that if Jerithan Cree returns to his position as First Lord there's a seventy-two percent chance we'll put things back in alignment, but there's only a six percent window for Jerithan Cree to resume his former status."

"Miss Emosh, what you are telling me is Jerithan will suffer a life in destitution along ninety-four percent of all his possible futures. And I must thread the eye of his life's needle to guide him through the six percent solution if I am to save our world."

Synja Emosh swallowed hard. "That's correct, sir. It's a significant challenge with no promise of triumph. It's all in the numbers. The math tells me the effort is sixteen times more likely to fail than succeed. But you are a great man..."

Crash, the sound of the Devil's Blacksmith's stone tumbler rang out through the darkness as it slammed into the mouth of the open hearth.

He roared, "Now it is Jerithan Cree and Reyne Brenton!"

A Sacrifice Worthy of Love

Outskirts of Topak: 9th Day of the Harvest Moon

Mithany

Conflicted, Mithany pitted her love for Reyne and her need to search him out against human decency buttressed by the demands of the Covenant of Absolute Universal Obligations. The competing claims on her soul struggled for resolution as an unending horde of Topak's refugees rushed past her and her friends. Overwhelmed by a broken heart, a riven mind, and consumed in pity for the thousands of refugees, a victor for control over Mithany's inner woman began to emerge.

She'd grown up wrapped in a community that honored the Covenant, cherished it, lived it. She felt, deep in her fragmented self, Reyne would tell her to abandon her quest to find him and to help these poor people. And she had the means to help them. When she left Hensdale, the Brenton orchard had been left in the capable hands of its general manager, Santander, with the harvest only days away. Her love for Reyne and all her years of dedication to the principles of a Covenant way of life built to a crescendo, compelling her to act.

It's a lot I sacrifice, my love. You know my heart. I can't just leave all these people to suffer. If even one of them died, knowing I could've helped, I'd never forgive myself. My sorrow would become part of me. It would taint our love... for me to keep on searching, knowing that choice meant suffering and even death to others. I've gotta do this for us. I know you'd agree.

Mithany made a fateful decision, and before she had time to second guess her new purpose, she turned to Trell and said, "Lift me up. Put me on your shoulders."

"What?" Trell said, looking puzzled.

Excited, Mithany smiled at Neladith. "Trell, please. Just do it."

"Alright," he said, grabbing Mithany by the waist, lifting her small frame and setting her buttocks on his shoulders.

Mithany raised her arms from atop Trell and called out, "Everyone. Stop. Listen to me."

Nobody did.

She tried again to get their collective attention, but failed. The crowd kept shuffling forward.

"Spetzer, Neladith. Help me. Make them stop."

Neladith sprang into action, followed by her puppy Spetzer. She extended her arm into the broad chest of an older man who responded by trying to slap her arm away. Spetzer copied her efforts, but somehow rested his outstretched arm and open palm on a young woman's breast. She kicked him in the balls.

With Spetzer bent over, the victim of his poorly disguised grope pounded away at his exposed back. The ruckus did the trick. People stopped in their tracks to witness Spetzer take a beating, although the scrawny-armed young woman delivered it with little force behind each blow.

Mithany seized the opportunity. She gave Neladith a nod and shouted to the gathered onlookers. "I can help you. All of you. Listen to me."

She fidgeted on Trell's shoulders, and her thighs squeezed tight against his neck. Trell helped stabilize her by firmly grabbing her legs. Her small frame didn't project her voice much beyond where Trell stood.

Neladith shouted, "Shut the fuck up! All of you. Listen to the lady." Her voice did carry. Many halted in place, blocking the forward movement along the road and causing those coming up from behind to do the same.

Without thinking of the logistics or how she would pull it off, she made a life-changing decision and shouted at the crowd, "My name is Mithany. I have an alphen orchard ready to harvest in a few days. If you have no food or nowhere to go, I welcome you to follow me and my friends to Hensdale. I can offer you endless alphens to keep you nourished and an open field where you can lay your head."

Of Topak's twelve thousand residents, Mithany estimated more than a thousand joined her, Neladith, Spetzer, and Trell on the foursome's return journey to Hensdale. Proud of herself for saving a small piece of the world, or at least setting her plan of reclamation in motion, Mithany beamed, walking alongside Neladith.

"Nel, do you think we did the right thing? He's still out there." Mithany left "he" hanging between them, knowing it meant one thing to her and another to Neladith.

"Not at all... Do I hear guilt?"

Mithany looked down and shuffled her foot along the dirt-packed roadway. "Maybe a little."

"Fuck that. You put aside your search because of some greater good you think you owe humanity. Can't say I agree with why you did it, but what the hell, we're heading home. Do what I do. I never look back. I make a decision, then move on. No regrets. No remorse. Works great for me."

The two walked in silence for a couple dozen yards. Mithany looked around at the trees lining the roadway in transition from green to the yellows, golds, orange, and reds of fall. The brisk autumn air and idyllic setting energized her spirit, driving away the guilty feelings haunting her thoughts.

She took in a deep breath. The familiar aroma of decaying autumn leaves sparked pleasant memories of harvests past in Hensdale. Mithany reflected on the small agricultural community. The villagers would be consumed with bringing in their various crops. Everyone would pitch in, and their shared efforts seemed to cement the bonds of kinship year after year. Like it did in so many rural communities throughout midwestern Kantos. *Before that asshole Chancellor's call to end the Covenant threatens to rip society apart.*

She didn't let such notions distract her. She tilted her head back and soaked in the special smell a second time. *Reyne's favorite time of year.* Contemplations of Reyne, autumn, and the annual harvest awaiting Hensdale warmed her heart. Moved by thoughts of love and friendship, Mithany slipped her hand into Neladith's, interlocking their fingers together as friends sometimes do. "Kinda ironic, don't you think?"

Neladith looked down at their entwined palms. "What do you mean?"

"All these folks... homeless. Because a bunch of angry people want to rip the Covenant apart. Here we are giving them back a little bit of hope *because* of the Covenant. It calls on us all, as an obligation, not as a choice, to help others for the betterment of the general welfare. Because of the Covenant they're homeless and because of the Covenant we're going to help them. Ironic? What's better than feeding a thousand hungry people?"

"I said it before, and I'll say it again. You're an exceptional little powerhouse, ain't you? And you have the most adorable cheeks." Neladith smiled. "What you're doing would never happen where I come from."

A strange feeling gripped Mithany. Without thinking, she released Neladith's hand and looked up off in the distance. "Reyne?"

"Reyne? What are you talking about?" Neladith asked.

Mithany felt Reyne's presence for a heartbeat, and then it vanished. "For a second there... Oh, it's nothing." Her mood rose at the sensation of him and sank just as quickly at its departure. She shook it off. "The Covenant is everywhere. What do you mean it would never happen where you come from?"

"The Covenant's influence reaches out only so far."

"You keep promising to tell me more about your home. We never seem to get around to it."

"Okay, happy to. Now's as good a time as any. But first tell me, it's not your orchard. And if Daedyn's not back, how you gonna pull this off?"

Mithany wondered, *She always says she's gonna tell me and then changes the subject.* Mithany squeezed Neladith's hand. Each of her fingers were half the length of the long, thin ones Neladith sported.

"Technically, I'm in charge until he gets back. I asked the general manager to run the show while I'm gone. Unless Daedyn returns, Santander—that's the guy's name—he's gotta do what I say."

"Giving a lot of the profits away to strangers so you can feed them ain't going to go over very well. It's a heck of a sacrifice of somebody else's coin."

"The Covenant doesn't demand its obligations based on profit or loss. In my heart, it's a sacrifice I make, worthy of Reyne's love. Coin's got nothin' to do with it."

Spetzer sauntered up to the pair. Wrapping his arm around Neladith's waist, he slid his hand down and pinched her butt cheek. With a satisfied smirk, he said, "It'll be getting dark in an hour or so. While it's light out, best to find a spot to settle in for the night. Know what I mean, Nel?"

"Everyone who heard you knows what you mean," Neladith said, removing his roaming, eager hand from her ass.

Mithany watched. Neladith's pursed lips and furrowed brow suggested Neladith's cost-benefit analysis of her time with Spetzer had tipped the scales into the loss column.

Mithany faced Neladith, ignoring Spetzer and effectively cutting him out of the decision-making process. "Spetz here is probably right. It's been a long day. If I remember, we passed a stream on the way here. Can't be a quarter mile more down the road and maybe a mile into the woods. Remember, we stopped at it on our way here? What do you think, Nel?"

Neladith piped up, also without consulting Spetzer. "Spetz, take a few guys and scout ahead for this stream Mithany thinks she remembers. Spread the word we're gonna stop for the night."

"Sure," Spetzer said, leaning in for a kiss.

Neladith backed her head from his efforts, leaving his closed eyes and puckered lips hanging in the air. "Go on. Take off," she told him.

Spetzer opened his eyes, looked around, and did as he'd been told.

As Spetzer raced away, Mithany gave voice to her observation. "All well with loverboy?"

"He's getting to be exhausting in the daylight. The nights are good, but putting up with him after we're done boning, I don't know if it's worth the effort anymore."

Mithany laughed. "It took you a couple of days to get there. Welcome to my world. I haven't been able to shake him for years. And, mind you, I never had sex with him. You've been my savior. Please"—Mithany held her hands together in prayer—"please, I'll get as much pleasure out of it as you if you keep it up, at least until we get back."

A belly laugh rolled out of Neladith. "All right. A few more nights. For you."

Mithany's prayerful hands held in tight to her chest, jostled back and forth. "Thank you so much, Nel."

"But it will cost you. Each time he makes me cum, I'll be thinking of you. When you see me tomorrow morning, with a big grin on my face, you're gonna know why. Then you're gonna picture me, nude, and you're gonna think about how I got such a big smile. Now, since I said it, you won't be able *not* to. Images of me stark-naked and excited are going to pop into your head. You won't be able to deny it. Ha!"

Neither the one-eyed wink Neladith gave her nor the scene she'd implanted in her thoughts had an immediate impact on Mithany. Her heart belonged to Reyne, whether here or not. Yet, Mithany's fragile state, masked by her recently acquired cheerful exterior, veiled the crushed and crippled soul underneath. Broken Mithany lurked precariously close to the surface. Neladith's tease brought its full attention to bear.

Neladith leaned in close to Mithany. "You ever been with a woman?" And gently nibbled at her ear. Mithany tried but failed to ignore the love bite. Her damaged soul quivered, if only in her hidden subconscious.

"Reyne and I have shared our bed with other women a few times. My doing, not his. But we do it together, never separately. So, yeah, I've been with women and enjoy it... but only with Reyne."

Neladith beamed back at her. "Good to know." She smacked her lips twice, offering Mithany a couple of flirtatious air kisses. "Wait a second, weren't you worried about your precious Covenant? I didn't notice any kids running around the ole homestead."

"Well, with the Covenant and all, we did it under the guise of two women sharing one fellow, but when bodies all start mingling, well, you can guess what happens. We were careful since I'm not approved by the government of Kantos for same-gender relations."

"Wow. Who woulda guessed? We both like fucking women."

"Reyne and I did it every now and then. Not a lot."

"You got me thinking. What say you... here in the forest... you and me?" She flopped her arm around Mithany's shoulder and pulled her in tight.

Mithany, a full head and then some shorter, her own shoulder poking into Neladith's side, tried to wiggle free. "I don't see a license number tattooed on you anywhere, and I don't have one. Maybe if Reyne were here..."

Neladith held them firmly together, side by side. "Fuck the license. We can get Spetz as the beard. I'm sure he'd love doing you and me both."

Mithany pushed off and gave Neladith's suggestion a full-body shivered. "Eww, never in a million years."

"Alright, no Spetz. Just you and me. That's how I'd really want it anyway. We'd be great together."

"My heart belongs to Reyne." Mithany froze as soon as the words escaped. She'd let her guard down. *Belonged. I should have said belonged.*

Neladith halted. Her eyes narrowed.

Trying to recover, her heart pounding, Mithany quickly added, "You know what I mean. He's only been taken from me..."

Neladith interrupted her by leaning in and tenderly pressing her lips to Mithany's.

Neladith's kiss came gently. Her lips soft, and as much as she wanted to repel the advance, Mithany closed her eyes and savored the embrace. Her damaged soul and broken spirit, yearning to wrest free from imprisonment, craved the connection, the touch, the bond Neladith's lips offered. She quivered as emotional electricity shot through her. But for only a second before the defensive mechanisms of her mind, unconsciously self-imposed to survive the love ripped from her, bloomed with thoughts of betrayal. She pushed back both Neladith and her fractured anima with a softly spoken demand, "No."

In spite of the rejection, a sweeping grin crossed Neladith's face. "Alright. No, it is. But I know you liked it."

Confused how best to respond to keep the façade of Reyne's death alive, to keep her interest in Neladith in check, to keep her impaired psyche from unraveling with the wrong response, myriad rejoinders raced through her mind.

Neladith's look told Mithany the would-be paramour had been studying her. *Taking too long. Answer her.* Mithany seized on one reply, and blurted out, "I'm only human."

Born in the kiss, a part of Mithany—hiding even from her own self-awareness—felt the attraction. She loved Reyne, and these new feelings changed nothing. But she longed for a lover's physical touch, to feel love in Reyne's absence. She missed him so much and her broken mind, without revealing itself to the part of her now in command, opened to the idea of an understudy. The broken-hearted, like Mithany, often make terrible decisions, especially when hiding from themselves. The damaged aspect of Mithany's soul counted on poor decision making.

In an effort to dispose of its imposed shackles, her subconscious set off the tiniest spark of desire. An internal battle, hidden from Mithany's own awareness, seethed for supremacy over the damaged woman's soul. One fought to break out, the other to maintain control. The battle raged in the millisecond world of thought.

Neladith's voice: "True, we are only human. But humans have needs," jarred Mithany's introspection. Like a referee stopping a fight, it brought the internal clash to an end before the damaged subconscious Mithany could gain a foothold.

Mithany heard the feminine, soft delivery in Neladith's reply—seductive and inviting. Mithany couldn't separate fear from excitement. Fear felt by the Mithany in control, titillation felt by her fragmented self. Whatever the cause, she had to get it under control. *Slow, deep breaths. Measured heartbeats.*

Seconds passed.

Neladith kept staring into her eyes.

The heat between them grew.

Mithany's thoughts wandered but for the deceit of her own divided identity. *When will you return? How long will we be apart?* Temptation tugged at her. She mustered her resolve. *No. It stops here.*

Neladith leaned in and whispered, "When I've been alone for too long, I need to release all the built-up tension. I rub one out, usually a few at a time to be honest. We could do it together, lying side by side. I take care of me while you take care of you. Wouldn't that be fun?" And she backed away, gazing into Mithany's eyes with a plea of longing in her look.

Mithany felt Neladith trying to burn lust into her heart. Despite Neladith's effort to reach deep into the pits of desire, Mithany stood fast, holding Reyne in her thoughts. The entombed, broken part of Mithany, in one last desperate attempt to evade the self-imposed imprisonment in response to Neladith's come-fuck-me look, set off the slightest flutter in her stomach with the image of the two women, lying side by side engaged in mutual masturbation.

No. Mithany demanded of herself, denying the tickle between her thighs. She played the only card she had and pleaded to Neladith. "Please, Reyne's been gone, taken from me only a fortnight past. I can't."

Mithany struggled to maintain mastery over her actions, unaware of her own mind's traitorous, duplicitous doings at play—a broken woman from the moment Reyne's hand slipped through hers and he walked away. The fractured psyche locked up, inched forward, threatening her mental grasp on control.

Neladith suggested, "If it's about breaking Covenant rules, I'll never tell."

The idea of sharing a bed without Reyne snapped her willpower back into place and slammed the door on the primordial efforts of her divided inner self.

"Please, Nel, I can't. Reyne has a hold on my heart. He might be gone, but I still can't imagine being with anyone but him. The kiss was nice, but please, let it go."

"Yeah, Very nice... Alright, I'll let it go, for now. But if I do stay around after I finish what I still have to do, and you've given me every reason to believe I have unfinished business, maybe we can circle back."

"Thank you for understanding," Mithany cheerfully replied, having unknowingly dispatched the attempted internal coup. Unaware of how dangerously close she'd come to returning control to the tattered mind of her broken soul, she asked, "What is it you have to do?"

"Oh, something I started even before I got to my cousin's apple orchard. Maybe they found it and took care of it while I been gone. Nothing for you to worry about. If it's not done yet, I'll get to it as soon as we get back to Hensdale. I'm sure I can wrap it up quickly."

Before Mithany could explore what Neladith meant by implicating her in the outstanding task, or what Neladith hadn't found yet, Spetzer rushed up to them.

Out of breath, he said, "Nel, we were searching for the stream, exploring into the forest. One of the guys found a dead body. We ran all the way back."

Mithany's hand shot over her mouth. Her heart pounded.

Reyne!

Horrified at the possibility it might be Reyne, she thought of him lying alone, dead in the woods. "Holy shit. Who is it?"

"Got no clue," Spetzer replied. "Come on, I'll show you."

Relief flooded through Mithany at the pronouncement: Spetz didn't recognize the identity of the deceased. *It's not Reyne.*

Neladith's brows raised high, eyes open wide, and a smile broke across her face. "I'm game. My dear Spetz, lead the way," she said, waving her hand towards the forest.

The three of them took off with Spetzer in the lead.

As they ran, Mithany asked, "Is it a man or a woman?"

Hunger

Teth: 9th Day of the Harvest Moon

Jerithan

Jerithan hadn't eaten since being thrown into the back of a wagon upon his unceremonious exit from Tandure, which he guessed had been several days ago. Frail, exhausted, and confused, the lack of food, or rather the search for anything edible, drove him to wander the streets for scraps. He considered begging, but that level of desperation hadn't set in, yet. He worried it would soon enough.

Safety demanded caution and trumped the growing call for immediate sustenance. What good was finding a meal if he died in the effort to secure it? Empty of would-be human threats, the unexplored alleyway held as little promise as the dozen or so he'd already foraged without success. Inch by inch, with careful intent, he poked his head around the next corner. A large dog hunched over and it appeared to Jerithan to be gnawing on something. He shied away from going head-to-head with the mangy-looking creature for an indeterminate prize, given his empty reserves of courage.

His stomach growled at him, most likely as much for his cowardice as for its demand to be fed. *Agghh. Shut up.*

The chance of recognition by any of the street-heathens as the powerful once-First Lord, played on his fears, competing with hunger for immediate resolution. He spied his own face while looking down at a puddle. Haggard eyes and sunken cheeks stared back at him.

"What's happened to you? Pull yourself together." He asked aloud of the man in the mirrored surface. The man in the reflection didn't respond; he didn't have the strength, and Jerithan already knew the answer.

Jerithan ran his hand across cracked lips, watching his likeness do the same. His tongue and dry mouth made new demands of him at the promise of water. The dirty brown liquid offered more than a mirrored surface. It held out the hope of relief from driving thirst. The sound of his own smacking lips and dry mouth resonated in his ears even before awareness caught up to his needs.

Maybe just a little.

With an open palm he brushed aside tiny floaters, too disgusting to contemplate their nature, wet his hand, and brought it to his mouth. He sucked on wet, soiled fingers, licked his dirty palm and rubbed what dampness remained over his lips.

He knew the danger.

Caution abandoned, he cupped his palm, scooped another handful from the brown pool, and supped the liquid into his gullet. His parched mouth delighted in the reprieve despite what might come of it. Too late, or too desperate, a hint of urine reached his tastebuds. Ignoring the offence, he scrubbed the wastewater remnants over his face. With a sleeve and bent elbow, he wiped it clean. Both revolting and refreshing.

Crash.

The noise seized his attention.

A man's voice rang out, "Shit."

Jerithan spun around.

The man staggered over a chamber pot.

Shit and piss spilled out. The man landed, face-first, into the soup of human waste. The unfortunate vagrant lifted his eyes to Jerithan, his face covered in urine-thinned, brown feces. Jerithan's heart pounded.

Fear drove him to conceal his face, despite the semi-cleanliness he'd only just achieved. The awful smell did nothing to deter him from acquiring his new camouflage. His hand reached into the slop at the bottom, grabbed a handful, smeared it from chin to brow, and ran off before the shit-faced man could stumble to his feet. Jerithan prayed it was only mud and hoped it would disguise his features.

Around a blind corner, Jerithan sped into another ragged backstreet of run-down dwellings. A door flew open and a burly man stepped into the street. Jerithan pulled up short of running headlong into the behemoth. Only a foot away, Jerithan crooked his neck to look up at the bearded monster of a man.

Jerithan prayed only his bulging eyes appeared through his mud-dappled mask. Terror hid underneath the hastily applied concealment.

To Jerithan's surprise, and much to his relief, the giant of a man smiled at him.

Yet caution prevailed, as Jerithan considered, *Never trust a man who smiles too much*.

Frozen in place, words eluded the dethroned First Lord.

"Who might ya be?" the man asked of Jerithan. "And why ya got dat shit all over your face?"

The loud blood-pulsing *lub-dub, lub-dub* in his ears almost drowned out the high-pitched vocalization coming from the man standing before him. A puzzling incongruence of a girly voice and hulking size battled for attention. The huge man's flame-orange hair of head and beard almost went unnoticed as caution and fear consumed Jerithan's thoughts. Orange pupils completed the man's color-coordinated facial ensemble.

Strange tones from such a large man, yet how Jerithan might respond to the question left him speechless. The deposed leader of the Temple of Life failed to construct a pseudo-identity for his life on the streets. Something, he should have thought of in advance.

He blurted out, "Keflyn." A childhood name Jerithan used when caught doing whatever got the younger him in trouble with the local constable. In the here and now, and for the foreseeable future, he became Keflyn.

"Well then, Keflyn, what brings ya to my corner of the world? I know most the folks 'round here."

He offered the man the one truth of his recent demise. "Just another guy made homeless of recent events."

Damn, I sound like a well-to-do. Tone it down, you idiot.

"There's lots of that goin' 'round," the big guy said with a chuckle.

Gentle tones, and the out-of-place high-pitched voice eased Jerithan's heightened state.

The jovial giant said, "Kinda ironic, don't ya think? Shantytown used to be the last place guys like you might want to enter. Now, it's the safest place in Teth. And that ain't sayin' much these days."

Jerithan, at first, didn't understand, but in a heartbeat, he pieced it together. Teth was in chaos. He witnessed some of it when escorted from the Temple Palace to be turned over to Derr. He suspected much of it at the hands of the residents of Teth's slums. And why would those causing the destruction of his city burn their own homes to the ground? They wouldn't. They would burn all the other buildings, but not theirs.

His inner voice chided him. *Make yourself sound stupid. You have to sound less intelligent.*

"I don't go for all that politics stuff. Just a victim of all this bullshit," Jerithan told the big guy.

Another laugh rolled out of the large man's belly. "I hear ya. Me too. Don't give a rat's ass. Just tryin' to survive. Day to day."

Jerithan replied in the local vernacular, or at least his interpretation of it. "Whatda they call ya, big fella?" *That sounded forced. Too much.*

"Nice ya should ask there, Keflyn. People in these parts call me Sir. Ha, only kiddin'. I'm Timble." He stuck out his hand for Jerithan.

Jerithan extended his, and the two men shook hands. "A pleasure to meet ya, Timble." *That came off better.*

"I'm just headin' out to pick up some grub. Nice to meet ya, Keflyn." Timble waved as he strode away.

Courage. Ask for food. Do it.

Jerithan gathered what resolve remained and called out, "I'm sorry to ask, but ya got anythin' you can spare? Been a few days since I ate."

There, I said it. Jerithan's heart pounded, waiting for edible salvation.

"Don't got much to offer ya."

Jerithan's heart sank.

Timble turned to face Jerithan, then added, "But I tell ya what. If you're still here when I get back, can spare half a loaf of bread. Don't got it yet. Goin' to get it."

Jerithan salivated at the promise, and a smile broke across his face.

"Can tell by that grin, you're likin' the prospect. Not sure how long I'll be. Stick around."

"Thank you... sir." Jerithan said, and with hope hanging in the air, an unexpected giddy chortle escaped his otherwise foreboding existence.

"Sir... Ha!" Timble laughed and walked away.

Jerithan watched Timble lumber from view.

Standing alone, cold and hungry, with the promise of food, the unthinkable happened. He heard it in his thoughts.

"Keflyn, that is new. I have missed you, Jerithan. How have you been, old friend?" the Voice asked.

Stunned, Jerithan stuttered backwards into a wall and slid down to the ground.

Jerithan sat with his back pressed against Timble's rickety front door, his folded knees pulled to his chest with arms wrapped tight around his legs. Cold leached from the hard dirt into his butt as gravel shards bit through his pants into his flesh. Like a lost little boy curled up in a ball, he rocked back and forth, the back of his head intentionally slamming into the door with each pass.

Where have you been? he pleaded to the Voice. *I needed you. You abandoned me.*

Stupid. Stupid. Stupid. He slammed his open palm into his forehead, over and over. *Why did I ever trust you? Get out of my head.*

Gurgle... gurgle... grrr... His empty stomach howled at him, relentless in its clamor to be fed.

Jerithan continued rocking, unable to answer hunger's demands.

Thump... thump... thump... Percussion thundered in his chest, hammered at his ears, and pulsed anger through his veins.

He bitterly rubbed his temples, pleading against all hope for it to stop.

Agghhh! I can't think.

Confusion attacked his thoughts and dissembled the perception of his new reality.

I'm a prince amongst men. Reduced to a beggar in the streets.

With eyes closed, his body rocking, he imagined himself in his bedroom at the Temple Palace.

He scanned the gritty, filthy street, dreading he'd miss an imminent external threat. An internal one, the Voice, had already snuck past his senses into his consciousness, unmolested. Since announcing its return, the Voice remained silent.

Potential dangers assailed Jerithan from within and from without. Like a coiled beast, his body remained curled in a ball as the back of his head relentlessly slammed into Timble's door as he rocked back and forth... *thud... thud...* again, and again, and again, his skull crashed against the door. His eyes darted wildly from side to side with each tilt forward.

I'm pathetic. How the mighty have fallen. The would-be Emperor of Tartica, reduced to a street urchin.

Thud... thud...

Now you return! I have no use for you. You abandoned me at a time of my greatest failure. What good are you now? Are you going to help me find my next meal? Big deal. Timble's bread awaits me.

Thud... thud...

You're not my god. You're not Father Sun. It doesn't matter anymore who you are. You might have been me, talking to myself all this time. So what if it turns out I'm just a little bit crazy.

Thud... thud...

Go away! his thoughts screamed at the Voice. *Leave me alone! Let me wallow in my misery.*

As he lamented in self-pity, a sudden percussive threat attacked his ears. *Footsteps!*

He stopped rocking. His entire being on alert, his muscles locked.

He nudged his head up ever so slightly to spy its source. Pressure pulsed against his veins. His eyes peered out from under his sunken brow and over his shaking knees.

A man walked towards him, of average size, minus orange hair.

Not Timble.

Jerithan buried his head between his folded legs. The muscle hidden behind his rib cage thundered wildly inside. The sound of boots on scattered gravel and dirt grew closer. *Clomp, clomp, clomp* struck at his eardrums.

The footfalls stopped.

Terror seized him. Each pulse from his thundering heart threatened to explode his eyes from their sockets.

The stranger demanded, "Get up."

The Voice broke in, *"Tell him to back off."*

With his face still hidden, Jerithan's full body began to shake. The coward within him remained firmly in control.

"I told ya to get up. Do it."

For only Jerithan to hear, the Voice demanded, *"Tell him to get lost. Trust me."*

Why should I ever trust you again?

"Just do it. Get up, stand toe to toe, and do what I said. Look him in the eye. Show him you are not to be messed with. Do it now before you get your ass handed to you."

The man standing in front of the shaking Jerithan commanded, "I'm roundin' up people for another protest. Ya been elected to take part. Just so ya know, you'll be demonstrating to end the Covenant. So either ya stands up in the next ten seconds or I'm leavin' ya here, beaten to a pulp."

"Your last chance. Do what I told you."

Heeding the Voice, Jerithan shot up. His mouth opened, but gripped in fear and flooded with adrenaline, his voice box failed him. Only a faint high-pitched "Ahhhh..." escaped.

The man, not much bigger than Jerithan, laughed and grabbed him by the collar. "Let's go."

Jerithan pulled together the tiniest bit of courage and shrugged free of the man's grip.

"Oh, that's how it's gonna be." The man slammed his fist into Jerithan's empty gut.

Pain shot through Jerithan; he doubled over and fell to the ground.

"Listen to me," the Voice ordered Jerithan. *"In one quick motion, raise up, fast. The top of your head will slam into him and we will take care of this beast."*

The agony of hunger compounded the pain delivered in the punch, snapping him free of fear. Jerithan shot up from the ground. His almost bald crown rammed hard against the man's jaw. Jerithan heard the man's teeth smash together at the blow.

The man stuttered back a few steps but didn't fall. Fierce, confused anger shot across his face. His arm cocked back.

"Hey, Griz, whatcha doin'? Let 'em be. He's with me," Timble shouted as he turned the corner.

"Fucker smacked my jaw," the man complained to Timble, rubbing his chin with the same hand and arm that had been readied for retaliation.

"Like I said, Griz, let 'em be."

The riot recruiter shoved Jerithan, slamming him into the wall.

Timble moved in and towered over Jerithan's attacker, who wisely stepped back.

"Sorry, Timble. Didn't know he's one of yours. Fine. But I got a quota, just like ya do."

Timble slung his arm over the protest organizer's shoulder. "Hey pal, don't worry 'bout it. There's plenty more where this one came from. Any problems, tell Nails or her people it's my fault. Remind her I'm doin' that thing for her. She'll know what it means." He laughed.

Griz replied, "She ain't gonna like it. She wants as many as we can round up at the riot. More damage that way."

"Let me worry 'bout that. Best be on your way," Timble directed, obviously outranking Griz in whatever hierarchy existed in the slums of Teth or within the Thuggery. Jerithan wasn't sure which one applied, but Griz did as he'd been told and scattered.

The Voice asked Jerithan, *"Timble's a big one. Your new guardian angel?"*

Leave me alone.

"Don't be like that. I have returned to help you get back all they took from you."

Impossible.

"Not really."

The promise lit the smallest spark of optimism concealed behind the veils of betrayal and doubt, leaving him all the more uncertain of the Voice's true intentions. He wouldn't allow himself to be used again, but, like Pandora's box, at the bottom, after all the horror of his new life had been unleashed, there, dangled before him by the Voice, the slightest bit of hope.

Timble interrupted Jerithan's internal conversation. "Leave Griz to do what he do. I promised ya a bit to eat." The big man opened his door, stepped back and said, "Please, you're my guest. Don't have much, but go on, ya goes in first."

"You trust this behemoth?"

More than I trust you.

Jerithan asked Timble, "The guy called it a riot. He told me they needed me for a protest."

"They're pretty much the same thing these days. Don't worry ya self. Whatcha ya waitin' for, Jerithan? Go on in." Timble smiled, holding open the door of his disheveled home.

Jerithan replied, "If you say so." And he walked up to the opened doorway, looking into a dark, empty space.

Jerithan realized too late: he never told Timble his real name. *He knows who I am!*

Jerithan stopped.

"This could be a trap," the Voice warned.

From behind, Timble pushed Jerithan into the room.

Opening Salvo

Tandure: 9th Day of the Harvest Moon

Derr

Rain clouds threatened overhead. The sunless sky hastened the effects of the cool damp air, doing its best to affect Druin Derr. He ignored it all. Derr stood before the second largest mansion in all Tandure. A five-column, three-story immense structure that the respected businessman, the apex elitist of polite society and the de facto leader of the Hidden Hand, Ja'Rou Chamette, called home. Of interest to Derr was Chamette's influence over the secretive organization standing against Adelle's acceptance of life beyond the confines of the Covenant. That would have to change.

A small brass ball just to the right of an elaborately carved fifteen-foot-tall wooden double door extended from the mansion's marble façade at the end of a short, thin brass tube. Derr gave it a tug, heard the loud resounding results, and waited.

A middle-aged gentleman, well-groomed and appointed, with coiffed brown hair, pink eyes, and armed to the teeth in the nuances of protocol, opened the huge front door to Derr.

Derr offered the man a curt, "Good day," then pushed the door open wide, stepped forward from under the front porch portico, and brushed the dapper man aside.

"Captain Derr, this is unexpected."

"That it might be. Nonetheless, I'll see Chamette."

"I don't believe my employer has you on his itinerary today." Chamette's personal assistant, a man of considerable influence afforded him by his position, spoke for the powerful Ja'Rou Chamette.

Derr looked around, remembering the familiar setting from previous visits. A commanding entrance, the grand atrium rose the full three stories of the home. A balcony jutted out from the third floor, overlooking the vestibule. Derr understood Chamette used it to establish dominance even before introductory pleasantries could be exchanged. The enormous foyer, larger than the average home, served its purpose to diminish all who entered. The ostentatious setting often played out with the manor lord looking down from his commanding perch, hands resting across the exquisite artisan crafted balustrade. Just not this day.

Derr advised Chamette's assistant, "I don't do appointments."

Armed with the Chancellor's authority, Derr held free rein to go anywhere, at any time, to see anyone he damn well pleased. Pre-arrangements for a meeting with Chamette would only serve to put the leader of the Hidden Hand on notice. *It's a cliché for a reason*, Derr considered. *Forewarned is forearmed.*

"I am happy to accommodate you. May I suggest we arrange for you to return on a day when I can fit you in his schedule? Perhaps next—"

"No, you may not. I'll see him now."

"Sir, as Master Chamette is otherwise engaged, may I be of some assistance to you?"

Derr ignored him. He didn't deal with underlings. As Captain of the KCG, he outranked everyone in Adelle, save Chancellor Tomelai and First Lady Kaythlin, and sometimes even her. Derr neither reveled in his own self-importance nor abused his authority. He simply pulled it out whenever circumstances required.

Civil, yet commanding, his deep resonating tone, as much as his words, demanded, "Where is he?"

"Sir, he is not available."

"He's available for me. Get him or I'll find him myself."

"I'm sorry sir, I can't allow you to do that."

Derr's powder-blue, cold eyes, stared down the officious attendant.

The threat apparently understood, the man swallowed hard, bowed respectfully, and said, "Please understand, he will have my head for interrupting him."

"You're in a tough spot. Either Chamette can have your head, or I can. Choose."

Visibly shaken, all pretense of positional importance had been swept out from under him. Reduced to the stature of a doorman, the fastidiously attired personal assistant shuffled off along the artisan-crafted, inlay floor. Derr followed close behind.

To the left and right of the pretentious entrance, elaborate archways gave passage to the east and west wings. A grandiose candelabra hung from high above. Derr pitied the poor bastard who had the job of getting up there to light, replace, and put out the hundred-plus candles each day. A huge, wondrous staircase, artistically hollowed out in the middle to allow access to the first-floor main wing that came back together above at the second floor, continued to wind its way along to the upper levels. Both men passed through, entering the main wing of Tandure's most elegant private home.

Portraits, tapestries, art, golden sconces, wood panels, and every symbol of affluence were on display. Derr knew the man well and understood the purpose of the extravagant presentation: to intimidate. In the heart of Adelle, among the elites of Tandure, wealth equaled power. The more of one, the greater the other. Chamette put both on exhibit, forcing all to see while en route to his inner sanctum. Most would be unaware; negotiations had already begun—advantage Chamette. But not today. Derr didn't give a shit about Chamette's pretentious demonstration. His unannounced presence in the man's den carried with it his own unspoken message—a threat.

"Captain Derr, may I ask you to remain outside the doors while I pop in to announce you?"

One hand on each handle of the two ten-foot-tall oak doors, Derr's guide held one in place and pulled back the other. Before the man could stick his head inside, Derr pushed him aside and strode into Ja'Rou Chamette's personal office. A masculine space dripping of luxury, the target of Derr's visit sat behind a commanding desk in a high-back chair with hands folded on the top. Derr knew the other occupant, seated in a chair across from the desk. The man was a local businessman of standing, but unknown to most he was also the ambassador, in all but name, of the Thuggery's interests in Adelle.

Without an invitation from Chamette, Derr sat in a chair next to the Thuggery's representative. Derr leaned back and crossed his arms over his chest. "Ja'Rou, we haven't spoken in quite some time." Derr turned to the man seated next to him. "You can leave now."

Chamette nodded, giving permission for the Thuggery's ambassador to remove himself from the tension-filled room. The man wasted no time and rose to exit.

As both a warning and to make sure all in the room understood Derr knew of the business at hand, Derr said to Chamette's departing guest, "Convey to Nails I will be speaking with her soon." All in attendance, aware of Nails's position as the Thuggery's chieftain, received Derr's message—he knew what they were up to.

Derr watched Chamette tighten his jaw ever so slightly. He was always watching.

Nails's liaison nodded and left the room.

Chamette's personal assistant opened his mouth to plead his case at the interruption. Chamette held up one hand to stop him.

Derr didn't know if there would be consequences for the lackey and didn't much care.

With a dismissive wave of his hand, Chamette gave leave to his assistant.

Chamette stood. A tall man, gray hair and mildly overweight. Although, given his large frame, he carried it well. Chamette walked to the bar, poured himself a drink, and graciously offered the same to Derr.

"No thanks."

"What brings you here?"

Derr's eyes followed Chamette as the big man gracefully made his way back to his throne. The older man gave away telltale signs of being annoyed. Derr suspected he'd broke in on important negotiations but let it pass. He had other, more important issues than those between the Thuggery and the Hidden Hand. "We both know why I'm here. Let's not begin our talk pretending it's business as usual."

"If we aren't dancing around issues, I can only assume since you've come to me, I have the better hole cards. Whatever it is you are here for? Speak frankly."

"Here's frankly for you. When you and I talk, you never hold the hole cards. I know what you do. When you do it. Who you do it with. Because I don't stop you, don't think it goes unnoticed." He paused, then continued, "I let you do it. And have never asked for a cut or anything in return."

Derr studied his opponent yet didn't detect any tells of surprise. He didn't expect any. Chamette, a worthy adversary, with extensive legitimate business holdings, presented himself as a respected pillar of the elitist community. Although unknown to most, with his active participation in illicit Thuggery interests across Tandure, Chamette straddled both worlds.

"Let's assume I accept your premise; you let me operate with a free hand. Why sully our relationship by bringing it up now?"

"Human nature being what it is will always reach for the outlets of illegal drugs like Dust, will always seek the outlet of the flesh trade—especially for the unlicensed Samers—and I could go on. The thing is, if not you, someone else would fill the void of human want that exists outside the boundaries of what society will allow. Since we'll never eradicate want for it, you handle it as well as I'm willing to accept. It's a business to you. You keep it as clean as possible, not without issue, but better than anyone else, most likely. You're the devil I know. Does that help you understand us better?"

"Somewhere in there is a compliment."

"Believe what you want. That's not why I'm here."

"Then why are you here?" Chamette took a long pull from his glass.

Derr glanced at the gulp that followed and wondered if it provided cover for Chamette's growing concerns. "You have disappointed me with your response to the announcement concerning Adelle's position withdrawing from the Covenant."

"Now, Captain, I've spoken of this and of our Chancellor, publicly, in glowing terms."

"It's not your empty public pronouncements that bring me here today. It's your efforts within the Hidden Hand to negate its implementation. Not to sound pedantic, you've hidden your hand well, but not from me."

Derr studied the big man's reaction. There wasn't one. Proof Derr's sources had the truth of Chamette's attempted deceptions.

Chamette didn't contest Derr's conclusions. "My compliments to the Agents of Derr. But look at it from my perspective. In the years to come, gutting the Covenant will be a boon to Adelle. Yet, in the short run—"

Derr cut him off. "Let's stop there."

"Druin, look at me. I'm almost an old man. How much time do I have to reap the benefits of freedom from the Covenant? Surely you understand. It will take more years to adjust than I have ahead of me."

Derr sat silent and listened.

"My holdings in the flesh trade to the unlicensed Samers would take a considerable hit. Without the Covenant, those seeking relations with their own gender will no longer need my surreptitious services. And, mind you, my clientele is from a class able to pay highly per assignation. Besides, I have pity for their plight. Forced to hide who they are. There are a lot of them, more than society thinks. I service those with much coin. It's *big business*. You're asking a lot."

"You're leaving out the coin you rake from the blackmail that follows those secretive rendezvous you arrange."

A *tsk* escaped Chamette. "Come now, Druin."

"What pleasures people take of each other is of little concern to me, yet it does concern the Covenant. Of course, putting the procreation requirements aside and eliminating licensing of Samers will diminish your brothel income and your one-on-one assignation-for-a-fee amenities. You understand Adelle could also legalize Dust, open government gambling houses, and kill off your loan business, both the legal and illegal, by offering government low-interest, short-term credits. How would losing all that business, as you say, impact an almost old man's ability to recover lost income?"

Smug in his reply, Chamette stated, "It can't be done."

"Why not? That's the beauty of one man holding all the reins of government. And consider this, would I be sitting here talking with you if all of what I'm saying isn't on the table?"

"Tomelai would never take such drastic actions."

"To eliminate the ability of the Hidden Hand's shadow efforts pushing against his edict pulling out of the Covenant, I assure you... he will."

Chamette's lips flapped as exasperated air whooshed from his puffed cheeks. "And what do I get in return?"

"Are we negotiating?"

"Come now. You know we've been negotiating from the moment you stepped into this house. The only thing that's changed is now I know what's on the table."

"There's more."

"What else is there?"

"There are the legal operations you run. Your banking houses where you launder and clean the Thuggery's coin. Many millions every year. Those charters are on the table as well. But I have something to give you in return for your cooperation and your influence. I don't just want you. I want you to bring everyone you deal with in line. I want the Hidden Hand staid."

"Impossible," Chamette demanded, slapping his large hand forcefully on his desk.

Derr didn't react to the resounding thud bouncing around the room. He angled his head to one side. "Have I come to the wrong man? The man who pushes his weight around when anyone dares to get in his way. You've accomplished so much without having to kill many people. Yes, I know who you've had killed over all these years we've known each other."

This time Derr did read surprise on Chamette's face. "You and I can come to an understanding without me having to ask you to join me at KCG headquarters."

A direct threat. "Let's not pretend I believe what you've said. You've kicked off a brilliant strategy. You work one side of the issue, Nails the other. You oppose the Chancellor's efforts to eliminate the Covenant in Adelle while the Thuggery under Nail's leadership supports killing it off in Teth. Together, you are positioned to collect coin from opposing factions with no real regard for whether the Covenant lives or dies."

The lump in Chamette's gullet informed Derr the man understood the stakes. But Derr didn't let it rest there. "I'm no fool. I can't expect you to be something you're not. There is no loyalty in you. None for your Chancellor. None for Adelle. None for the Covenant. To you, there's only the exploitation of circumstances to extract more coin."

"If who you say I am is an accurate portrayal, what then can I expect from you? Specifically, in exchange for my goodwill weighed against this lost opportunity to amass more coin. Putting aside your bluster of a KCG invitation, what are you offering?"

"Tomelai has called for releasing electrics on the world. The contract to build its infrastructure in Adelle will be huge. It could be yours. The promised coin from electrics alone should secure your cooperation."

"You and I may have different concepts of huge when it comes to coin."

"Many, many millions."

"Alright, go on."

"There's more to consider. Tomelai requires a standing army to defend his position. There will be numerous lucrative contracts to supply Adelle's military."

Chamette's face began to change ever so slightly. Derr kept talking while evaluating his opponent's reactions. "And if there's a war with Kantos or Greenlin, I'm sure you can guess, war racks up considerable expenses. An army consumes much, and war... I imagine even more so. You deal in ledgers. Which side of the soon-to-be-opened ledger do you fancy? There's more than enough coin in those government contracts to offset your losses from whatever you and Nails have cooked up. And enough to spread around to all the shadow-brethren of the

Hidden Hand you bring to heal. That is, if you all don't get too greedy or cut too many corners fulfilling those contracts."

Derr watched. Chamette's lips curled at the edges and his eyes lit up.

"Can I take a day or two to think about it?" Chamette asked.

"No."

"And if I say I'm not interested?"

"There's always KCG headquarters."

"If you take me off the board, someone else will step into my shoes."

"Of course they will. But you won't be around to see who it will be."

Angry, Chamette roared, "Don't you threaten me!"

In a soft voice, Derr said, "You're a man who understands reality. I don't deal in threats."

Silence hung in the air. Derr kept his focus on the big man's every movement, searching for the little tells that give away more than intended. Derr compiled all Chamette's body language and discerned surrender when his shoulders slumped.

As Derr watched the big man, he thought, *In the war that's coming, this is Adelle's first victory.*

"Look, Ja'Rou, I'd rather have you as a willing partner than a disgruntled accomplice. I'm here to make peace with you and the Hidden Hand. I can promise you a good share of the coin we are going to spread around. If you can build an electricity production and distribution network based on government specs, not only yourself but generations of Chamettes will remain prosperous. Can I count on you?"

"I suppose."

"I need more than that."

"Yes, you can count on me."

"Good. I'll be watching you, along with those who you bring into the light."

"I can't get all of them. You know that."

"Of course. Get as many as you can, and it better be most. The ones who hold out, who hamper our efforts to break from the Covenant—leave them to me."

"You are not making this easy. I can foresee several good people who won't bite."

"Never said it's going to be easy."

"Alright. We have a deal."

Derr slowly brushed his hands on his pants. "Now that's settled, I have one more issue I need your help with."

"What else? Haven't you done enough to me today?"

Derr paused before responding. He had one more person in his sights for the failed assassination attempt on Tomelai. Derr would extract his revenge. He told his new partner, "I'm going to need your help with Nails."

Enter at Your Own Risk

Reyne

Reyne's unconscious physical mass lay in an open field in midwestern Kantos, he presumed under the watchful eyes of Mera and Gina. In a state of sleep paralysis, Reyne's body and thoughts existed as separate entities. His mind passed through the enigmatic astral plane and the metaphysical impenetrable barrier to reach the other side where the Void awaited him. If anything existed beyond the absolute depths of ebony, darker than pitch-black, truly aphotic—absent a single photon of light—Reyne experienced it as he entered the Void.

Comprehension, defining the boundaries of whatever engulfed him or of the parameters of his own presence, eluded him. He may have filled the entire Void with his habitation of it or persisted as only a tiny speck within it. He'd shed his corporeal form until he'd reclaim it.

Perception of anything evaded his free-floating thoughts. Uncertain of movement, neither having the ability to initiate it nor sense it, given the lack of a single point of reference. Reyne may have been traveling at the speed of light or may have been anchored to the spot in the Void he'd emerged into. He simply didn't know. And strangely, he didn't care.

Reyne wondered if this was what death delivered to the eternal soul. Nothingness. Of all the promises to join the Community of Life after one's death, the asseverations of the Temple of Life rang hollow as he experienced existence without physical form.

Reyne contemplated how long it had been since he entered. It may have been seconds, minutes, or even years. The realization struck him in the all-consuming blackness: time did not live in this realm.

Consumed in utter darkness, Reyne should have been terrified facing the unknown, unaware if anything hunted him within the empty blackness. Yet, a calmness prevailed in spite of his circumstances.

Minus his physical form, the need to speak in his own head, to use his inner voice, word by word, vanished. Ideas, sentences, recollections burst into his thoughts as a single data dump at the instant of conception. He remembered Mera's lengthy instructions concerning navigation through the Void. Back in the glade, the delivery of Mera's words consumed more time than Reyne thought necessary, but in his present state of existence—as pure thought—the recollection, unabridged, was delivered to him through the Void's instantaneity without the need to unpack each word.

Mera directed him to focus on the image, the lifelike drawing of the physical place he sought to emerge on Evidar, and it would find him in the Void. He tried to lock the image in his mind, but so many events and people rushed into his thoughts. Daedyn, his brother, and Baide, his recently discovered sister, took hold. Both had been ripped from him. Reyne felt their familiarity in the Void. He didn't want to let either slip away.

Faint shadows of the life Daedyn would have lived bloomed. Hundreds and thousands of Daedyn's Probability Waves reached Reyne's understanding. A wisp of one future of Daedyn married to Mithany appeared and dissipated. None had substance, but wave after wave kept coming at him. Many showed him Daedyn's life where his brother escaped death. Daedyn as a thief, another as a wealthy aristocrat, while still another, so very faint, showed Daedyn as the First Lord of the Temple of Life. Pale, gossamer, unformed lifecycles for the lives Daedyn would never live, but that had been possible. Reyne could barely make out where one life fractured into a new direction, meeting up with and melding into another Probability Wave, another life path for Daedyn. Reyne tried to connect to any of them and even all of them, yet with each effort, Daedyn's life crumbled like sand through the metaphorical fingers of Reyne's essence.

Experiencing the Daedyns that would never be, a profound sadness permeated Reyne's existence in the Void. His gloom like a magnet attracting the awareness of thousands upon millions of other life energies through undulating, unseen forces passing through his perception. As though the forlorn all reached out to him at once in distinct voices, expressing their grievances for him to hear. Reyne understood them all. He felt them all. Their loneliness. Their jealousies. Their unrelenting, limitless depth of want. But more than anything, their pain.

Reyne's eyeless tears fell across his faceless cheeks. The accumulated suffering of humanity threatened to push Reyne beyond his limits of endurance. He suffered with them all for seconds, days, maybe years. Reyne couldn't know. Almost broken, his existence in the Void frayed and began to dissipate, exposed to the suffering of so many. He wallowed in his own desolation. All he had left of himself to hold on to: one hope, to reunite with the woman he loved.

Reyne transmuted his thoughts through iron will alone, turning away from the all-consuming sadness to his love for Mithany. His concentration on her did not waver. The taste of love blossomed. Though impossible to experience emotion as a flavor in the physical world, Reyne knew it to be the rich palate of their shared devotion. Sweeter than honey. More delicate than saffron. Deeper, richer, more decadent than the most mouth-watering chocolate. All in combination with the savory essence of Mithany exploded across his bodiless tastebuds. The sensation flooded through him. He relished in the exquisite, flavorful palate of love.

He held onto it. Savored it. Sparked by the flavor sensation of her love, it attracted Mithany's Probability Waves to him. Gentle and soft, more waves, then still more, caressed him. They kept coming. The darkness of the Void enveloping him began to give way, if only across an oasis. In the Void, a vision of Mithany stood before him. He recognized her surroundings—the road to Topak.

In every color across the spectrum, wave after wave rolled off her, danced away from her—all to no harm. Thousands of Mithanys emerged from where she stood. All moving away in every direction in the plethora of her radiating Probability Waves representing myriad life choices. Thousands of divergent Mithanys spread out into the future—all the possible futures she might ever live were there for Reyne to see. It overwhelmed his soul.

From moment to moment, the wave projections into the future changed, reshaped, reformed, and moved along into new destinies. Thousands and thousands emanating from her instant by instant. Reyne understood them all in their totality at their moment of creation.

Each projection of her future thinned in appearance the further from its point of origin. So many futures Mithany might experience took flight across Tartica, all at once. Reyne comprehended them all. He witnessed different Mithanys, sometimes as an older woman with him by her side, other times aged, childless, angry, and alone. In one future Mithany shared a life with the red-haired woman who murdered Daedyn. The two women loved each other, grew old together, and it horrified Reyne. To his dismay, he watched her die over and over in thousands of altered scenarios.

Killed by a soldier as war spread across the continent.

Horribly raped and murdered by Spetzer.

Her throat sliced open by the same red-haired woman who she might have shared a life with—the one who murdered Daedyn.

Each time, his sense of loss nearly broke him.

But there was love as well. So many versions of a future shared between them. Some with children, others without—growing old together. Reyne craved those more than anything he'd ever experienced.

The thousands and millions of Mithanys all grew faint the further life took them from the Mithany standing in the roadway. Reyne could get lost in any single Probability Wave of Mithany and play out an entire life with the woman he loved. However, a single Mithany-wave embraced his soul, and he knew it to be the one.

Reyne yearned to wrap his arms around her. Yet, without arms, he reached out into her thoughts and caressed her mind. A conflagration of bright, white-hot light exploded across the Void, or at least it lit up the oasis he created. Pure love engulfed him. He wanted to never let her go. And then, astonishingly, Mithany responded to his soft, gentle, mental caress of her life force. He heard her voice call out to him, "Reyne?"

At that instant, another presence in the Void slammed into Reyne's percipience—and invaded his mind. The sanctity shattered like shards of glass blown apart in every direction. Before he could tell her, *Yes, it's me, my love*, she vanished—ripped from him.

Reyne cried out, *Mithany! No!*

But she was gone. The connection collapsed—torn from his soul.

Another being from within the Void invaded his essence. Complete and utter blackness slammed into him. Like waves cresting in a violent storm against his unfocused mind, an untethered buoy in an ocean of never-ending thick black ink, he tossed about in every direction. As pure thought, whether he moved one centimeter or was scattered across light years, Reyne didn't know. But the tumult was real.

He reached out to moor himself against the millions of Probability Waves the Void threw at him. The invading force inside his thoughts attacked him at each attempt. Time after time, his efforts to coalesce a focused vision failed.

Fear and intense fury manifested in whatever found its way into him. Wherever his concentration took him, the entity followed. It chased after and into his thoughts. Not as an external pursuit from somewhere else in the Void, but from within his own existence.

The thing's anger, whether an organism, a substance, a cognition, pervaded his sense of being. Reyne also came to know it was terrified. He sought to hide from it and its fury. Reyne attempted escape after escape, yet the entity discerned his evasions at the instant each began.

The Void pummeled him inexorably from without while the entity scattered his thoughts from within. It went on for years, days, or maybe for only a few seconds, but it was without end.

Over and over, his soul cried out for Mithany as the entity shattered his every effort to secure a connection with her. The being recoiled in terror at his efforts.

Reyne tried so many times, yet the process repeated itself: escape, terror, pursuit, failure.

Reyne began to experience his mind fraying at the edges. Distress seeped into his awareness. If it continued, he would become nothing but wisps of dandelion seeds, blown away, his essence to be scattered across the emptiness of the Void.

And still, the mysterious entity assailed him.

Desperate anger screamed through every particle of his existence, real or imagined. The force of his outburst pushed the entity to the edges of his quintessence, along the fluttering threads of himself seeping into the Void.

Uncertain how long the reprieve from attack would last—seconds, minutes, all in a place where time didn't exist—Reyne faced a life-altering decision: return to the glade or move forward into Evidar. With his opportunity to act slipping away, he listened to his heart. The sooner he got to Evidar, the sooner he'd retrace his steps and return to Mithany—if he could figure out how to access Evidar through the Void without Mera's help. The latter, a huge gamble. But one he had to take.

Frantic, Reyne concentrated on the lifelike painting Mera provided of a specific location on Evidar. He had it in his mind's eye. He locked it in. Reyne reached out into the Void with the image in his thoughts. Hundreds and thousands of Probability Waves similar to that one image assailed him. Desperate, he sought the one that felt right. None did. So many waves confronting him, he foundered for life, for escape, for salvation, but not one of the multitudes of Probability Wavefunctions of that one scene connected with his core. He screamed without a voice, without a mouth, and wished he hadn't; the release set a beacon for the entity to trace back to his core.

He sensed its pure horror at the thought of his abandonment, to be left to forever wander in the Void. With the bodyless creature at his boundaries trying to pull him away, he smelled the one Probability Wave of his want. It burned his noncorporeal nose, bitter, harsh, dark. He sensed it to be the one. He found it. Or it found him.

Light grew around it. A small window opened in the ebony miasma of the Void and exposed Evidar to him. Revealed behind a thin gossamer veil, its Probability

Wave crested and rolled along to the open expanse of the dark, rocky destination he sought.

Escape was within his grasp, but the entity clamored to yank him back from the event horizon. From the outer limits of his mind, he sensed its ravenous anger, its unbound fury, its all-consuming terror at being left in the Void. Reyne struggled to deny its purchase of his soul, yet could not.

The wave that would carry him from the Void to his terminus, opened before him, and the invading force rushed at his core. Indecision locked him in place: flee to Evidar with the entity clinging to his soul or battle for freedom from it in the Void.

Like a rope whipped from one end, a crest rolled forward, then another, crest after crest, repeated endlessly. Each wave crest rode across the space between his existence in the Void to the open field on Evidar.

Reyne reacted too slow. The noncorporeal being slammed into him with the force of a hundred horses crashing against the chest of a single man. The entity gripped Reyne in a crushing hold at the instant he reached out to take possession of his escape atop his chosen crested wave. The entity's hold on him was like the force of gravity from ten thousand Earths. Reyne struggled to free himself taking his focus away from the collapsing Wavefunction's promised destination. Blackness drew in from the edges. Evidar started to fade.

No!

With every scintilla of willpower, Reyne shot his thoughts onto the evaporating Probability Wave crest rippling towards Evidar, with the entity in tow clawing at his soul—inseparable. Uncertain if death awaited him from the unwelcome passenger, the price of escape from the Void, he fled.

Winds a thousand hurricanes strong scattered his essence, ripping him from the Void.

He awoke back in his body. How long he'd been out, he didn't know. Reyne opened his eyes to discover a face, nose to nose, looking back at him. Absent his clothing, lying on his back, at the exact spot he pictured. A similarly naked Gina straddled across his chest. Her forehead pressed to his. No longer in the Void, the unwelcoming world of Evidar awaited.

Rest in Peace

Arek

Soft light drifted into Brenal's bedroom where Arek had settled in, recovering from injuries delivered by Neladith, by wolves, and by whatever else happened to him. Day after day, Arek woke, fed himself stale bread, gulped down water, consumed the mystery powder marked *For Infections*, and tested his leg. Time after time he found himself too weak, or it too damaged to put weight on the suspect limb, until today.

Arek's fever broke and his lacerations, gouges, and gashes, while still discolored, had their mounds of pus receded noticeably. Still open cuts competed with youthful stubble for his fingertips' attention as Arek ran them across his cheeks, his chin, his nose and his forehead, probing for scabbed-over facial wounds. Where sutured, the skin closed, although, eventually, he'd have to pull out each thread.

After several seconds of standing, with his full body pushing down on the right leg, the one missing a piece of thigh muscle shook and gave out.

Shit... I can do this.

He stood. His leg shook. His strength gave out. He collapsed.

He repeated the process: stand, shake, collapse.

Over and over Arek drove himself. Pain came along for the ride and screamed at his every effort, but it did not deter him.

With the help of walls, doorknobs, and whatever else he discovered along the way to prop himself up, Arek completed the journey from bedroom to kitchen. Arek wrapped a towel over the floor-end of the mop, broke off the other end to match his size, secured it under his arm, and made his way outside. The stairs were challenging, but holding onto his crutch and the railing, he took comfort in not falling on his face.

He made his way to Brenal's body. With each step, *Pain… Neladith*. Arek settled himself at the base of Brenal's beloved flower bed. Rock by rock, he dissembled it to entomb Brenal's body under a makeshift cairn. Once completed, he sat back on the porch's bottom stair. A pang in his heart touched his soul as he looked over Brenal's makeshift resting place.

As though Brenal might hear his words, Arek spoke aloud, "How many times did you and I sit here after one or another beatings my mom gave me? I was just a little kid."

Brenal didn't answer.

"You'd comfort me. I didn't understand why you cared, but you did."

Arek laid back against the other steps and looked up into the sky as though searching for Brenal in the heavens. "You always did your best to patch up the bruises. Body and soul."

He patted his hand on the wooden step. "You'd sit here next to me. Told me every time not to blame myself. You'd make me feel better about being me. I did forgive Mother, eventually, thanks to you. Mithany would never come to see you like I did so many times. Wish she had. You might have saved her, too. She's still a broken soul. Who knows what I would've become if not for you?"

Ignorant as a child to Brenal's true wisdom until years later, Arek's post-adolescent reflections told him the genteel country doctor kept him from a bitter, angry life. "You saved me then, and you saved me now. I wish you could be here. Mother might've damaged me, and you helped me heal… Another woman's brought it all back. I can't forgive Neladith. Look at what she's done to me."

Arek pushed up from the stairs, aided by handrails and his makeshift crutch. He looked out over the healer's body. Tears trickled down his damaged cheeks.

He wiped away the sting of salty water in his cuts. "You deserve better than this. Thank you for saving my life. I'll have justice for you. When I'm strong enough, I'm gonna bury you properly. I will always love you, my friend."

After saying a prayer to Teth and another to Mother Earth for his friend, Arek made his way to Brenal's bed. As he settled in, he considered, *One more day. Tomorrow I'm gonna track down the Judjurex. Walking to town ain't gonna be easy. Don't care how much it's gonna hurt. I'm coming for you, Nel.*

Depleted of vigor, sleep stole away the hell of his new existence at the instant slumber's veil silenced his inner voice.

Pain... Neladith... Brenal... made up his last conscious thoughts.

But No More

Evidar

Reyne

Reyne gazed up at Gina's face. Her forehead on his, two pairs of eyes locked on each other. Their bodies entwined in the exact position Gina put them in, back in an open field on Tartica, while pleading with Reyne to wake up. The denuded woman, her legs splayed open across Reyne's chest, screamed just seconds after opening her eyes and launched herself off his similarly unclothed body.

Evidar, as Mera described it, held the promise of immediate peril upon arrival, maybe even death. Despite Mera's warnings of Evidar's inherent dangers, lying on his back, Reyne remained calm. *Progress. One step closer. I'm on Evidar. This moves the needle forward.*

Gina reacted, flinging herself off Reyne from their entwined encounter. Reyne eyeballed her body and listened as Gina let loose a boisterous, unending yelp, all the while scampering about in every direction. Hands waving, arms thrashing, legs jittering nonstop, and incessant howling of unintelligible sounds spewed out of her as she mindlessly scampered about in circles.

Reyne instantly understood they'd transfigured to Evidar. It appeared to him Gina hadn't come to terms with her situation. Yet Reyne was puzzled at Gina's presence and why she had been delivered to Evidar on top of him. To his recollection, he'd been alone on the ground when Mera sent him into sleep paralysis, initiating his journey into the Void. While stupefied by the development, he didn't let confusion interfere with relief at having a companion to face the sallow world he found himself in.

Evidar hid itself from Reyne under a veil of darkness. A coal-colored sky painted everything gray; that is, everything Reyne could make out. Neither sun nor moon appeared overhead through the impenetrable, pervasive gloom. Dark as any night on Tartica, absent stars overhead, Reyne wondered if they existed at all or loomed behind the ash-laden atmosphere. The twenty or thirty feet his eyes could penetrate detected a barren, foreboding landscape. Eerily void of sound, surrounded by darkness, Evidar seemed like the Void incarnate. An acrid, foul smell hung in the air attacking his nostrils. The low-lying rocky terrain, stripped of all plant growth, showing itself in sable black, combined with the empty sky, the voiceless land, and the smell of evil to appear before him as a malevolent, living entity, intent on squeezing both hope and life from his soul.

But he wouldn't allow it to affect him. Reyne took comfort in surviving the difficulties thrown at him in the Void. Relieved he'd survived the other entity's pursuit of him across the black emptiness. And pleased he'd secured the singular Probability Wave to deliver him to his desired destination. *All things considered, could be worse.*

Gina stuttered to a stop in front of Reyne while her legs kept running in place, her arms swung at her sides, and her hands wiggled and juddered wildly. "What the...? How did I end up here? This is your fault, farm boy."

Reyne saw it coming when her legs stopped moving and she wound up to kick him. Too slow to stop her, Gina's foot dealt Reyne a breath stealing blow.

Whack.

She demanded, "What did you do to me?"

Reyne recoiled, grabbed his gut, and gawked up at her.

"Yeah, I'm naked. Get a good look," Gina said in a snit. "We got bigger problems. Focus on that, not my tits, dickhead." She swept her hand over the length of his prostrate, exposed body. "You aren't any better off."

"Look all you like. Doesn't bother me. Like you said, we got bigger issues. And don't kick me again." Reyne spun his half-truth, hoping to distract himself from her body and hoping to distract Gina from taking another swing at him.

Gina returned to her spasmodic dancing in place. "Aggghhh! I'm in the glade one second, and the next, I'm in total darkness floating in my thoughts. It was terrifying in there. Then, the next second I'm lying on top of you without a stitch of clothing. The sun's gone. It's dark all around us. Obviously, we're on Evidar. I'm not stupid. Mera sent you into the Void, not me. So how the hell did I get sucked along for the ride?"

Reyne sat up and wrapped his arms around folded knees. The one thing unnerving him more than the gloom of Evidar's sky—Gina, no longer prancing around, standing inches from his face, hands on hips. "Can you take a seat?" Reyne asked.

She didn't move.

"Please."

Same response.

"Gina, your, you know, is in my face."

She scrunched her face before settling alongside him. "We're adults. It's not a 'you know.'"

Reyne watched as she slowed her breathing and composed herself. "Hats off to you and Mera for finding a way to join me, but I don't understand how you got here?"

Gina's expression changed. "I've something I got to tell you."

"Something positive, I hope," Reyne replied, expecting more than the dour look on her face foretold.

"No. Something awful." Her lower lip began shaking. In a soft whisper, she forced out, "Mera's dead."

Reyne gasped, "No. It can't be." His heart sank at the news. "How?"

In the short time they'd spent together, Reyne's feelings toward Mera started in anger, bled into resentment, and only recently, shifted towards respect—after discovering Mera delivered him from certain death before his life even began. The revelation changed Reyne's understanding of Mera and his feelings towards the man followed. A pang of sorrow touched him learning of Mera's demise. Reyne closed his eyes, forming an image of Mera extracting him as a newborn from his dying mother's sliced-open womb. Reyne hung his head.

"An arrow meant for you from some red-haired Evidar cunt. Likely pierced his liver. By now he's bled out."

"Means he saved my life... again. Hey, thought you didn't like that word."

"I got no problem using it when it applies. I have issues when it's used to describe me. Thought you understood."

"I do now."

"I should be back there with him. But I'm here. The chance to fix him up, gone by now. Not even sure I could've saved him. I'll never know. I gotta live with that." Tears filled her eyes.

"Not your fault. Besides, got no idea how long we traveled through the Void. Seconds? Days?"

"Doesn't matter."

Reyne and Gina sat in silence for several long minutes. Reyne reflected on how Mera called on the past, once in Hensdale, once in Teth, to show him the two women from Evidar, both with red hair, one young, the other older—like the woman Gina described.

Gina broke their quiet reverence. She'd been crying softly to herself. She sucked in the snot dripping from her nose and ran the back of her hand over it, wiping away the residuals. "You know, I met him in my early teens," Gina began.

Reyne listened to her narrate several adventures she shared with Mera and how the two became close friends. Reyne and Gina now existed on the dark world of Evidar, and other, more immediate concerns demanded attention, but letting out their grief seemed more important. Reyne appreciated Gina sharing her more vulnerable side, even if most of her stories ended in either her or Mera killing someone. Finally, she detailed how she'd eliminated the red-haired Evidar woman who had taken Mera from them.

Gina concluded her final yarn, "From what Mera told me of the hunters sent after you, I'm guessing the one he called Dylla killed him. Doesn't matter, 'cause whoever she was, she's dead now."

Reyne pulled up a memory of the woman peering in the window of his dead little sister's bedroom. The sister he never knew, who'd been brutally murdered on the day he'd been born by the very woman Gina described. Reyne craved for the murderous woman to be the one now dead.

Softly Reyne said, "Wish I hadn't been such a dick to him in the beginning. Woulda liked to known him better. He's always gonna be a mystery to me. He's a remarkable guy." He reached out to Gina, resting his hand on top of hers.

Gina's voice cracked. Tears ran down her face. "*Was* a remarkable guy."

REVEALED IN DEATH

Quith | Neladith

Quith remained in the world of the breathing, he supposed, because he'd promised Gina to take down everyone from Evidar. She had vanished, leaving him alone in the forest. Selundra Quith recognized he was lucky to be alive. She was better than him, and it gnawed at his self-imagined superiority. He blocked it from preying on his thoughts, as he had a lot of figuring to do about his future.

Initially, Quith headed back towards Hensdale, thinking it the best place to begin his pursuit of his old boss, Dylla. Almost as soon as he set out, while traveling south in the direction from whence he came, he'd picked up a trail he thought might be Dylla's. The trail however, headed in the opposite direction, north. After a quick about-face, he was on the hunt.

Careless of you, Dylla, leaving clues for me to follow. Unless... it's a trap. This whole Reyne Brenton debacle hasn't been your finest effort. Two swipes at the man, we missed both times. That's on you. You put together our little unit of well-trained cutthroats. I wonder, Dylla, will the Devil's Blacksmith hold you responsible? Then again, I suppose you pinned the blame on me. But you haven't been able to find Reyne Brenton since. That's also on you. Looks to me like your ass is on the line. Won't matter, he'll never get to hold you accountable. I'm gonna find you first.

Before midday passed, Quith followed what he hoped would be Dylla's trail to a wooded area at the edge of a clearing somewhere north of Hensdale as best he could determine.

Fresh tracks. She's close.

He crouched at the edge of a clearing. A large boulder outcrop in the middle of an open field and a pile of something he couldn't make out caught his attention. He made a note to himself to check them out after he killed Dylla. *Too risky now. Too much exposure in the open.*

Quith listened to the sounds of the forest. Leaves rustled in the gentle breeze while insects sang their mating calls. Birds fluttered through the trees. Idyllic and peaceful, Quith hated it all. He preferred the emptiness of his world, devoid of the noises shed by joyous creatures. Every living thing in the darkness of Evidar feared predation in the shared struggle for survival. He strained to gather whatever his ears could collect. Detectable human movement wasn't amongst any of the forest's offerings.

Quith moved carefully through the trees, hiding, crouching, step by step. Traces of matted undergrowth and recently overturned fallen leaves pointed the way.

It won't be long now, Dylla.

Heel to toe, slowly, Quith crept closer.

Poking his head out from behind a tree, *A foot.* He looked deeper, *A leg.* He pulled back quickly fearful of exposing his position. He waited. He listened. Nothing. He peered out again, *A body!*

Quith rose and came out from his hiding spot. He approached the carcass. It lay face down. With his foot, and without regard for affording the dead any dignity, he rolled the corpse over. His joy in finding Dylla dead gave way to disappointment. He hoped to kill her with his own hands. *All things considered, dead is dead. I'll take it.*

Dylla's open eyes, now cloudy in death, looked back at him. Quith bent down and poked one finger into the pool of blood soaking into the forest floor. He squished the sample with his thumb. *Congealed, just a little. Too bad, someone found you first. I wonder who Mera, Reyne Brenton, or was it the same gal who found me?*

His luck had taken a one hundred eighty-degree turn. Three compatriots he aimed to slay were gone and two had been removed by others.

With his foot, again he nudged Dylla's remains. Quith spoke to her as though her cold, lifeless ears could hear the delight in his voice. "So, you were going to kill me, huh?"

An evil thought crossed his mind. He freed his dick from its confines, held the tip in one hand between thumb and forefingers, aimed it at her face, and pissed on her carcass. Steam from urine, hotter than the air surrounding them, began to rise off her body. After draining himself, followed by two shakes, he stuffed his privates back in his pants, tucking it in on the right out of habit. He stepped back to admire his work. It felt even better that her eyes remained opened to watch him defile her corpse.

Quith rested his back against a tree, near to where his once-leader lay, contemplating his next move. Now that Dylla was dead, his odds of living longer had greatly improved. With a two-fingered salute, Quith gave voice to his appreciation. "If this is your handiwork, Mera, thank you."

An hour passed as plotting and strategizing played out in his head. He kept coming back to Neladith Karlis. *What do you know? Did Dylla catch you up with the new kill list that includes me?* Before he could effectively lay out his next steps, he needed to understand if Neladith planned to come after him. *A successful op requires accurate intel.*

Feeling safer, although still careful, Quith paced while he considered Neladith and his next move. As he wandered about, deep in thought, an out-of-place object stole his attention. What looked like the tip of a strung bow poked out from under a pile of leaves. He glanced at the bow and then back to Dylla. Quith playfully asked Dylla's corpse, "Another piece of the puzzle?"

Quith took hold of the bow, confirming his suspicions. He asked Dylla, "Yours? Maybe your better's?" A rustling of leaves, off in the distance, pulled him from his speculations.

Footsteps. More than one. Sounds like three, maybe four.

Quith quietly moved away, bow in hand. Hiding behind a nearby slab, he watched a trio lackadaisically lumber along a path near to the spot Dylla's cold, urine-soaked body lay.

He locked onto them as they approached. *Be ready. Might have to kill all three.*

"Holy shit!" one of the men called out, stopping short. The same guy stuck out an arm to halt the other two in their tracks. "You see what I see? It ain't the stream we're out here lookin' for."

"Is that what I think it is?" the second guy stammered. His eyes opened wider than Quith had ever witnessed—for Tarticans, anyway.

The first guy kicked the second guy in the butt. "Depends on what you think it is, douche bag."

"You're an asshole. I never seen a dead body before."

Guy number three took control. "Enough, you two," he said walking up to the body. "Oof-dah. You smell that?"

Guy number one scrunched his face, "Agh! Guess it's true," he said, waving his hand in front of his nose to clear the air. "People really do piss themselves when they croak."

The third guy asked, "Either of you know who it is?"

Both shook their heads.

"Yeah, me neither. Wonder if it's one of ours."

Guy number one added, "I lived in Topak my whole life. Sure, it's a big place, but I never seen her."

The second guy asked, "Should we do something?"

Man number three shot man number two a derisive look. "What could we do for her? She's a corpse."

Guy number one grabbed a stick and poked the body. "She ain't getting' up. Whatda you think happened to her?"

Guy number two reacted. "Leave her be. Look at her neck. I don't like this. Let's get outta here. Screw finding that stream. I ain't sticking around here."

Man number three rubbed his chin. "We gotta show this to someone who'll know how to deal."

Quith stayed in place, curious what plans they had for Dylla's carcass. The trio left, and he remained secure from sight. *More visitors on the way: a chance for more intel.*

He didn't wait long, less than an hour. But when more people returned, Quith couldn't believe his eyes. Shock mixed with delight flushed through him. *Neladith. And she brought Mithany.* Quietly rubbing his hands together, he thought, *This should be good.*

He remembered Reyne's fiancée from his operational briefings and from meeting her at the Owls Neck Inn. Quith also recognized the man with them as guy number three who'd discovered Dylla's body earlier.

While Neladith's presence pleased him, it was also a bit confusing, and it raised more than a few concerns. She was too good for him to keep his head poking over the top of the slab. Fearful of being spotted, he hunched down behind the block, where he could only listen.

Spetzer, Mithany, and Neladith arrived at the lifeless body. Neladith knew the dead woman instantly, Dylla Weisner. She didn't feel anything at the loss of her operation manager's demise, but warning bells rang out for her own safety. Concern, mixed with a touch of fear, at the murder of one of her own put her on guard. Spetzer, Mithany, and Neladith stood over the carcass, staring down at it. With open eyes, the corpse stared back at them. Dylla's death demanded Neladith get a handle on it fast, before some unknown attacker could do the same to her.

Neladith's eyes darted about while her brain worked the scene and various plausible events played out in her imagination—all the while her companions kept talking.

Mithany said, "This woman's been murdered. Her throat's been slashed."

"Duh, obviously," Spetzer quipped.

Neladith smacked his arm. "Don't be a wiseass."

Mithany asked, "Do either of you recognize her? Is she one of the people from Topak?"

Spetzer said, "The two guys who were with me when I found her said they didn't think she's one of theirs."

"Nel?"

"Me? No. Never seen her. No clue."

Neladith completed a cursory risk assessment. If the threat remained nearby and fighting became necessary, Neladith didn't want to expose her assassin skills to her companions. It would mean she'd have to kill them both. A dead Spetzer was no great loss, but Neladith had plans for Mithany. She was her guide dog on the hunt for Reyne and besides, a growing desire to bed Mithany had taken root in Neladith's youthful, sexually inquisitive appetites. She told her fellow explorers, "Mithany, Spetz, I'm going to look around. I'm gonna see if anyone's still nearby."

"Wait," Mithany said. "What if they are? You'll be in danger. We should all go together."

"You two stay here. I'll be okay. While you guys check around for signs of how this could've happened, I'm gonna head over to that clearing over there, near the big rock and find out what that brown pile is. Can't make it out from here. I'll stay in sight of you both."

Certain Mithany wanted nothing to do with spending time alone with Spetzer, Neladith forged ahead regardless. "It's okay. You'll be fine. I'll be right over there," she said, pointing to the boulder in the clearing no more than sixty yards away.

Spetzer said, "Before you go, either of you have any idea how long you figure she's been here like this?"

"Doesn't seem this woman's been lying here for long," Mithany replied.

Neladith offered her observations. "It's just a guess, but it looks fresh. Half a day, tops."

Mithany gave her a questioning look. "How could you know that?"

"I don't. I'm guessing." Her training and experience with deceased bodies accurately pegged Dylla's time of death. Neladith turned to pursue the spot in the open field near a big rock, sitting alone out of place.

Neladith surmised the trio would need to head back soon with the sun going down, and that didn't leave her much time to figure out how Dylla was taken out. Neither Mithany nor Spetzer had her keen Evidarian vision in the dark. She walked toward the glade with the sun starting its descent across the top of the tree line.

She pondered Dylla's killer and what circumstances led to her demise. Few knew of their operation. Neladith eliminated Daedyn as Dylla's executioner. He was dead, if she read all the signs Mithany had been shedding. She eliminated Arek for the same reason—he was dead, too. The old doctor couldn't overpower Dylla. It couldn't be Mithany; they'd been together the entire time. She wondered if there'd been an argument between Dylla and one of her fellow agents. Not likely, but possible. Then she considered Reyne. *That bastard is still alive. I know it. But I don't see how he could've done this.*

The excursion to find Reyne had proven unsuccessful and had taken longer than Neladith expected, but overall, her purpose in joining Mithany had borne fruit. Her ops leader wanted confirmation of Reyne's state of existence. Neladith was certain she had ascertained it from an unknowing Mithany. During untold hours of long talks on the road to Topak, the petite powerhouse shed too many tells for Neladith to think otherwise—she just hadn't located him yet. And getting to know Mithany had turned out more inviting than expected. Neladith learned she liked Mithany, and the way life unfolded in Tartica. She even toyed with staying behind after the team completed the op. But such thoughts were for another time.

A more immediate concern required resolution, and who killed Dylla puzzled her. Given Reyne's newly discovered ongoing status amongst the living, Neladith pondered how a local bumpkin running a nut farm had the skills to slit the throat of an experienced assassin like Dylla. *No fuckin' way.* One candidate remained at the top of her list: the man Tarticans knew as Mera.

What appeared as a heap of leaves nestled at the base of the immense stone sixty yards or so away dipped from her line of sight as Neladith drew closer. The open ground of the clearing gently sloped down from the forest before ascending back up gradually. The clear sight she had from the trees gave way and her view cut halfway across the rock outcropping at the swale's lowest point.

Neladith walked to stand atop a small rise and immediately understood what looked like a pile of leaves from a distance proved more ominous up close. What she discovered surprised her. *Another body. Meratoruc?!*

Approaching with caution, as intel briefings provided to Neladith in preparation of the Reyne Brenton op suggested Mera was a sneaky bastard capable of feigning death to set a trap. Although the protruding arrowhead, along with the red-soaked clothing, made either seem unlikely. Even so, his well-earned reputation demanded vigilance. Not far from what appeared to be Mera as a corpse, a death she could take credit for given Dylla couldn't say otherwise, lay a clump of clothing.

Neladith readied herself for an attack and, with her foot, nudged Evidar's nemesis. *No reaction.* She took a few steps back, looked over the scene, then back to where Dylla lay dead, and contemplated the series of events that gave rise to it all. Of all the pieces of the story laid out before her, the pants, the waistcoat, and the boots rested on the ground as though emptied of their occupant concerned her more than all the other factors. *Is it possible Reyne made it through the Void? Clothes here, body gone? Could be other reasons for the clothing laid out like that, but with everything else going on around this scene, looks pretty certain. The pieces fit. Mera was watching over him. Dylla showed up. The two fought and killed each other and Reyne transfigured. Fuck, this ain't good.* Though a second set of clothing confused her.

Neladith bent down to check Mera for a pulse. He looked dead enough, but she had to be certain. Two fingers to his carotid revealed nothing she didn't expect. She pressed harder on his neck to determine if a faint heartbeat hid beneath. An excited call broke her focus, and Spetzer came rushing through the trees, arms waving about, running towards her position, Mithany right behind.

"Nel. Hey Nel. What's going on?"

Neladith reacted quickly. She shot up from her spot. She needed to prevent Mithany from seeing Mera's body at all costs. She yelled out, "Nothing here. It's gonna be dark. I'm coming to you. Stay there. Let's head back to camp."

The pair stopped in their tracks. Neladith sighed in relief.

Her thoughts raced. *Mithany can't see this. She can only know of one dead body. Not two. Not Mera's. She'll recognize Reyne's outfit. She'll know they were together and now Mera's dead. With Reyne's clothes lying here and he's missing, don't know what she'll do. Can't risk it. Too much at stake.*

Neladith turned her back and scooped up the pile of clothing. In haste, she stuffed it into a crevice along the back side of the out-of-place boulder. Neladith sprinted towards her companions.

As she sped towards them, she played out events in her operative trained imaginings. *Dylla and Mera fought. She shot him. He didn't go down right away. He killed her. Somehow, he made it back to Reyne before collapsing. The clothing*—she recognized the signs—*doesn't follow a body into another reality.* She had taken the trip once herself, popping into Tartica's version of Earth, naked as the day she was born. *Reyne was alive and Dylla had interrupted the pair in the middle of his transfiguration. It cost her her life. Only one conclusion. Reyne's in my world now.*

Neladith considered her next move. She'd dispose of the bodies after dark. *After I get rid of them, maybe I should just go after Reyne? Follow orders, that's what Dylla always said. No... fuck her... Life on Tartica would be nice...* Shaking her head she thought, *What, am I crazy?... the Devil's Blacksmith ain't gonna let me go that easy. But I would like a shot at fucking that tight little Mithany... I'm so close... I can feel it, can taste it. No. First things first. Get rid of the bodies. I'll figure it out after that.*

Neladith caught up to Mithany and Spetzer. A little out of breath, she bent over to rest. "Alright, you two." She straightened up and threw an arm around Mithany. Spetzer gave her a hurt puppy dog look. "Nothing over there but some animal carcass. Time to get back to camp."

"What about the dead woman?"

"We'll check around camp and see if anyone fitting her description is missing. If not, tomorrow we'll send one of the Topakers to the nearest village. Alert the locals one of theirs needs a proper burial."

Quith stayed hidden and listened to what he could hear. He needed more information about Neladith, more intel, so he followed the trio from a safe distance back to their camp. Quith, astonished by the mass of people gathered, stayed out of sight. As dusk overtook the mass of travelers, the horde completed setting up camp on the roadway. Neladith and guy number three retired to a tent. Quith listened to their conversation as best he could, but missed most of it. As night settled in, the sounds of Neladith in the throes of passion rang out and reached him in his hiding spot.

Lucky fellow.

The night wore on. Slumber fell across the campsite. It didn't surprise Quith when Neladith emerged, alone, and quietly began her travels back into the woods. Quith remained out of sight and in stealth mode, followed Neladith's return to Dylla's body.

Once at the mortal remains, she stopped, looked around, and announced, "You can come out now."

Caught off guard, Quith had to decide. He'd been exposed and lost the element of surprise. Was she baiting him to unleash an assault of her own? His choice: go out in the open to expose himself to an attack or make an attempt of his own to take down Neladith. He braced for an assault, stepped out from hiding, and let slip his ever-present gravity knife from his sleeve into his waiting hand. He left the bow behind. It would be his secret if needed later. "When did you pick up on my presence?"

She didn't move.

No attack. Alright then.

"Picked up on you tracking us after we left this place earlier. You're not as stealthy as you think. Back at the roadside camp I moaned extra loud for your listening pleasure."

"I wasn't the only one in earshot. I suspect the whole camp heard you."

"What? You think I was the only one getting fucked tonight? There's a thousand people. Surely someone else got lucky besides me."

As much as he would have liked to continue the discussion of her sexual exploits, he pressed on. "What are you doing here?"

Neladith didn't immediately respond. Instead, after a long delay, she said, "I could ask you the same question, and another, more important one. Did you kill her?"

"No."

She stated, "I didn't think so. Normally, I might be a bit skeptical, but since there's also Mera's dead body in the mix, yeah, probably not you."

Quith hadn't yet scoped out the pile of debris. Surprised, his head spun about, searching the area for Evidar's nemesis. "No. Where is he?"

"His corpse is near the big boulder in the clearing."

Astonished, in a long, slow statement, Quith said, *"Fuuuck me."*

Neladith shot back with a laugh. "Not with Dylla's cold, dead vag."

"Hah hah. The bastard's finally dead. Great news. Tell me your assessment of what happened here."

Neladith explained what she unearthed, her calculated assumptions, including her suspicion Reyne was still alive and that he'd transfigured to their home world. Quith noted Neladith seemed unaware of the new player who he speculated could have been responsible for Dylla's murder—Gina. He let Neladith's reveal of the events go unchallenged. He kept knowledge of Gina to himself.

When she'd finished debriefing, Neladith said, "Glad you're here. You can help me get rid of these lifeless lumps. The little one, Mithany, I don't want her to see Mera's body. While we're doing that, you can tell me what you've been doing and why you're here."

Quith asked, "Got a shovel?"

"Nope."

"Fire it is."

The two gathered twigs, sticks, branches, and several larger logs. They exchanged information back and forth as they worked. Quith lied in revealing Grafph's and Tylus's demise, offering Meratoruc as the likely cause. He withheld Agents Kebra and Harvin's arrival as well. She detailed why her opinion of Mithany's behavior and words supported the conclusion Reyne remained amongst the living and only after, Quith admitted to his discovery of Daedyn's body.

Quith determined, Neladith did not know of Dylla's kill order on him. Before deciding whether he needed to kill her, here and now, he wanted to know more.

Neladith said, "You haven't yet told me what you're doing here."

"After digging up Daedyn and discovering Tylus and Grafph were taken out, I set about to locate Dylla to update her on everything. With nobody around to tell me where she went, I picked up her trail only today. Found her here not long before your scouting party did. You showed up and you know the rest."

"Fair enough. Let's grab the bodies. I think we've got a good enough pile of sticks."

The pair first secured Dylla on the makeshift funeral pyre and, after grabbing Mera, unceremoniously swung his body between them a few times before flopping him on top.

Neladith wiped her hands on Mera's leg. "I have to get back before smoke or the sight of the glow hits camp. I don't think either will reach that far, but just in case. Mithany can't know I did this. So, before I set it ablaze, we have to talk about Reyne. I think one of us should return home and go after him."

"I agree."

"Who's it gonna be, you or me? Keep in mind, I've established solid cover with Mithany and the Hensdale contingent. Dylla always told me, 'Follow orders.' You're the ranking agent. What're your orders, chief?"

"You follow orders. That's rich. Let me think."

The two stood silently as Quith ran the options through his operative, trained mind. He first decided he didn't need to kill Neladith, at least not yet. Quith considered Neladith's skills with a bow at long distances and that she might be needed to take out Kebra. Plus, she did not know of Dylla's kill order on him, and there was no one left to tell her. If he ordered her to return to their version of Earth, when debriefed she'd reveal too much about doings on Tartica, of Dylla's killing and, most seriously, of Reyne's transfiguration, something Quith figured he'd leave to those in Evidar to discover on their own. Kebra and Harvin had their instructions from the now-deceased Dylla, and they wouldn't be returning north anytime soon. It all came together to afford him more time to complete his self-given assignment—to save his own ass.

Quith continued lying. "Tell you what. I'll return home to hunt Reyne Brenton down, if in fact he did successfully transition. You stay with the girl in case he didn't cross over and he's still here on Tartica. If he is, he'll meet up with this Mithany sooner or later. We'll cover all possibilities that way. I'll report in and let the Devil's Blacksmith know what you're up to."

"Good plan. Sounds about right."

Quith had no intentions of returning to Evidar. Agent Harvin held the top spot on his list of the soon-to-be-dead with Kebra's demise to follow. She would be the most difficult to execute, and he might need Neladith's help to achieve it. He'd tell Neladith some bullshit story about how Kebra killed Harvin and they needed to take her out. *Yeah, I'll save Neladith for last.* He just needed to keep Neladith uninformed and out of his way while he put the Kebra and Harvin pieces in place.

With a snap of his wrist, Quith struck a match and lit the dry leaves they'd packed at the bottom. Neladith followed his lead, lighting several spots along the base. The flames grew slowly, starting small before gradually igniting the branches above.

Neladith turned from the burn. "Alright, I'm heading back. Don't need two people to hang around to make sure it doesn't go out. Thanks, I owe you one."

"Yes, you do. Now, off you go. That's an order."

Neladith sped away. Quith, unable to resist the temptation to ogle her ass in departure, evoked the remembrance of her seductive moaning earlier. With his plan in place and three agents on his kill-list dead, Quith had little to occupy his mind while watching Dylla and Mera burn. His thoughts turned to Neladith and her sensual vocalizations that visually played out in his imagination as he stared blankly into the flames.

The fire grew hotter, snapping him back from his absent-minded reverie, and Quith backed off to the tree line to watch the fire do its work in the center of the clearing. As time passed, he observed flames shooting up from the center of the funeral pyre. He wasn't certain, but thought he saw something move within the conflagration. *Nah, just the fire settling.*

The pile moved again, and embers rose high into the air. *The shifting weight of bodies,* he told himself.

Impossibly, an arm reached out and somehow grabbed hold of a powerful flame. *Can't be. No way!* Legs shifted and swung out over the edge of the burning woodpile. Clothes appeared to be ignited on the rising cadaver. Quith's hands shot above his head and he interlaced his fingers atop his white pallet of hair. His jaw dropped open—wide.

A humanoid shape sat up, engulfed in the blaze.

Flames danced all around the moving carcass without consuming its flesh.

The ghastly human form lumbered off the crumbled fiery heap. Quith watched the other body on the bottom sizzle in the intense heat to be consumed by combustion, yet the risen figure brushed away embers clinging to its clothes.

The acrid odor of roasting human flesh wafted across the clearing, attacking his nostrils. Quith gagged. Hidden in the trees, horror gripped his mind. The dead body stepped away from the red-hot bonfire.

Quith's mind reeled.

He recognized the face.

Impossible.

His eyes went wild.

Mera's alive!

New Business

Teth: 9th Day of the Harvest Moon

Nails

Nails moved the Thuggery's headquarters to The Gift of Flesh Celebratorium after the fall of the city. She delighted in her achievement, sitting behind a huge desk, admiring herself at acquiring it. From atop her new perch, she closed her eyes and pictured herself squeezing coin from every financial transaction across Teth. Control over just illegal commerce proved too restrictive for Nails's ambitions.

The Gift of Flesh Celebratorium, now a home for Teth's dominant criminal organization, had once been the jewel in the Temple of Life's network of holy sites honoring the sacrament of procreation. An elaborate structure dedicated to one of Goddess Teth's six gifts to humanity and open to the faithful and non-believers alike. The Temple's Celebratorium offered participation in any number of procreation-oriented worship "ceremonies" with one or more of its acolytes at a predetermined donation rate based on one's choice of ceremonial pleasures. Licensed Samers and enthusiasts of heterosexual couplings mingled together in worship. A brothel by any other name, its splendor and noted cleanliness gone in the days since falling under Nails's control.

A Thuggery underling popped her head into Nails's newly acquired office. "Chief," the minion began, "there're two blokes here to see ya. Says they're here on biz. Say they represent someone named Dylla Weisner. I never seen 'em before. Ya want me to send 'em away?"

Nails rubbed her chin. She pushed her chair back from the large desk she'd inherited. "Nah, I know Dylla. Send them in."

"Right away, Chief."

While waiting, Nails's eye's darted around the room from one mural depiction to another, each illustrating a passage from the Book of Teth. Sacred images depicting the joys of devotion to acts loosely associated with procreation and other variations on that theme, but to Nails, the frescos denoted titillating scenes of erotica. Not much different from the acts dozens of paying customers were currently engaged in, rolling around in a pile of flesh spread across the rotunda just outside Nails's office door.

The ornate office's prior occupant, who previously managed the Celebratorium's affairs, succumbed to the wrath of a Citizen's Committee tribunal. Charged with enforcing licensing requirements to its Samer customers, her guilt Nails determined even before the offenses were announced. With the sham trial in the books and justice meted out, the woman no longer needed an office. Nails sent her on her way to explore the truth behind the Goddess Teth's promised Gift of Renewal.

Under Nails's leadership, the Thuggery opened the Gift of Flesh Celebratorium's doors to all comers. The license requirements for Samers, under the new management overlord of the once pristine holy site, were no longer enforced. The other five gifts the Goddess Teth bestowed on humanity, Knowledge, Life, Nature, Love, and Renewal, Nails held in less esteem—if she held them in any esteem at all. She adored, above all things, an item the Goddess Teth never elevated to "Gift" status. But Nails did now that she ran the city outside the walls of the Temple of Life Palace. She worshiped above all else the newly minted Gift of Coin.

The door opened to the Thuggery subordinate with two Dylla Weisner's associates in tow. "Chief, the little one here says she's Kebra. The big galoot calls his self, Harvin."

"Thanks, Caulky, I got it from here. You can go. Close the door behind you."

Kebra spoke up, "Thank you for meeting with us. Dylla sends you her well wishes."

"Ain't seen her in a while. But okay. Let's get to it. I'm a busy woman. What're you here for? She wants something, that's certain."

The pair strode forward. "We're…" Harvin began.

Kebra poked Harvin with her elbow. "We agreed I'll work this out with our host."

"You two pasty-white motherfuckers need to get your act together. I got a lot to do. Don't waste my time."

Kebra craned her neck up to stare down Harvin. Then turned to Nails. "My apologies. I'll get right to it. Our leader, Miss Weisner, has done business with you in the past. She speaks highly of you. She's sent us here with a proposition. Has another one of our associates approached you with Dylla's request?"

"No."

"That's too bad, but okay then. There's a contract she'd like you to put out to your entire organization, and there's an image of a young man she would like converted to a wanted-dead-or-alive poster. She's requesting you produce and distribute it across all of Tartica. As quickly as possible."

"You got my attention. Gonna cost you lots of coin." Nails waved her hand toward two open chairs on the other side of her desk. "Sit down." As the pair accepted her invitation, Nails scoffed inwardly, watching the petite woman's form get swallowed by the oversized seat. Once settled in, Kebra's head barely poked above the desk's horizon. Harvin, too large to fit, wedged himself in. He seemed preoccupied with one of the tapestry scene depictions.

Nails heard the woman's voice, "Thank you, Miss Nails," and laughed to herself as Kebra's mouth remained hidden from view, with only hair and eyes showing.

Holding up one hand, the Thuggery leader stated, "Just Nails."

Kebra withdrew the drawing of Reyne Brenton from her overcoat, unrolled it, stood, and placed it on the desk. "Dylla would like to employ your services to have several thousand of these copied and spread around. She would also ask that you issue an open contract on his head."

"Nice-lookin' fella. Sure you want to kill him?"

"Yes. As soon as possible."

"Could be done. Dylla got the coin? The wanted posters might be even more than the hit since you want thousands copied and you want it done fast."

"Dylla's directed us to pay double for the usual fee on the contracted hit and triple if it's completed within the week."

Nails leaned back, rested one foot on her desk, and locked her fingers behind her head. "Put the coin on the desk and I'll get started."

Kebra rested her palms on the work surface and leaned in. "Dylla has asked that you accept this on her promise to pay. She's always been good for it and hopes you can accommodate her request. She's in Kantos at the moment but expects to follow up with you within days."

Nails, a skilled observer of human nature, sensed desperation in the request. "I could. But, it'll cost her. I ain't runnin' no fuckin' charity. Four times the usual hit rate and six times if one of my people finishes this fellow off in the week. Not negotiable. Take it or leave it."

Kebra and Harvin faced each other. Harvin gave Kebra an almost imperceptible nod, but Nails caught sight of it and pumped her fist inside her thoughts. *Read that one right.*

Kebra turned from her view of Harvin. "Thank you, Nails. We'll pay as you've asked. What of the posting service?"

"Gonna take a lot of labor. If you expect me to take the job on spec, price goes up. And you're paying points every day until Dylla settles the debt. I'm only doin' this cause she's never failed to pay before." Nails looked out from under her lowered brow, pointed her finger at Kebra, and demanded, "She better not fuck me on this one or I'll see to it you all pay with your lives."

Kebra nodded her agreement to the terms.

Nails rocked her chair forward and slapped her hand on the desk. "Done."

The door opened and Caulky stuck her head through. "Sorry to interrupt ya, Chief."

Nails shouted, "What? What's so damned fuckin' important? Can't you see I'm doin' biz here?"

"Again, sorry, but that thing ya was lookin' for. One of our guys thinks he found it. Ya said—"

"I know what I said." Nails stood, waving a finger at the Evidar agents. "You two pasty-faces, we're done here. Leave the image of the mark on the desk, I'll get it done. Tell Dylla to get her ass over here with the coin right away. Now get out."

Harvin, from his seat, looked straight ahead at the still standing Kebra. He opened his mouth to speak. Nails saw anger in his eyes. Kebra's hand shot up, and she held one finger to her mouth, stopping Harvin from saying anything. She bowed to Nails. "Thank you for your time, ma'am."

Nails waited for Dylla's agents to exit the office. "Caulky, you sure about this?"

"Sounds solid. The finder sent a runner. Says ya needs to gets to it right away."

"That's just fuckin' wonderful." Nails rubbed her hands together as though an exquisite meal magically appeared before her.

Caulky asked, "What about the two jamokies that just left? Guessin' they brang us new biz. Anythin' I can do to get it started while yuz gone?"

Nails's smile had yet faded from Caulky's news. "Nah. What them dopes brought me can wait 'till I get back. So tell me about this exciting turn of events... where'd they find him?"

"Near the Shantytown section."

Dead Man Walking

Teth: 9th Day of the Harvest Moon

Jerithan

A squat, round figure sat in silence amongst the gloom of the shadows. Jerithan's chest pounded realizing Timble had discerned his true identity. At first, he didn't notice the figure looming in the corner. His eyes caught up with his hammering heart and opened wide at the discovery.

"It is a trap," the Voice shouted into Jerithan's thoughts.

Timble deceived me. I am a dead man walking.

"We cannot let that happen."

Timble, in his high-pitched voice, said, "Jerithan, I'm sure ya already know our guest. I sent word for Nails to join us."

"You son-of-a-bitch."

"Don't be mad, Jerithan, they tell me ya two know each other."

Nails stood. Still in shadow, her shape didn't change much from the specter she cast sitting down. She said, her ever present aggression poking through even when offering pleasantries, "Thanks much, Timble. Let myself in the backdoor."

The Voice offered Jerithan insight. *"Cannot trust anyone these days."*

Like I can trust you?

The Thuggery leader spoke, "Jerithan, I've been looking for you. It's like you disappeared for a week. But here you are. My man Timble recognized you immediately. Dirt-mask and all." She stepped forward out of the dark, with a broad grin pasted across her jowls. The hanging flesh mixed with her grotesque smirk made for a hideous appearance in the dim lighting, a visage as threatening as her words.

The Voice chided, *"You cannot let her sense your fear. You were First Lord. Face her now as the First Lord you still are."*

Jerithan considered the advice, swallowed the scraps of saliva gathering in his mouth, and did his best. "Nails, this is quite the surprise." He extended his hand to her.

The round woman let his offer hang in the air. After a few seconds, Jerithan let his extended hand slide down to his side, followed by another dry gulp.

Timble grabbed the pack on Jerithan's back. "Let's get this off."

Jerithan resisted.

Nails told the dethroned First Lord, "My friend, we can do this easy or hard."

Jerithan acquiesced, allowing Timble to remove his backpack. "Friend? Seems unlikely. And Timble, where is the loaf you promised? I have not eaten in days."

The big man handed Jerithan's pack to Nails.

"Got it right here." Timble's massive hands ripped the small loaf in half and offered the larger of the two pieces to Jerithan.

The Voice added, *"Last meal for the condemned?"*

Jerithan ignored the Voice and everyone in the room as his teeth tore into the first sustenance he'd had in days. He didn't take notice of Nails rifling through his belongings, focused squarely on the rapidly disappearing bread in his hand. Any flavor his brain might have registered as taste gave ground to his ravenous attack of the life-giving meal.

His mouth stuffed with the dry loaf, Jerithan mumbled, "Water?" Crumbs dribbled from his mouth as he spoke.

Nails held up a green vestment extracted from Jerithan's backpack.

"Water?" he asked again.

Timble poured a large cup from a dirty container, handing it to Jerithan.

He gulped it down. "Another," he said, handing the cup back to Timble.

Ravenously he chugged, caring little for the water spilling from the sides down his cheeks. Relief coursed through him. With what remained of the liquid dripping from his jaw, his open palms rubbed respite across his face. Jerithan looked out between his fingers, noticing all eyes in the room on him, judging him, and he wiped his chin with his sleeve.

The Voice confided, *"Their collective opinion of you means nothing."*

Again, he handed the empty mug to the large orange-haired man.

Responding to the Voice, Jerithan thought, *You are right. I have been freed of concern for what others think. I do not know why, yet I do not care. Let them condemn me. They mean nothing. Rabble.*

Nails held the garment up to Jerithan. "I'm gonna need you to put these on."

"To what purpose?"

"Haven't you heard? I'm now the chairwoman of the Citizen's Committee. We're running the city. It's in my hands. The Temple of Life no longer governs Teth outside the Palace, and the Committee has decided the Temple needs to account for its ways. Who better than you to stand before all and pay the price?"

Jerithan replied, "My dear Nails. Haven't you heard? I am no longer part of Temple business. I want them to pay for what they have done as much as you."

"Yes, but you, I fear, want them to ante up for what they did to you. I, on the other hand, want you to atone for what you've inflicted on all of us these past several years."

"I have done nothing but made your lives better," Jerithan politely added.

Nails tossed the green robe at Jerithan. "I dare say there are several thousand Samers who beg to differ. Then there are the breeding farms. I'm sorry, but you'll need to take responsibility for those as well. Your Order, the Temple, has held back humanity's progress for millennia, holding firm to keep civilization rooted squarely in Nature. Disallowing a better life for the poor while you and all your prudents live in luxury. Shall I go on?"

Jerithan let the clothing, the symbol of his once lorded Temple authority, fall to the ground. "I am no longer the man you accuse me of being."

Nails would not relent. "Believe what you want. All I care about, you were once."

"And will be again," The Voice told him.

Jerithan offered, "Then it is the Temple of Life you need to put on trial. It is the Covenant of Absolute Universal Obligations you need to hold up to the call for justice. I have served only as its steward. Its principles have guided our way of life almost fifteen hundred years and you want me to be the one to stand in its place for payment because now you take the position of disagreement? Your quarrel is not with me, Nails."

"Maybe. But you'll do."

"Nails, you and I both know you do not give a shit about any of those issues you have so eloquently spoken of. Yours is a different agenda. You care only of one thing, now and always: yourself."

"You're a brave man, I suppose. Saying such things to the woman who has your balls in her grip. But, let's say you're right. Don't matter. Don't change anything. I'm still gonna squeeze your nuts, hard, and you're still standing trial. Now put on the fuckin' robe."

In an act of defiance, Jerithan crossed his arms over his chest.

"I see the old Jerithan again. This is good."

Will it be good when she kills me?

Nail screamed at Jerithan, "Put it on!" Spittle flew from her flapping maw. Jerithan didn't move.

Still yelling, Nails commanded, "Timble. If he doesn't make a move to put on the green piece of shit in the next ten seconds, strip him of those rags and put the thing on him yourself."

"If this is about silencing me for your part in the failed assassination of Tomelai, you have nothing to fear from me."

The Voice noted, *"Very pleased to see you lie as well as ever. Tell her you have already spoken with Derr. Warn her Derr knows of her involvement. Give her a chance to get away. If you do, it might just get you out of this alive."*

I do not think so. She is vindictive and her self-preservation instincts are off the charts.

Nails said, "You know what they say about secrets between friends. Knowledge of the secret can never be eliminated, unlike the friends."

Jerithan attempted a deflection and to plant a seed in Timble's thoughts about the big man's own future. "What about my previous friend here, Timble? Surely you must be concerned about what he now knows. At some point you will have no choice but to deal with him. Like me, he's a dead man walking."

"Swing and a miss. He's paid well, and he knows what will happen to his daughter if he talks. Timble here would never betray me at the risk I'd put her to work servicing Gift of Flesh aficionados. A few years suckin' dick and fuckin' old men. Don't get me wrong, there's nothing wrong with either. I've dabbled in both a few thousand times myself. But when it comes to the art of oral gratification, I'm rather good at it and I quite enjoy it. Especially the power it gives me. So much trust literally placed in my hands. I get off on the control men willingly hand over to me. Gotta admit, though, things went bad for more than one or two of those trusting fellows. Don't fret, I left no one dickless who didn't deserve it. All things considered, let's just say I have no worries for Timble's ability to keep his mouth shut. Nah, the big guy here ain't ever gonna betray me. You, Jerithan, on the other hand, are a different story. Ain't I right, Timble?"

"It's just as ya say, ma'am." Timble nodded.

Nails continued, "If we're done, back to the issue at hand. I'm losing my patience. Now... put... on... the... fuckin'... robe."

"Suppose Derr already knows?" Jerithan said, positioning another card to play.

"There were only three of us who could've told him, and Razoal is dead. Not to mention every one of my men who died in the effort. Leaves me and you and I know *I* didn't say anything to Derr. You're the only leak I need to plug. And look at you, roaming the slums since being thrown out of the Temple. Simple math, Razoal's dead; you didn't have the chance to tell him, and I ain't said nothin'. Once you're dead, it's me and Timble here. And he ain't talkin'. Derr will never know. Enough of this. Time's up. Timble, when I get to zero, if he ain't dressed in green, put it on for him." Nails paused for dramatic effect before starting the countdown. "Ten... nine... eight... seven..."

Jerithan pleaded for a last-minute rescue. "Timble, you must know she will have no choice but to kill you at some point."

Timble didn't respond and stepped forward.

Fear squeezed his heart. The Voice spoke to him, *"You tried. You made your stand. We need to get out of this alive. I suggest doing what the fat lady says. We will figure a way out of this later."*

Jerithan remained motionless.

Timble came closer.

"... six... five... four..."

Timble stopped halfway along his path to Jerithan and reached for the door-knob.

Nail stopped counting. "Timble, you goin' somewhere?"

"No, ma'am. Just gettin' the door."

"I didn't hear a knock," she said, confused.

Timble pulled on the rickety handle.

The hinges squealed.

The door swung open.

Tandure's wealthiest private citizen, Ja'Rou Chamette, stepped through the opening and closed the door behind him.

The confused chairwoman of the Citizen's Committee spewed, "What the fuck? Chamette, what are you doin' here? You're supposed to be in Tandure, fuckin' things up over there."

"I have come all this way for you. Timble here has been kind enough to alert me where to find you. He sent word to my people as he did yours, less than an hour ago. I'll settle up with him later. Thank you, Timble."

Timble nodded.

Chamette continued, "Puts the whole 'he wouldn't betray me' speculation to rest. I heard you from outside the door while I waited. And then there's your involvement in Tomelai's failed assassination you spoke of. There's someone who would like a word with you about your involvement."

Nails looked to Chamette, bewildered, angered. "Chamette, you motherfucker. I thought we were partners. You're supposed to be on my side."

Chamette shrugged. "There are no sides. There's only coin. Aren't you the same woman who extracted payment from three sides of a two-sided issue? You recall your involvement in the Vote of Revocation? You took payment from Serco to keep prudents supporting Jerithan from getting back in time for the conclave. You took payment from Jerithan here to keep Serco's prudents from making it back to the city in time to vote, and in a surprise move, you took even more money from Derr to make sure the vote went against our friend Jerithan over there. You made it look plausible, just enough damage to all sides, but I know your orders allowed Prudent Hansel to slip through at the last minute. The deciding vote. Like I said, you and I know, there are no sides."

Jerithan exploded. "I'll kill you!"

He lunged at her but didn't get far. A large hand shot forward and Timble squeezed Jerithan by the shoulder in an iron grip, cementing the furious, deposed, First Lord in place.

Chamette swung open the door. All heads in the room spun to witness Lieutenant Willem Ferpratt, Derr's right-hand man, stride into the room, followed by ten other men and women of Adelle's KCG.

Change of Plans

Evidar

Reyne

Although the ability to track the sun's movement across the sky wasn't possible, Reyne guessed he and Gina had arrived on the dark world of Evidar less than an hour ago. If Mera's assessment was correct, the sun was still there; it was just hidden from view by the abysmal, oppressive atmosphere. Thoughts of Mera and news of the man's death hit Reyne harder than he'd expected.

He owed Mera his life. When the journey to Evidar was first proposed by Mera, Reyne considered making it a quick round trip, returning to Mithany almost as soon as he'd arrived. At the time, deceiving Mera to believe he'd taken up the cause to kill Evidar's Damus didn't bother him much—it did now.

At the moment Reyne entered the Void, he still hadn't decided: implement the plan to return to Mithany or stay on Evidar to do Mera's bidding. With Gina's appearance, joining him on the world forever in darkness, and with Mera gone, new considerations forced him to reexamine his planned deception.

The two set out to follow the map Reyne held in his thoughts in search of their Evidarian contacts, Aderlee and Siandra. But the landscape seemed different from what he expected. They needed clothes, food, and weapons. While his first priority was survival, Reyne second priority was to decide which course of action to take.

"Reyne, you mind if we sit a bit? I could use a pair of boots. My feet are killing me."

The two sat in silence, staring out into the murky world enveloping them. Reyne contemplated the melancholy invading his psyche while Gina rubbed her feet. Reyne mulled his options. Several long minutes passed in silence as thoughts of Mera added to the gloom and complicated Reyne's plans. With a snap of his head, Reyne piped up. "I might be able to return to our campsite on Tartica. But we got no way of knowing how long we spent in the Void. Could've been in there for minutes or for days. And since Mera's already gone, there's no going back to save him."

"The Void felt like an eternity to me."

"Plus, if I went back, I'd have to leave you here, alone. How *you* got here, neither of us understands."

"That's gonna have to be a problem for another time."

"Gina, the first thing Mera told me to do was to track down either a guy named Aderlee or a woman named Siandra. Shame we don't got a real map, just what's in my head. Nothing makes the trip but the body. Hence, the two of us sitting here in the buff," he said, waving his hands over his exposed skin for emphasis.

While seated, Gina pulled her knees to her breasts. Mirroring Reyne, she wrapped her arms around her legs. "For however long it took to go from that spot where I trained you to here, the time in the black emptiness was terrifying. Scared the shit out of me every moment I spent in the Void. How the hell did you handle it?" She shivered, and her entire body shook.

"I surprised myself; I handled the Void pretty good until something invaded my mind. For a second, I thought I could reach out and almost touch Mithany. But an entity crashed into me. When that happened, it broke off my connection with her."

"I don't know if the entity in the Void was me. Could've been. And that thing about Mithany, for the slightest second, I felt that too. In there, it was like I could sense another's thoughts forming, but when I tried to get close to the source, it would shatter into little pieces. I recall being so furious I couldn't connect yet terrified I'd be in there forever."

Reyne tilted his head to the side quizzically. "Huh. Wonder if it was you tracking me. Sounds like it. I think we just put together the first piece of the puzzle."

"That other presence I felt in the Void might've been you. But how did I get there?"

Reyne said, "I don't know. We'll figure it all out in time. I'm just glad you're here."

"Don't take this the wrong way. I'm not. I should be back there with Mera. I'm gonna miss him." She wiped away a tear. "Look at this place. It's miserable. You can hardly see anything through the darkness beyond twenty or thirty feet."

"Gina, I gotta be honest with you. I'm a red-blooded male. My eyes are gonna wander every now and then. Don't want to upset you, but they got a mind of their own. And whether you do the same thing, feel free to look, stare, or whatever. Doesn't bother me in the least. Until we find something to wear, we're gonna have to accept it. I'd be lying if I told you otherwise."

Through puffed cheeks, Gina let out a gust. "That's fine, I guess. Back on Tartica, of all the people we both know, who haven't either of us seen without clothes? It's just the culture we live in."

"True enough. Thank the Goddess Teth for the Gift of Flesh paving our way on Evidar."

"Yeah, that's one way to put it. Besides, I keep in shape, given my line of work and I'm proud of my body. Look, but don't touch. Those are my rules. I'm in charge. Nothing happens unless I say so. If you can abide by that, guess we can both live with it until we track down some clothes."

"I accept... and I can certainly see why you should be proud."

"You weren't shortchanged either. By the looks of that thing, Mithany is a lucky gal."

"You don't got to worry about the whole touching issue. Wouldn't be right. I intend to remain true to her. We're gettin' married as soon as I get back."

"We'll see how long that willpower of yours holds out, farm boy. Sooner or later"—she stood for him to get a full assessment—"all this might change your mind."

"Sit down. Don't see us getting bored. We got other priorities to attend to, like food and water."

Seated on a hard slab that went out in every direction to the limits of their vision—as permitted by the engrossing ebony veil—Gina said, "The way I see it, we're screwed. Mera got you here. He's gone now. Somehow, I got pulled along for the ride and even if we do find and kill this Damus, we got no way of both of us getting back to Tartica." She rested her chin on her knees and lamented, "We're fucked."

Reyne replied, "Look at the bright side. At least it's not cold. Ground's even warm. And I think I can get back to Tartica. Not positive, but pretty sure. Sometimes, not often, every now and again while I sleep, my mind gets separated from my body. I look down from above and see myself sleeping. Scares the shit outta me every time. So, I can get to what Mera called the astral plane. From there, now that I know how, I can get into the Void and back to Tartica from there. But, we gotta figure out how you hitched a ride so we can reverse the process if I'm gonna bring you back with me."

Gina's presence was a blessing and a curse. She had the skills to assist him in both survival and taking out this Damus person. The downside was getting Gina back to Tartica with him presented an entirely different problem, one he didn't have a solution for other than leaving her forever on Evidar to fend for herself.

"Remember back in the glade when you laughed at the idea of me running around stark-naked when I arrive on Evidar? You amused yourself at the thought of my jostling and bouncing privates? You hooted trying to picture it. Fell off that boulder because you laughed so hard?"

"Yeah, I remember. So what?"

"I thought about how you laughed at me while you yourself were running around screaming with your tits bouncing up and down. That bitch Karma turned the tables on you. Gotta admit, Gina, it was a hoot, just like you imagined." He finished with a big, toothy grin.

She punched him in the arm.

"Hey, that hurt," Reyne protested, and they both laughed.

Gina abruptly stopped, hung her head, and pulled her sitting posture into a tight curl. "Mera's dead. We got no food, no water, no clothes, it's dark as hell, we got no way of getting home, and we're Tartica's only hope to sweep some bad guy's plans into the shitter by finding a Damus we've never seen and got no idea where to search."

While rubbing his arm, Reyne considered his plan to leave Evidar behind with a quick turnaround back to Tartica. He wondered, *Am I the kinda guy to abandon someone?*

Daedyn, I need you more than ever. I miss you, brother. I should tell you, we had a little sister. Well, I guess she'd be our big sister. She was three years older than either of us. I don't give two shits what Mera's said about all that biological family stuff... you're my brother. That makes her our sister.

Bro, what should I do? You had a way of seeing things so clearly. I'm no assassin. Guess if I had to, I could do it. I didn't want any of this. I never believed Mera's claim, Tartica's in immediate danger. Might never happen the way he says it will. I just want to get back to Mithany. Let someone else save the world.

I think I know what you'd tell me. I owe Mera my life. I made a promise to him. Mithany will be there for me when I get back. You'd say, "Do the right thing. Don't leave Gina here alone." I hear you in my thoughts telling me, "Little brother, that's not the kinda guy you are." Ahhh, I get it. I know. You're right. Miss you so much, Bro.

Shit... Shit... Shit...

Change of plans.

With renewed conviction, Reyne reached out to take Gina's hand. "Mera said you're the best there is. I don't know how you ended up here, but since you did, I'm glad you're here. Together, we're gonna kill Evidar's Damus. After that, there's gotta be a way to get us both home."

REVELATIONS

THE WOODLANDS OF KANTOS: 9TH DAY OF THE HARVEST MOON

Quith

After the shock of seeing Mera rise from the flames, a trick Dylla's cadaver proved incapable of matching, Quith turned his attention to assessing the conditions on the ground. He dispatched the luxury of contemplating the existence of a man capable of cheating death; instead he focused on preventing Mera from effecting his own.

With Mera alive, Quith had an enormous problem. A life-threatening problem. Understanding coalesced in a heartbeat—based on hushed rumors of its existence coupled with Mera's repeated repudiation of Quith's every attempt to kill him—*That motherfucker's got the Soul Stone.*

Wish I knew that earlier. His body lying there on the ground, looking dead. Would've been a lot easier getting it off him then... a problem for another time. First, got to live through this encounter with that sneaky bastard.

No chance to slink away. He's seen me.

Quith raced to Dylla's bow he'd hidden from Neladith earlier. Dylla, being dead, didn't need it anymore. Unfortunately for Quith, any signs of where she'd left her arrows or her quiver evaded his expedited search. He needed more time to find them, but the situation didn't allow for it. He accepted his predicament, a bow without arrows. To the untrained, a useless instrument, but not to Quith. *I'll use it as a bluff, and if worse comes to worse, I can beat him with it.*

Quith struck an archer's pose with an arrowless bow in hand, hopeful Mera could discern only enough of his presentation to accept the feint. The fire consuming Dylla's carcass glowed, lighting up the night. The contrasting effects didn't reach out with enough strength to enhance Mera's outline in anything beyond a silhouette. "Meratoruc. With my bow I have you in my sights. But know this, I mean you no harm, old foe."

Mera walked down the swale and up to the top of the berm.

With one hand cupped to his mouth, the other holding out the toothless threat, Quith projected his words. "Seems your boy made it."

Mera turned his head, and Quith knew he'd heard him.

Uncertain of what the once-apparently dead man would do—engage in dialogue or attack—Quith tried to nudge Mera toward the former. "I'm throwing my bow to the ground. From this distance, I could have easily killed you. I mean you no harm. I just want to talk."

Quith held up the weapon for Mera to see and tossed it aside. Mera couldn't have known the weapon had been defanged prior to Quith's gesture of peace. Quith's threats of dealing death were as impotent as his arrowless bow, knowing all his prior efforts to end Mera's life had resulted in failure. He'd left Mera for dead before, but only now were the seeds of understanding beginning to take root—the Soul Stone.

Mera stepped forward.

Quith gulped hard. "Stay where you are. We can talk from here. I'm sure you know I got other weapons on me. I'd rather leave them sheathed. I know Reyne is alive and well. Your deception failed."

"What do you want, Quith? Make it quick. You'll be dead in a few minutes. I saw you that day with the blow-dart aimed at Reyne. I got lucky he lived. Not so lucky for you. Time to pay up. You killed his brother."

"And, just so you understand, I didn't kill the brother or any on your side."

"Technicality. You might not have pulled back the bowstring, but your team did. You stood alongside Neladith and directed her to take the shot."

Quith wondered how Mera could know. *Mere speculation? Not important.* "Sorry about the brother. Doesn't matter. Reyne lives, and from what I can gather, he's made it to my world. I'm still here. I didn't go after him. I don't care what he does. I'm out of the fight."

"Goody for you. Doesn't mean I'll let you live. Besides, I don't believe you."

Quith expected as much, but he had more cards to play.

Mera inched forward.

"Wait!" Quith shouted, holding up both empty hands.

Mera kept moving forward.

"STOP!" Quith demanded. Another lump slid down his throat. "Let me finish. If you still want to kill me after I'm done, you can try. But let me say my piece."

Mera stopped walking. "You got one minute."

"Dylla's dead. I killed her. Her body burned underneath you on the fire. I killed Tylus and Grafph too."

"We both know that isn't true. Tylus died at another's hand."

"Okay, yeah, you're right. I lied about Tylus, but I did eliminate Dylla and Grafph for you." This time, only half a lie.

"For me? I doubt that."

"Well, not so much for you. I did it for myself. Like I said, I'm done doing the bidding of the Devil's Blacksmith. We both know who I'm talking about. I can help you with *him*. Even though my team, Dylla, Tylus, and Grafph, are dead, he sent over two more. Both are very dangerous. I can help you with them."

With his clothes still smoldering, Mera said, "Why would you do that, and second, what of the shooter? The young woman with the red eyes and red hair. Haven't heard your update on her status yet."

How the fuck does he know about her? Quith wondered. "Like you said, the girl's name is Neladith."

"I know her name and who she is."

"Haven't seen her." Quith continued lying in pursuit of extending his life. He'd held Neladith in reserve to be used in the future if needed. Her game piece had to remain in play for the time being. He would kill her later, but not yet. "You sent Reyne into the Void, and he's most likely over in my world as we speak. I didn't go after him. That's got to account for something. And just as important, I didn't return to warn the Devil's Blacksmith. Calls himself the Architect."

"I know what he calls himself. I know more about him than you could ever imagine. I'm also aware an associate of mine caught up with you and let you live. She filled me in on your conversation. Not her best decision, letting you go."

"Maybe I let her live. Ever considered that?"

"Not likely."

"You already knew all this. I'm going after the two agents heading south. It's to your benefit, so why try to take me out now?"

Mera grinned. "Past transgressions. I owe it to all the people you've killed."

"You two are so much alike. It stunned me when I saw you rise from the flames. Then I thought to myself, he's got to have the Soul Stone. It's the only explanation there is. Now I understand why the other times I killed you didn't take."

"Reminding me of that doesn't help your case... Time's up."

Before the sound of Mera's voice reached Quith's ears, the man, fresh off the burning pyre, launched himself and raced forward. His clothing harboring glowing embers painted an ominous outline of orange pulsing dots that formed in the shape of a man, speeding through the dark of night with the silhouetted forest framing the backdrop.

Quith responded, rushing headlong at Mera.

En route, as they raced towards each other in the open field with fire blazing in the background, Quith snatched the dagger from its sheath along his pant leg. Just feet from each other, he feigned a killing strike with the blade at Mera's throat, certain his opponent's eyes would follow. With his other hand, he aimed an open palm at Mera's chest, intending to cripple Mera's ability to breathe.

At the instant Quith meant to strike, Mera dropped to his knees and swept his arm across Quith's feet, taking his legs out from under him. Quith's extended arms from his botched maneuver failed to brace his fall. Quith face-planted into the hard Earth with a crunching sound. His nose broke. Pain burst across his face.

His fingers opened on impact. His grip on the weapon, lost. It bounced from his reach. Blinding agony shot through his head into his vision.

Mera hit the ground. Embers spewed off his clothing. He sprang up in a flash.

Quith fought back the pain. He snapped into a battle-ready stance and wobbled unsteadily on his feet.

Mera shot forward, ramming his shoulder into Quith's chest. They both crashed to the ground. Quith slammed backwards into the hardened surface.

Mera tumbled into a roll. Jumped upright.

Quith struggled to regain his breath.

Mera lunged forward. His burning boot stamped down at Quith's head.

Quith spun. Mera's heel grazed his temple. Smoldering footwear slammed into hard earth. Cinders scattered. One caught skin at the corner of Quith's eye. The red-hot ember seared into his flesh. Quith screamed. He launched himself forward and upward, wrapping both arms around Mera's legs.

Mera toppled over. The back of his head crashed into the ground. He twisted free. Mera swung his elbow down to smash into Quith's neck. Quith squirmed away just in time. He rolled and smashed his own elbow into Mera's face.

Mera's head snapped back, yet he sprung to his feet. Quith did the same. At that exact moment, Mera drove his knee into Quith's groin. His nutsack screamed agony into his skull. His gut reacted of its own accord—pleading with his brain to wretch. Quith denied himself relief. His eyes darted left to right. He scanned the area for his blade.

Mera afforded Quith no reprieve. With open palm, he struck Quith's broken nose. Hot skewers slammed into his brain. Quith staggered back.

Mera swept up the wayward weapon. He lunged forward with blade in hand—straight at Quith's torso.

Quith saw it coming and punched down. Mera dropped the knife. With his free hand, Quith swept it underneath to catch the dagger as it fell. Quith swung his arm up, deadly blade in hand. He pulled up at the instant cold steel touched Mera's neck.

A drop of blood leaked out. Mera stilled.

Quith held death to Mera's throat.

Breathing heavy through his mouth, bloodied and half blinded, Quith said in a nasally tone, "You fuck! You broke my nose."

Mera shrugged. "Not drawing the knife across my throat. You want me to think you're a changed man?"

"I only want to talk. I didn't come here to kill you."

"You and I both know that's not why you didn't do it."

"Why then?"

"You're not sure you can kill me, and you need something from me. Neither of those lets you off the hook."

Quith threw the cutter to the ground. Stepping back from Mera, he bent forward, resting his hands on his knees. His chest rose and fell, sucking wind through his mouth to recover his breath; he tilted his neck up and looked to Mera, "Are we done here?" Blood dripped out through his nostrils.

Mera opened one palm to reveal a small push dagger. "You would never have had the time to open my neck. I had this little blade in reserve throughout our little tête-à-tête. Lucky for you, I had no need of it."

"Enough already. Look, I can help you. I got to eliminate anyone here now from my world and anyone else that comes over if I want to live. Otherwise, I'll be looking over my shoulder until the day I die. I don't want to live like that. I'm not on your side. I'm on my side, but my side is useful to you. I'm invested in your success. If you want to try to kill me when this is all done. Fine. We'll go at it again whenever that is. But for now, truce?"

"If I don't kill you, the Devil's Blacksmith will get the job done. You can't just walk away from him. You figure that one out yet?"

"That's my problem, not yours. Besides, he doesn't know yet. I have time. Today, it's between you and me."

The fighting doused the remaining life from Mera's smoldering threads. The ripped, torn, and burned clothing barely covered his body. The slovenly appearance did little to reduce Mera's stature in Quith's mind.

Dylla's funeral pyre continued to burn in the background, having borne witness to the battle and the parlay that followed. The eerie orange glow danced across Mera's form as he faced Quith. Mera told him, "I can agree to a truce... for now. You'll probably die sooner than later, and if you take a few more Evidar agents with you, all's the better."

"Why didn't you just say that? Why did we just go through all this?"

"You deserved what I dished out. From what my associate shared, I anticipated your offer to help. But know this, I wanted to take a measure of satisfaction from your hide. Wanted you to taste pain. I've done enough damage for now... so I accept your offer. Mind you, it's a temporary truce. And if you give me any reason to think otherwise..."

"Fine," Quith said in a huff. "To show you I'm not all that bad of a guy, there's a pile of clothes stuffed in at the base of that boulder. Guessing they're Reyne's, and there's an extra set, too. His stuff might be a wee bit big. It'll do."

Mera stayed quiet as he yanked the attire from its crook. He held up both sets of pants and tops. Quith's enhanced night vision followed Mera's every move. He wondered at the knowing look on Mera's face holding up the smaller of the two outfits. Mera stuffed Gina's outfit back in the crook, stripped, and donned Reyne's clothes and boots. The fit, a skosh loose.

Mera said, "So where are these other two agents you told me about? Let's not forget about Neladith either. You have Evidar hunters to eliminate."

Quith had achieved his immediate goal—to live another day. Long term, he had bigger problems. Once the Devil's Blacksmith caught wind of his betrayal, his life would be forfeit. Yet he wondered about the Soul Stone. *If I had it for myself, it just might help me survive the Devil's Blacksmith's wrath. New objective: get the Soul Stone.*

Get Settled In

Mithany

A thousand people or more all around me, but our home will be empty without you, my love.

Mithany couldn't stop thinking about those few seconds the day before when Reyne's essence caressed her heart. His connection to her fled as quickly as it first appeared. Her broken heart fed off the fleeting touch of Reyne's presence—real or imagined—that she'd experienced along the road to Topak. Almost home from her quest, familiar landmarks toyed with her emotions the closer she came to the treestone residence she and Reyne once shared with Daedyn. Her heart fluttered as she anticipated a glimpse of the orchard around the bend.

She focused on formulating an explanation to the Brenton Orchard's general manager, Santander. She'd have to explain why she'd returned with a hungry horde in need of food and a place to set up camp along with the whole *who the heck are all these people* clarification he'd expect.

On the return journey from Topak to Hensdale, the indigent caravan swelled by an additional hundred or more as they passed through one hamlet, then another. Many of the rural areas fared far better than the riot-plagued city of Topak. The mostly Temple-going religious faithful of the smaller communities had an advantage over the larger population centers. The relationships in rural villages that bred familiarity amongst close-knit peoples led to conformity by way of peer pressure enforcement. That, coupled with the fraternal nature of the agricultural way of living, with Covenant-based obedience as a core belief, withstood the initial onslaught of the unincumbered, rebellion-minded insurrectionists like those who destroyed Topak.

The wave of revolution sweeping across Tartica sputtered in the less densely populated countryside. Nonetheless, pockets of Covenant objectors from several burgs found their way into Mithany's band of homeless followers. The new arrivals were at odds with the core beliefs of the refugee horde. Human compassion held the day, owing to the shared need for comfort. Mithany hoped to maintain the status quo but understood a long-term peace between the factions unlikely.

On the outskirts of the property, Mithany caught sight of Santander's familiar grizzled round face with pronounced worry lines cutting every which way. His gray hair and his mostly bald crown brought a smile to her face when she spotted him on his daily inspection of the farm. She sprinted to the large hulk of a man as fast as her short legs allowed. Filled with joy, she slammed into him and instantly wrapped her arms around his protruding, bulbous waist.

Even before offering a greeting, Santander patted her on the back and asked, "I don't see Daedyn. Reckon you didn't find him."

Mithany pouted, "How about a hello? I missed you."

"I missed you too, dear."

"We didn't find him. Made our way to Topak lookin' for him. We came across all these people left homeless after they got burned out by rioters. I couldn't leave them without food. We have so many alphens. We can feed them. I had to bring them here. Can only hope Daedyn finds his way home soon." She lied about Daedyn, all in the name of protecting Reyne.

"How are you holding up, dear? You been through a lot."

Mithany hung her head, hiding her quivering lower lip. "I cry when I'm alone. I miss Reyne so much. My heart's broken. He's gone. Daedyn's gone." She buried her face in his chest.

"We all miss them, dear," Santander said, and kissed Mithany on the top of her head. He followed with, "Hello."

Not intending any harm, in response to his delayed greeting Mithany jabbed a soft love-tap to Santander's well-protected innards.

The uplifting surroundings of home, while enveloped in Santander's comforting bearhug, fed her need for human connection in the face of Reyne's absence. Her heart told her to curl up in a ball while her eyes peered out from Santander to look out over the approaching horde. The broken half of Mithany, driven from her own awareness, held at bay by her newly gained outlook for charity, remained sequestered, waiting for an opportunity to break free. But something was missing. Stepping back, her eyes darted from tree to tree. "I expected to see people everywhere. Where's the pickers Daedyn set up?"

Santander shrugged. "The harvesting crew never showed. We contracted for two hundred and fifty experienced workers. Chaos in the cities, I suppose. I tried to round up some locals. Got a few but you know, we're all farmers around here and they got their own crops to harvest. This Covenant mess is gonna cost us. I'm afraid we're gonna lose most of this year's crop."

Santander's large, close-set brown eyes, ladened with heavy, wrinkled bags beneath, opened wider and wider as more and more Topak travelers rounded the bend and came into view. "Dear, I'm starting to worry. How many did you bring with you and what are you hoping to do for them?"

"I brought along a few hungry mouths to feed. It's just a guess, a thousand give or take. Maybe you can put a few of them to work in some way? Even if the thousand-plus Topakers feed on nothing else but alphens for a week or more, there'll still be plenty to harvest." Although it would result in less alphens for charity, or barrels of nuts paid in kind to the Temple of Life's tithe master in the coming year, Mithany happily accepted the trade-off, as feeding the refugees was charity to her way of thinking.

Mulling it over, Santander rubbed the day's stubble of his chin. "It ain't a perfect solution. A thousand people who never did this before won't be the same as two hundred who know what they're doin'. It's gonna be old school, picking by hand, nut by nut. Won't be easy for them. They'll eat into the profits, but I guess it's better than watching the crop rot in the field."

"Thank you so much. You're the best." Mithany squeezed Santander's waist, not able to get her short arms all the way around his enormous gut.

Santander's belly jiggled as he laughed. "We'll get a full measure whether it works... after we see how much they eat."

"You'll see, this is gonna work. By the way, have you seen Arek around? He was supposed to join us in the search. He never caught up."

Santander shrugged. "No, dear. Ain't seen him since you left. I'm sure he's fine. You and I both know what he's probably up to."

Mithany closed her eyes, rubbed her eyebrow with two fingers, and took in a deep breath.

Returning to the refugees, Santander told Mithany, "They'll need some training. Not sure we can use any of the shakers. Takes teamwork and experience. Don't think they'd pull it off without losing a few fingers. The good news is, there's enough of them to do it the old-fashioned way: poles, ladders, and buckets. Yeah, we can make it work"—he paused—"but we're gonna need more poles."

Chuckles escaped them both.

Delighted Santander agreed to put the homeless to work, Mithany said, "I run a leather goods shoppe, so I don't have the slightest idea what we need to get this set up. There's logistics to work out."

"First thing we gotta do is set up a few dozen outhouses. It's gonna get messy around here real fast."

"Man knows his priorities."

"We got the shacks, you know, the temp quarters we'd have used for the seasonals, but that's not gonna be enough for the crowd you brought. It'll be snug, but I guess they could double and triple up. That'll still leave a couple hundred to camp out on the edges of the orchard. As for the shit holes, get a few guys to dig some trenches far from anywhere. Winds mostly outta the northwest this time a year. Keep that in mind. Do that until I can get outhouses put up. Meantime, people are gonna have to do their business out in the trenches. You know where the shovels are. Get them started digging. We don't have a lot of time before it's gonna get pretty stinky."

Mithany reached up, pulled his head down, and kissed his leathery cheek. "Thank you."

The pair parted ways for the moment, and the day progressed as best Mithany could expect, yet not without the occasional confrontation between her guests. Mithany put Neladith to work, elevating her to the unofficial position as field commander in charge of all indigents, tasked with implementing whatever Santander required of the refugees. Mithany recognized Neladith didn't take shit from anyone and slapped down several of the pushier men and women again and again, until all understood the concept, *You do whatever Neladith tells you to do.* Word quickly spread and things started getting better thereafter. Better, but still chaotic.

Mithany didn't object to Neladith when she put Spetzer in charge of shit-hole duty. Both of the women exchanged knowing glances at the irony of the assignment.

With Santander and Neladith muddling through the unwieldy deployment of tasks and personnel, Mithany made her way to Reyne's bedroom. She flopped onto the bed they shared. Her emotions cleaved of two minds, happy to be near him in spirit yet consumed with grief Reyne wasn't there to share their bed.

She ran through thoughts of waking each day wrapped in his arms. Of laying down with him each night. Of making love and how close together that brought them. And how she loved it when he nestled alongside her with his head resting on her chest, near her heart. She almost felt his fingers running through her hair.

Pulling a pillow over her face, she breathed in deep his familiar scent. It bypassed her nose and shot straight to her heart. Sitting up with his pillow wrapped tight in her arms against her chest, tears crept slowly down her cheeks.

The squeal of the front door hinges yanked her from the engrossing dreamworld. Palms pressed to her face, Mithany wiped away any sign she'd been crying. The internal pangs didn't recede in the endeavor. Mithany called out, "In here."

Within seconds, Neladith, with Spetzer a few steps behind, popped their heads into the bedroom.

Giving no attention to Spetzer's existence, Mithany said, "Nel, what's goin' on?"

"Some idiot smacked another idiot with a shovel. Now, one of the idiots got a big cut on his forehead. Didn't hear what they were fighting about and don't care."

Spetzer jumped in. "They didn't all agree on stuff about breaking free of the Covenant."

Neladith shook her head. "Who gives a shit?"

Mithany asked, "How bad?"

"I don't know which one said what."

Neladith looked at Spetzer from her lowered brow. "Don't be dense. She meant the injury."

"Oh, that. There's lots of blood. It stopped bleeding already. Well, the heavy stuff anyway. The shovel left a big gash."

"Nel. Spetz. I should go get Doc Brenal to check it out. The cut might get infected. With all these people, he's gonna be real busy the next week or two."

Neladith, sweeping her eyes around the room, said, "No. You stay here. Tell me where this Doc guy lives. I'll go get him."

Not Welcome

Jerithan

Jerithan jumped at every new encounter with street scum only to find relief when Timble greeted each with what appeared as a knowing smile. The pair navigated the streets of Teth headed to the Temple of Life Palace. Jerithan felt secure with Timble at his side as his guide and protector.

Jerithan commented, expecting Timble's thoughts in return, "There is not much you could say that would be more surprising than Ferpratt walking through that door earlier."

The Voice added his opinion, *"Are you sure about that? I can foresee many more events in your future even more alarming."*

Jerithan's inner voice replied in their ongoing sequestered conversation. *I do not need you offering running commentary. When you have something tactical or strategic to add, we can exchange thoughts then.*

"Is that really how you want to play this? I am back to help you regain what has been lost."

First, tell me, why did you abandon me?

"I needed time to reassess our situation. I was hasty in my untimely departure. I offer you my apology once more and am here for you now. Move on, my friend."

Move on? That is easy for you to say. You did not endure being raped. Agghh!

"Stay with me, and we will make all of them pay for what has been done to you."

Timble said, "Jerithan, are ya listenin' to me?"

"I am sorry. What were you saying?"

"I confessed."

"Confessed to what?"

"I knew ya from the second I laid eyes on ya. Keflyn, ha!"

Jerithan said, "You took a gamble leaving me in that alley."

"Nah. Didn't. Told a few of my boys to keep ya safe until I got back. Don't know how Griz slipped through. Knew you'd wait for me to get back with food. I had to leave ya there to set the trap for Nails and track down the good guys."

The Voice, seeing the world through its connection to Jerithan's mind, observed, *Look at this once beautiful city. It has been turned into a war zone.*

Jerithan disregarded the Voice, staying focused on Timble. "You set up Nails. Are you worried about her people coming after you?"

"Turn here. It's safer goin' this way," Timble said, taking hold of Jerithan's arm to direct him. "She treated everyone like she did me when she threatened my daughter. She rules by fear. It'll take a while before they figure she's gone. In the meantime, folks gonna be too scared to do anythin' she ain't gonna like, so I'm guessin' things are gonna be quiet for a few days. After that, who knows? Maybe they'll all be fightin' each other for her spot? That could be bad, could be good. We'll see."

"This one may not sound intelligent, yet he offers wisdom in his butchered manner of speaking."

Like the wisdom you once provided? You have not yet told me who you are.

"Who I am matters little. I am here to help."

You want to help. Tell me who you are. Until then, stay out of my head.

Jerithan's mind quieted at the demand, and he turned his attention back to the world of brick and mortar.

"Timble, you were there when Chamette reminded me of a debt I owe to Druin Derr of the KCG."

"Yup. Aware of that."

"What do you mean, you are aware of the debt I owe?"

"Like I told ya. KCG people reached out to me. Told me to keep an eye out for ya. Why do ya think I knew how to find Mister Fancy Pants, that Chamette guy?"

"Oh my. This one has been playing both sides. There is a lot going on under those orange curls of his."

"What are you saying, Timble?"

"Like I said. Kept Nails from messin' ya up." He slapped Jerithan across his shoulders. "Just lookin' out for ya, buddy."

"There is more to it than that. Be careful with this one. For now, my best advice is to keep your eye on him. He could be dangerous left to his own devices. Keep him close."

"I have been thinking, Timble. When I get back to the palace, after I put my vestments on once we are safely inside the gate, maybe I should employ your services. Would you like a job working for me? I could be in danger in there and could use a bodyguard."

"It'd be my honor. What's it pay? Nah, we can figure that out later. I accept."

"Now I am really worried. He signed on too eagerly."

Jerithan ignored the Voice's prodding and addressed the big man leading the way. "We need to go over some ground rules."

"Okay, boss. Should I call ya boss? That okay?"

Jerithan and Timble continued on their trek through the chaotic and burned-out streets of Teth, reviewing Temple protocol and duties of Timble's new position. The Voice offered unsolicited input to Jerithan, who provided nothing in return throughout the remainder of the journey.

After an hour of touring the once beautiful city, Jerithan Cree and his new security detail of one, Timble, came to stand in the very room where the vote of Revocation stripped the once-First Lord of his title. Its beauty he once admired now tasted bitter. He'd been asked to wait there for First Lord Serco upon gaining entrance to the Palace. The acolyte attending to Jerithan acted deaf and dumb, leaving all Prudent Cree's questions unanswered.

The Voice observed, *"Serco put you in this room to remind you, to humiliate you and to torment you with the notion he did this to you."*

His intentions, then, are met. It is an insult for me to wait in this room. He will purposefully drag this out. Salt in the wound.

"In time, my friend. We will achieve our revenge."

I am not your friend.

"I am eager to hear his words. Once I do, you and I can begin to strategize on a path to your reclamation."

The hours passed as Jerithan, now a prudent with little to no authority, paced.

The Voice prattled on in his head.

Timble, unmoving, stood in silence.

The door opened to reveal another acolyte. She spoke in the ear of the other who'd been attending to Jerithan throughout the long wait. After delivering the message, she departed.

Arms folded behind his back, the young attendant spoke. "Prudent Cree, the First Lord cannot see you today. He has asked that I lead to where Second Lord S'Leen will see you. Please follow me."

Jerithan replied, "I know my way around. I am aware of the Second Lord's office location. I will be fine. Thank you."

"Please sir, I've been asked to accompany you."

"Lead the way then. Timble, you are with me."

The acolyte stopped. "I'm sorry, sir. My orders are to escort you and you alone."

"Wherever I go, this man will be by my side. Otherwise, I will remain here until Serco finds the time."

"I mean no disrespect, Prudent Cree, yet I must insist you honor protocol while in the Palace. It's First Lord Serco, not Serco. And, please wait here. I will return shortly."

"How soon they forget. It is the nature of power. Serco now has it and we do not. The power will be yours again, just not today."

Jerithan returned to his paces while Timble stood quietly, waiting for the acolyte's return. A few minutes passed when he reentered the room. "Second Lord S'Leen will see you. Mister Timble, you may join us."

"Just Timble, young fellow. Just Timble," the big man said, and slapped the acolyte across the shoulders. "Let's go. Lead the way, my young friend."

Surprise shot across the aide's face.

Jerithan advised, "You get used to him, acolyte."

The young man led them to their intended destination and, opening the door, he said, "She'll see you now," then departed.

"Jerithan, it is so nice to see you," Second Lord S'Leen said, stepping forward to welcome her guests. "I've been informed this large fellow is Mister Timble."

Timble spoke up before Jerithan could stop him, "Just Timble, ma'am."

Jerithan quickly added, "My apologies, Second Lord. He is learning protocol and speaks when he should remain silent and fails to address you properly." He finished with a harsh stare aimed at his bodyguard.

"No offense taken. Jerithan, I've been so very worried about you. I am glad you are home."

"S'Leen, we have known each other for many years. Congratulation on your ascending to the honored position of Second Lord. I am truly happy for you. However, I must ask. You and I have been allies, and you voted against Revocation if I counted the votes properly. Why have you accepted this, supporting that usurper? I put you on the Council of Prudents, for Teth's sake." A touch of anger leaked out in his tone.

"I've always been and continue to be your friend. Please do not be angry with me. Much has changed in the short time you've been gone. I serve the Temple of Life and have been called to service in my new position. The Temple is at the forefront of all I do. And I suspect our new First Lord required someone from your camp to begin healing Temple wounds."

The Voice chided, *"Be careful here. We can hold on to this one. Let go your anger with her."*

Jerithan considered the Voice's advice before speaking. He adjusted his approach to Second Lord S'Leen, deciding the guidance from the mysterious presence inside his thoughts held wisdom. "I am sorry, S'Leen. Yes, you are right. The

Temple comes before all worldly concerns. You will fill the role with distinction. I am proud of you." Jerithan swallowed the bile rising inside him.

"Thank you, Jerithan. You've been my mentor, and I will never forget all you've done for me."

"Of course. I suppose you have spoken with Serco since I showed up today. He is most likely amazed I am still standing and even more so that I have returned to the Palace. He could have handled my return with more grace." He waved off the growing tells of an appending protest from Second Lord S'Leen and failed in his commitment to the Voice to keep his resentment to himself. "He didn't have support to strip me of my prudency. And now he hides, not being man enough to deliver what comes next. He sent you. Let's dispense with explanations and niceties; give it to me straight. What new role, new humiliation has he asked you to deliver?"

"Not wise, Jerithan. She is only the messenger. We will need her later. It is a cliché for a reason. Don't shoot the messenger."

S'Leen's sad eyes spoke volumes to Jerithan; she craved his approval and continued friendship. His reply delivered only his own selfish concerns.

He braced for impact.

The Voice pointed out the harsh reality and the challenges still ahead. *"If you were in Serco's position, would you allow yourself to remain in the Palace? Of course not. Whatever she says, be nice and accept what is to come. It is not of her doing. You and I will find our footing."*

The Second Lord said, "You are my friend, yet I am your Second Lord. I take no pleasure in assigning you to serve as prudent for the Temple of Life in the Kingdom of Adelle in its capital of Tandure, filling the role made vacant when the conclave elevated Prudent Serco to the position as our First Lord. Under different circumstances, the posting would be an honor. I understand you will not see it that way. However, it is what our First Lord has directed me to do."

Stunned, Jerithan lacked words to express his anger. His face burned red hot, and with clenched fists hidden from view inside the cuffs of his vestment, he opened his mouth to speak.

The Voice spoke first, *"Say nothing. Bide your time. Serco never expected you to return. You were supposed to die at Derr's hand. He cannot leave you inside the Palace. It is the smart play. He is not completely stupid. He is worried, not sure what to make of these developments. He probably thinks sending you back to Derr, the KCG will have no choice but to finish the job since you will be of no use to Tomelai in Tandure. We can use this. It tells me Serco is afraid of you. It portends of support for you within the walls surrounding him. A fearful opponent is prone to mistakes. I do not know how yet, but we will prevail. We just have to survive Derr. Take the posting and do not speak another word to this woman in your current state of mind."*

Listening to the Voice's assessment, rage coursed through him at being forced to return to where he'd been violated. In the days to come he would be required to smile and bow at the dynasty that contributed to his demise. From Tandure, he would be outside the sphere of influence inside the Temple Palace, unable to gain access to the necessary intel demanded by Derr in exchange for his life. Rancor, malignancy, deep-seated enmity roiled just beneath his skin. Jerithan couldn't speak even if he wanted to.

S'Leen broke the engrossing tension. "I'm so sorry. A coach awaits. You leave for Tandure immediately."

Delusions of Love

Hensdale: 10th Day of the Harvest Moon

Mithany

From Reyne's bed, Mithany looked to Neladith and Spetzer. She considered Neladith's offer to run over to the home of Doc Hollid Brenal and to bring him back with her to the Brenton family orchard, where an injured man needed medical attention.

The internal war over Mithany's psyche consumed her subconscious from the time of early childhood. Although never able to fully rid herself of the consequential damages of a brutal upbringing, with Reyne at her side, his love and support unwittingly helped Mithany maintain mastery over her broken soul. However, the defective side of her, like a bloodhound on the scent, forever searched for a way to escape its forced confinement, sniffing out the slightest of leads. The recent loss of Reyne's emotional support—from the lack of his physical presence—opened a tantalizing trail for her imprisoned subconscious to explore.

Neladith, unaware of Mithany's internal fractures, unknowingly assaulted Mithany's defenses at their weakest point and assailed her beleaguered-of-late hold on control—by way of her amorous advances. It connected to fears held deep in Mithany's core of abandoned love. Her mother's and now Reyne's. She knew Reyne loved her, yet his absence denied her, and his return, uncertain. Vulnerable, her repressed anima pursued the opportunity for escape. Subliminal feelings of love abandoned demanded of her an outlet.

A voice from deep within teased Mithany with a thought. *Send Spetz. Stay here with Nel.* The struggles raging within Mithany's ego, which her joyful persona currently held mastery over, gave way the tiniest bit of ground at the suggestion.

Without hesitation, Mithany said, "Spetz, why don't you go? You know the way. It's only a mile or so from here. It'll be quicker. If you run, you can be there in ten. Probably take longer to get back with the Doc. Would you mind?"

Spetzer failed to respond. Clear to Mithany, he waited on Neladith's approval. Neladith nodded her head and Spetzer replied, "Sure. Be back in a jiffy with the old coot."

Mithany, forlorn and struggling of a riven mind, waited for Spetzer to leave before turning her attentions to Neladith. "Thanks. I don't want to be alone right now. Being in his room brings up difficult emotions, but I can't find it in myself to leave." She reached out and took Neladith's hand.

"You know I could have gone for the Doc."

"I know you would. Just sit here with me." She padded an adjacent spot on the bed with her free hand and gently guided her friend to take a seat.

Mithany's cheery persona diminished against the onslaught of emptiness, alone in Reyne's room. The damaged, broken aspect of the love-abandoned woman pushed to break free from its subliminal confinement. It offered half-truths planting seeds of doubt. *Reyne's gone. It's so lonely without him. When will he return? If he's ever to return.*

She fought against her own mind. *No, stop. He WILL come home to me.* Although she'd pushed back, Mithany's heart yearned to feel Reyne's embrace, for his lips on hers. Her longing unleashed a deluge of emotion, of loss, of want, and the tiniest speck of desire took root. The surroundings inside Reyne's room, the bed they shared, threatened to overpower the joyful, forward-looking grip on control, holding back the delusions of her fragmented mind.

"Whatever you need. I'm here for you," Neladith said, stroking Mithany's hair.

A trail of tears broke free, and Mithany's sad eyes looked up, searching for a port to weather the love-starved storm brewing inside her. Neladith gently held Mithany's face and wiped away the stream of water from her puffy eyes.

The red-haired woman's tender stroke toyed with Mithany's desire for Reyne. She voiced soft cries, burying her head against the taller woman's chest. Her sobs grew louder, and she felt the warmth and security of comforting arms around her slight frame. She imagined them Reyne's.

Suffocated beneath her own internal mental mastication, the splintered facet of her mind pounded against the self-imposed psychological walls entombing it, demanding to be unchained. A voice uttered something off in the distance of Mithany's awareness, but the battle raging for control of her soul, preoccupied the attention of all her firing synapses, barely registering the sound of words.

Emotional damage inflicted by a violent, affection-withholding mother, left Mithany's psyche fragmented from an early age. All she ever wanted from her mother, she never got—love. What she did receive were frequent beatings. The damage compounded as she pursued affection only to be rejected time after time, year after year. She'd adapted as she grew, learning to bury deep the broken bits of her tormented soul. Yet, never able to shed them completely.

Inevitably, when as an adult profound emotional loss threatened, her irrepressible craving to be loved, a bane from the love-starved relationship with her mother, triggered the return of the broken part of her lying in wait.

Long fingers gently sifted through Mithany's hair. The tingle of the caress exploded across her vulnerable emotional state and sparked into her splintered self. Weakened, fragile, alone, and wanting, command over the tattered fragments of her mind slipped away. The incarcerated, unsettled, affection-covetous persona within emerged.

Quick to grasp control, free from self-imposed restraint, Mithany's broken soul, now in charge, immediately wrapped her arms tightly around Neladith's torso. A shuttering wail that enjoined the excitement of her defective mind's newly gained independence with the cravings of human connection involuntarily poured out. Thoughts of love for Reyne flooded through her like a tsunami slamming into a shoreline, overwhelming everything in its wake. Holding Neladith tight as though embracing Reyne, she anchored her love against the onslaught of emotions overpowering her grasp on reality.

She quivered at Neladith's warm body. Trembling, she freed the woman from her grasp, looked up, and searched the eyes staring back at her for Reyne's love. She coveted human connection in her heartsick condition. Neladith's face hung before her, but in her mind's eye, her damaged inner-self saw Reyne's. Somewhere in her cognition, she knew it was Neladith, yet she willingly accepted the woman as a surrogate for her missing fiancé. It was Neladith's body, but she imagined it Reyne's in the deluded, fractured psyche bequeathed to her by her thoughtless, uncaring mother.

Thoughts gave way to the dominion of desire, driven by a ravenous appetite to fill the empty void of abandonment. She ached for Reyne, and the love-deprived child in her wouldn't be denied.

Mithany found what she sought in the want of the ruby globes locked on her in return. Moving her hands to hold Neladith's face in her palms, Mithany, ever so slowly, moved her lips to rest on those of the eager proxy. Soft and gentle at first, hunger took control, and she pressed Neladith to the bed, never releasing her from their embrace.

Mithany's voracious hands explored Neladith's breasts as she swung one leg over the redhead's lanky torso. Small fingers of the diminutive woman scooped up the hem of her partner's shirt and pulled it over her head. She followed by doing the same with her own. Both exposed from the waist up, Mithany laid atop Neladith, breasts pressed firm against each other, and enthusiastically kissed the unknowing Reyne-stand-in.

Neladith flipped Mithany over on her back and pulled off the willing woman's pants. Freed from the bondage of clothing, the cool air kissed the delicate, wanting skin of her outer lips, and it set her groin ablaze. She ached for Reyne's touch in the gentle way he stroked her.

Mithany watched while Neladith shed herself of whatever apparel remained and stood at the foot of the bed for inspection. Mithany rose to her knees and scuttled towards Neladith's waiting body. The eagerness of the newly disrobed, upright maiden became evident as she moved one knee to the soft mattress and, with her hand, pushed Mithany prostrate on her back.

Neladith cat-walked along the sides of Mithany's legs and stopped at her minge, where she stroked with teasing fingers. Her mouth soon followed to Mithany's eager lower lips. Neladith's tongue began its exploration. Palms reached up and slid over Mithany's quivering torso, finding their way to waiting breasts. Through fluttering eyelids, the back of Neladith's head between her thighs filled Mithany's perception.

Mithany reveled in delight.

How much time passed while Neladith teased and toyed as an apparent expert cunnilinctor, she didn't know. Nor did she care. A pounding heart hid amongst deep breaths, heaving breasts, and rhythmic groans at each pass of Neladith's dancing, flicking, tormenting tongue. She craved release from the exquisite torture only to find her clitoric paramour stopping just short each time Mithany stood at ecstasy's precipice. The anticipation and stimulation built to a crescendo until she could no longer hold back the flood.

With the instantaneity of a spark, primal pleasure swept through her with explosive force. Her body shuttered. She released a thunderous moan—and cried out in ecstasy.

Over and over, wave after wave, she convulsed in delight each time her partner brought her to the edge and beyond. Her thighs squeezed surrogate-Reyne's head and held it tight each time rhapsody struck.

With intense breaths and light-headed, Mithany rolled to her side, took hold of Neladith, and laid her on her back. Their eyes met, and she kissed Neladith with all the passion caged in her heart for Reyne. Like a lioness hovering over her prey, she lapped at Neladith's rock-hard nipples and playfully teased them with her own joyful lips. Slowly, she kissed her way to Neladith's vulva, where her tongue found a home.

Time passed as Mithany licked and lapped at Neladith until the red-haired woman's thighs trembled. Neladith shot her fingers rummaging through Mithany's mane and with a sudden jerk, Neladith pressed Mithany's head against her quivering flesh, arched her back and came—hard.

Mithany didn't relent.

She slid her hands under Neladith's clenched buttocks, lifting her ass off the bed, all the while pressing her eager mouth against her partner's hungry quim. Gripping the loose bedding tight in her fists, panting, Neladith shuddered in rapture, crying out as Mithany brought her to climax, again and again.

Suddenly, the door flew open on squeaky hinges. Mithany lifted her head from between Neladith's thighs to look up at Spetzer standing in the doorway. His jaw hung open almost to the floor. His eyes bulged wider than Mithany had ever seen in another person.

He spit out, "What the hell? Nel, what are you doin'?"

Neladith yelled at the stricken Spetzer, "Get the fuck out, dickhead!"

Spetzer didn't move. Didn't speak. He just stared.

Mithany flopped on her back, and the two women laid bare, side by side.

Mithany watched his eyes roam over their bodies.

Neladith sat up and shouted, "I said get the fuck out," throwing her arm into the air, pointing to the exit.

His body juddered and he shook his head. "Brenal's dead."

The announcement concerning the death of the country doctor should have been additional fodder for Mithany's broken ego to feed off, to cement its control, but the opposite reaction occurred. It might have been she'd satiated her craving for Reyne, as provided by Neladith's body, or it might have been the momentary reprieve that secured the opportunity to regain command. Whatever the cause, the damaged part of Mithany, only just released, was thrown down in that short span to be shuttered away once more.

Mithany scooped up her clothes, pressed them firm against her body, and said, "The dear man. What happened?"

Neladith remained sprawled, unclothed, across the bed. She aimed her eyes at Spetzer and said, "You're a dick."

Mithany turned red and embarrassment rose up within her. "Spetz, can you step outside for a minute so we can get dressed?"

Neladith turned to her with a quizzical look. Anger rolled off her. "What the fuck does it matter now? He just got an eyeful of the goods you been hiding from him all these years, and god knows he's seen me in the flesh plenty."

Mithany's soft apologetic tone spoke volumes. "Please, Spetz."

Spetzer did as Mithany asked, leaving the two lovers alone.

Mithany kept her head down without looking up to the now standing, bare-assed Neladith.

The tall woman's fury scared Mithany. "Two minutes ago you had your tongue... "

"Nel, please... "

"And now you can't even look at me."

She didn't know what took hold of her and, suddenly, Neladith no longer functioned as Reyne's stand-in. Guilt at betraying the man she loved, overwhelmed her. "I'm sorry, Nel. I'm so sorry. I don't know what's wrong with me." Mithany's hands shook, trying to pull up her pants and she started to cry. "I'm not licensed. Spetzer saw us. Oh god, what if he reports me?"

Neladith walked over and wrapped her long arms around the shaking Mithany. "It's alright. You've been through a lot. Sorry I got mad. Get dressed and don't worry about Spetz. I'll make sure he never says a word to anyone... and if I have to..." Neladith didn't finish the thought. Instead, the buxom temptress stepped back, turned slowly in a full circle, and said, "Get one last look before I put all this away. We definitely gotta do this again." A broad smile finished the hopeful paramour's sentiment.

With eyes focused on the floorboards, turning them away from Neladith's denuded exhibition, Mithany chose not to respond to the open invitation. The corrupted portion of her mind screamed to be heard, to jump at the offer, to confirm the next rendezvous, but its voice went ignored and its access denied to any form of outward expression.

The women, now fully clothed, exited the room and sat down in the kitchen where Spetzer waited.

Mithany asked of Spetzer with tears in her eyes, "How did that poor man die?"

"I don't know. When I got there, I went inside, but the place was empty. On the way in, I had seen the pile of rocks in the front of those stupid flowers he likes so much, but as I was leaving, I noticed at the corner something sticking out. I pulled off a few stones and saw a sheet covering something. It was Brenal. Someone piled rocks on top of his dead body. Scared the hell out of me when I pulled back the sheet to see his face. I fell over, got up, and high-tailed it back here. Where, you know, I found you two fucking. What the hell, Nel, thought we had somethin'?"

Mithany saw the hurt in his eyes and heard the pain in his voice. Sadly, she understood its genesis as Neladith's lack of fidelity and not for Brenal's passing.

Neladith slapped her hand on the table. "What? We fuck a few times, Spetz, and you think you own me? That ain't how it is. If you ever want to see this cooch again, get over it. And don't you say a word about this to anyone. I'll fuckin' kill you if you do."

Spetzer hung his head.

Mithany reached out to rest one hand on Neladith's and, reluctantly, the other on Spetzer's. "The Doc was a good man and a friend of mine. I need to go to him. Spetz, can you track down Judjurex Tetrip? Tell him to meet me there?" She wiped her face of mucus and tears. She squeezed Neladith's hand. "We'll go together. Spetz, we'll meet you there."

STAY STRONG

EVIDAR

Reyne

Reyne did his best to fight off the constant despair, hunger, and everything else Evidar threw at him. The empty, dark, dreary gray world relentlessly attacked his senses while the ever-present offering the Gift of Flesh taunted him with dissembled his ability to maintain focus. He'd committed to staying on Evidar until the Devil's Blacksmith had been denied further access to his Damus, permanently and with prejudice, assuming the pair could even find the woman. Until then, Reyne and Gina were stuck in the soul-sucking reality of Evidar.

"Think my eyes are starting to adjust," Reyne commented, hoping idle chatter would distract his thoughts.

Gina replied, "Mine too. But my stomach hasn't. Can you hear it grumbling?"

Diverting his attention by fashioning wearable vegetation, Reyne continued weaving several large, light brown palm fronds into basic coverings. The endeavor offered respite from the constant desolation gnawing at his soul.

The pair sat across from each other constructing their soon-to-be native wear. With his concentration fixed on weaving, he attempted to smother both Evidar's gloom and Gina's unintended fleshscapade.

"Think these things are edible?" Gina asked of the long slender leaves they were using to style grass skirts.

Reyne continued weaving. "Mera told me about plants we can eat that grow with little light. He also filled me in on some of the animals unique to this place.

Still haven't seen a single creature. Then again, it hasn't exactly matched the map and landmarks Mera showed me."

Gina shrugged. "If we're gonna eat, our best hope is finding those plants."

"Keep a lookout for mushrooms, sprouts, and I think he mentioned wheat-grass. These leaves don't look like any of them. I wouldn't take the chance."

"As you say, but I'm real hungry. We need to find food... soon."

Reyne nodded in agreement and continued interlacing palm leaves.

"We've been lucky so far. Haven't run into any natives," Gina said.

"I don't know, I kinda look at it different. We've been *unlucky*. We gotta find someone who can point us toward Siandra or Aderlee."

Gina shook her head. "What, you think everyone on this planet knows every-one else? This ain't Hensdale, farm boy."

Reyne rolled his head back, waited a few seconds, then added, "Businessman who owns a farm. Not a farm boy. It's like the point you keep making, you're not a girl, you're a woman. Same thing. I respected your point of view, please respect mine."

Gina pulled her lips tight and shrugged. "We're in another world. This empty black place is miserable. Who gives a shit?"

Reyne mustered a fake smile, snapped his fingers while waving his arm and quipped, "You got it... girl."

She smirked, and half-jokingly shot back, "Bite me." But only half.

Reyne looked down at the progress he'd made on his palm-leaf clothing in the making.

Gina sighed. "Something I should tell you."

Apprehension kicked in at her announced warning. "Here it comes."

Big eyes offered a hint of disappointment on Gina's face. "Here what comes? Don't be like that. This is important."

"Sorry. Tell me."

"You've asked about my abnormal quickness. Mera unlocked something very rare that he saw in me during an Eye of Heaven connection years ago when he tried to get me into the Void. It's how I can move so fast. As he tells it, he did his mumbo-jumbo routine and flipped a brain switch in some Third Eye function that allows me to access enhanced brain-signal-muscle-response abilities."

"It's amazing how you can move so quickly. We're gonna need it more than ever here on Evidar if we're ever gonna save Tartica."

"Well, the thing is, it takes a lot of energy to pull off. I'm gonna be hamstrung until I know we have a source of food to replenish my body. If I turn on the burners and have nothing left in the tank, I may end up comatose afterwards. It's happened before. Not to worry, though, I'm better than most at average speed."

"Thanks, good to know. That explains why you eat like a horse. Glad it hasn't made a difference yet. Eventually we are gonna run into people. Gotta hope they're friendlies. At least until we find food."

"If Mera's to be believed, not sure this place has any friendlies."

Reyne concluded, "Then we gotta locate us some grub. Our search to find Siandra and Aderlee means running into people. If we're gonna survive, you gotta be at full strength."

"We've walked miles. The only plants we seen are these palm trees."

"Consider it our good fortune. These plant leaves are gonna make a great kilt."

Gina snickered. "Kilt? You can call it what you like. You'll be wearing a grass skirt. Time to get in touch with your feminine side, farm boy."

"This place is miserable. Let's do what we came to do and get out of here," Reyne complained.

"We're stuck here until we understand how I hitched onto your wagon through the Void. Until then, we're not goin' anywhere."

"You're not," Reyne teased.

"Don't even think about jumping ship, leaving me on this shithole of a planet all by myself."

"Just messing with you."

"First things first, get some food and real clothes, track down the contacts Mera gave you, and maybe they'll also know how to get me back to Tartica."

"You left out killing the Damus. Aside from that, I agree, someone's got to know how two bodies piggyback through the Void."

Reyne's opinion of Gina had shifted since they began their journey on Evidar. Although she wasn't supposed to be there, she proved a welcome partner. Her incessant taunting had abated, being no longer incessant. Reyne speculated Gina being out of her element in Evidar's threatening, barren darkness moved her to appreciate companionship, even his. Although he had not figured out why, from the moment they met, she was hell-bent on tormenting him.

"I'm hoping we get lucky and find one of those overgrown giant mushroom trees Mera told me about. Boy, wish we had a handful of alphen nuts right about now." Reyne's reflections brought him back to Daedyn and how his brother loved the taste and relished the savory nut with every bite. Years of eating the jewel of nuts wore on Reyne but not Daedyn. Pangs of emptiness at thoughts of his brother's death squeezed Reyne's chest, exacerbated by the foreboding veil hanging over the soul-sucking dismal gray existence he found himself in.

Gina's movement yanked him back from his thoughts; rising from her seat, she stood. Proudly holding up the makeshift apparel, positioning it up to her waist, checking out how it would look on her, she said, "It's getting there. How's yours looking?"

"Not as good as yours, but it'll do the job. Almost done."

Gina sat, butt on the ground, ankles crossed in front, knees apart, and returned her attention to the garment's final touches.

From his seated position facing Gina, Reyne looked over at her and said, "You mind not sitting like that?"

She looked down at herself to evaluate the perspective giving rise to Reyne's objection. She toyed playfully with him, her words dismissing his concerns. "Get over it already. It is what it is. Besides, we come from a world where there ain't no shame in nudity. On Tartica, it's everywhere. Can't see why it should bother you now."

Reyne's eyes lingered.

Gina added, "Doesn't mean you have to stare. We got more important things to think about. Find the Damus. Kill the Damus. Not my cooch."

"Human nature, I guess. Sorry. It's a red-blooded male thing."

"Yeah, I also remember you said something about difficulties controlling that thing sometimes. It seems to be taking notice of the view." Gina grinned, and from a closed hand, she flicked one finger straight up, mocking Reyne's growing problem.

Reyne, embarrassed at the rise in his lap, lamented, "Like I said, it's got a mind of its own sometimes. Now it's my turn to say it is what it is, get over it." He noticed her focused line of sight. "What, now it's your turn to stare?"

Laughing as she spoke, "It's rather impressive… gotta admit. Can't help myself. You know, the whole red-blooded woman thing. And it's got me thinking…"

Reyne huffed. "Ain't gonna happen. Like you said, we got more important things to think about."

"Your loss." She remained in exactly the same position that initiated Reyne's dilemma.

Reyne heard a hint of disappointment in her tone. He couldn't blame her. Gina had no ties holding her back. They'd come from a world whose mores encouraged free love, where the human form pervaded every facet of society, and he suspected Gina took all the *free* she wanted. It was obvious to Reyne, here on Evidar, the Gift of Flesh was ever-present, right there for her to grab.

"Can't wait until we get these kilts finished." Seeing Gina exposed made him long for Mithany to be close to him, to hold her in his arms. Yet he had to admit, Gina was an exquisite specimen of womanhood—physically, anyway. He found it hard to look away. His brain told him not to, but it wasn't running the show at the moment, and his eyes did as they pleased.

Flustered, Reyne rushed to complete their palm-leaf clothing, eager to purge temptation from his thoughts. He was on Evidar to reclaim the life he craved with Mithany, not to cheat on her with Gina.

Frustration tugged at him, and with herculean willpower he denied himself its release. He closed his eyes, holding onto thoughts of Mithany. *Stepping back from the brink… never easy.*

He reminisced how Daedyn loved to pursue the Gift of Flesh. While Reyne struggled to keep himself in check, Daedyn would have reveled in the constant nudity Gina flaunted. His gaze lingered. Her breasts stole his attention. He smiled thinking of his brother, and imagined how great a pairing of Gina and Daedyn would have made under the same circumstances. Reyne recalled some of the last words Daedyn spoke to him: *"You follow your heart. The Gift of Love suits you. I'll follow my dick. I just love the Gift of Flesh."*

Reyne considered himself adequate to fend off the challenge Gina threw at him. Where Daedyn would have savored it, exalted in it, accepted all Gina offered, Reyne concluded, *Daedyn was the better man for the road ahead.*

Reyne, to be true to himself and to be the man Mithany deserved, committed to remaining faithful, but lamented the constant onslaught of temptation attacking his eyes. The sight captured in his vision, coupled with the offering of it from its maker, railed against his resistance. Reyne held tight to his only true defense, love for Mithany. It would have to be enough.

Reyne began to comprehend the struggle Mother Earth set in opposition across all time and laid bare before him at Gina's calling: the enduring bonds of love pitted against the promised momentary pleasures of the flesh. One did not survive the other, here on Evidar or back on Tartica. Even if successful in killing Evidar's Damus, saving Tartica, he couldn't live with himself if he gave in to temptation—the cost too high. Surrender to lust and the unbreakable bond inherent in the true love for his soulmate Mithany would be forever tainted. In that revelation, he hardened his eyes against both Evidar's despair and Gina's promise of fleeting pleasures. Even with the promise of death around every corner, he could go to his grave with a clear conscience and with Mithany in his heart.

Gina had set aside her dislike of him, he guessed, not only because they needed each other in the dark reality of Evidar, but also because of the persistent exposure to his well-chiseled, muscular frame. The larger-than-average endowment he'd been afforded by nature's luck of the draw added to the effect. Maybe Gina would have been less distracted by him had Evidar turned out to be cold.

He never thought of himself as eye-candy, but given the circumstances, Gina must have stumbled into that conclusion with no encouragement from him. He was beginning to understand the point she'd made back at the Whispering Eye when all eyes seemed to follow her ass saunter across the room—now with her eyes on him, he didn't like it.

They had important issues to deal with during their time on Evidar. He didn't need or want the distraction Gina's exceptional unattired form tempted him with. By focusing his thoughts on killing the Damus, he hoped the effort might shift the blood flow to his brain, where it was truly needed. With his thoughts redirected at their shared predicament, he told her, "We're gonna need a plan to go after this Damus woman."

Still seated, Reyne gazed at Gina, only to find she'd assumed her prior position, butt to the ground, knees apart as she returned to weaving. *Stay strong*, he told himself, but his eyes didn't listen.

Gina whispered, "Shut up. Did you hear that?"

Chains, Nails & Love

Tandure: 10th Day of the Harvest Moon

Derr

Inside a KCG secret op's site, in a secluded room with thick walls designed to inhibit the escape of a single sound, Nails hung at the end of chains. Assembled in the room with the fettered captive, Derr, Chancellor Tomelai, First Lady Kaythlin, and their son, Loseff, sat comfortably, facing their prisoner.

Nails's attempted assassination of Chancellor Tomelai inside The Stand the morning of the Feast of Teth failed. Derr determined his efforts to extract payment from her would not. Pain first. Death later. Between the two, he hoped to insert a confession, wresting from her an admission of guilt.

Nails's legs, unable to touch the cold slab of a floor, spread apart at their limits, were shackled in place, as were her arms overhead. Excessive poundage pulled harder on her shoulder joints than the human body could endure free of excruciating agony. The grimace written across her face spoke of her misery, where her defiant silence did not. Cold and hungry, relief for either was beyond reach and would most likely never be satisfied for the remainder of her life.

The enclosure smelled of death.

Derr took the lead. "Wendolyn. Yes, I remember all those years ago when you went by a different name. Before your conversion to the darker side of commerce and your adopted moniker, Nails. I respect your silence. You know why you're here. You also know how this will end. But I have an offer for you to consider. The ending can be relatively painless, or I can stretch it out for days. Just confess your part in the failed assassination and we can end your suffering. Ferpratt is especially good at keeping one alive through his various endeavors, removing small pieces from you hour by hour. And, I have to say, you give him a lot to work with. It could take weeks."

In spite of the room's chill, sweat clung to Nails's skin, brought on from her body's reaction to constant pain. It dripped from her uncommunicative jowls and from taciturn chins. Her resistance highlighted Nails's ability to endure the torture they'd dished out. She smiled at the seated gathering.

Chancellor Tomelai turned to his son. "Loseff, you're here because you asked me about this very subject just days ago across our breakfast table. This is an ugly yet necessary part of ruling. It is time you know it for what it is and see it firsthand."

Loseff asked, "Where's Tane? Shouldn't she be here?"

"Your sister has seen other sessions like this one and knows what it will take to secure her place once it falls to her. To her credit, son, she preferred not to be here today and takes no pleasure in torture or ending another's life."

Kaythlin added, "My dear son, it pains my heart that you are here to witness this awful necessity, and as a mother, I hope you and Tane are of the same mind."

Hoarse and faint, Nails finally spoke up, "Blah, blah, blah, what a heap of trite bullshit. Just fuckin' do it already. Show the boy what cold-hearted cunts you really are. That's the real lesson he's gonna learn here today... mommy and daddy are cunts."

Derr watched. He let it play out.

Kaythlin stood and approached Nails. "I remember you, Wendolyn Trensher, when you lived here in this very city. We were barely in our teens. You were a year or two ahead of me and an altogether different woman then." In slow, leisurely, graceful steps, Kaythlin, her fingers dancing along a measure of chain, circled Nails. "Young, quite attractive, and always well dressed." With the back of her hand, Kaythlin brushed the side of Nails' sweat-soaked cheek. "Your family still flourishes in our capital. You had many suitors, if I recall."

"Yeah, and I fucked them all. What do you think there, young Loseff? Like what you see?"

"Not sure I can make out all the lady parts and the whole female look you're going for." Loseff smirked.

"Trust me, lad, the lady bits all work just the same. And don't kid yourself, a lot of men and women like a full-figured gal." Nails smirked back at him and did her best to shake her once firm, now flattened, saggy breasts. Clank after clank echoed off the walls in sync with the sway of Nails's gravity-inflicted, stretched-low bosom.

Kaythlin grabbed hold of the rattling chains holding up Nails, quieting them. "You had so much to live for. You had looks. Your family had wealth. You could have led a privileged life."

Derr saw anger in Nails and heard it when she squeaked out, "What do you know of it? All your rules. All your pretentious fluffery. I wanted freedom. To do what I want. I fuckin' hate all your prissy etiquette, you and all your high society elite fuckin' snobs. Think you're better than all of us. You elites think you know what's best for everyone else. And fuck my family, they're the worst. They wanted to fit in so bad. I hate them more than I do you."

Kaythlin bowed her head, walked away, and sat down.

"Loseff, wanna know why they call me Nails? I'll tell you. Everyone thinks it's 'cause I'm so tough. That's what they think now. But in my younger days, when I first got the nickname, I used to enjoy playing with balls. Tickling them from underneath with my nails. Still do. Drives some guys wild. Proud of that name. Gonna miss it."

Chancellor Tomelai stood. "I have heard enough from this foul-mouthed waste-of-a-life. Loseff, it is not our role to deliver the death stroke. Our role is to pronounce judgement. We can leave this to Drew and his people. Yet may I suggest you remain with Drew to see the outcome of these difficult decisions."

Derr said, "Leave it to the KCG, Rotti. I'll take it from here."

Loseff remained seated. "Yes, Father. If I'm going to lead an army into battle, kill the men and women of our enemies if called to, I need to see death. I want to see death."

Nails lifted her head. "Go fuck yourselves. I said all I'm gonna say. You can do your worst. You already have your minds made up. Nothin' I say's gonna change that. I ain't getting outta here alive, so I ain't saying nothin' else."

Derr faced his Chancellor. "Rotti, Kaythlin, you don't need to stay. You can leave Loseff with me. She's probably telling you the truth of it. I've seen many people in this room face death. She's most likely to remain silent. She took the whip yesterday. Her back's rather bloody. Handled it better than most. Didn't even whimper. We'll do our best for a confession, but I doubt she'll give us one."

Kaythlin looked at Derr and then to her husband. Derr saw the ruminations taking hold of Kaythlin's mind, given away by familiar tells written on her face only he and her husband were skilled enough to read. He watched her as he always did, and after all the years they'd spent in each other's company, he wasn't surprised when she said to her husband, "My love, this is not an issue for the state. This woman tried to kill a member of my family. You. Her actions make this a family matter, and family is my domain."

Tomelai attempted to persuade her otherwise. "Kay, it is best to leave this to Drew."

Derr laughed to himself, knowing his friend Rotti wasn't going to win this one.

"No, my love, I do not see it that way. I will hear no more of it." Kaythlin patted Tomelai's hand, then turned to face her son. She presented Loseff a kiss to his cheek. "There are things a wife and a mother must do to protect her family, Loseff. Love has no limits. It rises above god and country. That is the lesson you learn this day. Love first, today, tomorrow, and always."

Kaythlin got out of her chair, kissed her husband, and turned to Derr. "Druin, are you certain of what you said? She is not likely to confess?"

"We'll push her to the limits of pain the human body can endure. But yes, Kaythlin, it's unlikely she'll talk."

Kaythlin walked to Nails with slow, purposeful steps.

Nails looked her in the eye and followed it with an evil, prescient grin, as Derr read it.

Derr spied Kaythlin brush her hand along the placket of her skirt to expose, then to take hold of the long, thin, sheathed stiletto strapped to her thigh.

Pride filled Derr as Kaythlin held Nails's hard-knowing glare in her own. Kaythlin, a beautiful woman, strong, intelligent, warm, and elegant, yet as fierce and determined as any warrior.

Derr observed the First Lady unrelenting in the combative stare-down between the two powerful women. Nor did it come as a surprise to the captain of the KCG, that, without looking, being locked in the grips of an eyeball-to-eyeball confrontation, Kaythlin skillfully positioned the blade's entry point to pierce Nail's heart. Adelle's First Lady gracefully eased the knife into Nails's chest, impaling the cardiac organ of the Thuggery chieftain as intended... and left it there.

WHAT MIGHT HAVE BEEN

HENSDALE: 10TH DAY OF THE HARVEST MOON

Neladith | Arek

Late in the afternoon on a brisk autumn day in the first weeks of the Harvest Moon along a dirt-packed road on the way to the late Hollid Brenal's home, Spetzer, Arek, and Judjurex Tetrip approached from the east. Mithany and Neladith approached from the west. Brenal's dead body awaited them all.

Neladith hummed a pleasant tune, satisfied with herself having just shagged Mithany. The two women ambled along towards their destination. Mithany said little the entire trip, and Neladith considered her new lover's fragile state the cause. Neladith accepted silence from her newly acquired fuckbuddy and gave Mithany's solitude a wide berth.

Neither the bright sun nor cool air could dampen the immense satisfaction the Evidar agent took from having bedded both brother and sister while on assignment. Conquest, whether the thrill of killing a mark or the titillation of seducing siblings, delighted her dark soul. As far as she knew, Arek was dead, and Mithany was fair game for future amorous dalliances. She just had to hope her team made sure Reyne would forever remain out of the picture.

Clouds drifted overhead. The sight of it captured Neladith. Until transfiguring to another dimension, she'd never seen nor experienced white puffy objects floating in the sky. The pristine breeze smelled sweet to the woman who grew up breathing the acidic atmosphere of Evidar. Of the differences between the two worlds Neladith encountered, clean air held a top spot amongst the many reasons she'd grown fond of Tartica.

Hensdale's bucolic, simple way of life grew on her. Over time it gave birth to wondering if there could be a way to spend more days away from her own dark world. She enjoyed her role as an assassin, but the time between assignments came with the harsh realities of day-to-day survival.

Mithany, unknowingly, fomented hope in Neladith. For the second time in her life, Neladith had feelings for another living thing—if only for two women from different realities with the same face. Although Neladith had sexual encounters with many men and women in her short life, caring about any of them never occurred to her. With budding feelings for Mithany, Neladith was both unprepared and confused.

Time spent with the petite, brown-haired wonder roused Neladith's insides with a rarely experienced—save once before—spark of something more than lust that she didn't understand and wasn't willing to readily accept. But while roaming over Mithany's body with her hands, her lips, and her tongue, memories flooded back to another young woman Neladith once cared for, Mithany's Evidarian doppelgänger. Their lips, the same, their naked bodies almost identical in every way: hips, breasts, eyes, and the feel of her skin. The dead woman had been lost to Neladith in Evidar's harsh environment, but now walked alongside her, reborn in Mithany. The experience left Neladith confused, as her life in a world forever in darkness focused her every thought on survival and hadn't afforded her the necessary skills to understand or navigate caring emotions. Especially feelings for a Tartican woman commingled and muddled within the pangs of lost love.

Over the past several days on their trek to Topak and back, Neladith mentioned to Mithany several times she considered remaining in Hensdale after completing her unfinished task. Existence in the rural village was easier than where she grew up. She imagined a lifestyle that included planting apples instead of the daily threat of land skirmishes, battles over scarce food resources, and killing on behalf of a higher authority. Although she did love the thrill of the hunt and the exhilaration of a kill, Hensdale had its appeal.

Nevertheless, while her time with Mithany had been short, it had also been intense. Adding fodder to her musings, the object of her desire wasn't the only reason to spend days away from Evidar, but it was a damned good one.

Neladith's major obstacle to her contemplations of a better life, the man behind her assignment to murder the Tweener Reyne—the Devil's Blacksmith. *Cut and run would never work with him.* Quith and Dylla might have thought it a well-guarded secret, but she knew desertion had always been dealt with harshly. If she stayed in the realm of Tartica, she would be hunted interminably by her own people. Total abdication of her responsibilities as an assassin for the Devil's Blacksmith, not a viable option. *Although, splitting time between these two realities... I wonder if that's possible.*

Pulling it off held promise, yet not without danger. The perception of being anything less than totally loyal to Evidar's leader proved a death sentence.

There might be a way to do a little wet work for the Devil's Blacksmith, then hiatus between assignments on Tartica. Once Reyne's dead, hook up with Mithany as much as possible. The best of both worlds. I'll see what Quith thinks when I get back. Maybe I can sell him on assigning me to the Tartica contingent permanently. The answer is "no" one hundred percent of the time when you don't ask.

I'll find a way.

Mithany interrupted Neladith's introspections. "Nel, we're almost at the turnoff to Doc Brenal's home. Before we get there, do we need to talk about what happened between us earlier today?"

Neladith hadn't a clue how to respond. "What for?" She'd never had cause to transact in feelings and had no idea what to say. If she didn't care for the woman, it would have been a different reply. But she did care and didn't want to mess it up by saying the wrong thing. She took hold of Mithany by the hand, turned her one hundred eighty degrees to directly face each other and looked into her eyes, searching for signs of the woman of her desire's intentions.

Mithany's own eyes swept left to right, gazing back into Neladith's, and said, "The redness is fading. Guess I see it better in this bright light."

Neladith, pleased to hear it, assumed her natural coloring would complete the transition soon enough. But she never had time to find the answer to her question. Off in the distance, movement suddenly appeared between the trees with three men headed her way. Neladith froze. Recognition exploded into her psyche, and her world, her hopes, her dreams… crumbled.

Can't be.

She looked again.

No fuckin' way! Arek?

Her heart threatened to leap out of her chest.

Impossible. He's dead.

She squinted harder to sharpen her sight.

"Neladith? Are you okay?"

Shit, it's him. He's alive.

Those motherfucking idiots Tylus and Grafph. I told them to make sure he's dead.

I'd kill you both if someone didn't already beat me to it.

Copious amounts of cortisol flooded through her.

Her body screamed to her—fight or flight!

FUUUUUCK!

She didn't have much time. Seconds at best.

With the sun behind her, Neladith could see Arek and only hoped the strong rays of light, low on the horizon, prevented him from seeing her as anything other than a silhouette. Neladith grabbed hold of Mithany's shoulders and held her firm, away from seeing her brother's distant approach. "Hey, I have to run back. Just remembered something Santander told me to do. I'm a little worried he'll find out I didn't do it. You go on. I'll catch up with you."

Neladith let go and bolted without warning or without waiting for a reply. Speeding away, Neladith heard Mithany shout, "You can't expect me to handle Brenal all by myself! Wait, I'll come with you."

Neladith didn't wait. She sprinted into the sparse trees lining the well-worn dirt road to avoid Arek's ability to identify her. She quickly put distance between herself, Mithany, and Arek. As she sped away, she engaged her analytical, operative-trained brain, searching for a solution.

Mithany's protestations faded on the breeze, as did the life Neladith envisioned for herself. Her desires had barely taken root. They would never be allowed to bloom. *What might have been,* rattled around her thoughts as she ran. Her opportunity for a better life died in Arek's resurrection.

Sprinting between the trees, she considered killing Arek once and for all. Yet, he'd surely already given away her admission of murdering Daedyn. Mithany would never forgive her, especially since her real target was the man Mithany loved. Neladith couldn't get to Arek fast enough to keep him from Mithany's sight and couldn't kill Arek in front of her.

At Quith's direction, she'd embedded herself perfectly to detect Reyne Brenton if he returned. Failure to complete her assignment roused her ire. She fucked up, leaving Arek's death in the hands of two incompetent assholes. Quith would use it against her. He'd pin the blunder on her. *No, Tylus was his subordinate... he was in charge... it's on him.* Regardless of who bore the burden of blame didn't matter in the moment; she had to disengage from her assignment.

Fucking Mithany ever again was out of the question, and being there to kill Reyne Brenton if he ever returned was now impossible. Screwed from every angle, Neladith considered her only option was to return to the life she knew, on the version of Earth where she'd been born.

The sight of Mithany exploded joy into Arek's heart. Hobbling along as best he could, leaving Judjurex Tetrip and Spetzer behind, Arek made his way to his sister, who was hurling herself full speed towards him. Rushing headlong towards each other, Arek covered barely ten percent of the gap while Mithany quickly made up the rest. She slammed into his chest, almost knocking him over, wrapping her arms around his waist. The handcrafted crutch flew from its grip on impact.

Tears filled her eyes, she stepped back and, with love, punched him in the chest. "Where the hell have you been? You had me so worried. Oh my god, your face."

Arek held his sister's cheeks in his hands and kissed her. "Sis, you don't know how great it is to see you. I'll tell you all about it. I've been through a lot. For now, let's just say I'm happy to be standing here with you."

Mithany squeezed him tight.

Arek sucked in air between his teeth and grimaced. "Sis, not so hard. I've taken a few bruises since the last time we saw each other."

"I saw you limping... And your face... Oh my god, what happened to you?"

"Neladith happened."

"I know you all too well big brother. Was it a *good* hurt?"—she winked—"Things get outta control?"

"Bad hurt... She tried to kill me."

Arek looked down at his sister's dumbfounded expression. Her mouth gaped open, wide. She sighed. "No. Can't be."

"Sis, I saw someone take off. Who was that with you?"

As though confessing to a crime, she answered, "Neladith." Mithany's face turned red hot, even more than it had been only thirty minutes ago when it burned in the throes of climaxing.

Judjurex Tetrip, who'd sidled up to the siblings, stepped between them and in his direct way said, "Enough, you two. Arek, let's get to Brenal's body. Show me where he is. We'll get to this Neladith, soon enough. You can be certain of that."

Where's the Gratitude

Jerithan

Upon being forcibly delivered back to Tandure by First Lord Serco, Jerithan and Timble were ordered to remain at the front gate of the Chancellor's Mansion. Autumn air nipped at Jerithan's cheeks as Derr approached the waiting pair. Bright sunlight streamed into the open, expansive courtyard, and the smell of fallen, decaying leaves wafted along a gentle breeze.

Derr appeared to ignore it all, his focus aimed at Jerithan. "We had a deal. You were to secure information about Temple plans to deal with this Covenant crisis. If you can't deliver the intel, we're back to where we started. In your case, where your story comes to an end. Here. Today."

"Captain Derr," Jerithan began, Timble by his side, "this is not of my choosing. The moment I set foot inside the Temple Palace, I was denied access to any of the people who were once my supporters."

Derr's jawline tightened, his eyes narrowed, and Jerithan felt the harsh stare burrow into his brain. The KCG captain looked as though he took pleasure in it all. His words were of even less comfort to Jerithan. "You're useless to me."

Silence hung in the air. It amplified the once-First Lord's growing dread. Derr remained relentless, drilling focused eyes into Jerithan's fear. Jerithan broke eye contact, frantically scanning the environs of his predicament for a way out. Timble, his very large assistant, looked calm.

Breaching the quietude, Jerithan pleaded, "Returning here was not of my doing. You know that."

"Of your doing or not, it matters nothing to me."

Jerithan begged, "There has to be another way."

The Voice broke into his thoughts. *"My advice, do not sound so desperate. Project confidence."*

I am going to need more than that. How about something more concrete? I need to come up with more than confidence.

"Give me time, old friend. I just got here. I need more information."

Derr signaled to a nearby guard, who came to stand at attention by his side. "Please escort Timble to Lieutenant Ferpratt. They will have much to discuss."

"Yes, sir. Mister Timble, come with me," the guard said.

Confusion sprawled across Jerithan's face, compounded when Timble shrugged his shoulders at his new employer. "Hope to see ya later, boss."

Jerithan's jaw dropped.

Timble gave Jerithan a wink, turned, and strode off with the appointed escort. Slapping his huge arm on the shoulder of the guard, he said, "It's just Timble, young fella. Lead on."

Derr explained, "He's one of Ferpratt's men inside the Thuggery. We asked him, and others, to monitor you. Needed you to ferret out Nails. And you did. It all worked out."

The Voice cut into Jerithan's confused thoughts. *"This Derr is a sly fellow. I like him. He plays a deep game. But so do I... Keep your head Jerithan, this is not over."*

I was nothing but bait.

"Yes, you were unknowingly dangled at the end of a hook for Nails to bite. But you were also useful to him. We have to find a way to keep you functioning as a resource."

I played my part. Nails ensnared. Now he will get rid of me. Where's the gratitude?

Turning from his inner voice, Jerithan asked Derr, "What now?"

"One of two paths are open to you. Find a way to serve Adelle or you pay the price of your past deed. Either is fine with me."

Derr waved down another guard.

The Voice offered Jerithan hope. *I am familiar with nudging events towards a desired, if not altered, outcome. I am going to need everything you know to figure a new way forward.*

The guard quickly attended to Derr.

Derr told the second guard, "Please take this man to a cell in KCG headquarters. I don't want him here at the Mansion. Once Ferpratt is available, have him attend to our guest."

Guest? He called me a guest. That is a joke.

"Stay calm, my friend. Stay calm."

Easy for you to say. You can leave any time you want. I am the one going to prison.

"Yes, but for now, I am going with you."

Jerithan stated, "You cannot dump me in a cell. I am an official representative of the Temple of Life, here at the instructions of its First Lord."

"Let's just say you have been assigned official quarters inside the same place, that I, the esteemed Captain Druin Derr, use as a working office. It is an honor to share my facilities with you. As for your First Lord, you and I both know why he returned you here. He never expects to see you again, so you can forget the Temple coming to your rescue. Now, you can leave. This man will escort you to your cell."

CHOICES

Neladith

Plans within plans rattled around in Neladith's head as she ran. She sped away from where she'd left Mithany on the road, not far from the site Arek first appeared to her—alive. Raw ire burned at the *idiots* who'd failed to kill him, yet their failure no longer mattered. From every angle, Neladith examined her predicament, hoping to find a purchase to a future partially spent in Hensdale with Mithany by her side. To her dismay, the same conclusion unfurled at every imagined scenario. Arek lived, and that meant she was fucked.

Diversion. I need a diversion. I need time. Something to keep everyone busy and not looking for me.

Amid the hasty retreat, taking a breather along an isolated section of the Brenton farm not too far from where her life began to diverge, Neladith considered her options. The rest of her life awaited the answer to one decision—one choice—two different paths.

Neladith Karlis, Agent Arrow, the woman who murdered Daedyn, had delusions of a life away from the world of her birth—at least part of the time. The dark, kill-or-be-killed demands of the reality she once embraced, before discovering the country life in Hensdale so enticing. Escape from Evidar's hold on her, born in the flutterings of her newly discovered feelings for another woman, Neladith lamented, *She'll never forgive me...* and in that simple thought, she made her choice.

It's better this way.

Everyone I'd ever known's let me down. In time, Hensdale and Mithany would've too.

People suck. Always have. Always will. Doesn't matter what world they're from.

Fuck me. I never really had a choice.

Time to go home. The Devil's Blacksmith will welcome me with open arms. Quith fucked up, not me. I made a great shot. He's the one who picked the wrong target. His people let Arek live.

Neladith almost believed she was doing the right thing, returning to the Earth she knew: back to the thrill of competing for survival in a jungle filled with predators, where she saw herself as an alpha. She had the confidence and the skills to one day assume the role as top dog.

Her head told her she'd made the right decision while the rest of her struggled to overcome the sense of loss. Confused over which drove her to these feelings, a desire for a deeper connection with Mithany or the dream of taking up residence in a world offering comfortable surroundings.

Setting aside a life she could never have, along with a love that could never be, a solution to her immediate need for a diversion took shape.

It doesn't matter.

None of this is real.

Fuck 'em all.

She put her new plan into motion. A diversion to keep anyone and everyone away while she pursued a path into the Void and then home. But she needed time.

With the goal of creating an all-consuming distraction, she settled in away from the Topak refugees and set fire to Reyne's beloved alphen orchard, lighting branches and leaves in several places, ensuring the fire spread quickly.

That oughta keep those fuckers busy long enough. Let it burn. Huh, ironic.

Neladith turned her attention to her next two problems. Where to secure a safe sleeping environment for her transition into the Void and the townsfolk, who would eventually come looking for her after Arek shared his story of her murderous deeds.

Where to lay my head? Can't just fall asleep in the woods. Too many critters, and one of those Great Yetgnals might still be around. Need a building. A house. Could just break in anywhere. Nah, can't do that. Don't know who might come home for some stupid reason. Could go back to Mithany's leather goods shoppe. No, it'd take too much time getting there. I'd eat up my grace period. Two closest places, that Brenal guy's and the apple farm. Can't go to Brenal's. Don't know if anyone's there. Leaves only one choice. Back to the apple farm with dead Grafph. Risky? Not really. I'll be gone before anyone comes-a-knockin'.

Neladith weighed all the risk factors and calculated that no one would come after her in time to stop her from transfiguring back to her own world. Even Arek would be too consumed with saving Reyne's orchard, for Mithany's sake. She figured he'd want payback for what she did to him, but only after they saved what they could of Reyne's precious alphens. Neladith confidently believed Arek loved his sister more than his desire for vengeance—Mithany's needs would come before revenge.

Neladith set off at full speed for the homestead of two dead apple farmers. As she ran, one thought above all others comforted her; she'd outsmarted everyone.

Oh yeah, he'll come looking to retaliate, but only after the fire's out.

By the time Arek or anyone else comes for me... I'll be long gone.

So, you can all go fuck yourselves. I'm goin' home.

A dozen trees set ablaze one after another, spaced generously apart, seeded the inferno to come. Dried and split-open husks of the alphen nut-laden trees awaiting harvest took quick to the flames. Embers rose from the canopy and flittered along wind-driven pathways to ignite upon landing, consuming ancient and sapling hardwoods alike. What began as twelve separate fires blossomed into a conflagration in a flash.

Topakers, only days ago having escaped their burning city, were the first to catch wind of scorched-wood aromas wafting through the air. The initial sight of fire sparked terror in the itinerants occupying the makeshift campsite packed in tight together, spreading even faster than the flames dancing from tree to tree. Screams of panic en masse competed with the roar of the growing firestorm as the frantic indigents raced from the danger.

By the time Mithany, Arek, and Judjurex Tetrip arrived on the scene, having been interrupted at Brenal's by an urgent messenger sent by the farm's general manager, Santander, the blaze had grown out of control.

Horrified at the sight of her beloved Reyne's life's work going up in flames, Mithany screamed, "Santander! Where's Santander?"

Soot-covered, Santander appeared from between a line of alphen trees untouched by the mounting inferno. Stepping towards Mithany, he shouted over the roaring firestorm. "As soon as I saw it, I set up bucket brigades. Cisterns are full. That helps. The Topakers have been doing their best, but we're giving more ground than we gain by the minute. I don't have enough trained people to work all the pumping stations. We got three of them up and running. It's spreading faster than we can stop it."

Mithany pleaded, "Oh, by the Goddess Teth, help us." Her body shook. "Oh god, no." She'd lost Reyne, Daedyn had been murdered, Neladith tried to kill Arek, and now this. Her heart couldn't bear it. Her fractured mind couldn't process the pain, the loss, and now, the fire. She froze in place. Her stomach squeezed her insides like a hangman's noose around her neck. She couldn't breathe. Gulping for air, the bitter taste of burning alphens attacked her palate. Involuntarily, her fists clenched. With her head turned up to the sky, she let it all out in a horrendous screech.

Santander pulled up and grab Mithany by the shoulders. He shook her and stared into her eyes. "Mithany, dear, pull yourself together. I'm sorry, but there's no time for that." He turned to face the others. "You two, join the lines or help with the pumps. We need every able body. It doesn't look good. I think we're going to lose everything. I'm praying, with Teth's help, the firebreaks built into the orchard's layout... may be our best hope." Santander turned and sprinted away, disappearing back into the smoke enshrouded trees.

Tetrip followed the general manager's lead.

Words of losing it all seized Mithany's mind like an unmovable gear rusted against an unyielding socket. She collapsed to the ground, curled into a ball, and began rocking back and forth. The burning orchard mirrored her own life, and whispers leaked out, "Everything's gone. Everything."

Arek struggled to lower himself next to her. Lying beside Mithany, he looked into her grief-laden eyes. "You can do this, Sis. You're stronger than you know. I believe in you, and you know I'll always love you." He offered her a one-eyed wink. "And Reyne loves you. Now, get up. Do it for him. Go save his farm." He kissed her forehead.

The rocking stopped. Mithany didn't move at first. Like the times as children Arek always found her after another of their mother's brutal beatings. Pain only Arek understood. Comfort only Arek could give. His words caressed her soul. His presence with her there on the ground, sharing her misery, touched her deeply, like he always did. A smile grew slowly. She gently pressed her lips to his and kissed him. "I love you too. Don't know what I would ever do if I lost you." Mithany rose and brushed herself off. "You're right, I can handle this."

"Sis, help me up."

Mithany pulled Arek from the ground and hugged him. She turned to follow the men. Running headlong into the calamity, she suddenly stopped, turned around, and said, "Arek, come on, we need everyone."

The conflagration bellowed like a thousand furnaces off in the distance. Arek yelled back through the gathering smoke, "Neladith set this fire. I know it in my bones. Sorry, Sis, I gotta go after her. Got a good idea where she'll be. She won't be there for long. I gotta do it now."

Mithany threw up her hands, spun away from Arek, and raced off to join the effort to save the grove.

Before leaving the burning orchard, Arek hobbled his way into Reyne's home. Grabbing a knife from the kitchen, he armed himself. He considered what he'd do if he successfully subdued Neladith. He needed chloroform, and he knew exactly where Reyne kept it—for those times when a serious injury occurred to some unfortunate farmhand.

And he suspected where to find Neladith.

The journey was hard and took longer than he hoped. Both legs screamed at him for relief while the armpit supporting his makeshift crutch begged to be released of its burden.

Exhausted, Arek finally came to stand before the farmhouse. The place where he'd been tortured, violated, beaten, and where Neladith thought she'd killed him. Trepidation gripped his gut, shooting fear through his core. He froze in body and mind and might have never moved again, yet for the putrid fetor that slammed into him and stole away all other thoughts.

An ungodly odor poked at the hairs in his nose and threatened to unleash what little gathered in his stomach. Fearing the noise he'd make puking, Arek battled against his own reaction and swallowed down everything coming up. Stomach acids mixed with undigested food left an appalling taste in his mouth to compete with the putrefactive air attacking his nose and tongue.

Relief came in the guise of shifting winds brought on from smoke carried on a breeze borne in the Brenton farm firestorm. Arek reluctantly welcomed the aroma of burning alphens to compete with the odorous sent of death.

Off in the distance, billowing clouds of dark smoke loomed overhead. Peaks of monstrous yellow flames popped in and out of view over the apple orchard tree line from where Arek stood. The sight of flames stretching that high told Arek the effort to contain the conflagration was not going well. An inferno of destruction he suspected Neladith authored.

She proved herself more capable than him in their last encounter. He knew he stood little chance of winning a one-on-one fight, especially in his current physical state. Fear, uncertainty, nausea, and anger all rattled around in his brain, and he felt the weight of it as he hesitated to take his next step.

The door had been opened by someone before he arrived. He knew who.

A lump gathered and rode its way down his throat. The last time he was this frightened, a Great Yetgnal threatened to bite his head off and he shit his pants. He was close to doing so again. In the here and now, up against Neladith, in his diminished capacity, his chances were better with the Great Yetgnal of coming out of it alive.

I gotta do this. I WILL have justice for Brenal.

His best bet required stealth, sneaking up on her, if he had any chance at all. *Not an easy task for a hobbling gimp.* Having left his mop-crutch outside, depleted of vigor from the arduous trek, shaky on his feet, Arek slipped out of his shoes to muffle his approach.

Death reeked, and its lingering fumes attacked his eyes. Flies circled the body on the sofa. The sight of it appalled him as he stared at the dead man. A sneeze itching at his nose escaped every attempt to hold it back, but he clamped both hands over his mouth to minimize the damage it threatened against the silence.

Without the aid of his crutch, his thigh screamed into his mind with every step. The damaged leg shook, wobbled, and challenged his ability to stand, let alone walk. Sweat poured off him in spite of the brisk autumn air. His heart thundered in his chest as both fright and pain insisting of him to stop while his inner voice pleaded with his body for a temporary clemency. Gripping the far edge of the couch afforded Arek a momentary pardon. It granted a mercy to his leg, yet his fears weren't so lucky.

Thick vapors from the rotting corpse, palpable, were almost visible rising off the body. He begged Mother Earth for a stiff wind to sweep through the open windows and doors to carry it away. Like his prayers to the Goddess Teth, Mother Earth failed to answer.

He scanned the open area to the kitchen, basement access, hallway, windows, and a single closed bedroom door.

If Teth is with me, Nel's in that room and I won't have to do the stairs to the basement.

Arek fought an internal battle of physical agony holding him back pitted against steeled will driving him forward. Making it to the knob of the bedroom door, he prayed, *Please, Teth, silence the hinges.* A careful quarter turn and a gentle push gave him the goddess's reply.

Silence.

Thank you.

Arek peeked in to spy Neladith asleep in a bed against the far wall of the room filled with a hint of smoke in the air filtering in through the open window. Arek eased Reyne's kitchen knife from his back pocket but considered his options and returned it. From his other pocket, he withdrew a flask and a cloth. Poured one onto the other before going for the knife once more.

Arek had yet to decide which of the two he would put to use, approaching the sleeping assassin with a cloth in one hand and a sharp, killing kitchen utensil in the other.

Without making a sound, Arek hovered over the sleeping murderess.

His choice made.

One hand eased slowly towards the motionless body.

Cold metal against the delicate skin of her exposed gullet caused Neladith's eyes to snap open.

It Isn't You, It's Me

Evidar

Emosh

"Please come in, Miss Emosh," the attendant told Evidar's only Damus. The Damus had news for the man calling himself the Architect—everyone else called him the Devil's Blacksmith. "He is otherwise occupied at the moment, Miss Emosh. He will be with you shortly. Can I get you something to drink?"

Synja Emosh replied, "No, thank you. I'll wait. I've a very important update for him."

Time passed. Exactly how much, no one could tell precisely, given its nature as an intuitive construct within the gray environs of Evidar and further reinforced by the decentralized civilization's lack of any semblance of a stabilizing authority to impose a unified standard of measure. Miss Emosh, hands folded at her waist, stood for the duration, however long, waiting for the appearance of the man living beneath the yellow doored structure.

Hearth ablaze, deep purple and black flames licked at the darkness. The Devil's Blacksmith walked into the room and welcomed his guest. "Thank you for waiting. And thank you for alerting me to your findings, Miss Emosh."

"Certainly, sir. I'm quite excited."

"I am going to have a drink. Juniper spirits, a double. Can I offer you the same?"

"No, thank you. I want to keep a clear head. This stuff gets complicated to explain in terms that aren't as precise as the mathematical physics concepts that I used to construct my theoretical outcomes."

"Well enough then. Let us get to it. What have you discerned and what makes it so important you take me from my musings with Tartica's own Jerithan Cree?" He took a pull of juniper spirits from his tumbler, walked to his high-backed chair that looked more like the throne of a commanding lord, and with style, sat at his enormous desk.

The Damus began, shooting out words in rapid succession, as she usually did, "Interesting you should mention him. He is at the heart of it. He is part of it, anyway. Our world merging into theirs, well, it turns on the head of a pin. It is even more specific than the last time we spoke."

In his chair, the Devil's Blacksmith rested his hands behind his head, interlaced his fingers, and rocked his throne back and forth. "You caught me in the Void, connecting with Jerithan when you arrived. I pulled him from death's doorstep and found a way to get him back into a position of influence."

Excitement peppered each word. "Sir. Since you've reconnected with him, I've gathered a clearer picture. He may just be the linchpin to war in the other version of our world."

After another sip of his juniper spirits, the seated mastermind asked, "And you are thrilled at the prospects of war. Tell me why."

With a puffed chest, "I figured it out. All the other Damusi who came before me only hinted at the key. They offered advice on manipulating things to nudge Earth's timelines, their Wavefunction, this way or that, but I found the key to maintaining Coherence between our two realities—that is, until we can get them to the merge point. Me. I did it." She curtsied with arms wide, obviously proud of her discovery.

The rocking stopped, and the Devil's Blacksmith rested both arms on his desk. "You have my attention. Get to it, Miss Emosh."

Short steps propelled the Damus back and forth across the room as she spoke. "Okay, follow me. We need to keep our two realities in Coherence. You know, in sync. Until we both occupy the same space at the same time—Convergence. But our version of Earth has its differences from theirs: plants, animals, temperature, the Sun's energy reaching our surfaces, way different. So how have we stayed so close to achieving near-perfect Coherence? Only one possibility, offsetting variables have canceled out wave differentials and kept us close."

He pulled his elbows in tight, gathered his hands together, rested his chin on the newly formed pyramid, and stated, "You are drawing this out. I require the executive summary from you, Miss Emosh."

The Damus stopped pacing. "It all comes down to extreme heat on our version of Earth versus their version's excessive biomass. It doesn't make any sense. It shouldn't make any difference, but it does. That's why they all missed it. All my predecessors didn't see it. But I figured it out. Our heat and their biomass are keeping us in sync. And even better, their biomass is stable except for all the people. The other Earth's biomass keeps growing because the population on Tartica keeps growing. That's the variable. That's why war is so important."

"I need just a little more clarity, Miss Emosh."

"This reality's Wavefunction's modulation, its frequency, its crest, its amplitude is impacted by the buildup of heat on our planetary surface, and it is almost the same exact pattern produced in theirs but not driven by heat, but by their much greater biomass. Don't you see, we shouldn't be in anywhere near Coherence, but for these two major factors we still are."

"Miss Emosh, I think I understand. Two dissimilar variables that neither of our different versions of Earth share are independently producing similar results. Our planet and theirs continue to rise and fall in the galactic plane, traveling at the same speeds, producing the same wave pattern over light-years."

The dark, gloomy surroundings could not hold back the joy rolling off the skilled mathematician and prognosticator. "Yes! Exactly," she shouted, punching an empty fist into the lightless room.

"Are you certain of this, Miss Emosh?"

"Yes. Well, almost. I'm ninety-eight percent certain. I've seen many Probability Wavefunctions in the Void. Futures where Tartica suffers population collapse keep us in Coherence and eventually leads to a merger when they hit a specific smaller number of living people. Those where its population continues to rise, Decoherence is the result and we drift apart as two separate worlds, in separate dimensions... forever. I've also looked at some of the more successful timeline tinkerings in the past. Such as the times Tartica faced deadly plagues and viruses, introduced by our agents over the past millennium. Those were the most productive, pulling our frequency patterns closer in sync. We wouldn't be so close as we are today without those previous biomass reductions."

Up from his would-be throne, walking to his proud Damus, the pair stood face-to-face. "Very well done, Synja. I am proud of you." He extended his hand in a rare congratulatory offering.

The proud Damus eagerly accepted her leader's adulation, gripping the extended hand with both of her own. "Thank you, sir."

"This calls for a toast. You *will* join me." The Devil's Blacksmith poured drinks for two, and he handed one to his Damus.

"There's more. I shouldn't drink."

"I insist, Miss Emosh." Holding up his glass to celebrate the findings, he said, "To Miss Synja Emosh, our greatest Damus." Glasses clanked, and both swallowed their respective contents.

The Damus coughed, and the leader laughed. "Alright, please continue with the additional information you wish to share." He moved to the sofa and sat, leaving his Damus standing.

"Like I said, I'm excited. I've seen a small percentage of timelines where we merge after war consumes their world. A lot of people get killed off and poof, one Earth out of two."

"That is very good news. However, you used the phrase *a small percentage*. That needs further explanation."

"The Probability Waves I've seen in the Void where this happens, Jerithan Cree is a catalyst. A single point in time, along all the successful mergers, include this man at the fulcrum, tilting the fate of his world one way or the other. The timelines leading to a merger all branch off from that one point in time. That axis in time is now, but only after Reyne Brenton is dead."

From the couch, while seated, black eyes looked up at the Damus. "I will have to make sure I secure him to that outcome. I will have to be vigilant against this Reyne Brenton in his attempts to kill me before I can finish my work with Jerithan Cree. What new chronologies have you spied in the Void concerning Reyne Brenton?"

Ebony flames danced in the firepit and Evidar's de facto leader watched his Damus gulp hard at his question. "Say what you know, Miss Emosh. Hold nothing back."

Like a child trying not to urinate in her pants, Synja Emosh fidgeted wildly in place. "Well, it's just that... I have seen scenarios where this Reyne Brenton does succeed at, you know, killing you, and in several, the merger still happens. But in every Probability Wavefunction where our worlds come back into one, you have a Damus at your side. And a few where there is a Damus, but..."

"Continue, Miss Emosh, with your *but*."

"But... you're not always there in all of them."

"I thought you cannot witness your own timelines; you cannot experience your own Probability Wavefunctions."

"I can't, but I can calculate the probable futures of others. In the possible futures of those other lives, who the Damus is remains hidden from me. Yet, I have perceived *a Damus* within the peripheral existence of other lives, yours included. There is a Damus in all the timelines where we merge. In the Void, I don't experience your existence in every one of those same timelines. You are in some, not in others. And since I can't discern this Damus's identity, I must conclude it is me. It isn't only Jerithan Cree at the fulcrum of time; it is in combination, even more so, with Reyne Brenton. If this Reyne is successful in removing me, it doesn't matter what Jerithan Cree does or doesn't do. And if Cree doesn't move Tartica to war, Reyne Brenton's actions are immaterial. Both are required. These two men are interconnected with the futures of both Earths."

"If I am to accept your reporting on this, and not as an attempt to secure your own life against future failures, Reyne Brenton's success in killing me is not as important as I have been led to believe." Anger slipped out in his tone.

The visibly shaken Damus replied, "Oh, no, sir. His success or failure is pivotal. It's just that who he has success at killing will make all the difference. In other words, it isn't you, it's me."

The Devil's Blacksmith leaped to his feet. He erupted, throwing his glass, crashing it into the black fire, smashing it into hundreds of small shards. He seemed to grow even larger in anger. "All my efforts all these years, and whether our world ever emerges from the disaster of the Great Destruction falls to two insignificant Tarticans, Reyne Brenton and Jerithan Cree."

Synja Emosh's entire body trembled.

The Devil's Blacksmith roared, "Get out!"

Confessions

Hensdale: 10th Day of the Harvest Moon

Arek | Neladith

"I wouldn't move if I were you," Arek told Neladith. The cutting edge kissed the delicate flesh of her neck gently but threatened more aggressive action by the man wielding it. "Sure, you could try a quick maneuver or some special trick. Might work. On the other hand, might not. In which case, you'll most likely bleed out. So, like I said, I wouldn't move."

Neladith appeared to heed his advice; remaining still, she said, "I'm not dead yet. That's good."

"Not yet."

"Why?"

"Why what?" he asked.

"Why didn't you do it? It's gonna be harder now. Looking someone in the eye and ending their life. Few have the balls for it. Do you?"

"After what you did to me, got balls-a-plenty."

"I always liked you, Arek. We had a good time together. But I needed one simple answer to one simple question. You resisted and things got outta hand. You showing up today, alive, really fucked things up for me."

"Can't say I'm sorry."

Arek girded himself against the pain radiating down his leg. He knew he had limited time to stand while debating the past with her. Following Neladith's eyes, exploring the sweat covering his face, he had to assume she understood its cause.

She's stalling for time.

I remove the knife, I'm dead in seconds.

How did I get myself into this?

Stupid. Stupid. Stupid.

"You still haven't answered me. Why didn't you just kill me when you had the chance?"

Arek couldn't provide an adequate response inasmuch as he didn't know himself. He reached out with his other hand. "I will now, if you make a single move."

"I see what you got there in the other hand. Is that for me?"

Neladith remained motionless and, with Reyne's kitchen knife, he pressed it just hard enough for a drop of blood to ease out as a warning not to move.

Staring back at him, she didn't wince or gasp. The added pressure and resulting pain she let slide, unanswered. The two locked eyes.

With his other hand holding a wet cloth doused in chloroform, Arek pressed it over Neladith's nose and mouth. She didn't attempt to stop him.

Her lids eased closed, and she was out. Arek held it there a few seconds longer to ensure she hadn't feigned the expected reaction.

Along the edge, Arek sat on the bed where Neladith rested, subdued, with her mind in a fog from the chemically induced slumber.

Arek left Neladith lying on the bed, knocked out. After much effort and a few hits of fresh chloroform, he secured her arms and legs, tied to the corner posts with a rope he found in one of the nearby barns. The effort drained him while an overwhelming pain gnawed at him. Sleep called out to him. But he wouldn't be denied justice for Brenal.

Rest will come soon enough. First things first.

After a while, Neladith stirred.

Finally.

"Your head's probably a bit foggy. It'll pass. Reyne and Daedyn use this stuff dealing with bad injuries. People get hurt working on the farm every now and then. Glad I brought it with me."

Neladith breathed deep a few times, which Arek assumed its purpose to clear her nasal airway of the lingering odor and tang of chloroform. An offensive whiff of Grafph loitered about as well, despite the open window's endeavor to sweep away the offensive rotting stench.

She said, "Leaves a nasty aftertaste in the mouth. My mind is a bit jumbled. Bad for me, good for you. It solved your immediate problem and prevented another you never suspected. You should have used the knock-out juice the first time. You didn't need the knife. A bit too risky for a civilian."

"You're right. I'm new at this. Had to hit you a couple more times with the chloroform. Not sure how long it'd keep you sedated."

"Did the trick. You got me all tied up, and I didn't put up a fight. Couldn't, being unconscious and all," Neladith said, pulling at the rope tied to her hands secured to the bedposts. "What are we doing now? I'm getting the feeling you either don't want to kill me or don't have the stomach for it. Doesn't matter to me, I'll take reason one or reason two."

"I want to kill you. You murdered Daedyn. You tried to do the same to me. You caused Brenal's death."

"That's not true. Well, yes, I did kill Daedyn, but I thought it was Reyne and I never meant for you to die. Thought you expired while we were doing it. It just happened. I'm going to tell you something. I didn't have to take off my clothes back in the basement and I didn't have to ride you all tied up. Thought I might not get another chance and I wanted you one last time. I always enjoyed our time together. And as for Brenal, I had nothing to do with him."

"You messed me up pretty bad. I can hardly walk. Don't see it ever getting a whole lot better. And let's not forget, you didn't just ride me, as you say, you violated me."

"Violate? Are you kidding me? You were asking for it. Your rock-hard dick gave you away. I figured I'd take you up on your visible offer. One last hurrah between us. Never guessed you liked the rough stuff. I violated nothing."

Despondent, Arek responded, "What you think doesn't matter. I know what you did." His words trailed off to no more than a whisper.

"Then why are my clothes still on? Thought you'd want to take liberties with me like I did to you. A little payback. You know, revenge. Nothing's sweeter."

His voice lacked both strength and conviction. It reflected the downhearted surrender he faced, hiding just below the surface. "Thought about it. That's not who I am. I do hate you, but taking advantage of a woman isn't in me. I get them all willingly. I don't want revenge, just hoping for justice."

"You wouldn't be taking advantage of me. I'm one of your *willing*. Go ahead, slide my pants down. I'm game. There's something I should tell you first. Your sister had a nice technique. You know—I've had you both." A broad grin came over Arek's captive.

Arek's head hung low. His leg throbbed. Her attempt to provoke him failed.

Despondent at the realization death would not claim Neladith at his hand, Arek's heart bled at all he'd lost. He reached into his soul for internal comfort to ease the disappointment in himself. The one thing that gave him more peace than anything in his life, his source of happiness, and where he hid from the world, his sister's love. Their secret came out in the effort to ease his growing discontent. "I've had you both, too. So what?"

"Now that's a revelation. Wow! Didn't see that one coming. No pun intended. Hah. I get you're damaged. Figured that one out when the beatings started and your dick got hard, but not that sweet little woman. But... that kiss she gave you after you survived the Great Yetgnal. That was a hell of a kiss. Looked passionate. I should've seen it. And she fucked me, with Reyne gone how long? Yeah, guess she is damaged goods, just like you, only in different ways. I can see it now."

Soft soothing tones for the love he harbored for his sister emanated in his reply. "Mithany is a special soul, but she is more broken than you could ever imagine. Childhood scars never go away for some people. I've looked out for her my whole life. Someone had to. We've shared a lot. I was her first love. She was mine. Her choice. I gave in to her. In the end, she was right. I miss those days."

Neladith's eager eyes looked up from her prostrate position. "She's damaged in all the right places then. She's a little powerhouse and quite the lover. Does her fiancé know about you two or even how messed up she is?" The excitement in her voice died in the air, failing to pull Arek from his malaise.

Arek eased a breath from his chest that drifted out several long seconds between his lips. "No. I'm sure he loves her but doesn't have a clue the torment she endures to get by. The damage done to her, done to us both. She lives with it every day. She hides it well, always has. She's fragile on the inside. Tries to hide it on the outside. And nobody's damaged in the right places; don't be even more of an asshole than you already are. Going through the mess you created without me to keep her anchored, and with Reyne gone, no doubt she needed comfort. Given all that she had to deal with, gotta say, not surprised you two hooked up. Although if she knew what you did, it would've been a different story."

The expression on Neladith's face spoke to Arek before her words reached his ears when she said, "I *am* surprised. Not that I tasted your sister... but shocked... you two actually fucked."

"It doesn't matter what you or anyone thinks. You can't understand. No one can." Sadness dripped from his words.

"That's all well and good, and I love hearing about this stuff. Makes me want your sister even more. Gets me all excited. Think I'm wet. Want to check? Picture the three of us together in one bed; wouldn't that be fun?"

Neladith's response, as nothing more than prurient titillation in what he shared, saddened Arek. She missed or ignored the emotional pain in his revelations. He folded his hands in his lap, looked down at them, opened his mouth to speak, but the words didn't follow.

Neladith's tone changed. "All that aside, what are we doing here, Arek?"

Confusion bloomed across Arek's face. "Why aren't you scared? You're calm, even happy. And as usual, horny. You could be dead at any second."

"You confessed... so I will too. I've known this entire time you weren't going to kill me. I gathered that from the moment I saw you. You want to, but something's holding you back. I've known from the second you sat down that I'm gonna live long enough to leave this room. Your body language screamed surrender and your face, well, it gave you away."

Dejected with himself, Arek said, "You figured that out from the start, huh? ... I thought I could do it. Guess I'm just as broken as my sister. I should kill you, but I can't let myself. Think I'm just gonna go get Tetrip, the local civil enforcement guy. He'll take you in and deliver the justice you got coming. You should know, it's for Hollid Brenal. He saved my life and died in the effort. It didn't have to be that way... if you hadn't left me for dead."

"You could've croaked and none of that stuff would have happened to him. You could've just given me the info. It's your fault he died, not mine."

Arek screamed at her, "You killed him!"

He squeezed the knife in his hand. Temptation tugged at his soul to embed the blade deep in her chest. Knuckles turned white as he grasped the wooden handle in an iron hold, ready to strike, but faded to pink in defeat.

He let go of his hatred and his grip, dropping the knife to the bedroom floor. Desolation flooded through him.

In a calm voice he told her, "You ain't getting out of those knots. Bed's well built. Solid. You'll be here when Tetrip gets back."

Neladith asked, "Aren't you worried I'll tell everyone about you and Mithany?"

"You won't do that."

"You're not the same man I met in Owls Neck. I did this to you. Yeah, you're right, I won't be the one to reveal your secret. My way of saying I'm sorry."

"This from the woman I came face to face with in the basement of this very farmhouse. You're a psychopath. You say you're sorry, but I doubt you can feel anything."

"Your wrong. Your little village and maybe even Mithany woke something inside me. Like you, I've changed."

"Lies, all lies. You'd say anything to save yourself."

After Arek departed, the knotted ropes held, and the bedframe did its job.

However, tied to the bed, Neladith took comfort knowing no one would find her. No one living in Tartica, anyway. She had no intention of remaining secured in place to await Tetrip's arrival. Nothing had the power to keep her from sleep, then into the Void and finally onward to home. Unless, somehow, she'd be kept from slumber. No one hung around to do anything of the sort, and Grafph, dead on the couch, wasn't up to the task.

If all went as Neladith expected, Tetrip would find only empty ropes hanging loose from the bedposts and the clothing she wore laid out in the space her corporeal form currently occupied.

Neladith drifted off to sleep, into the realm of dreams where a clear-minded, astral projection—out-of-body experience—awaited.

A Life-or-Death Decision

Tandure: 10th Day of the Harvest Moon

Derr

Derr, Chancellor Madrotti Tomelai, and First Lady Kaythlin huddled in a private room inside the Chancellor's Mansion. The deposed former First Lord, dumped back in their laps, faced execution for his crime of attempting to assassinate Adelle's Chancellor. The meeting began with Jerithan elsewhere, under guard in the very cell inside KCG headquarter where he previously endured unthinkable indignities. As the trio's strategy session kicked off, Jerithan's death was a forgone conclusion.

"Can you believe that ungrateful prick Serco?" Derr lamented. "We put him in that velvet chair, and he throws Cree back in our face. Where's the gratitude?"

Kaythlin reached for Derr's hand. "Druin, it is clear to me First Lord Serco is asking Adelle to finish what he expected of us from the start. In delivering him to us the first time, Serco never thought Jerithan would live to see another day. He would like us to do what he is reluctant to do himself—end the life of Jerithan Cree."

"Drew, Kay's right. The question we need answered is not so much what to do with Jerithan Cree. We will dispose of him soon enough, but of what use to us is Serco? I am not pleased he failed to consult our people before returning Jerithan to me. Addressing the Serco issue will lay the foundation for any future need we might have for Prudent Jerithan Cree."

"Rotti, it seems to me Serco thinks he can do without your support. He may have just spoken the words, 'Fuck you. He's yours.' Thinks himself a little more important and more secure in his new role than he actually is. It portends ill of his intentions concerning the Temple's response to our Covenant withdrawal."

"I am inclined to agree, Drew. There is limited opportunity for Prudent Jerithan Cree to help us in any way under the present circumstances. That frees us to bring the Jerithan chapter to its rightful conclusion as justice requires."

"You and I are of the same mind, my love. Jerithan's place is next to Miss Nails." Kaythlin turned to face Derr. "My dear Druin, are we all therefore in agreement?"

"Sooner is better than later, Kaythlin."

Tomelai proffered, "However, the arrogance of Serco demands a response from the Kingdom of Adelle that both threatens his hold on power and makes clear there is a price to pay for opposing my will concerning both Jerithan Cree and our withdrawal from the Covenant. Kay, I am considering all options. I would like your input."

"Of course, dear. Let me take a step back, gentlemen. Adelle has pulled away from Tartica's founding document. The aftermath has not been pretty. There have been disruptions across our kingdom. Yet, we have fared better than the other nations."

Derr added, "Greenlin's capital building and much of its surroundings have been put to the torch. The countryside of Kantos is relatively untouched, although many of its cities have suffered Teth's fate. Kantos, Greenlin, and Teth are toothless in their current condition to hold us accountable."

"Thank you, Druin. I will continue. What you say is true, but that is likely to change. Fortunately for Adelle, it will take time for them to recover. Serco is hidden behind his gates. President Dimenk is battling insurgents who are demanding Greenlin also withdraw from the Covenant. Kantos's Prime Minister Larsed has been ousted. Our time to act is now."

Tomelai announced, "Our military buildup is progressing. Loseff expects to have no less than four thousand recruits assembled for training within a fortnight.

Our goal is ten thousand within a month. Samers are pouring in over the borders volunteering to join our cause."

Derr leaned back and crossed his arms over his chest. "That's good. I've made promises to Chamette that we need to make good on. I've given him contracts for uniforms, cudgels, bows, arrows, and swords. He's almost done constructing four separate barracks each housing twenty-five hundred, and he's broken ground on the stables for our future calvary."

"Druin, Madrotti and I have introduced Loseff to the Temple Archives—well, our copy of them. He has been directed to review books on historical generals from the Second Age with an interest in understanding strategy. He's been told to keep our copy of the Temple Archives a secret. Loseff was rather surprised at both its existence and the extent of the collection."

Tomelai asked, "Drew, what of weaponry? The Temple Archives are silent on weapons beyond those we currently use. Not a single book. Not even a hint. Is there anything you can think of that will give us an advantage?"

"Engineers have been working with explosives for the past few centuries, although no one's ever needed to convert them into weapons in all that time. My staff assures me it can be done. Rotti, you should know I already have some of my brightest working on prototypes. Once we create the mockups and test them, we'll ramp up production."

The Chancellor replied, "Let us be very careful. These secrets always have a way of getting out. A single blueprint copied or stolen by our enemies is a risk we cannot afford. Clamp it down. Limit the staff working on it and conduct your tests away from prying eyes."

"As you wish. But concerning strategy, Serco has the same books and is likely doing the same thing as we speak."

"For the moment, Serco is too occupied with consolidating his recently acquired power and is trying to hold his city in one piece." Kaythlin added, "He does not strike me as a man capable of attending to more than one issue at a time."

Tomelai remained quiet a bit before responding. "Serco is not the only risk. Letting the designs of weaponized explosive devices leak out could get me killed.

And I am not sure the KCG can stop a well-placed explosive. Let us be clear, the reason to deny access to munitions, from my perspective as the head of state, is that they can be turned back on the government. Consider, government can never again have absolute control over its people with such destructive implements at an enemy's disposal. It is in any government's best interest to keep those it rules unarmed."

"Point well taken. I will ensure the development of explosive weapons is classified as a state secret."

Tomelai asked, "And what of the other shadow players of the Hidden Hand who think they have influence controlling my country?"

"Rotti, if Chamette is to bring the elites to heel, and to keep them in line, we're going to have to feed them."

"And coin is what they feast on," Tomelai joked, but no one laughed.

"And you have plenty of it, Rotti. Chamette has his hand in the Citizen's Committee overseeing Teth now that Nails is gone. He plans to rebuild the city once everything settles down. He's looking at all this destruction as an opportunity to cash in. He's beginning to understand the financial gain in chaos and war. Even though he has considerable influence within the Hidden Hand, we need to open the treasury doors wider. The Hidden Hand has a lot of hungry mouths to feed."

The Chancellor's personal secretary opened the door and announced, "Lieutenant Ferpratt dropped off a message to Captain Derr. With your permission, Chancellor."

Chancellor Tomelai nodded. "Thank you. Hand it to the captain, then you are dismissed."

Derr read it aloud:

Captain, Prudent Cree has offered his services as an advisor to our delegation concerning talks between Adelle, Kantos, Greenlin, and Teth over the future of the Covenant of Absolute Universal Obligations. He believes advising Adelle on Temple of Life Protocols is an outdated position, but one Temple canons allow. He can serve Adelle's delegation, residing in the Temple Palace, and Serco can do nothing to block your appointment of him in such a capacity. He requests an audience and is hopeful for your approval. My input, Captain, is he seems genuine or as genuine as he can be trusted to do anything for anyone other than himself. Respectfully, Lt. Ferpratt.

Derr set the letter down, contemplating its contents.

Kaythlin ran her long, thin index finger over her lips. "He is a surprising individual."

"I give it to him, it is possible," Derr said. "Trusting him, that's another matter."

"I have never had need of it," the Chancellor responded. "But Jerithan Cree is correct. My father spoke of Protocol Advisors. The appointment has not been used in decades. Jerithan Cree was First Lord; he knows the rules. One question: How did he know about the upcoming negotiations? Do we have another leak?"

"My love, the man's a letch, a sneak, a self-centered human being, yet he is also very smart. My guess is he bluffed."

"Rotti, Jerithan's clever enough to figure the four countries are going to have to sit down and at least try to hash out our differences over the future of the Covenant, and what happens to trade if we refuse to return to the fold? Our grain production feeds the continent. Before it comes to war, he figured out, a parley's got to be in the works."

"Gentlemen, on its face, Jerithan's offer may be useful, but before we agree to it, may I suggest we explore all its ramifications, drawbacks, advantages and determine if it serves our ultimate goal of defending Adelle from what we anticipate is coming our way?"

The Chancellor nodded his agreement. As did Derr, although it wasn't his call to make.

"Kay. Drew. Using Jerithan can go very wrong. This is one of those pivotal decisions that only a Chancellor can make. I will need to examine this from every angle."

"Good," Kaythlin said. "I will arrange with the staff to clear our schedules. We will be dining here tonight. We are going to be here a while."

Tomelai grinned. "After we hash this out, I am going to have to do this all over again with my department heads. Kay, I may ask you to run that meeting."

Kaythlin rubbed her husband's shoulder. "You flatter me, dear, yet I defer to you. When you want something, you are hard to deny."

Tomelai leaned in slowly to kiss his wife. His hand settled on her thigh.

Derr watched. He was always watching, although this was one of those situations where he preferred not to. "Enough, you two. I know where this is going. We've got work to do. You can take each other's clothes off when we're done… after I leave."

"Of course, Druin," Kaythlin said, daintily wiping the corner of her lip with her finger. She offered a teasing smirk to her husband, yet never challenged Derr's premise concerning the events of the after-meeting.

"Thank you, Kaythlin. Back to the immediate fate of Jerithan Cree. We all know his final disposition. It's whether he gets a few more days to live, if we believe keeping him alive will help us achieve our objectives."

"Boys," Kaythlin began. "He will pay for his sins, just not today. I have an idea." With her eyes turned to her husband, she grinned. "With your approval, of course, but I think you are going to like what I have in mind for Jerithan, Serco, Greenlin, and Kantos. It involves Tane as well."

CRAZY EYES IN A DARK WORLD

EVIDAR

Reyne | Gina

It could have been evening or the middle of the day. Since making their way to the world forever in darkness, neither Reyne nor Gina had figured out the diurnal cycle. Constant hunger, ebony skies, and the persistent gloom of Evidar's despondent landscape had worn them down. While Reyne's eyesight in the dismal-gray environs had improved slightly, it was no match for the threatening, shadowy outlines of bodies that suddenly appeared huddled together off in the distance.

"Gina, there's too many of them," Reyne exclaimed.

"I tally seven."

"I count six pairs of eyes shining in the dark. Eerie. They ain't movin'. What do you figure they're doin?"

"Waiting to see if we're a threat. If they attack, remember everything I taught you. I'll go for the biggest guy. You go after number two. From that point on, it's a free-for-all."

"We need food, clothes, and we gotta find our contacts. We can't keep wandering around like this. Without the sun to guide us, who knows where we are? The mental map, as best as I remembered it, hasn't helped. Here's a chance for the locals to help us."

Gina stuck out an arm, holding Reyne in place. "Not yet. Mera said this isn't a friendly world. Folks struggle to survive here. He's told me stories of sneak attacks, lies in the promise of help, theft, rape, death, along with every other depraved behavior you can think of. And there are even wandering tribes that'll make us their next meal if we get captured. It's like nothing you or I ever experienced. It's utterly brutal. We got to be careful."

"When we're done here, you're gonna have to tell me why Mera never shared all those details with me." With cupped hands to his mouth, he prepared to shout. Gina yanked his hands from his face.

"He didn't want to worry you. Let me talk to them. A woman's voice may seem less of a threat."

"If they only knew you like I do, they'd know that's a bunch of shit."

Reyne towered over her. Gina's head almost reached the tip of his shoulders. Without her enhanced quickness, the pair was at a considerable disadvantage if the encounter came to blows.

She yelled out to the six pairs of small, silvery circles—Evidarian eyes reflecting in the dark. "We're looking for someone. We've come a long way. Hope you can help us."

Silence hung between Reyne and twelve glowing eyes. Whoever they were, their bodies remained covered in a nocturnal veil. They appeared like specters, human silhouettes outlined in gray against the black backdrop of Evidar's forever night. The height of each of the mysterious, apparition-like bodies Reyne discerned only by how tall each shiny pair of pupils stood above Evidar's hard surface.

The delayed response to Reyne and Gina came as six sets of tiny, pallid spheres off in the distance seemed to lurch forward against the backdrop of an ebony canvas. In unison, the Evidarians charged. A heartbeat later, Reyne recognized it for an attack.

"Shit!" Reyne exclaimed, looking down at Gina. "Who the hell are they?"

"How the hell should I know? But they're coming at us. I got the big one in the middle. Come on!" she yelled and sprinted towards the advancing herd.

Reyne followed her cue, racing into danger.

His kilt and her skirt, both made from the same palm-leaf material, flapped wildly as they ran on similarly constructed footwear. Three of the four sandals didn't survive the short journey even before the first blow struck.

Reyne, running right behind Gina, saw the biggest of the incomers pull back one arm with a fist aimed at her face. Racing forward, just feet away, Reyne could only watch. The attacker's huge anvil of a hand was inches away from striking its target when suddenly Gina dove for his legs and swept his feet out from under him.

Crash. He went down hard.

The big guy's temple slammed against the rocky terrain. He was out cold.

One down.

Five left.

Racing past Gina, Reyne thundered headlong towards the second largest attacker.

Charging at full speed, Reyne slammed a punch into guy number two's gut. The goon doubled over. But just as quick, he shot up, smacking the back of his head into Reyne's chin. White-hot pain swept through his jaw into his head. Reyne stumbled. Anger screamed inside his core. Rage gripped him. The blow—the pain—signaled his brain to unleash the primordial beast buried inside him, crying out to be set free.

The monster, inside a cage of pent-up wrath—borne of Mithany's love ripped from his life; borne of Daedyn's murder; borne of a sister and a family he never knew, brutally slain; borne of a craving to exact revenge—took control of Reyne's body.

Reyne attacked the assailant whose blow set in motion his transformation. Another thug joined in, pounding at Reyne's flanks from behind. Oblivious to the pain, he hurled an elbow at the rear attacker. The man's nose made a crunching sound from cartilage smashed against its own skull. Instantly, the assault from behind stopped.

Two down.

Four left.

Blow after blow, Reyne pummeled the man in front. The man collapsed against the onslaught.

Three down.

Three left.

In triumph, with both bloody fists raised over his head, Reyne roared. The monster within, not yet satiated, raged. Reyne, or what he'd become, scanned the melee and, without thinking, found his next target. Grunting, his nostrils flared like a wild bull. He shot forward, crashing into a woman. The two were driven off their feet. Reyne's large mass plowed her into the ground. The sound of air rushing from her lungs and the cracking of her ribs failed to register concern of any kind in Reyne's ravenous mind.

His eyes wild, he rose up. Fist raised, Reyne shrieked at the black Evidar sky. With savagery unbridled, Reyne scanned the ruckus for another to taste his fury.

Four down.

Two left.

Gina sprang up in an instant. Jumping on the back of an assailant who'd whizzed past her only seconds earlier, she wrapped an elbow around his throat. Her thighs squeezed against his flank. Wildly, he flailed backward punches at her head. One connected. Stars bloomed across her vision. Her gripped held. With her other hand, Gina searched out his eye socket. Finding her prize, Gina's thumb pressed hard against his eyeball.

Squish. It popped. She drove deep, dug in, and twisted her thumb. Gina's attacker screamed out in pain. Doubling over, he unknowingly flipped Gina from his back. The whipping motion flipped her small body through the air, legs whirling overhead. Gina's back slammed hard against the ground. Air whooshed from her lungs.

Gina clutched at her chest, gasping for breath. Before gaining control, an enemy descended on her. Her palm-leaf skirt was abruptly ripped away by the attacker. He pounded angry blows at her head. Her arms flailed wildly trying to block his rapid-fire assault. A fist crashed into her nose. Pain exploded through her. She went limp. Through fluttering eyes, revulsion gripped her as the attacker frantically yanked at his trousers. She faded out.

Gina recovered quickly. In horror she came to with a strange hand on her breast. Terrified, she saw his stiff dick in her line of sight—with clear intentions of feeding. Letting fly a deafening screech, she spat in his face. She wiggled. She squirmed. She raged. But nothing she tried freed her from what was coming.

The despoiler held both her arms in his one hand above her head. With his legs wedged between hers, his thighs strained to force hers apart. Pinned down, unable to move, she drove her knee into his ass from behind. The force of her blow slammed his body forward. His hand released her breast and shot out. With her feet, she thrust his knees out from under him.

His body went down. His face smacked in between her thighs while his hard phallus rammed into the unyielding ground. He screamed in pain. Gina squeezed her thighs, trapping his head where it landed. She wrapped her calves behind the back of his skull. Pushing his face even deeper into her groin, she prevented air from reaching either his nose or mouth.

Furious, Gina shrieked, "Is this what you wanted?!"

Her hands pressed against the unyielding rock slab. The force of the effort lifted her butt off the ground as she fought to suffocate her attacker. With his head firmly secured, it reluctantly followed her ass as it raised up. She felt the heat from his ears crushed against her inner thighs. The tops of his eyes, peering out over her torso, silently pleaded for release. Gina denied him. With every ounce of energy, the anger in her legs held him even tighter. If she could have, she would have cracked his head open.

His fists pounded at the ground and thrashed at her torso. But he'd been cut off from the acrid, dark air of the miserable world. Gripping her hips, he pushed against the force holding him. Her iron-willed grasp did not relent. He rolled his weight to the side trying to escape. Gina's body rolled with him. She threw all her strength into her legs, denying him even a single breath. Suddenly, his arms went limp, as did the rest of him.

Five down.

One left.

She extracted herself from the entanglement to look up, only to spot Reyne, crazy-eyed, charging towards her.

She didn't recognize who he'd become. An image shot into her mind's eye of Reyne out of control, just like back at the Whispering Eye. Gina sprung to her feet and braced for impact. Like she did earlier, she dropped at the last instant. This time, a half a second too slow. Reyne's charging knee drove hard into her side.

Thrown forward at the force of the blow, in agony she rolled. Reyne lost his footing, tripped, and slammed into her as he went down. His forehead crashed into the hard, rocky surface of Evidar's barren landscape. His eyes rolled to the back of his head, and he lost consciousness.

Writhing in pain, holding her side, Gina found herself trapped under his wilted, hulking body. Every muscle screamed anguish into her brain.

Gina wiggled free and rolled Reyne onto his back. She propped herself up. Leaning over Reyne, his kilt gone as well, she slapped his face, hard. "Wake up, you bastard. Wake up."

Before finding out the results of her effort to bring Reyne back, something crashed into the back of her skull. Gina fell forward on her back alongside an unconscious Reyne, and everything faded to black.

TRAPPED

EVIDAR

Reyne

The sight of unholy flames welcomed Reyne back to the conscious world. An unnatural ebony fire crackled and spit from a pile of sticks that did nothing to lighten the area or eliminate the musk of the despoiled air. Coming to, not only did the dark realm of Evidar have its hold on him, but he couldn't move. Not knowing where on Evidar he'd been taken or who held him captive, Reyne scanned his surroundings.

Gina sat athwart from him, ankles crossed in front of her, knees apart. Awareness in Reyne bloomed: Gina donned pants and a shirt. He did as well. How, he didn't know, but was grateful nonetheless. However, he wasn't as appreciative that both he and Gina were tied at their wrists with their arms behind their backs and secured to unyielding wooden posts. Their ankles were knotted, and their thighs were encircled in ropes affixed to stakes driven into the ground. Being tied up wasn't his only problem: he didn't know how to return Gina to Tartica, and she had no way of getting back without him. Until he figured it out—if he ever did—they were both prisoners of Evidar. His immediate assessment upon waking: he was trapped in more ways than one.

Confused, angry, and scared, he struggled without success for his freedom. Collecting himself, he looked across at Gina. "You okay?"

"My head's killing me, and my left side hurts like a son-of-a-bitch, but I'll live. You?"

"Right eye's tender. Head's pounding. Jaw hurts and I'm sore all over, but like you say, I'll live unless whoever's holding us has other ideas. How long we been out?"

"Don't know. Could've been hours, a day, who knows. Came to not long ago myself. Woke up all dressed. Speak quietly. Don't want to draw attention."

Reyne lowered his voice. "What're we doin' here? You see how many there are?"

"Only seen the one. Could be more. She fed me, at least."

"She say anything? Like who she is?"

Gina said, "Just told me to eat. I figured, being hungry as hell and all, why not? If she wanted me dead, why tie me up? So I ate what she put in my mouth."

"You ate. Great. Now you can do that speed thing you do."

"Not so loud, genius. And, no, I can't do anything tied up like this. I got souped-up speed, not souped-up strength."

"What do they want?"

With a scrunched face Gina said, "Duh, how should I know? Not sure it's a they, just saw the one."

"That fire is freaky." Reyne looked around. Seeing no one, he added, "At least we have clothes."

In spite of their immediate predicament, Gina smirked. "Don't get me wrong, I am too, but I have to admit, I miss the little guy."

"Little? Oh, that hurts. Aren't you the same gal who called it impressive?"

Gina leaned forward, as much as the ropes permitted. "Shut up, farm boy. You know what I mean."

Keeping his voice down, Reyne changed the subject. "What happened? How did we end up like this?"

"Good news... bad news. You pulled that berserker shit again. Like you did back at the Whispering Eye. You went all wild-man on a couple of them. I took a few out. Thought we handled them. Then, whack, something hit me from behind, and here we are."

"That sucks. I remember bits and pieces this time."

"What does that mean?"

"I was in there, but some mental thing snapped in my head. I couldn't stop it from taking over. It's like anger and hatred took control of my actions. A monster got out, and I went along for the ride. If I'm being honest with myself, I didn't want to stop it."

Gina said, "We gotta keep an eye on that."

"I can't control it."

"You got one hell of a shiner, farm boy. At least from what I can make out in this light. Never know if it's night or day. I hate this miserable world."

"You said you were hit from behind and got knocked out. Did you see what happened to me? How did I end up in la-la land?"

Gina shrugged—as best she could. "Don't know."

"Shhh." He lowered his voice. "Saw something move."

Gina whispered, "Where?"

He whispered back, "To my right. Your left."

"I know my right from my left, farm boy."

"Goody for you. Now shut up."

In the grayness, the dark outline of a body moved in their direction.

As the figure approached, Reyne made out the silhouette of a woman. The closer the form came, the ever-present darkness held the tall, long-legged body, tight in mystery. The woman moved with confidence, and Reyne found himself fixed on its swaying hips. Gina said something that hit his ears yet failed to register in his brain.

The lone outline came forward at a steady pace. Reyne shouted at the dark, shapely form. "Who are you?"

The phantom said nothing.

Several feet from Reyne and Gina, their captor pulled up to stand before the pair with hands on hips. His eyes scanned her from the ground up. Instantly, he recognized the face. Spittle and vengeance spewed out of him. "YOU!" he screamed.

Raging against his knotted prison with every scrap of vigor, Reyne struggled furiously to free himself to no avail. "I'll kill you!"

Point of Order

Teth: 11th Day of the Harvest Moon

Serco | Jerithan

First Lord Serco pounded on his desk. His nostrils flared. If not for the cavernous room, his anger would have rung through the Temple Palace hallways. "Second Lord S'Leen, how in Teth's name is that man sitting with the Adelleian delegation? I gave you an order to have him shipped back. What is he still doing here?"

"First Lord, with all due respect, I tried to do as you instructed," S'Leen meekly offered. "But I've been advised he will be serving as the Master of Protocol for the Kingdom of Adelle throughout the duration of the conference."

Pulling back from the abyss of anger, Serco asked, "What is a Master of Protocol? And what gives Adelle the right to seat that man at these pivotal negotiations?"

"I quickly looked it up. The position is allowed in Temple of Life canons. It is arcane but allowed. I'm sorry that you are only hearing of it now. I tried to find you as soon as I learned of it."

First Lord Serco demanded, "What is it?"

"In my review of the canon, it was established for the benefit of the Temple of Life. A high-ranking prudent may act as an advisor to an invited dignitary to ensure the foreign representatives adhere to our protocols throughout the process. It hasn't been used in over fifty years, but it's on the books."

With a heavy breath, Serco commanded, "Jerithan Cree is a sneaky bastard. Do whatever you need to, but get him out of my Palace."

S'Leen bowed her head. "Yes, First Lord. I must advise you, it will not be an easy task. Canon law gives the invited delegation the right to select who they want to serve as Master of Protocol while attending a conference hosted within the Temple of Life's Palace."

Serco blared, "Don't get wise with me."

S'Leen demurred, "Yes, First Lord." She paused before adding, "These will be delicate discussions, and Adelle is at the heart of the problem, having withdrawn from the Covenant of Absolute Universal Obligations. I cannot formally request his removal without creating a diplomatic crisis. An informal approach would be better, but my guess is Prudent Jerithan Cree is here for a reason, and Adelle will not consider any formal or informal request for his removal. I will endeavor to find another way, but it will take time."

"I don't care how you do it, just get him out of *the* Palace."

First Lord Serco stood before the gathered. Representatives from the independent nations of Tartica were seated around the large conference table. The same table Prudent Cree sat at when he was dethroned from his leadership position in the Vote of Revocation.

Jerithan seethed at the indignity and at his forced servitude orchestrated by the two men who placed him at the table: Garragent Serco, the author of his indignity, and Druin Derr, the master of his servitude.

Jerithan searched his thoughts for the Voice, only to come away empty.

Of course. Why would you be here when I need you?

Serco began, "Welcome, honored guests. We've much to discuss. No less of importance than our future as a peace-loving, faith-based civilization respectful of Nature and committed to the principles of life, repopulation, and respect for one another. As we all know each other, I will dispose of the traditional introductions and close with a request that we all honor and follow the prescribed rules of order. As host, I've allocated separate Palace rooms for you to use for privacy and set aside other rooms where select groups may gather to discuss side issues. As the representative of the traditional neutral party, I will lead our conference and will assume the recognized role as a mediator between nation-states when needed. My staff has prepared an agenda for our discussion, as your representatives have already approved, and I would like to—"

"Please excuse my impolite interruption, First Lord, as no disrespect is intended." Adelle's Ambassador to Teth, an elder statesman, Berik Dobchen, took the provocative step of interrupting Serco's opening remarks, setting the tone of the negotiations to come. The Chancellor-in-Waiting, Tane Tomelai, sat to his right. The gray of his pate, his practiced tone, and almost good looks combined to match his well-maintained physique. A prerequisite of the position, Ambassador Dobchen commanded attention when he spoke.

Jerithan reveled in the faux pas. He laughed to himself, *Whenever any words are preceded by "No disrespect intended," you can be certain disrespect will follow. Intended or otherwise, it was discourteous just the same... Good... It put Serco in his place right up front. It is never a positive sign when opening remarks go so poorly. Especially in diplo-speak.*

Dobchen continued, "It is my government's position Teth is not a neutral party to these proceedings, having a vested interest in the outcome and having taken the position that the Covenant must be maintained at all costs. This position is antithetical to that of Adelle's, and I must insist we recognize there be no established mediator. We are here to iron out how our nations move forward in a new world where each of us follows the Covenant in our own way or not to follow it at all."

More than one jaw dropped at Dobchen's statement, but it was Serco's that delighted Jerithan. Before the First Lord could respond, Greenlin's head negotiator jumped into the fray. "My esteemed colleague, Ambassador Dobchen, you may be knowingly or unknowingly setting the tone of these discussions. So let me be similarly as forthcoming. Your statement, much like your Chancellor's decision to withdraw from the Covenant, threatens to put asunder all the goodwill our four nations have enjoyed since the founding. I must insist we follow establish protocols and recognize Teth as the dually authorized mediator to these proceedings."

Jerithan probed his inner thoughts for the Voice. *Where are you? You're missing the good stuff.* To Jerithan's surprise, the Voice appeared in his thoughts. *"I am here, my friend. I was delayed. This is a wonderful start. You and I must keep them going in this direction."*

Not backing down, Dobchen replied to Greenlin's challenge, "To my esteemed friend from the great nation of Greenlin, whom I have known these many years, whom I respect, and with whom I have shared many a meal, please understand, it is my government's position that these are extraordinary times, and our efforts call for extraordinary measures. This point is non-negotiable, and I am authorized to withdraw from further participation in the absence of agreement on this point. Teth's position is known to us all, and the hopes of even the appearance of neutrality in any mediation with Teth at its center is tainted. We must all accept there are no neutral parties to these proceedings. Let us be honest up front. Honest negotiations are our only hope for the peaceful resolution of our differences."

The Voice offered Jerithan his assessment, *"Those are powerful words, and I love the part where Adelle threatened war in diplo-speak. Plus, when have high-ranking government people ever been honest with one another? There is always a hidden agenda lurking beneath their pontifications. When one diplomat demands honesty, you can be assured he is not offering any of his own."*

With his internal thoughts, Jerithan replied to the Voice. *When today is done, it will be my job to find out how far Serco is willing to take this. The Temple faith is rooted in all four Obligations of the Covenant. Preserving human life is at the center of it all. I can't see how he can bring Tomelai to heel without taking Teth to war. It would violate everything the Temple stands for. This is getting interesting.*

The Republic of Kantos's ambassador said, "Gentlemen. We seem to have gotten off on the wrong foot. Perhaps we might proceed along lines of agreement.

Cement what we all want from these discussions before we jump into the issues that separate us." After she finished, the ambassador from Kantos scanned the room.

The Voice suggested, *"This might get back on track. Do you have anything up your sleeve to get them back to bickering?"*

Each legation seated its lead negotiator at the center with supporting staff, two to the left and two to the right, having limited yet equal representation of five. Jerithan sat the farthest from Dobchen's left. The lesser position of all those accompanying the Adelleian ambassador. He rose from his seat to stand behind Dobchen and whispered in his ear, "Sir, there may be another way for you to consider. At such Temple initiated meetings where all nations are present to address Covenant issues, it's just like a Council of Nations meeting. By Temple of Life protocol, either there is unanimous consent, or any motion concerning Covenant business fails." Jerithan said his piece and returned to his seat. He looked up to find Serco's angry eyes burning in his direction.

Dobchen addressed the conference, "Point of order, please. I would like to make a motion. The motion is this: Teth is to be recognized as this conference's official mediator. I am willing to waive debate."

A smile crossed Serco's face. "I will entertain a motion to waive debate."

All agreed, followed by a vote to approve Teth as the conference's mediator with all the powers, rights, and privileges that follow.

The vote taken, Serco announced, "With Kantos, Greenlin, and Teth voting in favor of the motion and with only one objection from Adelle, the motion passes. Teth will act as mediator. I thank you for your trust in me."

Dobchen's head snapped in Jerithan's direction, and he shot a hard glare at the once-First Lord. The Voice chided, *"He thinks you have, with purpose, misled him, and in so doing jeopardized all of Adelle."*

Not waiting, Jerithan rose. "May I address the assembled? Point of order, First Lord. This is a formal meeting, with all nations present, to address issues concerning the Covenant. Temple protocol for a gathering of this nature requires unanimous consent for the motion to proceed, just like any agreement on the

Covenant that affects all nations. I ask the chair to recognize his mistake and also to recognize the motion has not gained unanimous support."

Jerithan watched Serco's face turn red. All eyes in the room moved quickly to Serco. Jerithan put First Lord Serco in a very difficult and embarrassing position and took great pleasure in it. The Voice said, *"Very well done. I especially enjoyed it when you mentioned it was a mistake."*

It felt good. Serco's in over his head.

"Although, my friend, Serco is not to be underestimated. He is the one in the First Lord vestments, and consider how he got here. Amateurish, yes. Unprepared, certainly. But still a deadly opponent."

Sounds of gentle, non-threatening tones flowed from the mouth of the Kantonian ambassador, known for her ability to bring people together. "Let us thank the prudent for correcting the misstep we've taken. We have, us all, seemed to have misplaced our rule books, but, yes, I believe, upon further reflection, the prudent is correct."

Dobchen stood. "Thank you, Prudent Cree, for bringing this to our attention." Dobchen looked around the room. "It has been a while since we've gathered in the Temple Palace under Temple protocols to address Covenant issues, but I also believe Prudent Cree is correct and I agree with the gentlewoman from Kantos. Unless there are any further discussions on this topic, the motion has failed, and for the remainder of this conference, there is no recognized mediation authority granted to any of its participant nations."

Jerithan had his victory, and he could see Serco ready to explode. The Voice broke into his thoughts, *"You won this round. He will devise something that will make you pay dearly for your interference of his authority and for the embarrassment. We need to be prepared. But, well played. You may end up as prudent in the middle of a cornfield, but it needed to be done."*

Prudent Jerithan Cree, proud of his petty conquest, as the uninitiated would judge it trivial, but in the parlances of high-ranking diplomats, it was an explosion, bringing to light the ineptitude and weakness of the Temple's new First Lord. He said to the Voice in his head, *A rookie mistake. If he knew what he was doing, it would never have happened. I will be ready for his reprisal.*

"*Are you sure of that?*"

FROM WHAT IS LEFT

HENSDALE: 11TH DAY OF THE HARVEST MOON

Mithany

The aroma of burnt wood wafted through the air, but for Mithany it registered as lost hope flittering on a breeze of devastation. Even more than the sight of it, the odor overwhelmed her.

The message it carried lingered in her nasal passage, where it attacked her senses and reached into her soul. She, along with Santander, strode through the mud of the water-soaked remains of the northern grove. As the pair inspected the damage, they weaved between rows of smoldering husks—reduced to stumps. The once vibrant expanse of alphen trees continued to dump gray fumes into Hensdale's pristine skyline. A hard-fought battle of inexperienced firefighters pitted against one of nature's unstoppable forces brought Reyne's beloved alphen farm to the point of near destruction.

Mithany reached out for Santander. They stopped when Mithany took hold of the general manager's hand. "Can you ever forgive me?"

The burly older man draped his arm around her. "Nothing to forgive, my dear. You didn't do this. In fact, the people you delivered, well, we couldn't have put it out without them."

Crackles in her voice, Mithany offloaded the guilt gripping her throat. "I brought Neladith here. Arek thinks she started the fire. If I didn't bring her along, none of this would've happened. It's all my fault."

"Nonsense, dear. You can't be responsible for the things other people do. Unless you had some clue in advance. And, let's be honest, you would never have delivered her to this place had you thought she'd do anything like this. If, in fact she did this." Santander pulled her in tight. Like a father, he rubbed her head, messing up her hair.

Condescending, maybe, she thought, yet she welcomed his comforting sentiments and embraced the lack of blame. The two took up their walking inspection once again. "How much is left?" she asked.

Santander, known for a direct style of communications, gave only a cryptic assessment. "More than we could have hoped for. Less than we need to survive as an independent operation."

"What does that mean?"

"The firebreaks helped. And getting the pumps going near the family home made a big difference. We saved about two or three acres. Alphen trees aren't like the giant sequoias that make up The Stand, which don't take to fire easily. Alphens, on the other hand—" Santander swept his arm one hundred eighty degrees in a complete half circle. "Well, look around, dear."

Mithany's eyes followed his gesture. "I hope Reyne can forgive me."

"I'm not much of a religious man. We saved the family burial plot where all the Brentons rest in peace. If there is any afterlife in the Community of Souls the Temple Lords preach of, I'm sure no one there will hold you responsible for any of this, dear."

A lump of guilt collected in her throat. Mithany swallowed hard her sin of misrepresenting Reyne's death in the face of Santander's kind treatment of her. Arek confided in Judjurex Tetrip the deception of Reyne's faked death. Santander would surely find out soon enough, and his trust in her would be at stake. He deserved the truth from her before everyone else. Once Tetrip took up his investigation based on Arek's confession, the entire village would know in a matter of days.

Concern gulped down her gullet, accompanying her guilt. Santander had always been kind to her. She had to share the truth with him now. Would he feel betrayed having been excluded from knowing it from the outset?

"You've treated me like a daughter in all the years I've been with Reyne. I've something to tell you. And I don't want you to..." She stopped. The words resisted her efforts to expose them.

"To what, dear? To be mad at you when you tell me Reyne is still alive? That Daedyn has been taken from us? Thank you for thinking you need to share with me the truth. I appreciate your trust, revealing that secret to me."

Dumbfounded, she looked into his eyes. *It's in the eyes. It's always in the eyes.*

In Santander's she found comfort, not anger, at the deception. Relieved, she asked, "But how?"

He laughed. "Do you think after all these years running this farm for their parents and then the boys, anything goes on here I don't know about? I knew from the start. I only wish I had returned from my trip sooner that evening. Daedyn might still be alive if I caught those bastards. I miss him. Daedyn was like a son to me."

Mithany spied his quivering lips: a pause that gave the griseous, older man a chance to push down raw emotions threatening to break free. She loved Santander all the more for it.

Santander collected himself. "I stole a moment from Reyne that night. He was leaning on a tree when I caught up to him. Just he and I for only a minute. He told me Daedyn had just been murdered and to stay out of sight the rest of the evening, no matter what, and to keep from being seen by Mera. Most important, he asked me to watch over you and that he needed to go away. Wasn't sure when he'd be back. He loves you too much to leave anything to chance. Hardest thing I ever did, staying put when he had the seizure that same night. Letting you walk off to Topak wasn't easy, either."

Mithany darted into Santander's oversized midsection and wrapped her arms as far as they would go around him. The big man, with his big hands, held Mithany tight. A minute passed and Mithany stepped back. She tilted her head to meet his gaze and choked up when she saw a single tear run down Santander's weathered face.

Mithany reached up and wiped away the salty stain from his leathery skin. The grizzled general manager smiled, and with the gentlest eyes Mithany had ever seen him express, he said, "You can't ever tell anyone you saw that."

She laughed. "Your secret's safe, but I think everyone already knows."

Not comfortable with his own feelings, Mithany guessed at why Santander diverted the pair's attention when he asked, "You hear that?"

"Yep. Sounds like my brother's voice." She yelled out, "Over here," before turning to Santander. "Thank you for being such a dear man." She squeezed him one last time and released him from their emotional exchange.

"Hey, Sis. Hi, Santander. What're you two up to?" Arek said, limping towards the pair.

Mithany ran to her brother and draped herself around him. "I'm so happy to have you back. Could've really used you on our trip north."

"Me too, Sis. Tell you all about it when we got time. Wanted to find you and let you know Tetrip went to get Nel where I left her tied up. But, she was gone when he got there. Says he'll put together a team to go find her, but they won't. I'm sure she's gone for good. It's my fault she got away."

Santander stepped in, separated the siblings, put one arm around each of their shoulders, and said, "Come on. Let's head back to the house. We have lives and an alphen orchard to rebuild... from what's left."

Love or Hate, Choose

Evidar

Reyne

Reyne tried with all his strength to rip free of the restraints holding him back from attacking the red-haired woman who'd murdered Daedyn. The Evidar agent Mera revealed to him in a vision of the past stood feet away but out of reach from receiving the justice she deserved because Reyne couldn't deliver it secured to a post. Hatred for the woman escaped the darkest pits of his soul.

With her hands on her hips, Neladith lorded over the seated Reyne, looking smug and satisfied with herself. Pointing at Reyne, she said, "*You*... are gonna kill... *me*?" as her finger turned back on itself. Taunting him, she laughed. "I don't think so. You certainly are a feisty one."

Reyne's nostrils flared with his intent: murder the bitch.

Her voice inflamed him, burning rage in his soul—feeding the beast within.

"I can wait here as long as it takes for you to calm down."

As though acid was thrown in his face, Reyne recoiled at the sound of her voice. Her words clawed at his eardrums. Every cell in his body demanded of him to rip her throat out to make it stop.

Gina made her own attempt at gaining freedom and while in the midst of her struggle she spat anger at her captor. "Don't be an asshole."

Neladith set a plate of food down between them and sat.

"I brought something along for you to eat. You're gonna have to settle yourself first. Big fella, you gotta be hungry. You both were out for about a day. My people kept you sedated waiting for me to get back. Good thing I showed up today. They were about to give up. Wouldn't of been good for either of you."

All the while Reyne's relentless endeavors to overcome his captivity continued without pause. The wild beast, from deep in his core, struggled to release its seething hatred for the woman and would not yield. Reyne released a scream of anguish that sounded more like a tortured hellhound than that of a human.

"This isn't getting us anywhere," Neladith said. She rose from her seat and looked towards Gina. After dumping the contents of the wooden plate to the ground, walking away, she said, "I'll be back when he calms down."

Yanking against her restraints, Gina shouted, "Not gonna happen!"

Neladith turned back and sauntered over to Reyne. After a quick sneer aimed at Gina, she crashed the plate into the side of Reyne's temple, mid-howl. His head snapped back against the blow and dropped to his chest—it hung there, limp, motionless, and silent.

Sometime later, Reyne woke and opened his eyes. Disappointment pierced his heart. The evil gray pervading everything delivered the news to his brain, *It's not a dream; you're stuck in this god-forsaken, miserable realm.*

Mithany existed a world away, and the bitter taste of Daedyn's and Baide's deaths lingered on the acidic air filling his mouth and lungs. He closed his eyes and wished it all away. Even before opening them, he knew the answer to his prayer. No.

Reyne lifted his head to find Gina where he left her before being rendered unconscious. She hadn't moved. She couldn't. Raw from yelling, his tender throat rasped out, "How long?"

"Hard to say. It's always night. Best guess, half hour or so."

"I miss anything?"

"A meal of some weird mushroom concoction."

"Suppose you two must've spoken."

"Yup."

"What the hell, Gina?" Through a narrow squint, Reyne glared at his partner.

"You're not gonna like it."

"Then spit it out and we'll deal with it." Reyne tilted his head back and puffed out a gasp. His lips flapped in the effort.

Gina paused before saying, "You did the wild-man thing again before she cracked you upside the head. Did you know that?"

"Yeah. Remembering more and more of it each time. Like before, another meaner me took over. The monster got out. Forget about that. Why am I not gonna like it?"

"You know, she could have killed us both already."

It sounded evasive to Reyne. His tone respectful, he demanded of her, "Gina. Why am I not gonna like it?"

"You should eat first."

Reyne tensed, tugged, and pulled at every restraint he'd been tied to. "Agggh-hhh! Spit it out!" he shouted.

"Understand, I'm on your side. I'm just the messenger." Reyne could see it on her face; she wanted him to actually consider what Daedyn's murderess had to say.

Reyne dropped his head in disgust. Speaking down at his chest, his questioning tone challenged the woman tied up with him. "Gina, really? She put an arrow through Daedyn's neck."

"You haven't heard what she had to say."

"Do I need to? She. Killed. Daedyn."

Gina commanded, "Look at me."

He didn't.

"Dammit. I said look at me."

He did, with stern, harsh, pulled-back, recessed eyes that he'd never offered her before. He looked out from under his brow, glaring at her like a predator lining up its next meal. The expression she gave in return told him she wished she hadn't.

Reyne gathered if Gina could have jumped back, she would have. A menacing tone seeped out in his warning. "Be careful what you say next."

Gina said nothing for several minutes as Reyne continued staring her down like a hunter fixed on his quarry. Neither moved. Gina broke first. "Can we start all over?"

Reyne surrendered, releasing his face as the harbinger of doom it portended.

Gina offered him a sweet persona, and in a cheery voice said, "Hey Reyne, welcome back. While you were knocked out, the mean lady came over and offered us a deal."

"Fuck you."

Surprised, she shot back, "Really? Fuck me? You had your chance before our captors tied us up and put clothes on us."

"You're exasperating. You know that?"

"Not so much. Never had this kinda trouble getting laid before... until I ran into you."

"You're pretty and all that, but you ain't Mithany."

"Since there's a chance we might not get out of this alive, I've got a little confession to make. Since you mentioned Mithany when we first met, you claimed you only wanted her. Mera and I decided that was your weak point: what I'd use to break you. Sorry, it had to be done. It was part of the process to make you believe you could take a life. I never got you past Mithany, but I did get you to accept that you could kill Evidar's Damus for her sake... if not for Tartica's."

Reyne yanked and tugged at his restraints. "If I could get outta these ropes, I'd come over there and kill you myself."

"As though you'd stand a chance... Anyway, I did it for your own good. So, don't be like that."

"Go to hell. Mera, too. I just started to like that manipulative bastard, even if he's dead. But you, how could you?" Reyne hung his head. Anger gave way to remorse.

"How could I what, try to make you want me? Turn your thoughts from Mithany? It wasn't personal. Mera said you had your head up your ass ever since leaving Hensdale. We had to change that."

"So, what am I to you? A weapon you wind up and point in the right direction?"

"I'm sorry, but yeah, that's how it started. Reyne, it's not like that now. Things have changed."

"What's changed is that you need me to get home."

"That's not it." She shook her head as a *tsk* escaped from her mouth. "You impressed me. That's what changed in how I see you now. You never wavered. Unlike every guy I've ever been involved with, you remained faithful to the one you loved. At least there's one of you out there who can be loyal in the face of temptation. As far as men go, you're one of the good ones."

"Is that what all your taunts have been about? Really?"

With a big smiley face, Gina admitted, "Can't blame a gal for trying. On the plus side, you restored my faith in men. That's gotta account for something."

Reyne rolled his eyes. "Gina, then what was all that bullshit at the Whispering Eye? Something about 'You don't know what it's like having a vagina' and all that nonsense."

"The things I said to you in the Whispering Eye are all true. It's just that... I don't really care. I've dealt with people gawking at my tits or my ass my whole life. Well, ever since they sprouted, anyway. I'm used to it. As I'm sure you've gathered, I don't think much of men other than Mera and now you. Women aren't any better, by the way. I've had my share of both. There's not much difference. That's why it's so easy for me to kill for money. As for that speech at the Eye, just wanted to get a measure of you. I give some version of that spiel to all the trainees Mera sends to me."

"I'll say it again, you're exasperating."

Gina continued, "Exasperating, that's a big word for a farm boy. And just so you know, you're the one who's exasperating."

Reyne tipped his head back, took in a deep breath, and released it slowly. "You win. I give up. What did Neladith say?"

Gina beamed through Evidar's despair. "Was that so hard? Did we have to do all this foreplay?"

"Out with it already. By the Goddess Teth, I'm thinkin' of leaving you here."

"Okay, farm boy. And I mean that in the most affectionate way. This is what we got."

"That's it. I've had enough of the 'farm boy' bullshit. I'm goin' to sleep and I'm outta here."

Gina relented. "Alright. Alright. She wants to make a deal. And how can you leave me here if you're not sure how to get back?"

"Oh, count on it, I can get back—I think. And you're pissing me off. How can you agree with her?"

"Don't be stupid. I don't. You're one hundred percent right. She murdered your brother. Even if it was by mistake, or she was just the hired help, doesn't let her off the hook. But, you and I aren't getting out of this alive unless we play along. You and me are on the same page. She's gotta pay for what she did... just not today. Given our current predicament, what choice do we have other than to hear her out?"

His hand clenched tight pushing against the ropes holding him back. Reyne took in several deep breaths through his nose, calming himself. "What's the bottom line?"

"She wants out. Told me she's pregnant. She said she wants to raise the kid in a world like ours. Wants a better life for her child."

"You believe that crap? She's up to something. I don't trust her."

"She might be lying. Mera says they all lie."

"Of course it's bullshit."

"Does it matter? Look, I don't know what her real plans are. What she did say is that she wants to live out her days on our version of Earth. That's all I really know. We talked. I figured it couldn't get any worse for us, so I told her why we're here."

"Gina, why would you do that? I thought you were smarter."

"She offered to help us. What we want fits with her plans. Not sure you heard of the saying in good old, tranquil Hensdale, but in the assassination business, the enemy of my enemy is my friend."

"She ain't no friend of mine. She's an enemy, always will be."

"Listen to me. She's got to get rid of the people who'll come after her if she goes AWOL, otherwise she'll never be safe. They're the same people we're after. If we don't agree, we're dead. Think about it. Why should she give us the chance? What, do you think she's gonna betray us? She could just off us here and now. Mera had it right: you're their target. But think about it, she hasn't put a knife in your chest yet. That's gotta mean something."

"Gina, that's all well and good, but she can do all that without us, and how do I let her live after what she did?"

"Yeah, she could go after them without us, but then she has you hunting her down, here in this shithole of a planet or back on Tartica. From her point of view, you have to be neutralized one way or the other. She's offering you the chance to walk away—alive. She wouldn't say anything else. As for you forgiving her. Don't. Go back to Hensdale when we're done here. Go on with your life after you, me, and Neladith kill the Damus and this Blacksmith asshole. Once back in Hensdale, get married like you planned, and forget all about her. What's the difference if this Neladith is on Evidar or in some out of the way village in a remote part of Tartica? You'll never see her again. Either way, you can forget about her."

Reyne looked lost. "*If* we can kill them... and that's a big if. Then what? Let her live? That's easier said than done. I don't know if I can."

"You better decide soon. She just stood up and is walking this way. She's been sitting behind you at the edge of my vision. I can just make out an outline. It's gotta be her."

"Think she's been listening?"

"Does it matter? My advice to you: it all comes down to one thing. You have to answer one question for yourself: What means more to you, love or hate? Here she comes. Time to decide. What do you want outta life, revenge for the past or a future with Mithany?"

Balanced on the Head of a Pin

Teth: 12th Day of the Harvest Moon

Jerithan

After peace talks broke for the day, at First Lord Serco's insistence, Prudent Jerithan Cree had been sequestered in a room away from the Adelleian delegation. Jerithan had done enough damage to Serco on day one of the conference and wouldn't be afforded further opportunities to do more that evening. Advising Adelle on Temple protocol wouldn't be required of Jerithan until the next day. With guards posted outside Jerithan's door, First Lord Serco left him no opportunity to seek out others in his Order.

Derr had offered Jerithan a simple exchange: if Jerithan could get useful data during the conference, he'd continue living. Serco made certain Jerithan spoke to no one in the Temple of Life and learned of nothing. Day one concluded in failure for Jerithan. Sure, he'd embarrassed his rival Serco, but he'd been unable to secure intel for Derr. His life hung in the balance. *Day two has to go better.*

After long hours and difficult negotiations on day one, a handful of minor trade agreements had been approved. At the prodding of the Kantos ambassador, the conference focused on the small items the four nations could agree upon with the goal of building on those minor successes. The participants skirted around the main issue: recognition of Adelle's withdrawal from the Covenant.

As the second day of negotiations began, as he did on day one, Jerithan took up his position at the table seated with the Adelleians. Everyone at the meeting continued to discuss myriad minutiae. Seated across from each other, with only a few standing now and again to emphasize the importance of an issue, hours passed with three of the four ligations pleased with the progress of the proceedings.

The conference took an altogether different direction when Tane Tomelai stood. The Adelleian ambassador Dobchen, seated alongside Tane, inconspicuously wrapped his fingers around her dangling wrist while looking straight ahead. Without taking visual assessment of the warning, she jerked herself free of his grip—but not unnoticed by Jerithan.

The Voice spoke inside Jerithan's thoughts. *"Adelle's senior statesman is worried. This is not planned. This may be an opening for us. Stay alert for an opportunity."*

Tane remained upright, waiting for all in the room to attend to hear her pending proclamation. The future Chancellor of Adelle glared at those who failed to heed her demand for consideration. In short time, Tane successfully quieted the conference attendees.

Tane's commanding tone, projected from a square jaw line inherited from her father, warned everyone in the room that playtime was over. "You all know me, so I will get right to the point. The work we've done here yesterday has laid the foundation for what we must do next. These minor agreements are well and good; nonetheless, we are here to set the cornerstone in place for our countries to move forward with the great Kingdom of Adelle absent from Covenant participation. Teth has been burned to a husk, the Provost's administrative building is destroyed. The capital of Kantos has been devastated. Across Greenlin's every city, there are revolts and uprisings. All these are in response to your collective intransigents that demand of you adherence to an antiquated document. And the entire time, we've been talking about minor trade agreements. Your evasive approach to the great issue of our generation threatens all humanity by this group's unwillingness to address what you fear. It is time we stand up as women and men, here in this room, now, and put this issue to rest."

The Voice said for only Jerithan's mind to hear, as he always did, *"This one means business. She is divisive. Her words will not bring people together. We should support her. The others will not. You must keep them from making peace."*

This Tane will be Chancellor of Adelle one day. She will prove useful in the future. If I live that long.

"*Maybe,*" the Voice advised.

Maybe what? She'll be useful or I'll live that long?

"*Yes.*"

Serco, who had spoken few words to that point on day two of the peace conference, slammed his hand on the table. "How dare you stand there and tell us we are cowards?! This mess is of your father's doing. He is the reason our cities burn and all of Tartica is in a state of upheaval. It's in Chaos. Our three nations have aligned to demand you put an end to your Covenant-abdication immediately... or face the consequences."

"*Well, my friend, perhaps she is more skilled than we think. She has forced the inexperienced new First Lord to show his hand before all the cards were dealt.*"

She drew him out with little fuss. Hat's off to Derr. His people knew just where to poke the bear.

The Voice added, "*And when to poke it.*"

Tane may have been well prepared by Derr, Kaythlin, and her father, but all eyes in this room are on her. I wonder if this young pup can hold herself together.

Tane shifted her gaze from Jerithan to Serco, folding her hands in front of her waist. "First Lord, I believe you've misspoken... again."

Jerithan observed jaws drop. In the world of diplomatic gatherings, polite code words ruled. Direct attacks were both frowned upon and considered poor form. He also understood only those taking an opposing position from the implied consensus were held accountable for violating ambassadorial norms. Dictated by conditions on the ground, Serco had free rein: Tane did not. Jerithan gathered from Tane's approach that Adelle's out for blood and cared little for diplomatic decorum.

Serco snapped, "Don't tell me what I've done, little girl."

Tane calmly spoke, adding further offence to her reply, "Insults, First Lord? Has it come to this? Adelle is here to resolve our differences. To find a peaceful way forward. You seem to desire exploration into causality and not towards resolution."

Jerithan could see the First Lord could not hold back his fury. "Big words. And yes, causality is important. Those responsible need to accept what they've done, and that factors into how we move forward to resolve our Covenant issue. To be even more clear, Adelle is the cause. Adelle has to accept our terms. You created this Covenant problem. You are required to bear the most weight in fixing it. It's always been this way amongst nations. It will be so now."

Realization struck Jerithan. He spoke to the Voice of his newly acquired appreciation for Tomelai's strategy Tane unleashed. *Derr and the Tomelais have played everyone in this room. Even placing me here to rattle Serco. If I did not hate them, Derr especially, I might be impressed. This is psyops level manipulation. She just set him up. Set us all up.*

"I am very impressed. I am looking forward to what she does next."

Tane leaned forward, resting her palms flat on the conference table. "You demand accountability, but offer none for your own actions." She ended by slowly turning her gaze from the new First Lord to the prior one. Everyone in the room followed her and Jerithan could only guess they all understood. "Esteemed First Lord, should we openly discuss the events leading up to Jerithan's removal from the velvet chair? Is that the accountability you speak of?"

Bitterness spewed from Serco. "You insolent whelp!"

"And what of the assassination attempt on Adelle's Chancellor, my father, the day of Teth's Feast? Temple of Life leaders played a role. I have it on good authority they initiated the failed murder attempt. Of course, in direct violation of everything the Covenant holds sacred, the Temple of Life set out to assassinate the leader of another independent country. Perhaps the Temple of Life has already taken the position that the Covenant's Obligation to preserve human life applies to everyone but itself? Is there a better definition of hypocrisy? What accountability does the Temple of Life offer to the Kingdom of Adelle for this gross violation? Let's be honest with each other, as Ambassador Dobchen suggested we all do." Tane gave Dobchen a knowing nod.

She turned to face Serco. "Isn't that where all this began? The single event leading us to the table here today, I lay it at the feet of the Temple. The Temple's own actions are evidence, proof it does not honor the Covenant. You demand Adelle adheres to stricture you ignore. How dare you, sir? I must ask, where is your demanded accountability for your Order's own actions?"

Serco flung his arm straight out with his index finger, aimed at Jerithan. "He did all of it. Not me. Him." A look of self-innocent relief plastered Serco's face for Jerithan and all to see. In his heated rebuff, the inexperienced First Lord, by his official standing, gave his implicit acknowledgement of the Temple's involvement.

The idiot just admitted the Temple of Life ordered the hit on Tomelai.

The Voice added, *"It is true. You and I did plot to kill Tomelai. Not our best work."*

True, but we never admitted it to anyone, especially to a crowd like this.

Tane continued, "That may well be, but *you* now sit at the head of your Order. You've admitted knowledge of the deed, and therefore it's your responsibility to make recompense for your prior First Lord's actions. What price will Teth pay for attempting to kill Adelle's Chancellor, just because he planned to introduce electrics? A proposal in opposition to Temple policy? You demanded accountability from Adelle, but it's the Temple's price to pay, to accept terms, as you've said."

Before First Lord Serco could reply, Greenlin's ambassador, an elderly, refined gentleman named Hasforn Kenic, came to his defense. "Now see here, young lady. You can't just throw around wild accusations and expect the leader of the Temple of Life to kowtow to your lies."

Tane's demeanor remained respectful when she turned to address the Ambassador's comments. "Sir, I ask you to refrain from derogatory remarks about my age and gender. I have given you no offense and see no reason you should speak in such a disrespectful manner. I will be Chancellor of Adelle one day and may remember your words when that comes to pass. As for lies, they are not." She again looked to Jerithan. "First Lord Serco has already admitted to his Order's involvement moments ago."

Hasforn shouted, "This is outrageous!"

Calm in her delivery, Tane nodded at Hasforn. "I would offer you an opportunity to take your seat, lest we start a discussion of a powerful woman, elected president of Greenlin, unlicensed for same-gender liaisons, having no children to qualify for a waiver, and who frequently engages in same-sex gratification in opposition to Covenant rules."

Hasforn spit back, "Salacious rumors."

Tane did not relent. "I can produce the requisite proof if it is so demanded."

Hasforn looked away to stare down at the tabletop. Everyone in the room had state intel of President Dimenk's frequent assignations with other women.

Unrattled, Tane remained resolute. "Then let me continue with my assertion. It appears Greenlin, like Teth, applies the rules of the Covenant to its populous but not to the rich and powerful. The elites are unbound from the Covenant. Ambassador Hasforn, you must certainly know the truth of what I speak. As such, Greenlin has already proven the Covenant's irrelevance within your own country, and you now demand Adelle adhere to the Covenant when your own leader does not?"

Hasforn Kenic took his seat.

Jerithan said to the Voice, *I always thought Dimenk liked the ladies. It has been rumored for years she has taken many female lovers. Would not look good for her political career for that one to leak out. Do as I say, not as I do. Not a popular position when you rely on votes to stay in power. Derr prepared his pupil well.*

The woman leading the Kantos delegation stood and opened her mouth to speak.

Tane slowly closed her eyes and shook her head from side to side before the Kantos Ambassador said her piece. Tane opened her eyes and locked them in a challenge. "It might be best for Kantos if you didn't."

The ambassador heeded Tane's warning and returned to her seat without speaking.

Tane told the gathered, "The Kingdom of Adelle is not innocent. Of all that I accuse you of, my country has done as well. We all regularly violate the Covenant to suit our ends. It is time we stop pretending. Adelle has taken the first steps at freeing our people. The average citizen of Adelle can now ignore the Covenant or follow it when it suits a purpose, as all our governments already do. You can continue to watch your cities burn. You can resist the overwhelming demand for freedom that has been unleashed across Tartica. You can dig your bunkers and invite your elites to join you in your resistance. In the absence of an agreement, we know the looming disaster facing Tartica. We can avoid what seems inevitable. Join me. Join Adelle. We can move forward together. A new and better Tartica awaits on the other side." Having said her piece, Tane sat down.

Silence hung in the air for several minutes.

Greenlin's representative spoke first. "None of us are innocent, as the future Chancellor reminds us, but my government is not prepared to abandon the Covenant."

The Kantonese emissary chimed in, "Nor am I. My government is not willing to walk away from the principles that bind us all. Kantos is prepared to take whatever action is necessary to secure the future."

The Voice demanded of Jerithan, *"Here is our chance. Give this Tane what you are thinking. It is now or never."*

With the Voice's advice ringing in his head, Jerithan rose and came to stand behind Tane. He whispered, "May I offer a suggestion? Is Kantos going to secure its own future or that of the Covenant? Her words are in diplo-speak and are evasive with purpose. Her true meaning will make all the difference to Adelle." Jerithan returned to his seat, having planted the seed.

Dobchen, from his chair, began, "We have all—"

Tane ignored Dobchen. "My esteem colleague from Kantos. Is it your government's position to keep faith with the Covenant and force adherence to its principles on the common man while flaunting their misapplication for the rich and powerful?"

The Kantos ambassador replied, "My country will continue to be governed by the Covenant of Absolute Universal Obligations, now and forever."

Tane pushed harder. "Neither Kantos, Greenlin, nor Teth can survive against their own citizenry with Adelle a beacon. As long as the Kingdom of Adelle walks a different path, your own populations will remain ungovernable. Surely you can see nothing but ongoing strife within your countries."

"That is correct. Kantos cannot survive under such conditions. My country is committed to do everything in our power to ensure the Covenant is applied across all nations."

"Greenlin concurs."

The Voice's excited thoughts shot into Jerithan's mind, *"You have done it, my friend. It is out in the open.*

"And what of Teth?" Tane asked before adding, "You are all hypocrites. Your governments are willing to engage in killing thousands from Adelle to bring us to heel, in direct violation of the Covenant's primary tenant to preserve human life at all costs. If you take such actions, the Covenant cannot survive. Don't you see? It is dead either way."

Serco opened his arms wide. "We have all agreed. Adelle must yield," he said, folding his arms over his chest.

Tane looked around the room at each pair of eyes. "Adelle will not yield. We will not return to the fold. Therefore, you mean to murder thousands. Because that is what you are going to have to do. Your elites will be safe. It will be the average men and women you send out as proxies to die for the desires and the protection of the few."

Jerithan sat stone faced and silent, as did everyone in the room.

The Voice told Jerithan, *"That does it. Tomelai sent her in here to ferret out what they were willing to do to save themselves, and she did it well. Adelle has its answer."*

Jerithan didn't reply. His own thoughts were gripped in astonishment at Tane's skillful ferreting out of the truth.

Tane nodded to the Adelleian delegation. They all rose. Jerithan followed suit.

She turned to Jerithan. "You must remain here. Neither the Temple of Life nor the nation of Teth are neutral parties in what is coming. As a prudent, high-ranking authority within the Temple faith, you are not welcome in Adelle."

The Voice broke into Jerithan's reeling thoughts. *"Tomelai just told Serco he is yours to deal with. And he is all but certain of the outcome."*

Terror gripped Jerithan's pounding heart. He looked to Serco, who grinned from ear to ear.

Tane stopped at the door before departing and turned to address the attendees.

"Then it's war."

Deal's a Deal

Evidar

Reyne

Reyne rubbed his wrists where rope manacles chewed into his flesh. Yanks, tugs, and struggles against the rough cord left nagging rope burns. Happy to be released from his bonds, Reyne stood to stretch his legs and shake out the cramps he endured from being secured in such an odd position. Now freed—along with Gina—Neladith placed no limits on their access to camp.

Gina stood, jiggled her arms and shoulders, and turned to Reyne. "Didn't think you had it in you. Thought we were both gonna die."

Folks moved about the area with little concern for the freed Tarticans. Mushroom caps the size of small trees set at the edge of an open expanse framed the outline of what Reyne assumed to be Neladith's tribal lands. Many of the caps served as roofs for the living spaces constructed underneath.

Reyne wondered why they didn't consider him a threat. It seemed out of place given the whupping he and Gina delivered to five of their clansmen. Reyne pondered another possibility; Neladith's word about the deal they'd struck neutralized him as a danger. And he considered that Neladith's word held sway amongst her fellow tribesmen.

"Gina, what choice did I have tied to a post? She constantly fiddled with that knife in her hand."

"Let's be honest, it didn't go down that easy. From where I sat, you did a lot of shouting, threatening, and even spit at her a few times. You pulled so hard against the ropes trying to get at her, I believed you were gonna bust free at any second… or at the very least rip that pole out of the ground. I was rooting for you, buddy."

"I'm still pissed she never responded to anything I said to her."

"Said? You didn't say anything. You screamed—more like screeched—every word. You went on like that for some time. Looked like you just exhausted yourself and eventually gave up."

"Nah, never gave up. Took that long for me to accept what I knew I had to do. Make the deal today… kill her tomorrow."

"She sat there, took all the shit you spewed at her. Just kept spinning that knife in her hand. Couldn't have been a more obvious message. She's one cold-hearted bitch. Gotta give her that."

"What the heck, Gina? How can you admire her? She killed Daedyn."

"Listen, farm boy, let's remember what line of business I'm in. Duh. I can admire her skills and still hate her."

Reyne shook his head in disapproval.

Gina rolled her neck. "You did what you had to do. She would've stabbed you in the heart if you didn't give in. I couldn't stop her. She kept me tied until the deal was struck."

"All I want is to hear her admit what she did."

"If she ever does, will it be enough for you to let it go? You really okay with this?"

"For Mithany, I can do this. Yeah, I'm okay with it. For now."

"For now? Reyne, you gonna do something stupid?"

"No… stupid's for another time."

Gina shook out her leg. The flesh of her thigh rippled with each air kick. "All things considered, well done, farm boy."

With his hands on his hips, Reyne twisted his trunk from side to side. "Don't start that farm boy crap again. I'm not feeling great about this deal. Daedyn deserves to be avenged."

Bent forwards, with hands behind her back, Gina continued stretching. "Yeah, that's true. We can always renege on the deal later. In my line of work, can't trust nobody and everyone going in... knows it."

Reyne rolled his neck as quick pops—like knuckles cracking—rattled off. "What bothers me is that she didn't say much. Didn't admit to anything. Seemed ignorant of what we were talking about. Only thing she kept on repeating, 'You agree or not.'"

Gina slapped Reyne on the back. "You're calmer now, back to mild-mannered Reyne. With a clear mind, together we can figure out what comes next."

"What you said to me about choosing Mithany kept banging around in my head between the screaming. I said that I'd do anything for her, and now it's real. Today, I gotta bury my hatred for this Neladith... we'll see about tomorrow."

"Like I said, didn't think you had it in you. You had the look of a killer in your eyes."

Reyne squatted with his arms straight out in front. As he bent down, his knee joints made a popping sound just like his neck. "And there's another thing. The woman Mera showed me when he did his magic mumbo-jumbo, pulling the past outta thin air, I watched her draw back the arrow that killed Daedyn. Neladith is the face I saw, but she had different-colored hair. And she had red eyes. I'll never forget those eyes. But not now... those haunting red globes are gone. It happened only a week or so ago. Was it all a disguise?"

Gina twisted her hips, stretching her muscles. "This place is darker than inside a squirrel's ass. Can't you be sure what color anything is."

Reyne stood on one foot, bent the other leg at the knee, up and down. "How do people live like this? It's miserable. Not a star in the sky, blocked out by shit in the atmosphere. Nothin' but an empty wasteland. And these giant mushroom trees are right out of a kiddie's nightmare."

"At least they put clothes on us. Look at the people walking around. This place is hot, and they're barely covered. At least one thing's similar to Tartica. Not the heat, the barely covered part." She laughed.

Reyne and Neladith reached an uneasy understanding. Reyne agreed not to kill Neladith—as if he could—in exchange for his life and for the life of Gina. For her part, Neladith gained two Tartican allies in her scheme to be free from bonded servitude. A tentative peace had been established with both parties working towards a shared goal: to kill the man Reyne called the Devil's Blacksmith and his Damus.

Reyne interlocked his fingers, turned his palms outward, and stretched out his arms as his knuckles popped in quick succession. "Laugh if you like. The deal we just made says I get delivered into the hands of the Devil's Blacksmith."

THE LAIR OF THE DEVIL'S BLACKSMITH

EVIDAR

Reyne

The ropes securing Reyne's arms and hands, tied behind his back, bit into his skin. An expert knotsman gave Reyne little wiggle room to move anything but a finger here or there, a few millimeters at best. The two escorts sent by Neladith to deliver Reyne—as they agreed—one on either side led him to an orange door entrance set in the otherwise pile of rocks. His sight had adjusted to the constant grayness verging on eternal midnight.

Into the lair of the Devil's Blacksmith, Reyne lumbered down the long, unilluminated staircase to be deposited in the middle of a room that included a man sitting on a large lounge chair at the head of a table, along with a bar, a desk, and a fireplace. Not that Reyne could make out much of it, being even darker than the outside world. Deep blue and black-purple flames dancing in the open hearth offered warmth but little light. As quickly as a yellow flare emerged from the burning logs, it got swallowed up by the competing darker flames. The birth of yellow light extinguished all too quick for Reyne to capture more than a glimpse of the man's face. Uncertain of what he saw, nonetheless, it gave him pause.

Reyne looked around the room and could make out shapes and a few particulars, but details remained hidden from his Tartican-born eyes. Death had come to many who ventured from Earth's Tartica to Earth's Evidar reality. Based on what Mera told him about Evidar, Reyne should've been scared, standing before a man who had killed so many and who was about to pronounce terms of his own execution. Yet Reyne remained at peace. If it came to it, he accepted his own death.

Death stalked him, and now it would set him free of torment and from his miserable existence without Daedyn or Mithany. Death had shadowed him his entire life, stealthily at first, more obvious of late, and if he were to face it himself now, so be it. He would deny Death any more pleasure or amusement toying with his life. At least he could buy Mithany's safety at the cost of termination from his own existence, believing Mera's tales of worlds merging to be far off in the future—if ever.

The man Reyne expected, the Devil's Blacksmith, sat on the plush chair as he spoke. "Gentlemen, you may go. Thank Neladith for her fine work. Mister Brenton, you present me with a bit of a problem. Your presence here portends bad tidings."

"Good. You've already fucked up my life. I'm hoping for an opportunity to offer you a taste of some Hensdale payback. And it's Reyne, not Mister Brenton."

Seated, the Devil's Blacksmith folded his hands across his lap. "It does not look as though you are going to have much of an opportunity to do what you so desire."

"We'll see."

"Determination. I like that."

Reyne walked to stand in front of the hearth with his back to it while he remained facing the man. "I gotta say, your voice, you sound just like someone I know. A bit more formal, but still familiar."

"We will get to that in a minute, Mister Brenton. You are here now and cannot do any more damage."

"Damage? Wish I could say I killed your people. But no, it wasn't me. Too bad. Maybe I'll just kill you and be done with it." While unable to delineate the man's features, the voice puzzled him. It hinted at something he didn't want to believe. Yet, he had an inkling. He had to see the face of the Devil's Blacksmith to be certain.

"My, you are ambitious for someone who has so little time left. You have admirable goals in your last few breaths of life. Most people get very nervous about now. You know, the whole 'I'm going to die, please, please don't kill me' routine."

Calm, Reyne said, "Death. I'm not afraid of him. He's been toying with me and my family for my entire life. I'm tired of it. If he takes me now, so what?"

"You surprise me. I cannot decide if you are brave or just stupid."

"Chalk it up to a little of both."

Laughing back at Reyne, he said, "What a shame. I suspect I could grow to like you. You are not pretending. You are not breathing heavy. Not sweating. Not pleading for your life. I do not hear your heart thumping in your chest."

"You talk a lot. Get to the point," Reyne demanded.

"I have known so many people who were, and I say *were* because they stood where you are standing now and did not make it out alive. They were hardened killers who did not have even a quarter of the courage you are showing me. They stood where you are standing right now, begging and even crying for another chance. But not you, Mister Brenton. That is good, because you should be aware I am not known for second chances. I would love to have you on my team, but we both know that is not possible."

"Haven't figured out how, but you should know, like I said, I *am* gonna kill you."

"I do not detect fear, but I can taste the hatred pouring off you. Again, too bad you were not born in my version of Earth. I could use a man like you. What a shame you have to die."

Reyne ignored the man's observation. "Since you intend to kill me in the next few minutes, how about you tell me what I'm gonna miss?"

Evil laughter erupted from the man Reyne knew to be the Devil's Blacksmith. "You have heard too many fairy tales if you think this is the part where I give everything away. That is not how life works. Besides, you already know the general outline of things to come."

"True. But what I still don't get. Why?"

The Devil's Blacksmith stayed quiet for a dozen or so heartbeats. "What I will tell you is that you have it all wrong, my young friend."

Reyne jumped in, "We're not friends. I'm pretty sure you're the asshole that ordered my death, killed my little sister, my father, my mother, and made the mistake of murdering my brother."

"I just may be that asshole, Mister Brenton. I have been responsible for many deaths. If your brother is amongst them, they all had a purpose. I cannot offer you an apology."

"Screw you and your apologies." Reyne showed his emotions for the first time.

The Devil's Blacksmith seemed to study Reyne before continuing. "Like I said, you have it all wrong. I am going to assume you know about the divergent realities of our two different Earths. I will also assume you were told my Earth is the bad one, the one that is the problem. Truth be told, your handler has lied to you."

Reyne said, "I can't see your face. Come closer."

"Do not be silly, young man. But before you die, I will show you my face."

"Now would be good."

"Let me continue. Yes, there are two divergent timelines. Two known versions of Earth. Created and separated at the point of the Great Destruction. They exist in different dimensions. The one who sent you here understands this, but that is for another time."

Reyne jumped in, "Another time. Thought you're gonna end me in just moments. What other time do I have? Now works for me."

"It is not important to you, Mister Brenton, so I will continue. What he has lied about is that this place is the true Earth."

Reyne interrupted, "You're tellin' me this shithole is the real Earth? My world is the copy?" It was Reyne's turn to laugh.

"Laugh if you like, but that is the truth. Why do you think this world looks like it does? This world took the damage from the Great Destruction. At the split-second a very large asteroid collided with Earth, it not only set the world on fire, exposed Earth's mantle, knocked our planet off its axis, gave birth to volcanic eruptions all over the globe that continue even to this day, filled the sky with heat-trapping gases, dust, and miniscule particles that block out much of the sun, but in that instant the asteroid struck, somehow, a second reality of Earth had been created and diverged along a separate timeline in another dimension."

"That's some theory. I gotta give you at least one thing. There does seem to be two worlds. I just don't give a shit about yours."

"You should, Mister Brenton. That long ago, cataclysmic devastation still chokes off sunlight to this day. Scientists, of the few who survived the Great Destruction, all now long dead, believed the heat from the open mantel combined with layers of particles trapped in our troposphere keeps in all the heat. They call it the Venus Greenhouse Effect."

Reyne struggled against the ropes hindering him. "Venus, shmeenus. Not my problem."

"Mister Brenton, I expect better of you. I am speaking of human life. Governments were swept away and never recovered. Civilization collapsed. Humanity collapsed. Earth's population was all but wiped out, save for the few of us living on Antarctica who survived the Great Destruction. What remains of humanity all these millennia later, in this, the original version of Earth, is like humankind's emergence from the Stone Age, but not with its future ahead of it but with its glorious achievements behind it."

Reyne's eyes were slowly adjusting. Squinting hard, he tried to make out the face of his tormentor. "I don't give a shit, but I am curious. Why is Tartica so important to you?"

"We barely survive from day to day. People from Tartica show up here every few years inciting those of my world with lies. I cannot have it. So, those like yourself, my people hunt down and bring to me."

Stunned at what he had heard, his mind reeled. It made sense, the reason Evidar existed as a dark, gloomy world, but how could he believe any of it? "You're right about the one who sent me. But he tells it differently. Guess it's just your word against his. I'm gonna go with his version."

The Devil's Blacksmith continued, "His words deceive you. The goddess you call Teth is no god. Although the first to discover the divergence, the existence of your alternate version of our Earth, she holds the honor as the first of our survivors to escape to it. Your precious goddess Teth is, or was, just an ordinary woman from my world. I have not seen her in a very long time."

Teth, just a woman from Evidar?

No way. Lies. All lies.

"Screw you!" Reyne shouted as his mind reeled.

"She came back here many times, taking other survivors she could find, guiding those capable of transitioning between realities and taking others with her who could not transition on their own but able to pierce the Void with her help. I suspect the man who sent you here followed her to your reality with something of mine."

He said, "the one who sent me," is from this miserable place. That's Mera.

Nobody can be that old and still living.

Impossible.

The mysterious man's rantings crashed into Reyne's belief system, the basis of Tartica's reality, its faith, the Temple of Life, its foundations in the Book of Teth, the Covenant, and if any of what he said proved true, it would leave Reyne's worldview in tatters. The words stole air from his lungs and hammered at his heart.

He looked about the room, his eyes wildly jumping about. Words escaped in a whisper: "Teth, from Evidar. Impossible." But the story of Teth the Devil's Blacksmith told him gave him hope. *If Teth took people with her through the Void, it can be done. I gotta know how she did it.*

The man Reyne believed to be the Devil's Blacksmith rose from his seat, walked over to stand a few paces from Reyne, looked him in the eye, and in a soft tone, said, "Impossible, no. Real, yes. True, absolutely. But what is this Evidar?"

Confused, Reyne's head listed to the left. "This shithole. Surely you've heard that's what we call this place."

"I correctly cite this world as Earth, yours being the copy. To those who have made it here from your world, we speak of this reality as Black Haven. It is of little concern. Your time is up, Mister Brenton."

Black Haven? That ain't right.

The man lit a yellow-flame match so Reyne could see his face, just as he assured Reyne he'd do right before he promised to kill him. Reyne's eyes bulged from their sockets as the small flame released an explosion of light into the luminance-starved room. The light, being consumed by Evidar's black nature, quickly faded. But not before recognition seized Reyne of the face before him.

"Mera?!"

Fuck me! I rode the wrong Probability Wave.

This ain't Evidar.

THE COVENANT

DECLARATION OF THE COVENANT OF ABSOLUTE UNIVERSAL OBLIGATIONS

In the course of history, when profound circumstances threaten the very existence of every man, woman, and child, we, the one thousand seven hundred forty-two souls that remain of Humanity must rise up and endeavor to take extraordinary and necessary actions to secure the survival of humankind. Foremost amongst these actions is to unequivocally set forth this Declaration of a Covenant, establishing the Absolute Universal nature of certain Obligations that each person owes to all others, without exception and in perpetuity, until such time the long-term survival of humankind is, without question, able to secure itself a future without concern for extinction as a species. We, therefore, set forth this Declaration, a Covenant of Absolute Universal Obligations, to be unencumbered by any law, be it Man's or God's in any form, by any government or by any religious authority, made by any man or any woman or on behalf of any community, until such time as a prognosis of the unconditional survival of our kind is secured.

First and principally among these is the Universal Obligation to Procreation, to spread the seed and nurture in the womb the future generations of humankind. It shall be the Absolute Universal Obligation, above all other laws, for all men and women between the ages of sixteen years and forty-five years to bring forward into this world at least three children attaining the age of fifteen years. Without exception, we recognize this Absolute Universal Obligation upon all but for those medically determined infertile by way of natural cause; for those that surpass the age of forty-five; and without regard for any individual's carnal desire to know another of one's own gender, each must endeavor to Procreate for the General Welfare inherent in the perforce propagation of our species. Recognizing the sacrifices that may be visited upon loving and caring souls, a general waiver may be granted to allow for the individual pursuit of same gender couplings, upon recognition in law of one's fulfillment of the Absolute Universal Obligation to Procreations having been attained. This waiver cannot be denied for any reason to any individual having fulfilled their Obligation of Procreation.

Second, and as well Absolute, we recognize the Universal Obligation to Preserve Human Life; to do no harm nor to place any human life at risk; to take no human life either by direct action or indirect action or by inaction, by any man, by any woman, by any child, or by any community or governing body at any level; to require intervention on behalf of any person having knowledge of another being at risk of imminent death, and to do so without regard for one's own safety, save death itself.

Third, and as well Absolute, we recognize the Universal Obligation to Promote the General Welfare. Incumbent upon all to effort a positive contribution to the wellbeing of the community of humanity through actions that may be recognized in a myriad of diverse services, products, or other unconventional efforts that Promote the General Welfare. Promotion of the General Welfare being Universal upon all humankind may take sway in and be all-consuming at all-time in some, while limited in others but rare moments in life yet Absolute and Universal, nonetheless is the Obligation to Promote the General Welfare. Reward nor recognition is the desired payment for the fulfillment of the Universal Obligation to Promotion of the General Welfare yet may be so without encumbrance by the will of man, woman, or by the force of community as expressed in laws or religious strictures.

Fourth, and as well Absolute, we recognize the Universal Obligation to the Natural Path. The Obligation to pursue life by way of the natural gifts of Earth's offerings to the exclusion of all else that is not firmly rooted in the natural world. We recognize the purported circumstances contributing to the Great Destruction and seek to begin a new path for humanity that enjoins us all towards a different, more enlightened course rooted in the Gifts of Nature.

These Declared and Absolute Universal Obligations are demanding of action by each and every person for each and every Obligation. We recognize that we cannot leave Humanity's future to the fortuitous whims of events or the inevitable consequences of humankind's collective or individual actions and therefore establish the Council of D'CAUO to speak as one voice for all humankind concerning the interpretation and implementation of this Declaration of the Absolute Covenant of Universal Obligations. In so agreeing, we bind us all; we remaining few souls, now and forever, along with all future progeny including any and all future governing bodies, persons, leaders, or religions, until such time as the future of the human race is secure and as such is so recognized by the Council or D'CAUO. So say we all declared this first day of the Summer Moon in the year eighty-six of the Third Age.

GLOSSARY

Acolyte: Rank of an initiate in the Temple of Life religious order.

Aderlee: (Ad-er-lee) Evidarian native supporting Edruk's effort to destroy the Devil's Blacksmith.

Arek: (Air-ek) The older brother of Mithany and a charming young fellow who is a favorite amongst the eligible women of Hensdale.

Baide: (Bade) Reyne's biological sister, killed twenty-two years ago at the age of three, in the year 1521 of the Third Age.

Brenal, Hollid: (Breen-ul, Hahl-ed) Hensdale's village doctor, serving the community for decades.

Celebratorium: A place where people go to celebrate each of the Six Gifts. Celebratoria, plural.

Chamette, Ja'Rou: (Shah-met, Jah-rue) An elite, wealthy older man living in Tandure and a powerful force within the Hidden Hand.

Caulky: (Call-kee) Thuggery associate.

Coherence: The fixed relationship between an object's wave properties that has been split in two, where each independent phase of waves radiates in separate but identical frequencies.

Covenant of Absolute Universal Obligations: The founding document created by the survivors of the Great Destruction to bind all of humanity, the few who remained, and all in perpetuity until such time as a self-sustaining population can be achieved. Its dictates apply to all governments, all religious orders, and all human beings as an absolute obligation that must be followed without exception. Its principles are revered throughout Tartican civilization, and it serves as the basis of the Temple of Life religion.

Daedyn: (Day-din) Reyne's deceased brother. He lived with Reyne and they ran the alphen orchard together as business partners.

Damus: A mathematical genius of Evidar, capable of applying complicated equations to predict the flow of events through time.

Derr, Druin: (Dur, Drew-in) Captain and leader of the KCG. Childhood friend of Chancellor Madrotti Tomelai. A harsh, serious, single-minded man dedicated to his sole purpose in life, keeping Tomelai safe.

Devil's Blacksmith: Also known as the Architect. An Evidarian leading the effort to alter the version of Earth from which he hails.

Dobchen, Berik: (Dod-chin, Bear-ick) Ambassador to Teth, representing the Kingdom of Adelle.

Dimenk, F'Saad: (Dem-ink, Fah-sod) President of Greenlin. She has no children and was elected by its citizens to a life term as President.

Dylla: (Dil-ah) Regional leader from Evidar overseeing all operations on Tartica to eliminate anyone thought capable of transitioning between the dimensions of Earth to her home world.

Edruk: (Ed-ruc) Reyne's birth father. Died before Reyne was born.

Emosh, Synja: (Ee-moe-sh, Sin-jah) Evidarian woman of exceptional abilities in mathematics and physics. Declared a Damus by the Devil's Blacksmith.

Ferpratt, Wilem: (Fur-prat, Will-um) A senior Lieutenant in the KCG. Trusted ally and right-hand man of Druin Derr.

Firache: (Fur-ach-ay) Fire beings that hide from human perception. They live a fire in all its forms.

Gifts of Teth: Six Gifts bestowed upon humanity by the Goddess Teth: the Gift of Love, the Gift of Knowledge, the Gift of Flesh, the Gift of Life, the Gift of Renewal, and the Gift of Nature.

Grafph: (Graff) An assassin from Evidar and member of Dylla's unit.

Great Destruction: Event in Earth's history approximately fifteen hundred years ago that brought an end to the Second Age of humanity and nearly wiped out all life on the planet.

Griz: (Gr-is) Thuggery associate.

Gwerther: (Ga-were-the-er) Reyne's adoptive father. Died a few years before his wife Pachelle when Reyne was young.

Hansel: (Han-sell) A prudent serving on the Council of Prudents.

Harvin: (Har-vin) Agent of Evidar.

Hasforn, Kenic: (Has-four-n, Ken-ick) Ambassador to Teth representing the nation of Greenlin.

Hidden Hand: Loose association of wealthy elites in Tandure who appear to be upstanding members of the upper class who operate in the shadows to manipulate governmental bureaucracies, press, and other legitimate civic functions to influence and subvert governments policies to suit their needs.

Jerithan: (Jer-eh-than) First Lord of the Temple of Life. He believes he is doing God's work in his own way.

Judjurex: An elected civil servant tasked with the responsibility to investigate, arrest and determine guilt or innocence of anyone accused of an offense or criminal act.

Kaythlin Tomelai: (Kayth-lyn Tom-eh-lay) First Lady of Tandure and wife of Madrotti Tomelai. Maiden name F'Shiyn. She is loved by the citizens of Adelle and is smart, charming, and attractive.

Kebra: (Keh-breh) Agent of Evidar.

Kingdom's Chancellor's Guard (KCG): The KCG is the secret service, quasi-spy agency, and intelligence gathering security organization tasked with maintaining the safety of Adelle's Chancellor, Madrotti Tomelai. Under Capitan Druin Derr, the KCG has the authority to explore any avenue of inquiry, detention, or interrogation in fulfillment of its mission.

Kiple: (Kip-ul) Leader of the Kingdom of Adelle's national police force.

Kwuinan: (Coo-in-anne) He is the de facto leader of the secular government of Teth with the title of Provost. Appointed by First Lord of the Temple of Life and answers to him or her in all matters.

Larsed, Hrotitem: (Lar-said, Hor-o-teat-um) The Prime Minister of the People Republic of Kantos. Leader of the democracy and elected Prime Minister by a majority of Chamber of Delegates.

Lorique: (Lore-eek) She was a suspected Tweener living in the coastal town of Jarouhar and was killed by Evidar agents.

Loseff: (Low-sef) Son of Madrotti and Kaythlin Tomelai. Second in the line of succession to the position of Chancellor for the Kingdom of Adelle.

Lume: Crystal that glows green light after being exposed to sunlight.

Madrotti Tomelai: (Ma-drot-tee Tom-ah-lay) Chancellor for life of the Kingdom of Adelle. Physically fit and dedicated to power. He is sometimes called Rotti by only one man, Druin Derr.

Marvo: (Mar-voe) A well respected and senior Prudent serving on the Council of Prudents.

Mera: (Meh-ra) Mera whose full name in Meratoruc, is Reyne's mysterious protector. Little is known of his background.

Mithany: (Mith-an-nee) Reyne's fiancée. She grew up in Hensdale. She is petite, competitive, and the sister to an older brother, Arek.

Nails: Head of the loose confederation of outlaws, thieves, and various criminal types known as the Thuggery.

Neladith: (Nel-eh-dith) Young female Evidarian assassin, capable of moving between earthly dimension, sent to Tartica to kill Reyne.

O'Hurn: (Oh-hern) A prudent serving on the Council of Prudents.

Pachelle: (Pah-shell) Reyne's adoptive mother and Daedyn's birth mother. She died when both boys were in their teens.

Prudent: Highest rank in the Temple of Life religious order but for the positions of First Lord and Second

Lord.

Quith, Selundra: (Kw-ith, Sa-lun-dra) Mister Whitetop. He reports to Dylla and is the on-site field leader of the Evidar ops team tasked with eliminating Reyne and all other known or suspected Tweeners.

Razoal: (Rass-ole) He is a prudent and ally of Jerithan serving as Second Lord.

Reyne: (Rain) A young man, almost twenty-two years old and the owner, of an alphen nut orchard on the outskirts of Hensdale. He is polite and well-liked by the community. Currently engaged to be married to his childhood sweetheart, Mithany.

Rotti: (Rot-tee) See Madrotti.

S'Leen: (Sah-lyn) Prudent serving of the Council of Prudents. She is an ally of First Lord Jerithan Cree.

Santander: (San-tan-der) General Manger of the Brenton alphen orchard. He has the reputation of being a gruff and demanding boss.

Serco, Garragent: (Sir-coe, Ger-ah-gent)) Prudent assigned to the Kingdom of Adelle and who sits on the Council of Prudents.

Signum Circulus: A religious gesture made with the thumb moving in a circle around the heart and the hand coming to rest over the heart. It is a ritual to invoke internal peace through divine reverence.

Silia: (Sill-ee-ah) Biological mother to Reyne.

Spetzer: (Spet-zher) Lives in Hensdale, same age as Reyne, and since childhood, has a thing for Mithany.

Sura: (Sue-rah) The wife of Hollid Brenal. Died long ago.

Tane: (Tain) Daughter of Madrotti and Kaythlin Tomelai. As the oldest child, age twenty-one, she is the heir apparent Chancellor of the Kingdom of Adelle.

Teth: Patron goddess of the children of Earth in the realm of Tartica. Daughter of Father Sun and Mother Earth.

Tetrip: (Tet-trip) An older man serving as Judjurex of Hensdale.

Thuggery: Loose association of criminals in Teth.

Timble: (Tim-bull) Thuggery associate.

Treestone: Wood product that tranforms into stone once treated in a special brine.

Trell: Young man, native to Hensdale, and a member of Spetzer's inner circle who frequents the Forest Maiden Inn.

Tweener: A person with the ability to move between the two known alternate dimensions of Earth, Evidar and Tartica.

Tylus: (Tie-lus) Assassin from Evidar and a member of Dylla's team.

Wendolyn: (When-dah-lyn) Last name Trancher. See Nails.

Acknowledgments

I would like to thank the many people I've encountered on this adventure who have been mentors, educators, and supporters. To the readers of the early draft, whose input helped improve the story, including Roger and Mark, thank you. To the editors Ciara, Lucy, and Kim, whose expertise contributed immensely—I could not have gotten this far without you, my heartfelt thanks.

To my loving wife Louise, thank you for your understanding and patience. To my wonderful children whose creativity knowingly and unknowingly contributed here and there.

Books By R.C. Vielee

The Utopia Falling Saga
Utopia Falling: A Darkness Rises
Chaos Ascending: A Feast of Betrayal
The exciting conclusion to be published in the winter of 2024:
Convergence Waking: Forge of the Soul Stone

Visit my website to read a preview chapter and more.

https://www.RCVielee.com

About the Author

Robert Vielee

Robert grew up in a small town in northern New Jersey.
He is married with four children and now lives
with his family in Pennsylvania. Before turning his
attention to writing, Robert's creative drive took him across
North America as a freelance nature photographer—while
holding down a day job. He loves nature, reading epic
fantasy, and most of all, his family.
Connect online with Robert on his author website

RCVielee.com

Newsletter